To my Friend/Se...
Please read and enjoy

Agatha Helen Caller

The Two Worlds of Ms. Anna

illustrated by Donald Barrie

HELEN COLLIER WITH MEOW AT THE HELM

iUniverse®

THE TWO WORLDS OF MS. ANNA

iUniverse books may be ordered through booksellers or by contacting:

iUniverse
1663 Liberty Drive
Bloomington, IN 47403
www.iuniverse.com
1-800-Authors (1-800-288-4677)

ISBN: 978-1-4917-7313-0 (sc)
ISBN: 978-1-4917-7312-3 (e)

Library of Congress Control Number: 2015912231

Print information available on the last page.

iUniverse rev. date: 08/19/2015

Dedications

This book is dedicated to the women who have passed through my life impacting it in many ways most importantly, my mother, Susie Pearl Green who taught me that persistence and a determination would always get you to the finish line. I want to thank you Ma'dea for teaching your children that because you start out in a train box car does not mean you will end up there.

To my husband John who believed that one day my books would become best sellers, I thank you for your faith and belief in my writings. To my deceased twin brother Eugene Green I will always feel your presence in every word I write and in the children you left behind. To my daughters and son Susie, Shenee, and Weslynn and Mylo thank you for believing in my writings and helping me along the way. And to my sisters Elsie, Lavonda, and Pearl our lives together have been filled with many unforgettable memories. I love you all.

To my friend Guerry Hoddersen and all the Radical Women and Men working to protect the rights of every person believing that we are all one human race on this earth no matter what our differences are. Thank you Ethel Mitchell for you guidance and believing in me always. Dale Golden and Deborah Jordan I want to thank you both for opening the door to my divine journey and the path I shall forever follow. Associate Professor Jane Pernell it was you who urged me to step out beyond my comfort zone to see that no race of people is all the same. I shall never forget Julie Buren who spent so many incredible hours getting me started on this project. Thank you, Venesia Hornsby for brainstorming with me about the design for my cover. Weslynn you have a gift for looking into the unseen to make sure it works. Maraget Barrie thank you for being a writing friend and never letting me forget I am blessed. And thank you Donald J. Barrie your cover set the stage for the rest of the book. Teresa Ms. Anna and the story of her life give us food for thought just as you said it would if I would just get it out there. Paris Williams the daughter of the late writer J. California Cooper helps me to keep it real. Nation Homes your belief in my writing has pushed me to the finish line.

Thanks you all my readers and friends. You can always email me at helencollier@yahoo.com or go to my website www.helencollierwriter.com

I am honored to be a part of the African American Writer's Alliance & the Northwest Writers Association

SUSAN SEYKATO SMITH

Of all those who have shared in my writing experience I must thank Susan Seykato Smith who stood as a shinning light pushing me to excel beyond my known potential. Because of her love and devoted attention to detail, this book as been born.

Author's Notes

Magical Realism gives the reader a view of life outside of the five senses. **"Ms. Anna and the Tears from the Healing Tree"** my first book in this Trilogy started the process. **"The Two Worlds of Ms. Anna"** is the second of a three-book trilogy of Magical Realism. It takes the reader into three generations of love lost and redemption while allowing us to view those generations from the inside out. *You are welcome to come set with me in my parlor but remember it is my parlor we are seated in.*
Author

No one can expose the hidden secrets of other cultures without piercing the dark secrets of his or her own. Helen Collier/Meow, Other books by Helen Collier Meow *Looking For Trouble by Meow, Ms. Anna and the Tears from the Healing Tree by Helen Collier with Meow at the Helm*

Prologue

It had taken several days for Raymond Forlorn to escape the watchful eyes of his wife and son. Leaving them still asleep in the penthouse suite he had reserved for them, he hurried over to the apartment he shared with Anna. There was no Aretha Franklin or Kenny Rogers to bring pleasure to his ears. The rooms were dead silent. His eyes caught sight of a note in the middle of the bed. The place where they had shared their warmest memories sagged under his weight as he sat down to read the note. The ringing phone stopped him. He reached for it, hoping it would be Anna. The voice coming through the receiver asked to speak to Mrs. Anna Bradley. After hearing that Anna was not home, the caller asked to speak to Raymond Forlorn, the person listed as the emergency contact if she could not be reached.

"I am he," Raymond replied. The caller went on to tell him, "There were two patients here with the same name taking a pregnancy test. A mistake has been made. The test indicates she *is* pregnant." The caller apologized for the mix-up, but Raymond had already dropped the receiver as he read the note in his hand.

My Dear Beloved,

The ball is over. The coach has once again turned into a pumpkin. Ray, my love, it was well worth the trip. I'm returning you to your wife and child because with them is really where you have belonged all along. As for Ms. Anna, well, she can never go home again. Too much has happened. Maybe I will turn to that convent. I shall never forget the time we shared together or the things you have saved me from and helped me overcome. There was no baby for us. I went today and checked.

NAMASTE: I honor the place in you where the universe resides. A place of hope, love and peace, The Old Head has been good to us.

Forever, my love is yours,
Ms. Anna

Raymond Forlorn reread the note that told him Ms. Anna was out of his life forever, going somewhere she knew he would not be able to find her. He shook his head, realizing she was gone carrying his baby she had been told did not exist. Looking back on the bed, Raymond's hand covered the black widow spider as it crawled along. He started to apply pressure.

Don't kill it! The echo of Anna's voice rang throughout the room. From between his fingers, the spider, its orange back glowing, crawled away and soon disappeared from sight.

Chapter One

—⟋⟍⟋—

When Anna went to return her keys to the owner who held her lease, she continued past his office and walked in the direction of the apartment her and her lover Raymond Forlorn had shared in Las Vegas. As soon as she entered, her mind tumbled backwards a week ago. She had gone to the bank to deposit the contents in the attaché case Raymond had given her into his safety deposit box only to discover he had forgotten to give her the key. It was probably because they had held each other so tight while making love way into the wee, wee hours of the morning that he forgot.

Anna remembered pushing his blonde hair back to gaze into his gray eyes. She felt the tingling of his mustache as his white lips melted against her full brown ones. He held her close reminding her that she would soon be his forever. She would be twenty seven that coming October and he was already thirty. The plan was that they would soon divorce their mates and marry each other.

The last time Anna had seen her handsome husband was four years ago when she caught him was in bed making out with three women. Anna lost her baby falling down a flight of stairs running to get away from him; she had not laid eyes on him since. Raymond had already filed for his divorce. All she needed to do was file for hers. It had been the plan until the supernatural force that controlled her life had come to her in a vision while she sat in the bank's Safety Deposit room.

When she was fourteen years old the pulsating brain surrounded by thirteen revolving eyes she had coined the Old Head had come to earth from the outer world and taken over her life. While she searched for the key in the bank it had revealed to her that soon she and the Young Chemist, the name the Old Head used to speak of her lover, would go their separate ways and she must continue her journey without him. The sign she would see was the Old Widow spider standing in its web. The warning had slackened Anna. She hurried back to the apartment upset by its warning. Raymond she had thought to herself would have to deposit the contents of the attaché case himself because she was not going back there.

Leaving the bank Anna had driven back to the apartment. As her mind traveled back in time, she remembered stopping just as she got inside her apartment. Another shock awaited her. A young petite white woman stood inside. Her flaming red hair fell in soft curls around her shoulders. Had it not been for the four inch black heels she wore they would have been the same height and size. Dressed in a grey tailored suit, frowns gathered in the woman's brows as she turned her green eyes to stare at Anna. Anna realized it was her lover's wife. What was she doing here? Anna had wondered. She had left Raymond for dead five years ago, insisting that his features had become so horrifying she could not stand the sight of him. She even had a memorial for him as though he had died.

Stunned beyond words Anna quickly turned her attention to her lover. He stood just below the six feet three inch shelf against the wall, the blonde hair on his head touching his shoulders just the way she liked it. His white biceps looking thick and tight as he held out his arms from his shirtless body in a hopeless gesture, wearing only his pants something she had believed he must have slipped on having been in bed naked when she left him.

Anna had looked towards the white woman now gazing at her dark brown slender legs and thighs up to the pink hot pants Anna wore. Had it not been for the thick towel tossed around her neck the woman would have seen the shape of Anna's full brown breasts bubbling over the top of her halter, a hundred and twenty pounds at five feet five inches wasn't too bad to look at Anna thought as she had listened to his wife reprimand her for coming into her own apartment without knocking. Realizing what she thought she must be Anna eased the attaché case down about to give her a reality check.

Just as she was about to speak, a young white boy around ten years of age entered the room. His head shaved as clean as the palm of her hand. After commenting on the cookies he was eating then drinking milk from the glass in his hand, the child began telling Raymond whom she then realized was his son about the places in Las Vegas he would like for his father to take him because he would soon have to return to the hospital a place his son said he hated. As soon as the boy had finished speaking, the Old Widow appeared behind him. She stood in her web the orange light on her back turning from orange to blood red. When she saw the Old Widow Anna knew the voice that had come to her in the bank had not been a trick of her mine. The time she feared had come to past. It was the sign the Old Head had warned her would come letting her know she must leave her lover and continue her journey alone.

Anna sighed feeling her tears slip down her cheeks as the scene from the past faded. Today the sound of the Old Head's violin instruments that had played when they had been most intimate filled her heart. Today it played a sad love song that told of two worlds apart, worlds that could never come together. The sound of each string inched out the fears and hate that would forever keep them apart. She stood listening to it remind her of every person who had come in and out of her life those last four years, all gone now. All were people she might never see again on this earth world. Her tears began to flow as she looked around what had once been her home.

Every corner burst with memories. Void of all their belongings, the rooms stood empty. Her fingers pulled at the drawers that had held their clothes. Nothing lay inside. Where, she wondered, had he taken the books? Her love for them filled her heart. No racing forms cluttered the table—the forms had given her a reason to complain that he needed a maid, which was most surely not her. Even the neatly made bed looked as though no one had ever slept there. It seemed as if it might all have been a dream she had finally awaked from. Anna turned to leave but the ringing phone stopped her. Picking it up, she thought: If this is Ray, I don't know what I will say. It's too soon and too hard letting go.

"Hello?" Anna said then held her breath thinking it was her lover.

"Ms. Anna, it is I, the Madame from the Repair Your Body Spa." Anna stood stunned, hearing the Middle Eastern woman's voice—the last person on earth she expected a call from.

"I heard some anonymous black woman found a cure for the Tack Disease that has been the cause of so many deaths of horses all over the world."

How could she possibly know it was she who discovered the cure that saved the lives of those dying horses? Anna asked herself, realizing it had something to do with her call.

"As soon as I saw and heard Monsieur Forlorn speak of the black woman who had found the miraculous cure, I knew the woman had to be you; even here in my country it has made a great impact. Why don't you come see me and get a spa treatment? On me, of course; I need someone to ease my boredom. No one does so like you, my friend, advising me on how you Western women live free." Anna said nothing. "Tell the Madame, how is your love life with Monsieur Forlorn these days?"

"I have no love life, Madame. It's over and done with. He is gone." Anna sobbed out of control while holding the phone, unable to say anything else but knowing it would be rude to hang up.

"Come to me, my dear; there is comfort here. Your ticket will be waiting at the airport. Simply mention your name and the Repair Your Body Spa. Come; please do so, Ms. Anna! Our lives' coming together has been a most extraordinary occurrence.

****

Anna soon found herself on an international aircraft, leaving the country for the umpteenth time, going to a world that would provide the solace she so desperately needed. She changed flights twice before reaching her destination. The Madame's chauffeur met her when she landed and led the way to the waiting limousine. After embracing her, Anna settled inside beside the completely covered woman next to her. Only the Madame's eyes peered out from the white hooded robe and hijab she wore.

They rode in silence as Anna stared out beyond the darkened window of the limousine at the ox-pulled wagons. Barefoot children ran along the dirt road beside the limousine as if trying to beat its speed. People walking by stared at the vehicle from scarred, weathered faces that indicated their struggles in this strange forbidden land. Those faces she sat hidden from reminded her of the tears of the Healing Tree. Drenched in its powers, Anna remembered her weird hallucinations as she sat before an old brown-faced man who forbade her to swat a fly he believed might be his mother. Crawling up his legs were bugs he stated were his relatives. She had walked through him as though he were a ghost as the strange powers of the tears filled her mind with weird hallucinations. A sigh escaped her lips. It was indeed a bizarre and different land, yet it had become a part of her journey. Her eyes widen as the magical dome appeared in the distance. It was adored with thousands of tiny rainbow colored lights crowning it. Anna felt the Madame slip her hand into hers as if to reassure her that soon all would be well. They did not speak a word to each other until they reached the privacy of the magnificent spa where women coming from all over the world spend enormous amounts of money to rejuvenate their bodies.

After a refreshing shower and an hour massage, Anna slipped into a comfortable white robe, as did the Madame. In the privacy of a tiny room with only a small sofa and table, she filled Anna's cup with tea. The Madame's brown hair that had been covered hung down her back. Her light brown eyes stared at Anna as though pleased by her visit. Anna looked at the tiny woman that could not have been more than five feet in height. Her olive face looked ageless as she peered at Anna. Sipping the potion tea she had been offered, Anna knew her healing had begun.

"You would be a famous woman by now, Ms. Anna, had you disclosed your identity. Why do you choose not to be known? Your work stunned many countries that have been unable to find a cure for that horrible disease that was taking the lives of so many horses." Anna listened to the broken English coming from the lips of this Middle Eastern woman whose questions caused her to realize that the Madame did not understand American culture, especially the black culture from which she had come.

"My family knows nothing of the work I've been doing, Madame," Anna replied, watching a shocked look appear on the Madame's face as she began to explain that her family knew her only as an accountant, the wife of an up-and-rising politician, the daughter of a well-known restaurant owner, and the mother of two children. What she had done and what she was capable of doing beyond that was unknown to them. They would never understand the work she had done or the man in her life at that time. The Madame held a look of surprise, even though Anna knew she was already aware of her breakup with her husband and the reasons for it.

"Your brilliant mind should not be hidden away. It is a blessed gift from the God spirit, my dear, not to mention how many people all over the world have benefited from the cure."

Anna sipped some more of the hot tea, allowing it to cool in her mouth as she gazed at the Madame. Smiling, she shook her head, letting the Madame know that if her mother knew of her work and that it had profited even one white person, she would rather every diseased horse in the world had died. She assured her that few knew the Anna she knew. Informing her that if the news reached her city that a black woman had found a cure for that disease it would never enter the minds of the people there that it might possibly have been *her* cure. That is the way it must remain, she insisted, as she sat her tea cup down, only to have it refilled by the Madame as she refilled her own.

"My dear, it is a gift that should be shared with the world; there is no telling how many lives you may one day save."

"Madame, you still do not understand my world. What I have done would not be something to be proud of but rather a violation of a code I had broken."

"I do not understand, my dear. Please explain."

"My saving animals that are important to whites would not have sat well, especially with my mother and others who share the same sentiments about whites as she does." The downcast look the Madame gave Anna caused her to share with her the reason for her mother's hatred. By the time Anna finished informing her of her mother's tragic life, the Madame was truly shaken by all she had heard. After finishing their tea, the Madame suggested rest for them both.

****

"Is there something you are keeping from me, my dear?" the Madame asked the next morning, staring at her as they sat on their mats after they had finished their meditation hour. Clothed in a short white robe, her legs tucked under her, Anna frowned at the Madame, hunching her shoulders in reply as if to say she had no idea what the Madame referred to.

"Why, my dear, you look radiant. I retain my exceptional treatments for mothers-to-be and, of course, important females who have their journeys unfolding in ways that are extraordinary. When you are in with a lot of round bellies, don't become apprehensive; just know you are indeed in one of the two categories." The smile appearing on the lips of the Madame suggested to Anna that she was indeed impressed with the cure she had discovered to save the lives of those dying horses.

Two weeks into her stay, Anna looked forward to the warmth of the covered rocks that lay against her body warming it and the cool ones after she left the hot room saturated with sweat. She was informed that an hour of stretches would add elasticity to her body as well as keep it young and vibrant. The herbal tea expanded her mind, as did the small parcels of food—just enough to add to her health, but not too much so that it added pounds to her limbs.

At last, Anna found it easy to fall asleep without fretful dreams of him. As a matter of fact, she began to realize that she had been freed of a problem that had troubled her since she and Raymond had become an item. Had it not been for that sudden break between them, she would have been forced to make a decision she did not have the courage to make. Running from it for four years had led to a dead-end street with no way out.

Best of all was that there was no baby for her to worry about having to abort. Without Raymond in her life, it would have been the only possible solution to a problem that would have alienated her from the family she dearly loved. She and the Madame went around and around, but she knew there was no way the Middle Eastern woman's culture and her culture would ever come to an agreement as to what was in the female's best interest. It didn't really matter what the Madame thought, Anna reminded herself. She was free now—having escaped the warning of the Old Head and its thirteen eyes.

"FREE!" she screamed, hearing the echo of her voice as she slept alone in the small room with only a bed and table. Her laughter followed, and every day she kept reminding herself she was free, until the Old Head and its thirteen eyes came to her in a dream, telling her it was time for her to once again begin her journey.

Chapter Two

―∞―

Anna feared the plane would crash any second. Imagining herself as Jonah in the biblical story, she remembered how her mother had repeated the parable to her when she wanted to make a point that concerned learning. Moving with the turbulence, she allowed her hand to feel the white scarf given to her by the female ranchers in Kentucky where she worked developing the healing Tree serum that cured those dying horses. Thinking of that time in her life, she thought she had surely lived in the belly of the whale. It had now spit her back into the world she had left four years ago. What would it be like?

When she had come to visit her children during the time she was away, her mother kept reminding her of the change she saw in her daughter whom Anna knew her mother had once thought to be timid and meek.

"'Who is this new man?' her mother kept asking. "'I want to know the man who has given my gal such an uppity attitude.' Anna remembered her saying. Her father simply looked at her and smiled as he shook his head when she denied that any such man existed.

If only she could ease her heart of his memory—stop the wild tapping inside of it when she thought of him. She had to forget if she was going to survive in this world she was returning to.

The three ladies from Momma Lucy's Salon had come to help her pack while they listened to the recent events in her life. With everything shipped away, she had thanked them, saying that she must leave before he came looking for her, hoping to rekindle their relationship. Each left her with her own words of wisdom.

"'Ms. Anna, you have been a star in our lives, helping us get our finances straightened out, not to mention all the fun we've had with you and your heavy man. Baby, I hope you don't go back to that man you left behind,' Momma Lucy said, blowing smoke from her cigarette.

"'He's not the icing to wrap around your cake. You have found love in an unexpected place with a man who has taken you out of the harshness of our black world, allowing you to enjoy love even some rich white women never experience in their lifetimes. You will miss him. We will miss you. I think it's time that I take a trip back to Texas and see what family I got left there.' Momma Lucy's eyes filled with tears as she embraced Anna.

Even Madria, as hard and cold as anyone in her understanding of life, allowed tears to slip from her eyes.

"'Ms. Anna, if I taught you anything, I taught you not to be weak. Use your wits when others try to treat you like a sucker. Let them know you demand to be respected even if it means you must pay in some way. You are nobody to be pushed around. Promise Madria you will never again be caught weak.' Madria dispensed her advice while placing her switchblade inside Anna's bra.

Anna looked at her Italian friend with endearment as she felt the switchblade Madria had placed there, and she promised that she would never allow anyone to disrespect her without standing up for herself.

While standing with her long legs apart, tossing her blonde hair behind her back, Linda smiled at her. "'You were down for him in his weakest moments, and he was down for you when it mattered most. I can imagine your saving his horses has placed you at the center of his heart, not to mention that you saved his life. He loved you, Ms. Anna in a way men are seldom able to love a woman.'

"I loved him, too—no, I still love him, Linda, but life must go on." Linda reached down, taking the black horse on the gold chain in her hand.

"'What are your plans for this?'

"I should have given it back to him, but the letter was gone when I returned to the apartment, and I knew he would not be returning because he thought I was also gone."

"'Wear it for him. After all, no one will realize its value but someone who knows him. Where you are going, no one will know. Keep it safe, just as he kept you safe. We will miss you and your heavy man.' She smiled, telling Anna of her and Madria's plans to go to Italy to visit Madria's family when Momma Lucy headed south.

"'Don't forget, you're still a kid learning about life,' Linda added, inhaling smoke from the cigarette between her lips.

"I will wear it, Linda, and I won't forget. Thank you for all your wisdom and advice. Although I am not good about writing, I will call and let you know when and where I settle in." They left her standing there with tears spilling down her cheeks as she watched her life suddenly change right before her eyes.

Now, seated in the cab that was taking her to her parents' home, she thanked God her life had been spared and that the plane had landed safely. Rain poured outside the window. Lightning streaked across the sky, cutting through the air like a whip, and the roar of thunder followed. The vibrations of the Old Head pierced her mind as she listened to its voice whisper within the unsettling storm brewing around her.

"You must once again enter into the world you left behind, Daughter. It will no longer be the world you remember, nor will it welcome the person you have become. The twists and turns of your journey back in time will open secrets locked away. Your earth mate will serenade you, wanting you to come and mate with him again."

Anna's laughter filled the cab, causing the driver to turn and stare back at her in surprise. "Serenade me? I want no man in my life again. I'm done—finished with the lot of them," she whispered to herself.

"The Old Widow's young shall lie in your palm to protect you from all things that would harm you, Daughter. Keep her close."

Anna listened to the Old Head. Her heart increasing its tempo as the roar of the wind made the cab shake. Had the Old Head meant for her to return to Jake? Surely not! Her thoughts were interrupted as the cab slowed in front of her parents' home. Looking out into the rainy night, she saw the light from a cigarette fly through the air and knew her father stood waiting for her.

Handing the cab driver payment for the trip, her father walked with him to take her luggage from the trunk of the cab. Anna stood with her father in the rain as they watched the cab drive away. Hurrying up the four steps out of the pouring rain, Anna lowered herself onto the porch swing. It moved just as it had done thousands of times before, carrying the weight of many bodies in the days when this house had been her home. When her father brought in the last of her luggage, Anna followed him inside.

At two in the morning, silence filled her parents' home as if no one lived there. Taking a seat across from her father at the kitchen table—the place where matters of importance in most black homes in Session were discussed—she looked at him. He was a clean shaven tall dark man, which is where her mother informed her she had taken her skin tone from. Though she took her color and dimples from him, she however had not taken her height from him. He stood tall and lean at six two with no fat around his middle. He always wore a gray Stetson hat when he was out and about. She looked at him and the wet hat on his head with tears falling from her eyes.

"Baby Girl, what happened with you and the white man? Did he do you dirty?" he whispered, blowing smoke up into the air.

"Daddy, he wants me still. I just could not allow him to have me—not with his wife once again in his life and his son so sick. I had to leave him, but I . . ." Anna's tears continued to fall as she attempted to get out what she needed to tell him.

"Baby Girl, I just don't understand how you could have possibly fallen in love with this Southern white man. Black women are not supposed to fall in love with white men, especially Southern ones," her father whispered, handing her a tissue and then taking out a Lucky Strike and lighting it. He quickly blew out smoke, shaking his head while looking down at the floor. Anna bit her bottom lip in an effort to control her emotions.

"I have loved him for as long as I can remember. He has always had a place in my heart, even when I didn't remember him. It happened because of a promise I made and had to keep, Daddy."

"From what I've seen of him, he's a nice guy—a gentleman, I would say. From the things he has done for you, he is definitely a guy I would want for my daughter if he were a black man. It's not that I dislike him, but his white skin and southern background speak of a history no black man can forget."

"Daddy, why does he have to pay because he has white skin? It makes no sense to me," Anna cried, causing her father to hand her another tissue to dry her eyes.

"You would have to give up your mother. While I could accept him and his presence in your life, it would kill her. The horrible history whites have played in her life would forbid her ever accepting him under any circumstances—you do understand that, don't you?" Anna watched him pat his shirt pocket for his Lucky Strikes, even though he had not finished the one he was smoking.

"What is this about me?" Anna quickly wiped the tears from her eyes seeing her mother enter the room

"Lord, ya done brung my prodigal daughter back to us. When all them boxes come in, I knew my baby would be home soon." Anna looked at her mother through her tear filled eyes and realized that too much time had passed since they had last seen each other. Her mother almost white in color looked as beautiful as ever, but she seemed to have aged. Her waist long brown hair seemed grayer than Anna remembered it. The light hazel eyes that could cause her heart to tremble stood dangerously alert. The Creole blood running through her mother's veins made her a woman always ready to do battle if matters became serious between her and an adversary. Though most of Session loved and adored her mother, many knew the dangerous enemy she could become. Looking at her now standing six feet, Anna remembered stories told by her father of the bigger and stronger women she had cut down to size with that straight-edge razor she kept nestled beneath her breast. Her mother carried a scar down the right side of her back from one such encounter. If her mother allowed her to look, Anna knew she would find the famous pearl-handled straightedge razor still nestled there.

"Lord, Baby Girl, if you don't look like a million dollars," her father said, hurrying to change the subject. The tightness of his hug and the kiss he placed on her cheek let her know he understood what was in her heart.

"Daddy's Baby Girl has finally come home. You are might pretty to these old eyes, like you just stepped out of Hollywood." Anna managed a smile as her father held her at arm's length as if examining her just as her mother had done.

"What them doctor done did to my gal, huh?" Anna remembered telling her parents she was seeing a doctor to help her deal with life better. It was the one time her mother did not ask about race. She guessed that her mother assumed the doctor would have to be black.

"Not too much, Momma, but helped me get better," Anna, answered, watching her father walk from the room. Her heart sank as she noticed the bend in his back that had never been there before. It suddenly occurred to her that she must remember to question her mother about his health.

"Jake Jr.? Are they here?"

"Now gal, you oughta know for sho'. Ain't nobody gonna be keepin' them babies but yer daddy and me. Go on in thare and take a peek at 'em," her mother said as she followed Anna into the rooms where her children slept.

"I will be quiet. I don't want to wake them . . . not at two o'clock in the morning." Even though she always talked to them twice a week, it had been a year since she had last seen them. At six years old, her son had grown into a miniature picture of his father. She forced herself not to kiss him for fear of waking him. Moving from where he slept, Anna entered the next bedroom and stared down at her sleeping daughter who was wearing bangs and two ponytails like Anna had as a child. If she woke up, her eyes would sparkle and the dimples would deepen in her cheeks like Anna's own and Anna's father's. The twins would soon be seven; she must think of some special way to surprise them on their birthday, she thought to herself.

After a long tub bath, Anna dried off, slipped into a black silk gown, and climbed into the bed that had once been hers when she had lived with her parents. Her tears flowed but they felt good. At last, she was home to stay. They had had a clean break. All she had to do now was to get on with her life—if not in Session, then somewhere else. She could not look back. Her life with him was all behind her now. No one knew about the white man that had been in her life but her father, and she knew he would never tell.

* * * * * * * *

Anna woke the next morning to wet kisses all over her face. Both of her children giggled as they covered her with more kisses. She gasped at the changes in her babies who were now school-age children. She hated that she had missed their formative years. Both sounded excited as they examined the material of her purple satin housedress that was thrown across the foot of the bed.

"Momma, we never want you to go away again!" her son exclaimed, his arms tight around her as he held part of her housedress in his hand.

"Did the angels take good care of you like Grandma say they did, Momma?" her daughter asked rubbing a part of her mother's purple satin housedress against her cheek.

"I think maybe I had at least one angel watching over me."

"Was the angel nice, Momma?"

"Don't ask stupid questions," Jake Jr. interrupted. "Only devils are mean, like grandma says. Right, Momma?" Anna smiled down at her children.

"Jake Jr. is right; angels are nice."

"Well, I don't care how nice she was—we don't want her taking care of you anymore! She kept you way too long!" Sheri' said, smiling up at her mother and showing the dimples that were so like her own.

"Momma, Sheri' is right," Jake Jr. agreed as he helped his sister squeeze their mother.

"Now what ya chilen go wakin' yer Momma up fer? She got in late last night and she needs hur rest. Git in thare and git ready for school."

"But Grandma, it's Momma's first day home. We want to stay here with her," Sheri' quickly replied to her grandmother's demands.

"Ain't no need of ya lookin' and beggin', Anna Jeff Drake Bradley, dese younguns talk wit ya most ever day ya was gone. Anyhow, I got some talk fur ya and it ain't nothin' for thay ears to be hearin'." She turned to the children. "Git up like I done tole ya 'fore I come as to gittin' my switches on yer butts. Ya can see yer momma adder school, now git." The children scrambled up, hurrying out the room with unhappy looks on their faces.

When the house was emptied of both children and Anna's father, her mother took a seat beside her at the kitchen table after making a cup of tea for them both.

"Now gal, seeing as how yer daddy and dem babies is gone, ya can come clean and tell yer Momma bout dat man ya done took up wit out thare in Nevada dat ya keep pretendin' don't exist." Anna looked at her mother, thinking she had not lost her ability to get straight to the point.

"Momma, what makes you think a thing like that?" Anna asked, looking down into her cup of tea.

"'Cause Momma's gal ain't never called asking fer one red penny. Stead ya sent money I knew had to come from somewhares. Thare ain't no job ya got dat 'llows ya to send five thousand dollars a month home, least none dat I knows of. Whare on earth did ya find such a man, gal?" Anna listened to her mother whisper, even though they were home alone. "Hare ya is now back lookin' like one of dem brazen women on a magazine cover, like yer daddy done said."

"Momma, there is such a thing as work, you know. Women work outside of the home all over America these days. Without Jake keeping me under his thumb, I realized that there is something I'm good for besides jumping to his beck and call." Anna drank from her cup, her eyes averted as her mother rose, walked over to the kitchen door, and closed it as though afraid someone might hear her next words.

Turning back, she asked, "Ya ain't done gone out to dat sinful place and got rid of dat baby ya was carryin', did ya, gal? No matter what dem white devils tells ya, it's a sin 'fore God." Anna's mouth opened in shock at her mother's disclosure but she remembered her cantor for getting to the point.

"Momma, I'm hurt that you would even ask that. I told you when we first talked over the phone right after the accident, don't you remember? I told you then what happened. Do I look like a baby killer? Goodness, Momma, I do remember some of the morals I was taught." Anna breathed easier, seeing the smile reappear on her mother's face.

"I tole that Negra man of yers I didn't thank ya could ever do a thang like dat."

"What's Jake been saying? He'd better not bring that lie to me, knowing how I fell down those stairs at Barb's apartment."

"Chile, it was all over Session by mornin'. Worst talk than dat storm what come up. And ya don't take adder yer Momma—no damn woman woulda run Annabelle 'way from hur home. She woulda seen the edge of dis hare razor first." Anna looked at the pearl-handled razor her mother took from under her breasts and thought of the switchblade Madria had given her. It took her back to the night she and Raymond had had their worst fight. She did not want to be reminded of that night ever again.

"It was all over town how she done run ya off. I tole dat man of yers if I ever was tole he done taken up with the likes of dat whore agin, he'd never be welcomed hare with us or dese babies." Anna looked at her mother and saw the warmth for her in her eyes.

"He done come to me cryin, I tell ya. Tole me he was sorry for showin' out thata way. Swore 'fore God he ain't touched no woman since ya been gone. I thank he railly gone make ya a better husband now." Anna listened in shock as she realized that her mother expected her to take her adulterous husband back after having been gone for four years. Her mother might believe his lies, but she sure didn't. The thought that he had not touched another woman since she left him was unbelievable; and even so, she did not care. It was over between them.

"Momma, he's crazy if he thinks I want him back. While he's telling you those lies, what he doesn't know is that if he had been your husband, he would be dead right now."

Her mother's eyes narrowed. "And so the hell would his whore gal."

"I'm thinking about swearing off men for the rest of my life, Momma." The two women's eyes met. Anna blushed at her mother's grinning face. "I'm serious, Momma."

"Anna Jeff Drake Bradley, when dat body of yurs gits dat ole, I won't be round to see it. Ya may not tell yer Momma, but thare was some colored man warming dat body of my baby at night." Anna gazed into her mother's eyes and remembered lips reaching for hers and hands under the covers playing in her most sacred place, a body moving inside of hers— not colored, but white. Cold chills flowed through Anna as her mother's eyes locked with hers. She rose and stretched, covering her open mouth. "Momma, I must be suffering from jet lag. We'll have to talk later," she said, allowing her housedress to slip down her back as she started out of the room.

The sound of glass breaking caused Anna to turn back seeing that her mother's eyes had grown large as she grip the edge of the kitchen table. Tears flooded her cheeks. Anna rushed towards her seeing her fall back into her seat.

"What's wrong, Momma?" Anna asked, hurrying to her side while picking up the broken glass.

"Ya back is as smooth as a baby's bottom. All dat marring on it gone. Oh God, how I prayed for my baby's back to be smooth again. Ya never shoulda gone thare. It's all my fault dat it happened," she listened to her mother whisper, a stricken look on her face as she shook her head in anguish.

"Momma, you don't have to feel bad about my back any longer. I had an operation that fixed it."

"When and whare did it take place, gal?"

The answer stuck on the end of Anna tongue. "Momma, I don't want to discuss my back now. I'm too tired she said rising as she disposed of the broken glass."

"Was it yer man done it for ya, gal?"

Yes, Anna thought to herself, her mother and her lover's cousin Julia Mike had a lot in common, getting to the bottom of the matter, but she had lots of experience avoiding giving answers. Pulling her house dress up over her shoulders, she turned away from her mother.

"It's beautiful now, Momma. That's all that matters, isn't it?" Anna asked, looking back to see her mother wipe tears from her eyes.

****

That afternoon, Anna rose from a much-needed nap to called Momma Lucy, letting her know she had finally arrived home. After dropping the receiver in its cradle, she sighed, disappointed that Linda and Madria had already left for Italy. Anna wanted to thank Linda for her advice about white men. With the help of Raymond's precious wife, she had been able to make a clean break without either of them getting shortchanged.

Anna had no regrets. She had gotten out of the affair with no entrapments. No one would ever know she had been with a white man except her father. It would be her own private secret, a secret she knew she could never share with anyone else.

That evening, she listened to her mother warn Jake Jr. and Sheri' not to reveal to their father that Anna had returned home. She quickly intercepted the conversation.

"Momma, I don't care if Jake knows I'm home. There is no love for him in Anna any longer. He's just another man out of my life. I thought you knew that by now." Her mother still insisted that she call him and let him know she was back before he found out from other people.

"Talk is cheap, gal; I'll know when he's with ya if ya forgot him or not."

Kissing her mother's cheek, Anna replied, "I'll bet you a good ten dollars he'll never sleep in Anna's bed again."

"Gambling is sinning, but yer Momma will take dat ten if'n ya don't live up to what yer be telling hur." Her mother cocked her head and stared at her. Anna realized that her mother was not prepared for the daughter she was listening to.

****

Unfamiliar streets caused Anna to lose her way to her friend Dee's home. Session had changed so much that she had trouble finding the grocery store she had visited regularly before leaving. At last, she saw a familiar sight. Driving up into the parking lot, she parked, got out of her mother's brand new 1977 cream-colored Lincoln, and made her way into Forals, Jake's old hangout. Someone in there would be able to explain what had happened to Pine Street, she thought to herself.

Walking inside Forals, Anna asked the bartender she knew named Rags about the street. The strange way he looked at her caused Anna to realize he did not recognize her.

"About three years ago the street name was changed to Malcolm X Drive," he told her as she turned to leave feeling the men's eyes on her as the eyes of other men had fell on her in the years she had lived with Raymond Forlorn.

"Where the hell did you come from, baby?" Anna looked at the man she knew as Mike White, one of Jake's poker buddies when he wasn't playing blackjack. It surprised her that he would speak to her in that manner. She realized that he did not recognize her either.

"My mother, if you must know."

"If all your momma's babies look like you, I gotta start coming over to help babysit," he replied, laughing along with the other black men in the bar who sat staring at her.

"Yeah, ya got that right, man, good as she lookin' and what's the name of that purrfffumm?" Rags asked as he and the other men seated at the bar sniffed the air.

"I don't think Janet would like it if she found Jake Bradley's wife being babysat by her husband, do you?"

"Anna Bradley, shitttt!" they all shouted in unison. "You damn sho' don't look like that woman got run outta here," Mike White insisted, staring at Anna as she removed her white fox coat and placed it across her arm. The red satin dress she wore hugged her body. The white diamond collar on it glittered for the men whose mouths stood open as they stared at her with wide eyes.

"I was told you got run out of town by them shelter women," Rags said, still eyeballing her.

"Now I wonder where you got that erroneous information," Anna replied, smiling at the men with her dimples reflecting her mood.

"I don't recall offhand—just a tidbit of info I picked up in passing," Rags said, covering his lips as he shook his head and let his eyes gaze down at the slit on the side of her red silk dress.

"Seems to me you picked up some bad information," Anna replied, moving closer to the door.

"Well, I sho' heerd it." he told Anna. "Somethin' bout you and that Barb woman you tied up with run you off. Folks round here looked for you a long time, guess 'cause of all that bread Jake put up as a reward after they found your car burned and you not in it."

"Well, you let it be known that Anna Jeff Drake Bradley is back in town. See if you can drop that tidbit of information in passing," she said, smiling as she walked toward the door with the fox now tossed over her shoulder. Rags raced to open the door for her.

"Damn, Mrs. Bradley, you sho' nuff don't look like the same woman Jake Bradley married, and you sho' nuff smell good enough to eat. Mmmmmhummmmm!" Rags said, still gazing at the slit up her dress. Anna walked out the door, leaving them all smelling the air that was now filled with the Wild Passion perfume her lover had always replenished because he also loved its smell. Soon, Anna knew, Jake would know she had returned.

Chapter Three

—ᴍ—

The streets had changed so much that nothing looked the same. Driving up into Dee's front yard, Anna looked around at all the changes that had taken place there. A new burnt-orange Oldsmobile had replaced the 73 green Chrysler, and Anna knew it had to belong to Dee. It was her favorite color. Getting out of her mother's car and stepping into Dee's yard was like coming home to a friend she had always missed. Dee's children's swing set she noticed had switched from her yard to her next door neighbor Shirley's yard. She guessed Dee's children had out grown it.

Anna walked up to Dee's front door and remembered that she never kept it locked during the day, a turn of the knob and it opened for her. She walked into the familiar living room with all its brown and orange furnishings and on into the kitchen where she heard voices and smelled the scent of peaches cooking. She knew Dee was making peach jelly one of her favorite cooking projects. Dee and Shirley sat peeling peaches and did not see her enter the room. A small boy and a baby sat at Shirley's feet. The baby was pulling at the older child's hand trying to get some of the peach he was eating. The toddler Shirley had brought to the shelter with her, Anna surmised would be old enough to be in school now. Both women looked up at the same time causing Anna to flash a smile.

"Anna!" I can't believe it's you!" Dee screamed, as she jumped up from her kitchen table and grabbed and hugged Anna. Anna squeezed her caramel colored sister in law a woman two inches shorter than she. Smiling as she noticed that Dee still wore her fancy looking purple and pink fingernails. Her short bobbed hair cut had not changed something that enhanced her large brown engaging eyes. Anna squeezed her sister in law she was so glad to see her.

Anna saw Shirley, Dee's white friend who lived next door, staring at her as she picked up the baby reaching for her. The young boy jump up and grab Shirley's leg when she entered the room. Shirley rose tossing her blonde hair behind her back looking nervous. Her hips spread from her small waist leading down to large hips and legs. Several inches taller then she, Anna looked into Shirley's wide blue eyes and knew the room had suddenly become uncomfortable for her. Both women marveled over the full-length white fox coat she wore. Dee spread it open wider to gaze at the Paris designer's red silk dress that gave Anna a provocative look.

"I'm going, Dee," Shirley said, reaching for her baby's bag as she sat the baby back on the floor. Anna watched as Shirley gathered her belongings. Walking over to where she stood, Anna touched her arm.

"Shirley, I thought you told me you were a sister when you came to the shelter needing help four years ago," Anna said as Shirley continued to gather her children's belongings.

"She is a sister, Anna. Besides you, she's the best friend I got," Dee answered for Shirley as she, too, stood staring at Shirley.

"I'm not talking to you, Dee; I'm talking to Shirley," Anna said, as the white woman again tossed her blonde hair behind her back.

"I am a sister," she said, staring hard at Anna. Anna knew she was waiting for the negative remarks she thought would come from her. Instead Anna stretched out her arms.

"Well, I do believe sisters hug when they greet each other, am I right or wrong, Dee?" Anna saw a wide smile spread across Dee's lips as she and the white woman hugged.

"Mrs. Bradley, you smell so good with your gorgeous looking self."

"I'm no longer Mrs. Bradley to you, Shirley. I'm Anna. Can you handle that, sister girl?"

"I can handle it, sister girl," Shirley said, smiling. Anna looked down to see her son asking Shirley for his crying brother's bottle. She almost lost her composure as she recalled that her own child would have been about his age if she had not fallen down those stairs at Barb's apartment. Kneeling down, she scooped up the crying baby.

"He sounds as though he is hungry. Where is his bottle, Shirley?" Anna asked as she ruffled the curly brown hair on his head. Anna smiled devilishly at the two women staring at her. Their mouths fell wide open when she kissed the crying baby's cheek.

"A bottle, Shirley. I did say the baby wanted his bottle, didn't I?"

"Sure . . . I mean yes," she answered, sounding more than a little shocked.

"You and Dee just continue putting up those jars of jelly while I get this baby to sleep." Anna walked toward Dee's bedroom with the baby in her arms.

"Oh no, Mrs. Bradley, I mean Anna. I wouldn't want him to throw up on that gorgeous red dress you are wearing."

"Please," Anna said, waving her off. "There are plenty more where this one came from." She left with the baby in her arms smiling at the two women stared at her with their mouths still hung open. Anna knew that they didn't know *this* Anna. The woman they remembered would not have acknowledged Shirley, let alone touch her biracial baby.

Shock them and shock them good—you have been shocking yourself for the last four years, she told herself, looking down at the child as she fed and then changed him.

He soon slept soundly. She kissed his smooth tan skin as she ran her fingers through his thick hair so much like his mother's, only curly while Shirley's lay straight. Shirley's eyes were blue; his were brown like his father's.

Anna's mind went back in time to the many places where she and her lover's bliss had continued to flourish after the three nights in the cabin. Their hearts raced as he moved inside of her, asking if she was with him. Right before the pond incident, they had discussed getting more pills before becoming sexually active again, but there just had not been time. They flew off to the Caribbean where they lay naked on a sailboat in each other's arms under the moonlight, thinking of nothing but the moment.

"Anna, just as sure as hell we are going to make a baby," he had whispered weeks later as they lay breathing hard in bed in a suite in Morocco at Mix's villa.

"We can always go sky diving, baby. Can't make a baby doing that, can we?" Anna answered, not caring about the baby they might make just as long as her lover continued to quench the fire he had been unleashed in her body since he had pulled her out of that pond by the cabin. Now thinking back to that escalated passion, Anna had to admit she had wanted his child because she had believed he would be there to love the child just as she had believed he loved her.

The Old Head had seemed worried that the pond held a powerful dark potion that would make her body desire his and eliminate her will to use caution, which would take her on many twists and turns on this journey of hers—twists and turns she could not escape. Thank God, her pregnancy test had turned out negative. She had been afraid that she had pushed her luck too far in not heeding the warning of the Old Head—but not enough to replace those birth control pills they had tossed out the window.

As Anna kissed the sleeping infant in her arms, she asked herself what she would have done if her belly had been filled with her lover's baby shuddering at the predicament it would have caused her.

She puzzled over his wife believing her to be a mere servant simply because she was black. Well, Mrs. Forlorn, she thought to herself, even though my race of women might not have been who you thought your husband could desire, you would have had to move over had my belly been filled with his baby because you would have then discovered what purpose the master still used his servants for down there in Las Vegas. Anna sighed, allowing her tears their freedom. Count your damn blessings, white woman, and be thankful you gave him a son, because although I was beneath who you thought your husband would sleep with, you damned sure were not above whom I thought I could take him from.

Lying next to the sleeping infant, Anna trembled at the thought of what his baby would have done to her life without him in it. After some time, the sound of her breathing could be heard along with the baby's.

When Dee woke her, Anna looked over and saw that Shirley's baby was no longer in the bed next to her.

"I told Shirley not to wake you, girlfriend. You have been sleeping two hours. I was going to let you sleep longer, but I am too curious about what you have been up to. You walked in here looking like a movie star. Now tell me, are those real diamonds you are sporting, especially those balls glittering in those ears of yours? And sister girl, where the hell did you get that fine-ass coat from?"

"What did you do with all the clothes I sent you via Momma, Dee?" Anna asked, sitting up in her friend's bed.

"Child, I got them packed away. I knew I couldn't explain them to Fred. He would have asked too many questions, but since you are back, I will start wearing them—you can bet on that!"

"Dee, you are crazy," Anna said, laughing at her friend's explanation.

"Anna, tell me the truth. Don't lie. I need to know every detail. Don't leave nothing out, not even a gasp, do you hear me?" Anna followed Dee eyes as they suddenly grew large as she covered her mouth.

"Dee, who the hell have you got in our bed?"

"Hello, Fred," Anna said, placing her feet on the floor as she watched her brother in law's green eyes scan her as if trying to identify her, just as the men at Forals had done.

The oldest of her husband's brothers, he was the only one clean shaven, very fair skinned, and the tallest of the three brothers standing lean but muscular at about six feet. His eyes, Dee told Anna had danced their way into her heart. He still wore his hair Anna noticed in thick waves combed to the back of his head down to his shoulders. Dee stood a little taller than his waist and always complained that she was always looking up.

"Don't look at her so stupid. She's your sister-in-law, Anna, fool."

Anna watched Fred's eyes light up as he stared down at her, exclaiming that she looked like a different woman and how much joy his brother would feel when he discovered she had returned. Anna said nothing as she listened to his unwelcomed comment on her husband's feelings about discovering her return. Twelve years her senior Anna had always had a lot of respect for Fred who was six years older than James and ten years older than Jake. He was the one the two younger brothers went to when trouble came their way. Though he was by far no angel himself, Anna knew many times his wisdom kept both Jake and James out of trouble when they listened to him. Fred would take up the fight for his younger brothers, verbally or physically and had the resources to go the distance. He made it a point to know everyone in town worth knowing. Both Jake and James knew Fred would call his brothers on their wrongs whether they liked what he had to say or not.

"God, baby, she looks so different—I would not have known her on the street," Fred said, still staring at Anna with his mouth open. Anna wondered what in hell had she looked like before she left.

"Damn right, she does not look like that homely-looking woman she was before she left—ain't that good! Anna listened to Dee tell her husband. "Jake is going to be knocked off his feet. He won't know her cause you look nothing like the Anna that left here sister girl."

Anna listened to Dee question her husband as to why he was home so early.

"Baby, I need to borrow the Oldsmobile; my car's starter has gone bad," Fred said, continuing to stare Anna down as he reached for the keys hanging on a hook by the door.

"I have a doctor's appointment, Fred. I need to use the car myself."

"Maybe, Anna won't mind taking you. I see she's driving that big fine new Lincoln her mother sports around town. I was wondering what brought her over," Fred said, still gazing at Anna with a big grin on his face.

"Sure, I'll take her," Anna agreed, rising from the bed. Anna could see doubt in the look Dee gave her.

"Dee, I'll take you there and wait on you, okay?" Anna said, reaching for her white fox coat.

"Damn, Anna, what you been doing?" Fred asked, whistling as he rubbed the soft white fur.

"Working, fool, just like you," Dee said, ushering him out the door.

"Okay, Anna, but you know how you are," Dee said once the door shut behind her husband.

"How I used to be, Dee, not how I am now, okay?" Anna saw that Dee still maintained a doubtful look.

"That husband of mine bought me that car because he really wanted it for himself, sister girl. Let's go before I'm late."

****

Anna smiled at the women seated in the doctor's office as she and Dee took a seat. Soon after they arrived, Dee was called. Anna looked around her at the women also waiting to be seen. Dee was right—before she had left Session, she would never have waited for her because the panic inside of her would have been too intense. For her own appointments, she had to be assured by the receptionist that she could walk right in at her appointed time. No longer did that Anna exist. She had changed inside and out. The women smiling at her would not have been able to do so with the old Anna.

She was glad she had left her coat in the car; she did not want to appear overly dressed in a doctor's office with women she thought were probably struggling to care for their families. Even though everything seemed smaller and the women seemed not so sophisticated, it felt good to sit among them unafraid. The woman seated next to her mentioned that she was four months pregnant and then spoke generally to everyone concerning her affair with a married man.

"Honey," Anna listened to her say to no one in particular, "when I want to get the motherfucker out of the house to come see me, all I got to do is call his house and cuss his old lady out. He's sittin' there listening 'cause that's the way we planned it." Anna sat stunned at the woman's admission of her deed and more shocked at the listeners' agreeable responses.

"Half hour later, we laying up in bed together." Anna looked at her grin as she sucked from the cigarette between her fingers, ignoring the No Smoking sign on the office door.

"She should have her number changed," responded a younger black girl with long purple acrylic nails.

"Hell, the bitch done had it changed five times. He just brings it over to his honey plum . . . that's what he calls me. I wait about a month and then start calling and cussing her ass out again. He keeps right on coming like always. The dizzy broad ain't caught on yet that that's his cue that I want his ass." Listening to the assessment of the woman's admissions bring laughter from the other women seated in the office caused Anna to wonder what she had come back to.

"Well," said a young girl Anna guessed to be in her late teens who sat with a baby in her lap, "once my man was out with his wife, Anna sat her mouth ajar listening to what she told the women waiting to be seen by the doctor. "I came into the joint and told my man there was some guys outside wanting to see him about helping them get their car started 'cause of him being a mechanic and all. When he got outside, we went across the street to the motel and made love for almost an hour."

Anna almost spoke—she was so shocked at such a young girl's admission. Where had she been not to know these type of women existed in Session?

"We goes back, and he gives his wife some money he said he made fixing the man's car. The frown on that chick's face for having to wait so long soon disappeared. Once he even left her inside the bar while we made out in his car. I wouldn't be nobody's wife." Anna shook her head, realizing either she had been gone too long or not long enough.

A pregnant teenager entered the conversation. "Most of the time, you don't have to worry . . . shit, the wives are going through so much shit at home, they are glad to git his ass out of their hair for a while, cussing and beating the hell out of 'em. Anyway, what man wants his wife when he has sweet little thangs like us on the streets?" She could not have been out of high school, Anna surmised, slowly shaking her head in disbelief.

"My brother went with me over to my man Jimmy's house to get him out to be with me." Another woman seated across from Anna spoke up.

"Shit, I wanted a piece of his ass." Anna listened to the young woman maybe in her early twenties say. "His wife thought my brother and I was sho' nuff thick the way we were all hugged up. We got us a good fight going. She asked Jimmy to take me home so my brother wouldn't hurt me. My baby comforted me all night long—what the hell do I need with a single man?"

"Ain't that the truth!" said the only white patient seated in the office. Anna looked at the thin blue-eyed female with black hair. Before she had left Session, no white woman would have had the nerve to come into this black doctor's office. It let her know the people in Session were certainly playing catch up. "I like to hang out in the wife's house, wear her shit, even her panties, have him in her bed." Anna could not help but think of Barb and how she had disrespected her home.

"Damn, you get personal with your shit," said the black girl with the purple acrylic nails.

"I ain't gonna call no names cause most of you chicks in here know him. He is well known around town. 'Bout five years ago," she said, lowering her voice, "this black dude I was hanging out with was some kind of good looker. Like I said, I ain't gonna call no names cause I wouldn't want to blow his cover. He told me once when we were out getting high off some fire that his wife hated whites so much she couldn't stand the sight of them. I told him she would have a fit if she knew what he was doing. He said he never had to worry about her believing he would have a white girl. I could do a blow job on him he was wild about, and he could make love like no other man I have met since." Anna stared at the white woman, feeling what the Madame would call pure disgust.

"Once when I hadn't seen him in about a month, I got up enough courage to go by his house," she said, singing out Anna's old home address like it were her own. "Up there where the good money biddies live," she said, in an attempt to help the women locate the area in their minds.

"Hillside?" The young girl with the acrylic nails asked.

"Yeah, that's it all right," the white girl said, blowing smoke from her cigarette. "I asked to see the lady of the house. Hell, I didn't know what I was going to say to get out of her where he was. Anyway, the kid that came to the door told her it was a white woman. She had him come tell me that her husband took care of all their business. I asked where he could be reached because it was important that I get in touch with him right away." The woman blowing smoke from her mouth never saw Anna's change of expression as she continued to tell the group how the child had come back to the door with the address to Jake's new office location.

Anna closed her eyes and shook her head listening to her say that when she got there and confronted him about giving her the brush off; he quickly denied any such thing. She said that he asked her how she got his new address. She grinned as she told the group of women that she told him how she got the number and that they went for another three months getting it on because his wife's hatred for whites had prevented her from coming to the door. The white woman concluded by telling the women that all his wife would have had to do was take one look at her and she would have known what was up. Everyone in the room laughed except Anna.

"Oh," said the young pregnant girl, "I like those kind, thinking they so high on the hog. Shit, we in bed with their men more than them."

I wouldn't doubt that for a minute, Anna thought, as she continued to learn from the women in the doctor's office.

"All they have is expensive vibrators and that kinda shit," insisted the young teenager. "Probably screwing each other; ya'll know how way-out those high-class bitches is with they lovin'. Go for all that unnatural shit." Laughter spread through the room. Anna noticed that even the receptionist joined in the laughter as she ignored the fact that the women were smoking.

"It's a shame they can't deal with what's real," the young white woman said as she pushed her hair back laughing with the women. At that moment, Anna was no longer in the waiting room but back with the Madame, listening to her words that she now realized were so true ringing in her ears.

"'Anna, the female is the most precious creation God gave this earth, but when she allows her tongue to become filthy and her body to be used like a sewer, she becomes the most disgusting beast on earth.' Her face flashed before Anna and then disappeared. Anna blinked, understanding at last the Madame's meaning. Looking up, she saw Dee coming out into the waiting room. Rising, Anna looked back at the females still in conversation. She shook her head, thinking they didn't have a clue.

"I was worried you would leave me," Dee said as they drove away from the doctor's office.

"Why would I leave you, Dee? Anyway, I got an earful from those women back there in the doctor's office—they left a lot to be desired. Their conversation about the games they play on men's wives is not cool at all."

"Street whores, sister girl. You know our word for them."

"We wouldn't entertain them with a slither of our breath!" they both shouted in unison.

"Probably got diseases we ain't never heard of, huh?" Dee asked, nodding her head as if assuring her they did. "The men who are paying those hustling whores for treats ain't gettin' nothing special, I'll tell you that. I am still shocked you didn't leave me."

"Why would I do that?" Anna asked, looking over at Dee as they walked to the car.

"Oh come on, Anna, I can remember when I would have had to beg you to take me, and I wouldn't dare ask you to wait for me. You bet I was nervous that I was going to have to walk home if I could not reach Fred after you told him you would wait for me."

"I'm not like that anymore, Dee. I keep telling you I have changed," Anna replied, looking ahead at the oncoming traffic as she drove them out of the parking lot.

Anna listened to Dee tell her how she and Shirley about went through the floor when she walked into the house and hugged Shirley not to mention picking up her baby. Asking Anna if she had seen the shocked looks they gave her. Reminding her that before she left, she would not have touched that baby, and if she had looked at Shirley, it would have been as if she was a leper. As a matter of fact, Dee told her she hardly dealt with anyone except her and that bitch Barb.

"Please, Dee, don't ever bring that name up to me again. She did a job on me I have yet to live down. I thought by now she and Jake would be an item." Anna turned to look at her when Dee laughed telling Anna that, if she called Barb's name around Jake, he'll get up and leave the room. Then she let Anna know Jake had been in a bad way. She shared with her that her brother in law now limped in his right leg from where Barb had shot him that night she caught him dirty. Anna frowned wondering why her parents never mentioned it to her on her visits. She continued to listen to Dee tell her Jake had been out of town since last week. And that he should get back the next night."

"Never thought I would see that man shed a tear over you the way he used to dog you, Anna. But when no one could find a trace of you, he cried so hard about how Barb set him up and how you fell down those stairs. We thought we were going to have to have the fool committed."

"There will be no more dogging Anna will take from another man ever again. The next man Anna gets, if there is another man—which I doubt—will have to live up to standards I have grown accustomed to since I left here."

"Come on, sister girl, out with it. I want to hear everything about those four years, not just that evasive shit you have been giving everyone. There was another man, wasn't there?" Anna pulled into the nearby shopping center, stopped the car, unzipped her dress, and turned her back to Dee.

"No way! All those horrible scars are gone! Your back looks as though it has never had a scar on it!" Anna felt her friend's hands slide down her back and heard her gasp as she whispered, "It's smoother than my back!"

"He did this for me—even helped me regain my memory." Anna smiled as she turned to see the stunned look on Dee's face.

"Are you telling me, Anna Bradley that you know how those scars came to be on your back? Anna felt her dress being zipped up as her hands tightened on the steering wheel. By the time she finished telling Dee how her mother beat her and why it all happened (leaving out the Old Head's part and Raymond's race), they both were in tears.

"Momma doesn't know I know what happened to me or her part in it?" Anna said thinking of her mother, realizing how hard it would be on both of them to have to relive that scene and the horror of it again "I couldn't tell her. It would be too hard on both of us reliving it all. Only Daddy knows I know."

"I guess it's best to leave it as it is," Dee said as they drove away . . . Wait, there is Harriet Tubman's Park drive into it There is parking down close to the lake," Dee said, pointing to where she wanted Anna to drive. "I love sitting near the water; I believe it has healing powers—anyway it relaxes me," Dee said as she got out of the car. Anna followed her along the lake seeing others strolling by. Birds flew over the water and ducks dunked their heads down, looking for food the water held. "Come on, Anna, out with it," Dee insisted as they walked along the water's edge.

"You sound like Momma! Goodness, Dee!" Anna replied, still not giving up any information.

"Where were you? With your man. Your mother believes you were! Damn you, Anna, I gotta know. I've listened to you tell me about your dreams for so long."

"The man I was with helped me through so many tough times, Dee. I'll always love him for that."

"What the hell! I knew it! Anna you were with some strong-ass brother—I just know it. Tell me, girl, before I die!"

"Dee, I've traveled to places I never dreamed I would ever see in my life; I've been to countries like France, Italy, Austria, England, Sweden, even Switzerland."

"You are kidding me! A brother did that for you?" Dee screamed as she jumped in front of Anna, walking backwards, looking at her with her hand covering her mouth.

"I kid you not, my friend. I even learned to see something in me worth living for. You know . . . what we used to believe only white women get."

"You don't have to tell me. No name calling?"

"Never!" Anna said.

"No getting cursed out for living?"

"No way!"

"No beatings and kicking the way some of the women around here get from those fools they are married to?"

"No way—everything had to be just right. Even when there were arguments, most were settled peacefully between us. When we walked down the street, everyone knew I was his lady. I received the respect that came from being his lady, sister girl. He made sure of that."

"You mean the brother's not two feet ahead of you and you running to keep up?" Anna shook her head no as she stretched out her arms, a big grin on her face.

"That brother had to be heavy. Better than those dreams you had about some white dude, sister girl. Fred done already wised me up about them white dudes."

"What do you mean, Fred wised you up about white dudes?" Anna asked, a frown starting on her face.

"My baby said white men are built to handle only white women. There is no way they can handle or satisfy a sister. Why you think white women are running down brothers? He says it's 'cause white men got a handicap in bed for real. No sister is going to put up with that shit. Fred made it clear to me that's why back in the day they had to take a sister—now they have to pay." Anna had to laugh, thinking to herself it was the same thing Jake had told her about white men something she believed to be true until she took that airplane trip with her lover. She started to enlighten her friend until she heard the soothing voice of the Old Head:

"Daughter the thoughts of one mind become collective thinking for all minds on your earth world. Allow her to embrace what she believes unless you are willing to tell secrets no one knows."

Anna swallowed hard and let it go.

"Why did you leave a brother that together, Anna?"

"Dee, have you forgotten I am a married woman? And even though he filed for his divorce, I still have to deal with mine. Plus it turned out he had a sick son. It was fun but nothing lasting."

"Was it hard letting go?" Dee asked as they continued to walk around the park.

"It was just fun, Dee . . . just a fun dream," Anna insisted, more to herself than to Dee. They walked without talking for a while, and then Anna stopped and turned to face Dee.

"Dee you and Shirley are really close, as I recall, once upon a time you had no use for white women. I always wanted to ask you what made you change and become friends with Shirley?" Dee looked at Anna hunching her shoulders as Anna remembered Dee had a habit of doing when asked something she had to think about. She watched Dee walk closer to the water, causing the ducks to hurry away.

"When she and Tony first moved next door to us, I'd walk past her and not speak when she spoke to me even though Fred and the kids would speak to her." Living next door, it was hard to get past her without us running into each other. Sometimes I would look out my back window and see her and Tony her husband standing talking to Fred while she pushed my baby in her swing or see her playing basketball with my boys." Anna watched Dee look down at the water as if trying to figure out herself how their friendship began.

"Fred told me I was acting like those white crackers down south and that was not like me cause he believed I would speak to a dog if it spoke to me." Anna listened to Dee say, her eyes casted down at the water they walk along side. "One day she came knocking on my door," Dee finally said. "When I opened it, she asked me what color did she have to change to for me to speak to her because she sure as hell hadn't done a damn thing to deserve the shitty way I was treating her."

"Whoa, what the hell did you say?"

"'Bring your ass on in here and let's talk I told her. I found we had a lot more in common than I realized, Anna. Shirley, I discovered, keeps it real. I don't have to watch my back around her 'cause she always has it. Between the two of you, I have no other friends I trust. She's a real sister girl Anna." A sigh escaped Dee's lips.

"As I recall, you had a few black sisters you called friends."

"Unlike you, they dropped me as soon as they saw her at my house more times than they thought was necessary. Told me, 'Cut the bitch loose! We don't want to see her at your house again.'"

"Damn, that's some heavy control."

"The next time they came, she happened to be sitting in my living room watching the soaps with me. After calling me a black ass white loving bitch, they turned around and walked out the door. I threw Shirley an orange, locked my door, and said good riddance." As Dee walked backwards, Anna noticed a big smile spread across her friend's face. "Anna, it's Friday—the kids don't have to go to school in the morning—let's go out and party tonight. I no longer need a sitter. It will be fun. Oh, I forgot," Dee paused, "you don't go out, do you?"

"What time will you pick me up, Dee? I want to go home and spend time with my kids."

"Be ready at eleven o'clock, sister girl; the fun don't start 'til midnight."

****

Anna knew she had returned to the black world when she walked into Session's largest nightclub called the Lion's Den with Dee and asked for a dry martini. Anna noticed everyone was dressed in evening wear but after her request they stared at her as though she was a stranger invading their circle. She smiled and took it all in.

"Give us two rum and cokes. Anna, this is Session; they don't even know what a dry martini looks like around here."

"Sorry," Anna said, thinking how strange it was to be sitting in a small nightclub compared to the glamour Ray had gotten her accustomed to. In those jet-set spots, people of all races stood shoulder to shoulder. This nightclub had only two or three whites seated inside it. Black on black brothers and sisters stood wall to wall. The band was playing while a singer sang BB King's *The Thrill is Gone*. The floor was filled with dancers. Because she had seldom left home, Anna never knew there was a place where that many black people gathered together. As soon as they were seated, two women stopped at their table.

"Who is she?" the women asked, staring hard at Anna with frowns on their faces as though they didn't like the competition she might bring.

"Jake's wife, Anna, don't you remember her?" Dee asked, laughing at their shocked looks.

"Hey Dee, where is Fred?" A man interrupted the conversation, with Anna noticing him staring at her.

"Max, Fred is at home with his kids. And by the way, this is Jake's wife, Anna. Don't you remember her?" The man's mouth fell open as he continued to stare at Anna in disbelief. Anna looked at him and then away from his staring eyes.

"Let me excuse myself. I don't want no beef with Mr. Bradley about his beautiful wife," Max said, continuing to smile down at Anna as she cringed listen to Dee tell him she was Jake's wife.

Anna waited for the man to leave then said to Dee. "Dee, I wish you would stop telling everyone in Session I'm Jake Bradley's wife like I am his property, damn it!" Anna rolled her eyes at Dee, seeing the smile widen on her friend's face.

"Sister Girl, you are now in Session, and whether you want to believe it or not, Session is Jake. He owns everything but the barbecue restaurant and your parents' house. Between him and his brothers, this is their town."

"What the hell has that got to do with me?" Anna asked, frowning at Dee.

"Whoa! You have changed. It may not make you a bit of difference, but it sure as hell will make a difference to the man who gets caught up messing with Jake's wife. I'm telling them up front so there can be no lying that they didn't know."

"I'm going to have to leave here, Dee," Anna said, unhappy with how she kept telling everyone she belonged to Jake.

"Come on, Anna, let's get into the soul train line," Dee said, jumping up and grabbing Anna's hand.

"Girl, you know I don't know how to dance like you do," Anna said, resisting.

"Just do what I do and you'll be fine," Dee said, pulling her up on the dance floor as the dancers filed down the line doing whatever they wanted to do to get to the end. The floor was already packed with people dancing all over the place. This was Session, and Anna realized it was bumping and grinding. The music was loud and intoxicating. Voices filled the air with people trying to talk over it. Looking at Dee, Anna found it not so difficult to keep up with the rhythm and the beat of the music just as she had learned belly dancing on a South Pacific island after drinking sweet intoxicating Tequilas that made her want to do wild, naughty things with the man in her arms.

Finally, getting to the end of the line, she felt delighted at her ability to get into the rhythm Dee had set up for them. No one knew, and she sure was not letting any of these black people whose lives centered on gathering together in a club to move their bodies at least once a week know that she could not dance like them. Walking back to their table, they ran into Terri and Joy. Anna gasped as her mind spun back to walking in on the two women and Barb in bed with her husband at Barb's apartment.

"Who's your friend?" they asked Dee, looking at Anna in the dark club. Dee kept on walking not saying a word. They stared at Anna. She cut her eyes back at them, walking by as if they were trash she needed to move away from.

"I don't think they recognized you, but if they did, they are going back to tell Barb for sure," Dee said, as she ordered another round of rum and cokes for them.

"That doesn't bother me. Let them tell her. What the hell is she going to do to me, Dee? Not a damn thing! If they know what's good for them, they will stay far away from Ms. Anna—that's for sure!" Anna said, drinking down her rum without coke as if it were water.

"That's for sure, Ms. Anna, now let's have some fun. The night is young and my friend is back." They toasted the air and drank their drinks, laughing at all the fun and excitement going on around them.

It was four in the morning when Dee drove up in front of Anna's parents' home. Never in her life had Anna done so even when she was grown and single. Anna looked to see if there were any lights on. Aretha Franklin's "Rock Steady" played on the car radio. They got out dancing to the music, bumping into each other like they had at the club. Anna, remembering the belly dance, did a short rendition for Dee, who burst out laughing.

"Damn, girl, that is the kind of dance I need to use on Fred's ass," Dee whispered to Anna.

"Dee, you will have him screaming all night long, sister girl. That dance is dangerous in bed." Laughing, they placed their fingers up to their lips, indicating they should be quiet before they woke up the entire neighborhood.

"Anna, tiptoe in now; you have never come into your parents' house drunk. And sister girl, we are buzzing."

"It is called intoxication, Dee." They gave each other a big hug.

"Damn, Anna, it was fun going out with you. We got to party again real soon. It's nice having my girlfriend back in town." Anna pulled the comb out of her hair and allowed her hair its freedom, shaking her head as well as her body as she threw her hands up to the sky. Pretending they were again going through the soul train line, they stifled their laughter so they would not wake the neighbors.

"I had a ball, Dee! Just think, all the time I lived in Session, I never went anywhere, never got to know the city or its people until tonight. I met so many women who remembered me from running the shelter. They were so happy to see me—asked if I planned to open the shelter again. Of course, I don't, but it was nice to hear them say they were glad I came back." She and Dee hugged again, and then Anna hurried inside the house, waving at Dee from the door.

Inside her bedroom, Anna, feeling the effects of the liquor, turned her thoughts to her former lover. In Switzerland she had sat in the tram's car with him all snug in layers of warm clothing while looking down at the skiers sliding up and down the slopes. Everything was so white—like Christmas, she had thought to herself at the time. Then suddenly she had heard Aretha's voice fill the small car with "Respect." Looking up at him, she had smiled, squeezing him closer to her.

"You had them play that for me, didn't you?"

"I thought since we were so far away from home, you would like to hear someone familiar." There had been no shame in kissing him deeply. The other couples did likewise. Later, at dinner, she overheard someone say in French that two thousand dollars had been spent on dinner.

"This is not having dinner, Ray."

"What is it we are having, may I ask?"

"Why, honey, it is Funzooing."

"What the heck is that?"

"Baby, it's the consumption of an expensive meal, of course. Didn't you see how that man sent his meal back because he did not experience the ecstasy he expected? For that much money, he is not eating—he is Funzooing." Taking her next bite, she stopped with the spoon still in her mouth as she heard Aretha's *You Make Me Feel like a Natural Woman* fill the dining room with her soulful voice. All eyes looked around. Smiles replaced serious looks and laughter warmed the wintry surroundings. She looked at him. Finishing the morsel in her mouth, Anna took his hands in hers.

"Let's hurry and finish—I need you closer to me." Soon, they found their way to the mountain lodge suite awaiting their return. When Anna walked through the door, Raymond took the fur-filled coat from around her shoulders. Aretha's "Doctor Feel Good" greeted them. Light from the cozy fireplace helped them find the bed as they allowed Aretha to finish the night for them in high fashion.

He still lived in her dreams, wooing her into his arms. It had been fun and, yes, dangerous at times. The Old Head had guided their lives into one adventure after another. She realized something about their sex life had changed after their return from Kentucky, from her body; the liquid had always flowed into him. Like a life-giving substance, it had sustained him, filling him with strength. He needed so much of her. The Old Head had allowed their love life to be filled with wild orgasms, so much so that they would wake not knowing when or how their climactic trip had ended. When he had pulled her from the pond and made love to her, Anna had felt for the first time the flow of his semen as it rushed upward inside of her. She had been worried because what at first had seemed abnormal had become normal, as if her energy still fueled his life. The sudden change startled them both. He seemed happy that at last he had assumed control over their lovemaking.

In her intoxicated state, she slipped into bed naked remembering how they slept still reflecting back on their adventures. His blue Corvette would stop in front of their apartment in the wee hours of the morning. She would turn to him half asleep, needing his lips on hers while her hands worked to unbutton his shirt. By the time they entered the apartment, it would be all they could do to make it to the bed. With these vivid moments so alive in her mind, her head spun as the liquor's high made her feel its effects.

Anna dreamed she lay naked in her lover's arms, his hands moving over her body, causing her to give in to the passion coasting through it. She waited to hear the sound of the violins' stringed instruments that would carry them over the peak into an unconscious sexual ecstasy. When the music never played, Anna realized it must have been just a dream. Her body now danced to the tune of a different but familiar tune—one she could not quite put her finger on, but even in the dream, her body ignited with the need to have him inside of her one last time.

Early the next morning, she lay still in a dream-like state. Feeling movement next to her she thought one of her children had gotten in bed with her. Rising to see which one it was she fell back onto the bed in shock.

"How did you get into this house?" she hissed, snatching the covers over her as she gazed at her husband's naked body next to hers.

"When I was sick, your parents allowed me to stay with them. It stood to reason I should have a key to the house," he said a big smile on his face as he reached under the covers towards her.

"Get your ass out of my bed, damn you! Who allowed you in my room without my permission?" Anna asked, moving out of his reach.

"This has been my bedroom whenever I came to stay with your parents." Before she could respond, their children ran in, jumping on the bed and hugging both of their parents.

"Jake Jr.! Now we have both our momma and daddy. I'm going to tell my friends at school."

"So am I, Sheri'. Daddy, will you take us to the Forest Park Zoo like you promised you would? Mom can come with you. Won't it be fun?" Jake Jr. asked, laughing along with his sister as they sat on the end of the bed with happiness glowing in their eyes.

"As long as we can skip that snake house, I sure will," Jake agreed, smiling over at Anna.

"Jake Jr., having both parents is sure a lot better than having just one and the other never around when you need her, isn't it?"

"Yeah, especially when Grandma does not feel like coming along on one of our all day field trips at school and Grandpa and Daddy are working and can't go." All of this ran through Anna's mind as she reminded herself she had been an absentee mother. Her children's assessment of her part in their life did, hurt to hear.

"Go and get dressed. I think your mother and I can manage a trip to the park for our children," he assured them, glancing over at Anna as she watched her children hurry out of her bedroom.

"Fred come calling, telling me I better get my ass back home 'cause my wife had returned looking good enough to eat," Jake said, reaching for his underwear as he rose from her bed. "I thought he was kidding me and told him if he didn't stop shitting me I would be on his ass. He told me 'If you don't get your ass back here ASAP, you ain't going to stand a chance because she is going to be gobbled up, fool.' Then he told me "'Dee and her are at the doctor's office right now.'

"I caught the first thing out, smoking that deal I was supposed to wrap up. Nothing was as important as having my wife home. My eyes stretched like balloons seeing you out on the floor at the club, dancing through the soul train line with Dee, drinking strong liquor like you had been drinking all your life. Rags tagged me about how you smelled so good, the need for a woman came alive in his old ass. And I'll be damned, you are beautiful," Jake said, glaring over at Anna.

"But by no means am I to be compared with Diana Ross, am I?" Their eyes met. The smile on his face let her know he remembered comparing her to the beautiful movie star–singer.

"You are more beautiful than any damn woman, Anna Bradley. I know I fucked things up for us, but believe me; I have paid for it a thousand times over. And I have missed my wife."

"All the women here in Session at your disposal and you missed your stupid little Anna—a woman you couldn't wait to get the hell out of your life," she replied pulling the covers tighter around her.

"As soon as I set foot in Session, the dudes couldn't wait to sit my black ass down and tell me of this new fine chick in town. A woman claiming to be my wife, a chick so fine even Rag's old ass sat cheezing back at the mention of her. I couldn't imagine no woman smelling so good five men had different names for the sweet scent of her body. Where the hell have you been all this time?"

Anna watched her husband as he slipped into his pants; still bare from the waist up he looked over at her. It reminded her of the last time she had seen him as he had stood struggling to get into his pants in Barb's apartment. His hair no longer cut close to his head, had grown so long that the curls he said he hated fell in his face. A full mustache covered his upper lip; his caramel skin tone gave him the look of the young gigolo who had cornered her in Italy. She had to admit her husband was still as handsome as the day she had left him, but there was no way some other woman was not nursing his wounds. Anna reached for her dressing robe. Slipping into it, she tightened the belt.

"Look, Jake Bradley, I don't owe you an explanation as to what I have been doing or my whereabouts. The marriage we had was finished the day I walked into Barb's apartment and found you in bed with three women who were supposed to be my friends. Taking her rings from her finger, she shoved them into his hands saying, "I made a point of wearing them so that I could personally give them back to you— the only business I have with you is in court." Anna fumed at the way he continued to smile as he stared at her. She watched him reach and pick up the dark green evening dress she had pulled off the night before, bringing it close to his cheek.

He smelled and embraced it as though it was on her body. A soft whistle flowed from his lips as he lowered the dress, reaching his hands inside her jewelry box. The stones he lifted from it glittered in his hands.

"Who the hell have you been with?" he asked, staring at the glittering stones.

"Nothing I've done since I fell down those stairs is of any concern of yours. I need to dress so that we can take the kids to the zoo as you promised them we would. Now get out of my room!"

Chapter Four

—⚏—

The smell of wild animals filled the air. Thousands of Saturday visitors invaded the Forest Park Zoo grounds—Anna imagined it to be the worst day for visiting the zoo. It reminded her of Las Vegas on a hot summer night. Movement was shoulder to shoulder. The zoo shows were filled with children screaming and clapping at the animal's performances. Trainers did their bows, putting her children in the best of spirits.

Jake swung the cane in his hand around, taking a step afterwards. Even Dee's telling her of his limb did nothing to ease the shock of seeing him having to use that cane. She could not help but understand what he had meant when he said he had suffered a thousand times over. To have been shot in a way that allowed anyone seeing him to realize that tragedy had to have been a hard blow for her husband, a man she knew enjoyed the pleasure of women admiring his beautiful body.

The kids now stood in line waiting to get cotton candy from one of the food vendors close to the bird house.

"I never understood the eighty–twenty rule until you caught me dirty," he told her as they waited in line with their children to get treats. She couldn't help but stare at the cane that supported his weight.

"I don't understand what you mean," Anna replied, realizing that it didn't make sense not to talk civilly to him because the children would pick up on it—especially Sheri', who seemed to notice everything.

"The old man used to tell Fred, James, and me about that rule, especially James. He'd say, 'Boy, one day you are going to meet a woman who will be loyal and trusting. She'll have your back, letting you know that no matter what she loves you unconditionally. Once in a lifetime, rarely twice, will you find such a woman." Anna took a deep breath not wanting to hear any of what he was telling her but knew with her children there she must be civil.

"Because of a certain quality she possesses, you will want no other woman but her to be yours because you know she will take care of you and whatever children you are fortunate enough to have. If you have a little sense and luck, she will become your wife—this eighty-percent woman. Then there will be that twenty-percent woman. The flashy, good-looking woman who makes you want to take her to bed just because she is someone other men grapple after wanting to have for their own. You won't want to keep her—just know that you still have what it takes to catch her interest, telling yourself you have control of the situation. In your heart, you know she will never be what your eighty-percent woman is. But still you feel you must have her, thinking you can split if it gets too serious.'" Anna thought of his father who had to learn that lesson after Jake's mother died. He had not been the best husband, yet Anna thought of him with endearment, a man who had treated her as her own father did. He had died before they married. She knew him to be just as his son stated.

"Sheri', get one cotton candy. It's okay to get a hot dog and pop, but I don't want you overindulging in sweets; it's not good for you," Anna told her daughter who asked for everything in sight.

"Go on, I'm listening, Jake," Anna said, turning back to him.

"I always thought he wasn't tight enough when it came to women, except my mother who he treated rotten. The ones I saw him with after she died always seemed to be in control of their relationship, with him allowing them to run his game. Lots of women wanted him, but if he had a woman, she was the only one he would allow his attention after Mom. Reminds me of how your father treats Mrs. Annabelle. I damn sure thought the old man was stupid, and I had the nerve to tell him just that."

"What did he say?" Anna asked, taking the hot dog Jake Jr. asked for but could not hold because he had his cotton candy and a large drink. Jake reached into his pocket to bring out money to pay for the children's food. Finding a table, Anna saw the looks of happiness in the eyes of her children as they smiled up at Jake and her.

"He said, 'I know you think I'm henpecked 'cause I keep myself one woman, treating her pretty good if she allows me. But if you lose that eighty-percent woman, your entire life falls apart right before your eyes, boy. You'll see yourself stripped down to a shallow, empty man, wondering how in the hell you managed to get to that point.' I laughed at him, thinking him a fool." Anna watched Jake rub his lame leg.

"I must have been your twenty-percent woman because I don't think I fulfilled anything for you, Jake Bradley," Anna replied, wanting to not feel the sadness gathering in her heart as she watched him wince at the pain his leg caused him.

"You fulfilled everything for me. In fact, you were the best thing in my life. I was just too stupid to realize it. I had no patience for anyone's needs but my own. Had it not been for the kids here, I would have tossed it in. They were all I had left of my hundred-percent woman, the woman I always loved but didn't appreciate. No other woman will I ever love but you, and no matter how long you have been gone, you are still my wife," he said, his eyes penetrating Anna's.

Listening to her soon would be ex husband Anna knew Jake had not been listening to a word she had been telling him.

"I have changed Jake. My memory returned while I was away. I have other interests that have nothing to do with us getting back together again."

"Did he help you with getting your memory back like he helped you smooth out that beautiful back of yours?" Jake asked, looking so hard at Anna that she turned away.

"Jake, we are here so the children can have fun," Anna said, ignoring his question.

"Daddy, let's go to the reptile house. I want to see the snakes. They will allow you to hold one if you ask."

"Hell no, Jake Jr. I'm not going anywhere near no damn snakes. They are the only thing that I cannot stomach. Ask your mother to take you over there. Now that she has changed, she probably has no problem going anywhere."

"Come Jake Jr., I'll take you there. Your father has a horrific fear of snakes."

"Was he bitten by one, Momma?"

"No, boy, and I don't intend to be," Jake said as he walked away from the direction of the snake house.

"Well, I'm staying with Daddy. I hate snakes, too. They are nasty looking and grimy," Sheri' insisted, frowning as she grabbed her father's arm when Anna and Jake Jr. turned to go toward the reptile house.

****

Although Anna enjoyed reuniting with her children and parents, she was not happy with Jake continuously trying to woo her back to him. Her parents reminded her that no matter what his past transgressions were, she was still legally his wife—a fact she apparently had forgotten. She would be in an attorney's office to correct that legality as soon as possible, she assured them.

Late one Saturday morning, she returned home to find him waiting for her. "Where have you been, leaving home without saying where you were going? This is not like you. I've never known you to do anything like this before. I've been waiting for you. I need you." He followed her into her bedroom smiling at their children who stood watching them.

"If you touch me," Anna said as he reached for her, "I will cut your heart out!" Anna watched him stop as his arms immediately spread, looking at Madria's switchblade pointed at him.

"Well, I'll be damned; look at this wife of mine. You have changed. I know I deserved your walking out on me after what happened, but I've paid dearly for that mistake."

"I want a divorce, Jake Bradley! After that, I'll be taking my kids and leaving this damn town of yours."

"You say what?" He stepped toward her.

"I want a divorce, damn it! Now get the hell out of my room and find yourself a lawyer," Anna hissed, pointing the knife in her hand at him. He grabbed her hand, causing the knife to penetrate the skin of his chest. Blood poured from it.

"Stick it in me, goddamn you . . . you've already ripped my heart out telling me some shit about taking my kids." The knife pressed deeper, causing blood to flow down his shirt. Her mind flashed back to Raymond and the blood pouring from his arm after she had cut him.

"Oh my God!" she whispered, trembling as the warm blood seeped down his chest on to her hand. She let go of the knife hearing the sound of it as it fell to the floor. Her fingers pressed against the blood flowing from his chest.

"You bring your fine black ass back here looking and smelling like a million dollars, telling me you're going to divorce me and take my babies away from me after I've waited four goddamn years for your return?" Fear overcame Anna as she looked up into Jake's distorted face, his tears splashing on her hands.

"I want you back home with me and our babies where you belong—otherwise, kill me now." His tears were coming fast as he ripped the dress she wore off of her. "You are my wife and I want you!"

Later, Anna laid there her exotic perfume now mixed with the scent of their recent sexual encounter. She had made a serious mistake thinking she could handle him. If it were not for the embarrassment to her family and her children, all of whom she knew loved him and wanted them to rekindle their relationship, she would have alerted the Old Widow's young to kill him for taking her as he had, but her children played just outside their door. The happiness she had seen in their eyes had prevented her from screaming out.

Momma Lucy's face flashed before Anna; her words rang in her ears: "Baby, I sho' would hate for you to have to go back into your own world. That heavy man of yours done spoiled you for any other man, especially one of your own kind down there in a black town."

"Who have you been going out to meet, Anna?" Jake asked his hands sliding over her smooth back turned to him. He stopped to kiss it from time to time.

"I don't know what you are talking about," she replied, removing his hand from her as she pulled the cover up.

"What happened to our baby, Anna? Did you miscarry due to the fall and accident, or did you deliberately get rid of it to spite me?"

"Get your ass out of my bed!" Anna cried, turning to face him as she forced herself to look at the bloddy knife wound she had caused. His hand slid over her stomach as he pulled the covers back and planted kisses all the way down her stomach to her hairline.

"That perfume you're wearing—it's driving me nuts." Tightening his hold on her, he cried out, "Please tell me there has been no other man . . . that you are still mine alone!" With his wet face on her stomach, he kissed where the child had once been. "Those fucking bitches fucked up our marriage!" He hissed. They set me up so you could find me with them in Barb's apartment. Her husband cried so hard it was all Anna could do not to reach down to him, her own tears falling, as he moved further down to the area of her vagina. Anna froze. He looked up. They stared at each other.

"You once told me oral sex was disgustingly filthy. Is there nothing the motherfucker didn't teach you?" Anna's eyes enlarged, remembering how her lover had shaved her clean every time the hair began to grow, afterwards tantalizing her with kisses there.

"You don't know what you're talking about. I had to have it shaved after I lost my baby and never allowed it to grow again. Get out of my room and leave me alone." Anna pulled the sheet up over her. Jake grabbed the sheet and ripped it.

"Your back . . . it's as smooth as silk. How many times do I have to ask you where you got it done? It must have cost a mint!"

"If you don't go, I will," Anna insisted, snatching her housedress to put it on.

"I'll give you time, Anna, to realize our marriage is not over, but don't take too long. I plan to have you back home with me and soon."

Chapter Five

"**M**omma, if you're not using the car today, I would like to. I need to go shopping." Getting no answer, Anna looked into her mother's grinning face.

"You can just wipe that grin off your face because I'm not going back to him."

"Yeah," said her mother, pocketing the ten dollars Anna laid on the table. "Jus' like ya was gonna swear off sex. He'll git ya back and it won't be long at the rate he is goin', gal."

"You want to bet on that?" Anna replied, staring at her mother.

"Naw, I betta not—don't wanta send ya ta hell plum broke." Giving her smiling mother a look of disgust, Anna accepted the car keys and walked out the door.

****

A week later Anna walked back into her parent's home. Her mother was just setting the table for dinner. Speaking to no one, her chinchilla trailing behind her as she filled the room with the noise of her four-inch silver heels and sweetened the air with her Wild Passion perfume Anna headed for her bedroom. "Anna, whare in the world have ya been? We all thought ya done left for good agin when ya called tellin' yer daddy to pick up my car at the airport."

"Momma, I told you I was going shopping; don't you remember?"

"Dat was a week ago, gal."

"I had to travel to Paris to have my designer get new measurements. He seems to think I have thickened up a bit."

"Whare's the clothes?"

"They are being shipped to me."

"Are ya tellin' me ya went all the way to another country to git clothes?" Anna noticed the look of shock on not only her mother's face but also her father's and Jake's as well. They stood with their mouths agape listening as her mother questioned her. Her children ran over and hugged her, commenting on how beautiful she looked. But they had been concerned that she might not come back to them for a long time. Anna held them close to her, not wanting to hurt them in that way again.

"Now Momma, you wouldn't have your daughter going to Kmart for her clothes any longer, would you? What would people think?" She cut her eyes over at Jake and winked at her father as she walked toward her bedroom.

"How ya come 'bout dat kinda money, gal? And ain't nothin' wrong with Kmart's clothes. Goin' to some other country to git clothes made fer yer self. Don't sound like nobody colored I knows."

"I worked long, hard, honest hours, Momma," Anna said, thinking of the long hours spent at the ranch as she developed the formula that had saved the lives of the thoroughbreds there. She paused at her bedroom door as her mother spoke again.

"Do you plan to . . .?"

"Eat with the family? Of course Momma, I shall eat with the family after I've freshened up a bit." She looked again at her father, who smiled and shook his head.

****

It felt good walking along the park path with Dee. The sun reflected rainbows in the lake, and although nothing had gone as she had planned during the month she had been home, Anna remained hopeful that it would. The lawyer who had taken her case had suddenly taken ill. She would seek someone else, of course. She wanted the divorce as soon as possible so she could get on with her life.

"Anna, what are your plans?" Dee asked suddenly as she took a seat on one of the benches near the ducks that stood feeding on bits of bread thrown out to them.

"What do you mean, what are my plans?" Anna asked, taking a seat next to her.

"You remember how you explained to me about cutting to the chase? You know, talking straight up to another woman when you have something you feel she needs to hear?"

"Yes, Dee, I know what cutting to the chase means," Anna said, thinking about where she had first heard the phrase. "What is it I need to hear?"

"Anna, you have forgotten how business is done here in Session and who the main players are." Anna saw that Dee looked not at her but at the water beyond. Something was up; she knew how Dee operated. When she got serious, it was time to listen.

"What is going on that I don't know about, Dee? I know you know. Now I tell you all my business, so come on out with it, sister girl."

"You are not a friend, Anna; you are more like the little sister I never had. I know I can lay this on you and not worry about it going nowhere, am I right?" Anna could tell the way the conversation was going that something serious was up.

"Whatever you tell me will be just between you and me if that is how it has to be," Anna answered, waiting to hear whatever it was Dee had to tell her.

"Jake has gotten it into his head that you are seeing the man he thinks you have been with all that time you were gone. He believes you brought your man here to help you get his kids." Anna's eyes widened as she grew alert while she listened to Dee. "You remember that guy you told me saw you coming out of the shopping center here in Session—the one who tried to hit on you?"

"I remember. He said that if he weren't a married man, I would be a woman after his own heart. I smiled and thanked him. He told me he was about to take his wife and kids on a trip to Disneyland. I told him I might do the same with my kids once I got settled. It was just a casual conversation, nothing more than that, Dee. Why?"

"He got his ass beat real good for that conversation. Jake, Fred, James, and Jay Man took that nigger's ass out. He is in the hospital right now. Once they realized he wasn't your man, they told him he better not even think about taking up with you."

"What!" Anna gasped as her mind growing alert to what was being told to her.

"Yeah, and you know that lawyer you tried to get to take your case?"

"Yes. What about him?"

"Jake sent Jay Man to see him. You know how Jay Man looks, don't you?"

"No, I've never met him, Dee."

"Well, if things keep going the way they are going, you will be meeting him real soon. Fred told me he told your lawyer if he sent his boss any shit about a divorce, he would kill him and his entire family—even his dog if he has one."

"You are kidding me, Dee!" Anna responded as she stared at her friend in shock.

"I don't know how you thought you were going to come back here as anything but Jake's wife."

"This is my home just like it is his, Dee. I told him we were finished as husband and wife, and that's what I meant. I don't care what he does." Anna thought about how upset she had gotten with Dee because she always told men who showed interest in Anna that she was Jake's wife. She had realized then that she must get her divorce as soon as possible so she would not hear the words "Jake's wife" come out of Dee's mouth ever again.

"Well I care. It's my husband out there trying to help Jake keep men away from you. Someone is going to prison or will end up dead, and I don't plan for it to be Fred. Damn, Anna, I have to admit that I thought you would have gotten over what happened and you and Jake could get back together, especially since you know how to act like a wife now," Dee said, refusing to look at her.

"I don't like how you are coming at me with that statement you just made," Anna countered, staring at Dee.

"Anna, with God as my witness, you know you hardly cared what Jake did back then. I mean, he would come tell me how he asked you to let him do things with Barb that any woman who loved her husband would have questioned. You never did—and when you were told by your mother and me that you should question them, you just ignored the warnings even though it was plain as day that shit wasn't right in your house."

"I trusted him and he betrayed me," Anna replied, her eyes now slits as she stared back at Dee.

"Anna, tell me, and I mean tell me the damn truth. Did you allow the man you were with for four years to go out with other women because you trusted him? Did you encourage him to spend time with other women like you did with Jake because you thought they wouldn't make out with him? Come on now, out with the truth. I'm saying no, because you knew any woman, especially a single woman, would replace you as his woman as soon as she could. And I bet you weren't having it, just as I wouldn't with Fred."

"That was because . . ." Anna started to say, but Dee interrupted her.

"You were preoccupied with this white guy in your dreams, and your lost memory had you all messed up, not to mention whatever that was messing with your head. If Jake had not been stupid enough to depend on Barb to use birth control, you would still be letting her do what you should have never allowed any woman to get away with, knowing you should have been doing those things for your husband yourself."

"Just what should I have been doing for that low down unfaithful husband of mine, Dee?"

"You should have been the one going places with him instead of always saying to take Barb like she was his wife instead of you. When he asked you stupid shit, you should have called him on that shit—things Fred would have cut his tongue out before asking me to have some other woman do for him—things I, as his wife, am supposed to be doing. Anna, you just looked past it like you were in another world. Did you do that with the one you just left? Let me hear you say you did." Anna looked at Dee, her mind flashing back to the five-inch scar her former lover would wear the rest of his life, a living testimony of what she did not allow in her relationship with Raymond Forlorn.

"You are telling me all this to say what, Dee?" Anna waited as Dee took a deep breath and stood up, looking down at her.

"What Jake did to you was low down and dirty, but he had help from you doing it whether you want to admit it or not. While I'm at it, I might as well tell you this, too." Their eyes leveled as Anna turned to face her. "There is one quality you certainly have like Mrs. Annabelle."

"What quality is that, Dee?" Anna asked, attempting to digest all her friend was telling her.

"The inability to let go of the past. You've got to forgive Jake and yourself for those things you've done to each other; otherwise, it is your children who are going to suffer, Anna."

"What do you mean suffer? When have my children suffered?"

Every day that she was away from her children they suffered. Dee shared. Telling Anna how much they missed her. She had made up lies to keep them thinking Anna had to be away from them and would return soon, she told Anna as she tossed a rock into the water. How soon she did not know, but soon. Anna listened as she shared that Jake has been a good father to their children, but they needed her in their lives, not her mother acting like she was their mother and not her.

"You don't understand, Dee. You have Fred and he . . ."

"He is what?" Dee asked. "You think you are the only one who has had to get over shit? When I was seventeen, he got me pregnant and told everyone it was not his. Back in the day, we all lived in the same neighborhood. Had it not been for Jake's little ass coming by and hearing me and my mother fighting about me being pregnant, I would have been out on the streets 'cause Fred was with his other woman—one I didn't know about until it was too late.

I slept on Jake's bed while he slept on the floor until his parents discovered me there and made Fred do what was right by me. Oh, I could have told him I didn't want him anymore, but it wasn't about me—it was about my baby and who would help me raise this kid his father didn't even want until Fred Jr. was born. Oh, and by the way, I wanted to name him Jake, but Jake said no, he wanted his own son to have his name one day." Anna looked at Dee, realizing her friend had just shared something very personal with her, something Dee would not have wanted anyone else to know.

"I'm not taking Jake back if that's what you want me to do, Dee, so forget it."

"Then go away from here, Anna. You are not like us anymore. Even before you left, you were different, but at least you understood how the grass was cut. All you came back to Session with, sister girl, is the face you left with—and even that has changed. You have forgotten how the game is played here because now you are more like Barb and them guys." Anna's eyes became slits again.

"Not in their sluttish behavior, but in your attitude about yourself. You know, like it's all about you."

"What are you talking about now? Damn you, Dee!" Anna snapped, not at all happy with being equated with Barb.

"Look Anna, I'm not trying to sweat you, but you know how Barb and them guys are with this women's lib shit, acting like it's all about being the same as men. Anna, don't give me that look. Men and women are different, at least here in Session we are." Anna could hear the Madame's voice saying the same thing.

"Cut to the chase, Dee, say what's really on your mind. How am I now?"

"It's about you—first, last, and always. You think Barb thought about her son when she was trying to take Jake from you? You think she cared about his family? Hell no. All she cared about was how good he felt in bed."

"I'm not like that and you know it," Anna said, turning away in anger.

"Damn it, Anna, it was me, your children cried to when they missed you, asking if you were ever coming home to them and their dad. It was me who tried to help them understand that you did love them and wanted their happiness above everything but that you were going through something that took you away from them. I told them you would be coming back to them and their dad. What did you want me to do, tell them the sordid details of Jake's affair?"

"Well, I do care about my kids, and I did come back to see about them," Anna said, her hands hugging her arms.

"Short visits in and out for a day or two. And no, you didn't care—not the way they needed you to care about them. You are so into yourself and your own needs even now that you haven't even bothered to notice how happy they are or why. In their minds, they believe everything is all right between their mom and dad. Too young to understand your and Jake's split back then, they don't want to think about your leaving them again or living without their father. He showered them with love and attention, never saying one bad thing about you to them, even though he begged me to tell him if you were with another man—something I would not have told him even if he threatened to kill me."

Anna swallowed hard and shook her head, thinking about her long absence and the impact it must have had on her children; they hardly knew her. She could hear them in her mind bursting through the door every day since her return asking if she was still there. She remembered how irritated she became because they always wanted Jake along on their outings.

"Anna, even your mother realizes you are no longer one of us. You have become like the women out there. Remember what Mrs. Annabelle used to tell us when we sat and listened to her at the Women's League? It is not about us—it's about having God in your life and family and doing whatever it takes to keep family together, even if it means sacrificing something you have believed all your life. Sometimes you do things just because you know we as black women have had to take it upon ourselves to do for our family no matter what." Anna had been there that day when her mother spoke about having the love of God in one's heart and remembering the importance of family. She had not understood all of what she had said, but she had heard her.

"Remember telling me once that we rowed with oars while the outside world rowed with motors? It is still true of us here in Session. We are like a country within a country. Our rules work for us. You were once one of us, Anna. Barb, Joy, and Terri never were."

"Now you are saying I am not one of you but them, is that what I'm hearing you say, Dee?"

"I'm saying not only do you look different, you think different. You have forgotten what it is like to be one of us. Your actions show me that you have become so modern that the things we value no longer have value for you. Sister Girl, you even sound white."

"What?" Anna asked stunned by Dee's analysis of her. "Tell me, sister girl, what does white sound like?"

"Oh my God, Anna, I'm still your friend, and friends must tell each other the truth as they see it. I'm willing to agree to disagree because I know you think I am wrong in my assessment of the situation." She stopped Anna as she opened her mouth to speak. "Hey, I am not saying your change is a bad thing—I don't see you taking what you took back then, and I'm glad of that. But I will tell you something."

"Say it, damn it! Get it all out so that I know where we stand," Anna told Dee, her eyes hard on her friend as she waited to hear what else would come out of Dee's mouth about her.

"I go to work on my job as a respiration therapist for one reason and one reason only."

"And that is?"

"That is to help my family, Anna. My home is the only place I feel safe and at peace. And no, Fred ain't no angel, but he heads my home and that is what matters to me." Tears began to flow from their eyes as they walked back to the car. They didn't speak until Anna drove up in front of Dee's house and Dee opened the door of Mrs. Annabelle's car.

"I love you, Anna, I swear to God I do. But the way things are going, someone is going to get killed or hurt because Jake is not planning to give you up without one helluva fight. And I do mean one you are not going to like. I don't want my husband to get caught up in some dangerous shit that might cost him his life or his freedom." Anna listened to the door slam as her friend turned from the car and walked into her home. Starting the car, Anna knew it was time to go see her father.

Chapter Six

—⟋⟍—

Anna's nostrils absorbed the smell of her father's famous barbecue cooking. Huge pots of greens, beans, and spaghetti stood next to all sorts of desserts in containers behind the counter waiting to be served. She forced a smile as her father untied his apron and hurried around the counter to embrace her. She knew huge amounts of his barbecue sauce were being sent to restaurants and stores in other states.

"Isn't she the prettiest little lady you have ever seen?" he said so loudly that the crowd of guests eating looked up smiling.

"Daddy, you are embarrassing me again," Anna whispered, smiling in spite of the tightness in her chest.

"Well, I have to tell the truth, don't I?" he asked, kissing her dimpled cheek.

"Daddy, I need to talk to you privately if that is possible."

"Hey Dan, Baby Girl and I are going back into my office. Take care of anything that comes up."

The young man smiled as they waved at each other. She remembered him working for her father as a teenager after being placed in detention for stealing food from a grocery store. His mother was a drug addict at the time and could no longer care for him. Now she ran a daycare center, having changed her life around thanks to the Women's League her mother headed.

Walking into her father's office reminded Anna of the veterinarian's office at Raymond's ranch down in Kentucky—everything was neat and in place. Offering her a chair, he took a seat in his office chair. Anna looked away from her father attempting to control her emotions, but the tears started coming so fast she could not stop them. Her father quickly grabbed tissues, and she began dabbing her face.

"Anna Jeff Drake Bradley, this is not the happy woman I saw in New York City. Now tell your daddy what is wrong."

"Daddy, things have become too complicated. I thought I could just come home, get my divorce, take my children, and leave. It's not happening that way at all. Jake has taken it upon himself to make it difficult if not impossible for me to leave here with my children," Anna said. She was about to tell him what her husband had done to the man she had briefly met and the attorney she hired but realized she had sworn secrecy and dare not divulge what Dee had told her. Her father would be on Jake in a second—that she knew for sure. Jake would know it had to have come from Dee. No, she had given her word. She could not go back on it.

"Daddy, Dee thinks I have changed and that one of the qualities that I lack is a forgiving heart. She believes I am partly to blame for what happened between Jake and me, and worse still, that I have placed my own feelings above my children's feelings." Anna looked away from her father as tears continued to spill down her cheeks. "I don't know what is right any more. I love my children. I would die for them. But go back to Jake? Daddy, I don't want him after what I saw and was confronted with in Barb's apartment." Anna listened to the deep intake of her father's breath as he stared at her.

"You don't want him, Baby Girl, because you are in love with another man."

"*Daddy!*" Anna uttered shocked at her father's announcement of her feelings

"When I sat in that restaurant and saw you publicly kissing Mr. Forlorn as though he were your husband, I knew my Baby Girl had changed one hell of a lot. You could have bought your daddy for a sack of potatoes. I was stunned—beyond stunned—looking at my daughter, who wouldn't allow her father to kiss her in public let alone her husband, embracing a white man in a way that would set any man's heart afire. I kept asking myself. Is this my black daughter? It can't be." Anna watched the frowns gathering in her father's face as she listened to him express his feelings about discovering her relationship with Raymond Forlorn. "I had to admit to myself that the old you had vanished. In her place was a woman so enmeshed in her relationship with this white man that even I had to wonder if you had ever loved your husband at all? I have never witnessed you give him the affection I saw you giving Mr. Forlorn."

"Like how, Daddy, if I may ask?"

"Like a woman who had fallen in love for the first time, Baby Girl." Anna watched her father shake his head as though he were still in shock. "It was written all over your face and his. No one else mattered. I continued to wonder if you had ever really loved Jake. If you did, it was never with the passion you gave to that white man. A man you held in your arms as though he was the only man who had ever existed in your life." Anna looked at her father, her mouth open but she could not utter a word. "What is it about Mr. Forlorn that has him etched in my daughter's heart? I asked myself. Make no mistake about it—he is etched in there still."

"Daddy, his name is Raymond, and he is young enough to be your son; yet you speak of him as though he were an old white man I had latched on to," Anna countered, turning her head from her father and letting out her own deep sigh.

"He and I had a serious talk once I discovered the real state of your relationship." Anna turned from the look her father gave her.

"And Daddy, what did he say?" Anna asked, turning back to face him.

"It wasn't what he said at all; it was what I said to him that placed the relationship in perspective, Baby Girl."

"And what was that, Daddy?"

"The fact is, as long as he can't give you his name, you're just another woman in his life, just as Barb was in Jake's."

"Daddy, it is over," Anna insisted, crying again. "I am no longer in his life. I just want to live my life without it being so complicated." Anna wiped more tears away.

"I can't fault Jake for wanting you back. I guess he is like everyone else around town who has been shocked at your transformation. Believe me, for those of us who knew you before you disappeared, it has been one hell of a shock—especially for Jake and your mother, by the way."

"Momma is just used to me allowing her to control my life. This time she wants me to get back with that no-good husband of mine."

"As for having a forgiving heart, I think you will accomplish that in due time like I did," her father said.

"Daddy, your heart has always been forgiving."

"You think so, Baby Girl? That year in prison was not easy. I blamed your mother for what happened. I was already in prison when she returned from hiding you down in Louisiana. Having seventeen years with the railroad turn into incarceration was no easy change." It was hard for Anna listening to her father express his pain at having to spend a year in jail for something she had done.

For the first six months, Anna listened in shock to her father tell her when her mother came to visit him in prison he wouldn't even speak to her. That he would just sit there staring off into space and asking how Anna were doing but had asked nothing about her mother and how she was doing. She sat stunned when he admitted almost hating her mother. It had taken he admitted someone who noticed his treatment of her to tell him, "'Man, if I had a woman looking as good as her coming in to see me every visiting day, I would not be treating her like shit. She looks beat down. Whatever she's done, she is begging for forgiveness, and for you to survive in here you must give it to her because you had to have loved her at one time.' Anna knew her father saw the disturbed look on her face when he shared.

"I didn't get better all at once, but I got so I could ask her how she was making it."

"What did Momma say? I know that hurt her to no end. She loves you as much as you say I love Ray," Anna replied, her thoughts now turned from her own problems.

"You know your mother has a degree in English. Anna sat speechless she never knew. "She can speak perfect English—in a southern voice—but perfect when she is passing. She had her hair permed until it lay straight. Got her a job with the courts as a legal clerk and found her a white female attorney to befriend."

Anna sat there in shock listening to what her father reveal her mother's contradictory actions finding them unbelievable except she knew her father would not lie. Shaking her head Anna, remembered that Dee had reminded her of her mother's speech about doing whatever it takes so that the family survives. Anna looked at her palm and rubbed the orange spot that she had not noticed since her return. Thunder roared and lightning flashed in her mind as the vision appeared. Had her father not sat there and told her, she never would have known the white woman she looked at was her mother.

Even the attorney gave no indication she knew her mother wasn't a white woman. As she listened to her mother tell the woman her father worked for her mother's family and that he had gotten into some trouble. Anna looked in shock at her mother, a woman who would not look at a white person without disdain, befriending the white attorney as though they had known each other for years. She shook her head in disbelief as she listened to her mother talking to the attorney about her father's incarceration and how to go about getting him released as they sat eating together in a restaurant like good friends. This had to have been the ultimate sacrifice for her mother.

"The day I got released, your mother and I came here and got settled. We bought the restaurant with the eight thousand dollars we had saved. She then went south and brought you back with her. The only thing that spoiled a perfect return were the scars that still marred your back from those switches she used to beat you with. I was glad to have you and her back, and I decided as long as you were alive, I would have to deal with the rest and get on with living.

"It was her idea that I start a business of my own. She didn't want me having to explain that year I had not worked. It was the best idea she has ever come up with. In fact, it saved my life after she had almost destroyed it." Anna listened to her father as she realized there was still much she did not know about her parents' lives.

"If that inmate—whose name I don't remember to this day—had not called me on my behavior, I would not have had the good life I enjoy today. Your mother has many problems she has yet to overcome, but when it comes to her family, she does what is necessary like most black women have done down through our history—whether we as black men give them credit for it or not. I had to forgive her for her shortcomings and realize I have my own. I never stopped loving her; I just didn't want to admit I still loved and needed her."

"Daddy I don't love Jake any longer not because I am in love with Ray but because of his infidelity. My life is worse than it ever was—I can't straighten it out living here—not with Jake in my face. No matter how you say I have changed, you witnessed him coming in and out of my home, and the woman he was with sure was not your daughter! No matter who I am in love with now, when I considered myself his wife, I never cheated on him and was devoted to him as his wife. His deceit would have destroyed my life had it not been for that white man you call Mr. Forlorn." Anna gave him a daring look. "You are right, of course. Ray will always have a place in this heart of mine. There will probably never be another white man in my life, but I will never take that deceiving husband of mine back—never! So you can put my forgiving him out of your mind!" Anna's eyes narrowed as she felt her anger rising. Her father took her hands in his saying.

"Your mother says you have come home acting like a privileged white woman."

"Like she has not acted like a privileged white woman around blacks as long as I have known her!"

"That's because . . ."

"Her skin is near white, Daddy." Anna quickly interjected, "And you and other black men think that gives her a right to be privileged while mine being dark doesn't give me the same right." Anna rose, staring down at her father. "The white man I was with let the world know that I was as privileged as any woman, no matter what her skin color was. It's just you black men who think only white women deserve to be privileged." She pulled open his office door, ready to walk out of it.

"Don't you walk out of that door, Anna Jeff Drake Bradley! Not on your daddy—don't you dare!" Anna stopped, her tears freely flowing again. He rose took her into his arms and closed the door as he pulled her back inside.

"Flying home on that plane, I kept asking myself, what the hell am I missing here?" Anna stood listening to her father tell her how her relationship with her white lover had caused him so much pain. "My daughter embracing this white man as though she had been with him longer than she had been with her husband. Kissing him like it was what black women did every day with white men." Anna felt herself blush, remembering her father was well aware of her intense hatred for all whites before Raymond came back into her life.

"When Mr. Forlorn called me with concerns about your health, I agreed to see him after he told me things only you would know if your memory had returned. Listening to this Southern white man, I assumed he was a doctor of sorts showing concern about my only child. He led me to believe you had somehow been placed in a hospital up there in New York, and that was where I would have to go and see you. I didn't mention it to your mother, feeling I should first come and see for myself how you were. Oh how glad I am that I did that!

"Nothing on this planet prepared me for what took place. We were seated in that restaurant, and you placed the barbecue I brought you in his mouth and pressed your lips against his and publicly kissed him after the two of you finished it as though he was your husband, as comfortable with him as if he was as black as me. Baby Girl, I was in shock weeks after I returned, looking at your mother and wondering where I would have to bury the both of you if she found out. I must admit I believe something unnatural happened to you I just don't know when."

Anna took a deep breath as she listened to what her father's meeting with her and Raymond had been like for him, a black man from a black world. The Old Head had taken her life to another level one her father would never understand. Her hatred of whites had been close to that of her mother's hatred of them before that supernatural force had taken over her life.

Her father continued as Anna sat there remembering everything. "I wondered how you two really met. I thought that from the looks of it, this man has money he will never need. Where did you really meet him?" Anna shook her head, turning from her father. "You told me he taught you briefly at that rich prep school I had you attend. You said that until you met him on the highway, you had not seen him since that time. Seeing the two of you together in New York, I have to wonder how much of this relationship with this Southern white man you left out. And to tell you the truth, Baby Girl, I would prefer you to be with Jake again than to have you continue this relationship you had with the white man. Our history with whites is too cruel, especially with white Southern men."

"Daddy, he is not a part of that history. And what about Momma? Was she just a woman you knew other black men would desire because she looks so white? Was that the reason you married her?" Anna listened to her father's sigh as he returned to his seat and indicated with an outstretched hand that she should return to hers.

"When I think about my life with your mother, I must admit I was like most black men I know—proud to have a woman so beautiful, at least what we consider beautiful, who other men wished to have as their own but couldn't.

"That is, until the day I walked into your bedroom in Kay, Massachusetts, and saw those bloody whip marks on your back. I hated the day I ever laid eyes on her. At that point, I think I wanted to kill her for what she did to you, not to mention the resentment I felt for having to go to prison. All of that happened because of her obsessive hatred that almost destroyed both our lives. You were hit the hardest by losing your memory and having your back marred. From that experience, I learned the true meaning of real love, and it isn't a warm feeling that always gives you pleasure, Baby Girl."

"What is it then, Daddy?" Anna asked realizing love is more pain than she could bear.

"It's loving enough to give up that which brings more pain than happiness and realizing that life is what it is."

"And that is?" Anna asked, pushing for the answers she needed to help her understand her own life.

"Learning that just because you walk out of your door planning a short trip to the store does not mean you will end up there and not elsewhere—perhaps in a place already predestined. What looks desirable on the outside may become undesirable once you're on the inside. In the end, you have to live with what others who want what you have may never see or know." Anna saw a faraway look in her father's eyes as if remembering the pain in his life because of her mother.

"My love for your mother has stood a lot of testing. It may be that the love you seem to have for the white man must also have its time of testing. Time will tell if all Mr. Forlorn has come to is a pleasant memory soon to be forgotten, Baby Girl, and I must admit I damn sure hope so."

Listening to her father surmise the intimacy of her relationship with Raymond Forlorn, Anna closed her eyes and remembered how vivid and real the dreams had seemed before they had met up again on that highway. With her memory gone, it would have appeared that he, too, would have been lost to her. But for nine years, the Old Head and its eyes had made sure his presence never left her. As soon as her eyes closed, she was with him, sailing on his sailboat as teenagers. She watched him adjust the sails, his black swimsuit contrasting against his white skin, then she rose and asked him, "Where are we going, Teacher?" Her purple bikini barely covered her youthful breasts and body. He turned, staring down at her.

"Why, Ms. Anna, we are going to find God. I must ask him what purpose he had in mind when he bound our lives together, allowing us to be with each other in a way no one can destroy." His smile brought a smile to her lips as he handed her a long-stemmed red rose, kissing her as she lay back while the warm sea breeze sealed them off from the rest of the world. Yes, Anna thought to herself now, seated there with her father, the Old Head had anchored their lives together in such a way that no living soul could part them. They were one even when they lived apart. What the Old Head had planned for them seemed to have ended. She wondered what, if anything would bring them together again. Looking at the worried look on her father's face, Anna's thoughts faded.

"Daddy, you haven't smoked one Lucky Strike since we have been sitting here," she said, breaking the silence.

"Your momma has been sweating me to stop or at least cut down. You women are always stopping a man from his pleasures," her father said, smiling as he showed her an unopened pack of Lucky Strikes. "As for you and the white man, he is a nice guy, but his loving you is too dangerous. Your having a relationship with him, especially here in Session, will get you killed, Baby Girl. And I do mean dead. As for Jake, your coming back here looking like you stepped right out of a Hollywood fashion magazine has brought him to his knees. I have never seen him so humble. But he is still a man with pride. I don't want to spend another second in prison, but if he hurts you, it will come to that."

Anna rose. "You forget, Daddy, that had it not been for the white man's love for me, I would already be dead out on that highway. His pulling me from that burning car before it exploded is the only reason you have me here with you today. Or have you forgotten that? As for Jake, I don't intend to do anything but let him know I no longer want him, but I certainly would do nothing that might cause you harm in any way. You have already been through enough because of me." Anna embraced her father again.

"Daddy, I think there is something else you have forgotten."

"What's that, Baby Girl?"

"Had you not placed me in that private prep school, I would never have met that rich white Southern boy." Her father smiled, shaking his head. Anna turned again from him and walked out the door.

Chapter Seven

—◆—

Anna arrived home at 12:30 that night to find Jake watching the late news with her father. A sigh escaped her lips. How, she wondered, was she going to make him understand she was not going back to him? She had driven around most of the evening, trying to stay away until he left, but when she drove up, she found to her dismay that his red Cadillac was parked in the driveway.

Ignoring his glances, she walked straight into the kitchen where her mother sat peeling apples for the pie Anna knew she planned to bake the next day.

"Whare ya been, coming home dis late at night?" Anna could tell from the look in her mother's eyes that she was upset.

"Riding around, Momma. Nothing's wrong with that, is there?"

"Got folks worried 'bout yer whareabouts," her mother insisted, placing the cut-up apples in the refrigerator.

"Momma, I'm a grown woman. I know my way home when I get ready to come."

"Anna," her mother said, looking hard at her, "yer talk scares me. Since ya left hare ya don't seem nothin' like my gal atall."

"Life goes on, Momma. Jake is the last person on my mind these days. I come home; he's here. I leave and come back; he is here or has called checking up on me. I find myself either sleeping with Sheri' or crawling in bed with you and Daddy because he will not leave."

"Chile, ya know how it is wit da men 'round hare. To Jake it would be somethin' he couldn't live down lettin' his wife git taken 'way from him. The men dat didn't try and git ya for thayselves would pity him thanking it's 'cause he lame ya don't love him no more. Po' thang, tryin' so hard. I pity da po' devil myself," her mother said, shaking her head.

"If it had not been for you, Daddy, and my children, I would never have set foot in this town again. I don't want the po' devil, and as soon as I decide where I want to set up a new residence, I'll be leaving this town with my children, damn him!" Anna said as her anger rose realizing she would have to leave Session for good in order to rid herself of this husband she no longer wanted.

"Anna Jeff Drake Bradley, ya mind yer tongue in dis hare house. Done got out thare with them fast wild women and become loose with yer talkin'."

"I'm sorry, Momma. I just don't feel good right now. I'm fed up with people telling me how I have changed and become someone else. Before I left, it was 'Anna you need to change; you are too soft.' Now that I am what you said I should be, you still aren't satisfied. It's time I am pleasing Anna and not everyone else, Momma," Anna said rising.

"I hear what ya sayin' yet I don't want ya hurt, gal, and he is still yer husband—is ya forgettin' dat?" Her mother placed her hands on her small hips and stared at Anna as she rose and turned to leave.

"He won't be for long, Momma. You can believe that," Anna countered on her way to her bedroom. Jake rose from where he sat with her father and followed after her.

"Where the hell have you been all day and half the night?" he asked, closing the door behind them. Anna could tell by the look in his eyes that he desired to have her again—something she did not plan to allow.

"My goodness, Jake, wasn't it you who said that sitting around the house all day was going to make Anna an old woman before her time? I think it was that night you were at Forals playing cards with the boys, leaving your little dumb Anna waiting for your ass all day. We wouldn't want Anna to become that old woman you told her she was going to become sitting her ass at home now, would we even though she worked everyday of the week for you at your damn construction company?" Anna turned her back to him.

"Just listen to this wife of mine, talking as strong as a goddamn bottle of granddaddy and five sniffs of coke. Look woman, I left a meeting where we were working out plans for a . . ."

"I don't give a damn what you left or why," Anna snapped, interrupting him. "Anyway, it amazes me that of all the times I came to Forals after you,

you had the nerve to tell me you were a grown-ass man and knew your way home. And you didn't plan to come home until you got goddamn good and ready. Remember telling me that? Well I'm a grown-ass woman and I sure as hell know when I want to come home." She watched her husband shake his head.

"Before I left here, I couldn't get you to go to the dime store with me. I come back here after four years and I can't move for you up in my face," Anna said, taking a seat at her vanity while looking at herself in the mirror as she applied lipstick to her lips. "Now come on—since I don't give a damn, let's hear about that lucky lady of yours you have hidden away. I just wonder if you laid her ass up on that water bed I always wanted you to lay mine on, or is she sleeping in my heart shaped bed wearing my clothes the way Barb had the nerve to do? Bitch could tell me more about my lingerie that you could. Every damn body rated better than your damn little scary-ass Anna. A bitch, according to your words to Barb, who was only good for sitting behind a desk. Isn't that what you told the whore when you had her lying in your arms in my bed wearing my lingerie?" Anna felt her anger began to stir. "Remember the nights you took me over to my parents' house from work so you could take the car and then pretended like you had to work late and forgot to come get me? When in reality you two were at our house turning flips in our bed? Laugh at me, will you?" Anna hissed, gazing in her mirror at her husband's reflection as he continued to shake his head, realizing he could not handle the change in her. "You can tell your new whores," Anna said, kicking up her leg high so that he had a full view of her smooth dark leg in the air, "little scary Anna has new lingerie and you better believe they won't be stepping up in my new house wearing my shit no damn more."

"I guess I deserved that," Jake said, as Anna watched him take a seat on her bed. "Tell me, Anna. This new lover of yours . . . did he lay your ass on one of those water beds you always wanted me to lay you on?" Anna had to take a quick breath, thinking of Mix's penthouse villa and that waterbed she flowed to paradise on with her lover.

"What the hell do you care who laid my ass where? You sure as hell didn't," Anna said, rising and lifting her robe off the bed. "I've got things to do, things that don't include you laying your ass around this house, because there ain't shit you can tell Anna she don't already know or hasn't heard before," Anna said, reverting back to the black slang spoken in Session that she knew her husband understood.

"I see that the motherfucking nigger has not only given you a smart-ass mouth, he has lifted that head of yours higher than holy hell." Jake moved over to where Anna stood, his hand moving up her leg where the split lay open. "How did that lover of yours go about helping you conquer your other problem?"

"I have no idea what problem you are speaking of?" Anna insisted, feeling his hand moving up her leg and reached out to stop it with her own.

"I know damn well you haven't forgotten your seething hatred of that almighty white devil you could never stand to be near." His voice sounded just above a whisper as he continued to move his hand up her thigh, disregarding her attempts to stop him. "You must have been forced to come in contact with some whites." Anna closed her eyes and turned away, only to feel Jake pull her head around to face him again.

"I think you had better go," Anna said, staring him down.

"You haven't answered my question. Now that you've learned to use that mouth of yours and hold that head of yours up so high, I'd like to know how you found a solution to your white-hate problem, goddamn it!"

"I no longer have a white-hate problem, if I ever had one. I can handle myself with anyone, white or black . . . it makes no difference."

"All those damn years I lived with you, you were never able to handle whites on any level; your passion for hating them was second only to your mother's hatred—something you had grown to love, Anna Bradley!" he hissed. "How the hell did the motherfucker manage to get you off of that kick . . . I couldn't get you to go with me anywhere whites might be remember that?"

"I don't owe you an explanation for anything. If you insist on staying here, I'll be leaving." Anna jerked her arm away from him. Opening a drawer, she threw her luggage upon the bed throwing her clothing inside.

Without warning, she felt herself being pushed against the wall, a handful of her hair in Jake's hand.

"Anna." He spoke so quietly she could hardly make out his words, yet the harsh sound of his voice felt like a knife cutting through her skull. She thought for sure when he turned her loose, all the hair in his hand would be on the floor. "Do you think I care that we are here in your parents' home?

I will kill your black ass right now. Whatever that motherfucking nigger has been doing for you, he can't do it no more . . . not here! If he wanted to keep you, he should have kept your motherfucking ass wherever the hell he had you. Coming to lay up with another man in Session will get your ass and his killed quick and in a hurry, you understand me woman?" Anna saw rage in the face staring into hers, and she began to fear what he might do to her.

"His ass will be dead before midnight and so, goddamn it, will yours!" Anna's memory slowly returned to the danger Momma Lucy, Dee, and even her father had warned her of. There was no "let us discuss the problem rationally" with men like Jake. No matter how they hurt you, if they didn't want to let you go, you were never left in peace unless you left and left for good. She felt herself being pushed on the bed, with his hand around her neck.

"Just who the hell you think this is you're talking to woman? Some motherfucker off the street? I am your goddamn husband, like it or not, and I will blow your ass off the face of this earth and then stomp the hell out of what's left into the ground! That motherfucker has fucked your goddamn head up thinking you can come back here talking to me like I'm nothing but shit."

All of a sudden, a loud scream brought everyone in the house running. When Anna took the children the next day to see their father in the hospital, he lay all swollen up. Sheri' and Jake Jr. cried and cried. Anna knew the spider's bite had not been lethal. She didn't want him dead—just out of her life.

Anna had smiled as she watched the Old Widow's young crawl from under Jake's leg when he jumped up. The rest of the family had run in the room trying to find out what was wrong with him. Anna walked out of the room with the Old Widow's young once again embedded in her palm.

****

It was the first time she dared go there without him, not knowing what she would find when she got there. But there was no other place she could find refuge, not without something awful happening. Jake had been released from the hospital a week later and was, of course, staying at her parents' home.

The apartment appeared just as they had left it. Even the Bunsen burners stood as a reminder of their time together. Her hands touched the massive library of books she loved, realizing that he had brought all of his books there from their apartment in Las Vegas. It had been the best for them. Mixing and developing formulas brought a new and different passion for their lives together. The tears from the Healing Tree had worked magic for her. Using that remarkable brain of hers, as Momma Lucy liked to call it, she had been able to cure those animals. All because of her love for chemistry and physics, her life had blossomed with him. She walked into the bathroom and saw written on the mirror with her lipstick, "I LOVE YOU, MS. ANNA, RAY." Taking her lipstick from the vanity, she wrote, "I LOVE YOU, RAYMOND FORLORN, MS. ANNA." Tears seeped from her eyes as she thought about her return to Session.

The family she loved found her uncomfortable and hard to take. She had been right in how she explained it to the Madame. They would have had no understanding of her work and what she had accomplished or what she might one day be capable of accomplishing. All she was to them was Jake Bradley's wife. To her parents, that's all that seemed important. She had to admit she was no longer one of them. That old Anna they had known had vanished. Her plans had to be changed. Taking her kids away from there would be the first thing on her agenda as soon as she determined her next place of residence, which surely would not be anywhere near Session.

Anna showered and changed into one of the dressing gowns she had left behind. What her father had said about her feelings for this white man left her asking that same question. What was it about him that made her want to fall into his arms and stay there forever? The Old Head had wrapped their hearts together so tightly that she wondered if she would ever be rid of the desire she had for him. Walking to the large bay window, she stood looking out, soon feeling his presence in every cell in her body.

It came back to her, leaving Momma Lucy's salon that night the women had been on her about her heavy man and what she planned to do if they split. There was something about the Old Head's warning that had worried her. Driving up to the apartment she had sat in the car for about five minutes feeling the tightness in her chest. She could not stop the tears from falling. The split was coming—she could feel it. There was nothing to stop its coming—she just knew it. Composing herself she had wiped her face dry, got out of the car and walked up the stairs into the apartment. Her heart had felt so heavy she had wanted to turn around, but there was nowhere else she could go. Aretha's voice could be heard coming from inside. Turning the key, Anna had let herself in. Stopping at the door, her eyes had widened as her lips parted. Raymond had been leaning over, lighting three scented candles on a white cloth-covered table with a bouquet of two dozen white and lavender orchids surrounding them. Dinner had been prepared for her. Dressed in black casual slacks and a black shirt that opened midway down, he had smiled at her as he ran his hand through his hair. She knew he hoped it pleased her.

"Ray . . ." was all she could think to say as her purse fell to the floor. In his arms, she had smelled the Wild Passion cologne. It had smothered her body with desire as it tantalized her senses. With their lips sealed together, they had eased their way into the bedroom, allowing their clothing to slip away.

Months later, she still heard the sound of her voice echoing his name over and over as he made love to her entire body, something he knew would cause her to beg for the ecstasy only he knew the secret to. Senseless to all outside influences, Anna listened at last as her heart slowed its beat. She remembered the feel of the warm water covering her as they had lathered each other, stopping only to kiss again and again. Finally dried and robed, they had eaten the meal he had had catered in as the scented candles filled her nostrils with the need to make love again. The wine had chilled her lips as she drank from his glass and he from hers. He pulled an orchid from the vase and gently placed it under her nose as he reached to caress the chain around her neck.

"'It shall not be removed unless it is given to our first born. Please make me that promise.' She had been given no chance to answer, feeling lips that tasted of sweet sugar when he pressed them against hers. Soon he had lifted her from where she was seated, taking her again into the bedroom where his body warmed hers all night long.

Anna felt her tears falling as her mind returned to the present. Suddenly, the familiar blue fluorescent light filtered throughout the room.

Anna spoke. "Old Head, you have left me with nothing. I have no one here I can turn to. What is it about this journey that I'm not understanding?"

The thirteen revolving eyes and that pulsating brain circled the apartment where Raymond had serenaded and made love to her before taking her to Kentucky—a journey within itself that she would never forget. The scarf given to her by the women in Kentucky now in her hands, Anna read the words again and again as she had done so many times since leaving there: THANK YOU MS. ANNA FOR YOUR HEALING TREE TEARS. GOD BROUGHT YOU TO US.

"Old Head, tell me where God is taking me next," Anna, whispered.

"Look and see, Daughter. Allow your mind to expand and the spirit of the universe will reveal much to you."

Anna looked at the scene below. It was the Lion's Den; the nightclub Dee had taken her to when she first returned to Session. A woman stood at their table talking to Dee. It must have been when she had excused herself to go to the ladies room.

"'Dee, when I stayed in the shelter,' she listened to the woman say as she blew smoke from her cigarette, looking at Anna walk away, "'I didn't see Mrs. Bradley that often because she stayed busy in her office. But I remember one day we were bitching at each other—name calling, ready to fight over some food someone said some bitch had taken. She walked out of that office and looked around, and I remember her words as if she just spoke. 'What is all this dirty foul language I'm hearing out here?' We started explaining what the argument was about.

"She said, 'In Africa, which is where all our ancestors came from, the women come together around the common pot, breaking bread together in love. There is no separation of me, my, or anyone else's. If one ate, they all ate right out of the common pot.' Sister girl, we all looked up staring at her. She placed her hands on those tiny hips of hers and looked at us. You know she always wore those wide gathered colorful skirts with those pretty matching blouses. 'Now what is it going to be?' she asked. 'Do I get some hugging up in here or will I have to call Jake Bradley and demand he close this place down?'

"'One of the other women looked at the only white chick there and asked,' 'What about her, Mrs. Bradley?' "'She had looking with disdain at Shirley who had just come in to the shelter the day before.'

Anna was startled back to the present, "Old Head, unknown to me, even then you controlled my life." Anna realized that at the time she hated having allowed Shirley into the shelter, remembering the vicious attacks her mother shared with her of how whites used violence killings to sooth their fears and hatred of the black people they held in their power. At the time she had seen in the eyes and stance of the black women at the shelter that she had had the same kind of power as to how they would treat the white woman by her signal to them.

"Yes Daughter, it was my eyes that allowed you to look into the earth creature's heart and see the fear she felt holding on to her young one as the other earth creatures stood ready to act in the direction your words would cause them to follow. Moving into your heart, the emotion that is in the winds of the universe you earthlings call compassion became so intense inside you that the power of your words moved the others to feel it for the earth creature they stood ready to destroy."

Anna shook her head. "Old Head, you stopped me from a vicious, heartless act. Their attack would have been the same as the horrifying deeds committed by the whites in my mother's past life and I would have master minded it having the same power over the black women's minds as the evil whites who had power over the thinking of other whites."

Anna had known she had no desire for that kind of power over anyone's life, saying at the time to the women, "There are white Africans in Africa believe it or not and as long as she is here with us she is another sister, a white sister but a sister just the same.'

She watched the distain looks of displeasure turn to looks of compassion for each other as they all embraced and walked back towards the kitchen together. Barb, Terri and Joy of course thought it had been Jake who had allowed Shirley's stay and that Anna had no control over her ability to stay or leave. Anna remembered hearing them discuss the white woman's coming in something they welcomed thinking she hated It. Anna listened to the woman say, "'we all started laughing and hugging.

"'That Mrs. Bradley was something else. You didn't see her that often, but let me tell you, she ran that shelter. She never let Barb and them guys dog us or put us down. She is the reason Shirley and I developed a friendship. I figured if she allowed her to come to our shelter, she must be okay. Look at her now—coming back here with her badass self looking like one of those Hollywood movie stars—ain't that 'bout a bitch.'

"Look further, Daughter—see the world of your children and listen to what's in their hearts."

Anna listened to her daughter talking to her brother outside the hospital room where Jake had been taken after the spider had bitten him. "'Momma don't love our Daddy any more, Jake Jr. She hates him.' Anna watched as tears flowed from her daughter's eyes

"'How do you know, Sheri'?' Anna heard her son ask.

"'I heard her say so. He's always trying to make her love him. She doesn't want to.'

"'Well, if she doesn't love him Sheri', how do we know she loves us?' Anna listened to her son ask. "'She's been gone from us as long as she has been gone from our Daddy.'

"'Well, she says she is going to take us from him so he will never see us again. That's all I know.' Anna looked at the stern look in her daughter's face.

"'I don't want that. I love Daddy. I love Momma. And I don't want to leave granddaddy and grandma; they are like our parents for real.' Anna watched her son shake his head no as he wiped tears from his eyes.

"'We'll just have to run away once we get to where she takes us, Jake Jr. I never want to leave Session. All our friends are here. And leaving my daddy is not something I want, do you?' Sheri' said, as more tears washed down her face.

"'No, Sheri' I want them both,' Jake Jr. answered. Anna listened to her children as tears flowed from her eyes. Nothing she had planned had been successful.

"Look even further, Daughter, to see in the heart of the human creature that deceived you. Listen to what is in his heart. See the pain his deception has caused him."

Anna looked to see Jake at their home, the one she had left and never returned to. He sat with only his white undershirt and a pair of khaki pants on at the dining room table, about to take a bite of food when his brother James walked in. James was the darkest of the three brothers no lighter than she, Anna thought as she looked at him take a seat at the table in front of Jake. James and Jake were the same height, five eleven. James was the middle brother and thought by many to also be quite a handsome man. His thick black hair lay in close cut waves on his head. A full mustache covered his top lip All three brothers had naturally curly hair, Jake shared with Anna, that the texture had come from their Native American heritage on their mother's side and the white grandmother on the father's side. Jake and James were the closest of the three brothers. Jake, Anna soon learned always wanted to be thought of as being as handsome as James. He thought James the better looking of the three. He commented more on his good looks than on himself or Fred having once informed Anna before she met James that James had a way of staring at a woman with his light brown eyes that made her feel she was being swept away and he declared, that women fell to their knees when his brother raised his left brow and smiled showing his pearly white teeth with his hand messaging the goat tee under his lip. Though she had known her husband adored his brother, Anna never felt swept away by him. She also knew he had been disappointed that Jake had not married a lighter skinned woman his wife Lois a woman almost as light as her mother had conveniently shared with her. He never said much but he was a furious political fighter and had been a high profile member of a local black militant group until he and Jake became councilmen for their districts in Session.

Anna watched him take a seat in the chair in front of Jake saying. "'Man, we are going to need you at the meeting tonight. You know them niggers are not going to vote on who can come in here developing unless you give the okay. It's like they can't think without you, Jake,' James said, taking a seat at the table across from Jake.

"'I ain't going no damn where until I get my wife back. That's all I'm interested in right now man. Until that business is taken care of, the city can fall apart.'

"'Damn, Jake,' Anna listened James say, "'can't you see the goddamn bitch don't want your ass no more,' Jake rose, pulling out a gun from the drawer next to him and cocking it as he stood staring hard at his brother who rose with outstretched arms when he saw the gun.

"'Motherfucker, I don't give a shit if you are my brother. I will kill your damn ass coming into my home sweating me. Disrespecting my wife by calling her anything but her name, which is Anna Bradley, ain't gonna cut it—not if you want to live, it ain't. You understand that shit?' Jake said, his voice rising. "'As much as I could say about your white looking uppidity wife, you have never heard me disrespect Lois ever, have you?'

Anna listened to their conversation alarmed that Jake would pull a gun on his brother.

"'I'm sorry, man, I was wrong. You are right. She is still your wife, but the woman has changed so much. The Anna I remember was sweet, gentle, kind, and so loving to you. I declare, man, she loved you more than Lois ever loved me. You could get her to do anything, and she fell for all that shit you used to tell her. Fred and I laughed at how you could get out of the house when we couldn't. I do believe some other nigger has gotten to her, man, and ruined your game for you, brother,' Anna heard James said as Jake lowered his gun and placed it on the table in front of him.

"'Yeah, man, that's exactly right. I fucked up my own marriage thinking I was all that and nobody else mattered but what Jake's ass wanted. She reminded me of that shit, man.' Anna watched him beckon his brother to return to his seat as he returned to his.

"'I thought it was all about me. Put her down—made light of her looks and her book smarts. Called her dumb when I knew inside she was a helluva lot smarter than me and had a lot more insight on what was going on. I dismissed her like I did everyone else getting in my way when Jake Bradley the man wanted to do his thang. When people give you too much power and glory, that's what it comes to, brother. That bitch Barb made a point of telling my wife how we made out in this house in our bed. Anna let me know the times I did that shit to her, man.'

"'I would have stomped Barb's ass in the ground before I let her get that shit out, man,' Anna listened to James tell him. "'Course now I would never be so stupid as to have no outside woman coming into my home. Too damn risky and it shows no respect for your home or wife. You are the reason I religiously use condoms. I can't afford nothing coming back to bite me. Women get to loving what you're putting down; they might let a baby slip in that says you belong to them. What did you say when Barb spilled her guts and chilled your game?' Anna listened to hear his reply.

She watched Jake look across the table at his brother. "'I couldn't say shit, man, not with that big-ass gun she had pointed at Anna. I didn't realize until that moment how much she hated Anna and was itching for me to give her the least reason to kill her. What she told on me I knew was all true. With me standing there looking like a goddamn fool, I guess she knew I wanted her to shoot me the way I was feeling, but she also knew I was not about to take no chances on her killing Anna and our baby.'

"'Well little brother, the way things are going, looks like you're going to have to kill to get her back.'

"'Yeah, I'm thinking it's going to take a killing. You know man Anna had the nerve to waltz into her parents house telling us she had been to Paris France to buy clothes.' Anna watched James eyes grow large. Laughter flowed from his lips as he leaned back in his chair.

"'The only place my wife had been was with that big time nigger's ass she brought back with her,' Anna listened to Jake tell his brother.

"Probably somewhere making out right up under your nose," James replied. Anna smiled as she thought back to the blue-eyed spiked green haired male designer in Paris smoothing his hand over her body as he took measurements to assure her a snug fit.

"'I gotta kill that nigger's ass. Got my shit and if it takes that, I'm game.' Anna listened to Jake reply, lifting the gun from the table and pointing it over his brother's head. If only that were true Anna thought remembering the deep frown that had creased her husband's forehead as he had walked up into her parents' front yard with his hands in his pockets. She had stood looking at her new white Porsche the dealer had just delivered. He had stopped, inspecting her newest purchase.

"'Your nigger bought that and had it delivered to send me a message?' He had asked as he stood checking it out. She had refused to answer. "'Sooner or later, we're going to meet up, me and your motherfucking nigger, Anna!' Anna took a deep breath, praying that would never happen as she continued viewing the scene between Jake and his brother.

"'You had a good woman, Jake. You just did not appreciate her. That nigger just showed you what to do with a woman like Anna. You brought that shit on yourself, brother.'

"'Don't you think I know that, man? And while you are talking about my ass, you better learn from my shit. Neither of us listened to the old man—thought he was a fool talking about appreciating some eighty-percent woman. I had a ninety-percent good woman. Everything a man could want in his woman, my Anna was to me. I just didn't care to see it. I was out there looking for that ten-percent body, thinking I could have it all. Now look at me. I ain't got my wife, which means I ain't got shit but a lame leg. Some other nigger saw what I refused to see in my wife, told her things I should have been telling her, gave her things I should have been giving her.

"'The motherfucker found the secret to making her body sing to his when it should still be singing to mine. I did that to myself, man. I have no one to blame but me. My kids have suffered because of me feeling like they lost their mother, but no one has suffered like I have.' Anna saw him reach for his cane as he looked up at James and wiped tears from his eyes. "And you, motherfucker, better think about what I'm telling you and stop whoring around on Lois. It's going to catch up with your ass.'

Anna watched a smile appear on James' face. "Lois has never been as gullible as Anna was. I have to really be slick with her. I know to give her the attention she needs. I learned that from observing how sloppy you treated Anna, thinking your shit didn't stink. You talked to the woman like she had a tail and was still back in slavery, only it was your slavery and you were the master.

"'Fred and I used to laugh, thinking one day you were going to get yours. We just didn't know how' Anna observed James' smiling face turn serious as he looked at his younger brother. "'We never believed she would be coming back here looking like every man's dream woman." His laughter rang out in the room.

"'Yes, I guess every nigger in town wants to see Jake lose her. I was always the dude with the know-how, had it all going my way. Now my wife is back in town looking like a hundred-percent beauty queen, as you well know, and I am the zero-percent fool following after her.'

"'As soon as I get my hands on that nigger's ass that kept her those four years, I'm going to thank him for taking such good care of my wife, and then I'm going to kill his ass right in front of Anna and take her home with me. The nigger is right here in Session, having her whenever he pleases. I got business to attend to, so don't come in here sweating me about no meeting because until I get my wife back, Session can fall to the goddamn ground I wouldn't give a damn.'

Anna's mind became her own as the visions from the eyes vanished, leaving her once again to her thoughts. The apartment held too many memories. Anna felt Raymond's presence in all of the rooms. The warmth of his body covered hers. Desire for him made it impossible for her to think clearly.

Tired of nothing to do but avoid Jake, Anna decided she would dress up and go out. There had to be somewhere she could have some fun in a place other than Session. She remembered Dee taking her to Fire Mount City on one of their nights out. It was far enough away from Session that Jake would not look for her there. He had always talked about how undeveloped it was.

She took out her gold and silver evening gown, remembering Raymond had had a famous designer design it especially for her after her back miraculously smoothed out and became beautiful. The dress was the only one of its kind. When she had stepped out in it to let him view it, he had had reservations about it; he thought it was too provocative. They agreed she would only wear it in his company, but he was no longer in her life. This would be her first opportunity to show off in it.

Anna left the apartment, driving her white Porsche, thinking it would be foolish to waste the dress and such a beautiful evening alone in the apartment. Getting out of the car, she slammed the car door shut and strolled into the nightclub, determined to think of something other than her present situation.

The Top Hat nightclub in Fire Mount City was no comparison even to the Lion's Den in Session. It was a small building. One large sign stood outside announcing it. Other smaller ones naming liquor sold inside were pasted on the windows. Loud band music could be heard from the outside. Inside the club a long round bar stood with stools around it. For the club to be so small, lots of guests stood inside, many of them dancing out on the small dance floor. She took a seat at one of the tables and ordered a set-up of Remy Martin cognac, a drink she knew they should have in stock. Looking around, she noticed the guests smoking marijuana like it was no big deal. She dared not smoke in the home of her parents, but she had wrapped two black gold joints while in the apartment, knowing where Raymond kept the hash Mix supplied him with. When the waitress came by, she asked if all the customers were allowed to smoke marijuana inside. Getting a yes nod, Anna soon found herself floating as she looked to see the image of her lover's face.

Hearing a voice asking if he could take a sit, she looked up. An attractive light-skinned black man took a seat next to her without waiting for her permission to do so.

"I'd like to share some of that fire with you, or would you like to try some of mine?" he asked, as Anna handed him her half-finished joint without answering him.

"That glimmering gown you are wearing dazzled my eyes. I thought maybe you and I could hang tuff together tonight baby," he said, smiling at her as he moved his chair closer.

"I'm not interested. Please just take the joint and leave me to my thoughts."

"Ain't no way, baby. How can I allow a beautiful fine chick like you to sit here all alone without my protection? Who knows who might come and try to snatch you up?" Anna looked at his thick mustache and thought again of her former lover . . . the man even became him for an instant, causing her to reach out and touch the hair on his upper lip. He smiled, moving even closer.

"Where the hell did you get this fire from? It smokes smooth as clean air."

Anna looked to see that his hair was wet. In her car, she had watched the lightning run across the sky as though chasing something. Thunder sounded close behind. It must have started raining outside, she thought to herself. All her worries lay in the recesses of her mind to be picked up later. Anna blinked back tears as the image of her lover vanished and the stranger next to her became himself again.

"Sugar, why you looking so sad? Whatever the nigger's done did to you, baby, you got me rapping strong to you now. Why think on that pain when pleasure is here to take its place?" He smiled as he sucked in more of the potent black gold hash she had given him.

"I am fine. Please, I want to be alone." His hand moved, touching her bare back as he bent to sniff behind her ear.

"Where have you been all my life? That's sweet smelling shit you are wearing is enough to drive a man nuts. Damn, your man must be crazy letting you loose to roam, but you got me protecting you now baby." Anna decided it was time for her to leave and spend the remainder of the evening in the safety of the apartment. She turned when the intruder's lips reached for hers.

"Motherfucker, I wouldn't do that if I were you." Anna's hands covered her mouth as she looked down to see her husband kneeling between them with his cane in one hand and a gun in his other hand, his eyes hard on the man about to kiss her.

Looking behind them, Anna recognized James and Fred. Another twisted-faced man she did not know appeared out of nowhere and in seconds pulled the man up and began walking him toward the door.

"Let's go, Anna," Jake said, standing over her, his gun now by his side as he leaned on his cane.

"I'm not going anywhere with you. What does it take for you to realize that it is over between us? We are through Jake Bradley. Finished goddamnit! Why can't you understand that?" Anna screamed seeing the determination in her husband's actions and the excitement in those seated in the club looking on in wild anticipation.

"Yeah, Anna, I understand. What I am wondering is how much it is going to take before you understand." The gun now stuck between her breasts was not a very large gun, but she definitely saw it was a real one. The eyes staring down into hers had a death look in them just as they had in their last encounter.

"Shoot me down now, Jake Bradley." Anna screamed! The old Anna is dead, and the new Anna doesn't give a damn. So shoot away!" Anna rose; her arms open as she dared him to pull the trigger. She stared him down while noticing the other night club guests turn to give them their full attention.

"Hey Jay Man, kill that nigger's ass right here and now. You don't mind if I kill him, do you, Anna?" Anna looked at the large odd-looking disfigured man holding on her intruder. There was something dement in the way he gazed at the man he held hostage. Quickly he cocked his gun to kill her intruder as Jake had asked.

"In here or outside? I'm ready to put him in his grave right now, man." Anna listened to the man Jake called Jay Man hiss like a vicious animal as though anxious to kill the man at that moment and thought back to Dee questioning if she had ever met him.

Looking around her she could also see the nightclub's wide-eyed guests who sat and stood, staring as though they hoped he would shoot. All would swear to not having seen a thing—that was the way it was with the blacks in the world she had returned to—something she knew only too well.

"What he do, man?" someone shouted from in back of the club.

"The motherfucker has come here to take my wife while I'm sick in the hospital, man." Anna saw the sudden interest rise in the eyes of those around them.

"What! Kill that motherfucker's ass right now! No good son of a bitch!" someone shouted.

"Look at that poor brother walking on a cane. Yeah, kill his ass," others in the club began to echo. "White ofay-looking motherfucker," Anna heard someone scream.

"Yeah…kill his ass. He deserves to die trying to take a crippled man's wife." Anna felt her heart began to pound as she listened to a woman at the bar shout, getting an "amen" from the crowd of onlookers.

"I'm asking one last time. Let's go, Anna!" Anna saw something in Jay Man's eyes that told her the man he held at gunpoint would be dead any second if she didn't leave as Jake had asked. Grabbing her purse, she walked with Jake outside. Standing against the outside door of the club, Anna stared as they pushed the man toward an unfamiliar white and blue Buick. Jake lifted his hand as if to slap her but stopped himself. The thunder she heard roaring in the sky was not her imagination, nor was the lightning that chased it. Her tears mingled with the rain as Jake screamed in her face, "Goddamn you, woman, you've gone damn wild, haven't you? I told you the other night how things were going to be. I'm down on my death bed and you bring this motherfucker to my town to taunt me. Your lover will have to die because you are so hard to convince."

"Die? What do you mean, die? I can't hang with that kinda action man. Hell I . . . I just met this woman tonight, and I sho' nuff ain't about to die for nobody I just met," Anna listen to the man say.

And he was going to protect her Anna thought to herself. Dee telling her if things kept going the way they were she would meet Jay Man came back to her. She now stared at the horrifying looking man pushing her intruder into the back seat of the car between Fred and James, saying, "Motherfucker, we killin' your ass. Ain't no use in you begging 'cause you gonna die tonight." Anna felt herself chill at the sound of his deadly voice.

Jake pushed Anna up front between him and Jay Man. She twisted to look behind her at the man and at the large guns Fred and James held at his head, causing her to remember Dee's warning to her.

"I must admit, my man," Jake said, "you sho' nuff did a wonderful job taking care of my wife. I am impressed."

"Where we gonna lay his ass open, Jake?" Jay Man asked driving off. Anna shuddered as the hideous face turned toward her. One eye was closed and the other twisted. His nose was smashed inward and looked like a donut between two hands. Huge thick lips hung loose from his jaws. He showed no pity for the victim now in their possession. Anna feared for the man's life as she began to realize Jake's mistake. The Old Widow would intercede only if her life was in imminent danger.

"We are taking this nigger's ass to the river Jay Man and kill him. Lets fuck him up good before he dies." Anna shuddered at the thought of seeing another killing. "Now, Mrs. Bradley, I'm going to make a believer out of you so you'll know I mean what I say when I say it. I see that's what it takes for a woman whose ass has become as tough as yours. Talking about killing you, I'm killing your man's ass!" Jake's voice resounded throughout the car causing laughter from the others.

"That's the shit I'm talking about," Jay Man said. "I want to kill my ass a motherfucker tonight. You don't have to get your hands dirty, Jake. I'm your man for the job." Anna sat stunned as she listened to the demented man's words.

Lightning filled the air as thunder took its turn shaking the earth. Her body trembling, Anna thought to herself, this man has the mind of a lunatic. Soon she saw neon signs from Tora light up the water that rippled in the dark night like some giant monster waiting to consume any would-be victim.

"His shit will be through when I put this lead into his ass. And you, Fred and James, when I get through plugging this bastard, take him to the river and sink him so they will be a long time finding his ass . . . about seven or eight years . . . maybe longer." Anna again heard Dee's voice telling her someone would get hurt or killed over her, and she did not want her husband to be a part of it.

"Please man, I never touched this woman . . . didn't know her name before you mentioned it." Anna watched Fred place the gun closer to the wavy hair on the man's head as he reached for the door handle, a man who had been talking just a little earlier about how she needed protection. Tears fell from his eyes. His nose dripped tears and mucus. She felt sorry for him. At first, she thought Jake was bluffing and would never go so far as to kill a man, especially one he was not sure she had been with.

"I never touched her. I swear to God, I didn't! I don't want to die, man, not for no reason!"

"You . . . man, you are one of those niggers I hate. Sitting here on your sorry ass crying like a goddamn baby. You know you can't say you didn't know she was married. She had my rings on her finger until she returned them to me, probably with your insistence." Anna watched the man kneel between Fred and James as he continued sobbing out of control. Jake turned to Anna. "Now look at your great lover. The motherfucker is on his knees crying like a baby. Nigger, please, you can save those damn tears 'cause I'm sho' nuff burning your ass! You had her for four years . . . now you want to come here and rub it in my face that you took something from Jake Bradley. Think I'm going to lie down for that shit? What I'm going to do is see what you do when these bullets fly up your ass."

"I know what he's gonna do Jake— shit and die! Please don't let him beg his way out of it," Jay Man urged as laughter again rang out in the car. Anna shook her head turning away from the cruelty of his words.

"Man," the guy continued to plead, "you're wrong—don't do it!" Anna began to realize things were getting serious . . . she could see the man thought his life was going fast, and she now thought the same thing, especially with that agitated fool Jay Man wanting him dead she thought to herself. She listened to Fred and James laughing in the back seat.

"Hell Jake," James said, "if he wants to do the killing let him."

"Yeah, I'm about letting the brother do the killing since he wants to," Fred added.

She realized that Jake really thought this man was Ray. He was planning to kill him just like he told his brother he would do if he caught them together.

"Jake, the man is telling you the truth. He is not who you think he is, I swear!" Anna insisted, as they dragged the man out of the car and on to the muddy river bank

"Come on, nigger, get your ass over here and let me get this shit done. Fred, you and James go find something to sink him with while Jay Man and me drag this motherfucker closer to the river and put these caps in his ass." The rain poured down hard as the man slipped and fell in the mud. Anna ran behind them screaming.

"Jake, he's telling you the truth. He has never touched me in his life . . . we just met tonight!

"Let's kill this motherfucker's ass now, man. Knowing Anna, she'd lie for the son of a bitch just to save his life." As they continued to drag the man, his legs limped under him. Anna watched Jay Man lift and carry the kicking man to the destination of his death.

"Man, please, pleasssseee don't do it! You are making a mistake. I never saw her before tonight, I swear it!"

Anna watched as Jake grabbed the man, telling Jay Man to let go of him. He put the gun to the man's head. "Die now, motherfucker. And while you are dying, remember nobody takes nothing from Jake Bradley and live to brag about it."

"No, Jake!" Anna cried, pulling him as hard as she could away from the man. "I swear to God on my mother's grave, he is not the man. I swear on our children's lives that this is the first time I have laid eyes on this man." Anna screamed, watching Fred and James running toward them carrying large bricks in their hands. Her friend's warning would soon come to pass. She knew she had to do something quick. "Please don't kill him. I've learned my lesson . . . honest to God, I have. I will come back to you as your wife. Don't kill him!" Anna pleaded. "If you kill him, knowing I am telling you the truth, I will leave and never return ever."

"How do I know you are telling me the truth that he is not your lover? How?" He stared at her, keeping the gun pressed against the man's head. Anna's mind quickly wondered back to the motel room and the two men with guns pointed at them who wanted to take her hearing Raymond after pushing her behind him, tell them they would have to go through him first.

"How, Jake? Because you never would have gotten out of that club alive if I had been with the man I left. He would have stood fearless before you even if you had an army of guns aimed at him. One of you would have died right there in the club because he would have laughed in your face.

He fears no man living and would face death without blinking. He has already killed to protect my life. Make no mistake about it. You would have caught hell trying to kill him." Wanting to save the man's life at any cost, Anna had blurted out the words, and there was no way for her to take them back. She hated it, but now he knew for certain there had been another man in her life all the time she had been away from him. Anna watched a smile appear on her husband's face as he dropped the man's arm letting him fall to the ground. Jake walked over to Anna.

"Drag that motherfucker's ass closer to me," Jake told Jay Man.

"Now you say if I let his ass live, you're going to do what?" Anna took a deep breath and stared at her husband who stared back at her. Jake cocked the gun, his finger on the trigger.

"Ohhh pleeeeassseee, lady, please don't let him kill me, pleeeassee!" Anna saw in his eyes that he was pleading for his life as both Jay Man and Jake pushed their guns against his temple. If this murder was ever discovered, Dee's family would be destroyed and so would her family's name be shamed.

"I'll come back to you as your wife," Anna hurried to say.

"This you swear on your daddy's life?" Anna gave no answer. Jake pushed his gun inside the man's mouth.

"Yes, I swear on my father's life—I'll come back to you." As Jake pulled the gun out, Anna saw blood flowing from the man's lips and knew he had lost some teeth. Jake shouted, his voice in a rage, "Do you, my sweet little wife swear on the lives of those two babies I gave you that you will come back to me and give our marriage another chance without my having to worry about you running off? Do you swear this to me before my friend, my brothers, and this nigger's ass I'm about to kill if you don't?"

Anna listened to the man sobbing pitifully in fear of losing his life, knowing Jake meant to kill him if she didn't agree to his demands. In the mix of the thunder and lightning and the downpour of rain, she lost all resistance. She could not allow the man to die . . . not even for her own sake. There in that nightclub, looking and smelling so enticing, she had lured him to her. He did not deserve to die because of his desire for her or Jake's rage at not being able to sway her back to him. Most importantly, there was Dee who had alerted her to this very night. Too much was at stake.

"I swear, Jake, on the lives of our children. I will give our marriage another chance."

Jake said, as the butt of his gun sounded against the man's head. "Take this nigger and beat his ass real good," Anna watched the man fall to the muddy ground. "He will think hard and long on this night. Maybe he will remember to keep his lips on his own wife if he's got one. Do you understand that shit, my man?" Jake asked, pulling him up to face him.

"Yesss, mann, yess, I understand!" Anna looked away from the man who was still crying pitifully as he collapsed down on the ground between James, Jay Man and Fred.

Struggling up the hill Anna looked at her ruined dress as Jake pushed her into the blue and white Buick. Soon Jay Man let them out at Jake's red Seville in the Top Hat's club's parking lot insisting to Jake he better hurry back before he missed the ass kicking.

Jake turned to Anna once they were inside his car. "How the hell do you think I felt getting a call from Jay Man asking me if it was over between me and my wife? Telling me I'd better get my ass down to Fire Mount City quick 'cause I ain't got no play left no more. He saw you when you first walked in the door. The engine roared as Jake gassed down.

"I couldn't believe my eyes, standing in that club with my damn brothers and friend watching my wife sitting in a joint smoking grass with some street wet nigger. Before your sudden disappearance, you wouldn't have even allowed the shit in the house, let alone hit the streets smoking it yourself." Anna shuddered at the harsh laughter that rang throughout the car. "My old Anna has vanished into thin air, leaving you—a too-damn-smart-ass-sophisticated woman in her place," He looked over at Anna.

"It takes a tough-ass woman to tell a man with a gun pointed in her face to shoot—in fact, you dared me to shoot your ass. Did that nigger you were with ever threaten to kill your ass when you came with that smart-ass talk of yours?" Anna envisioned her lover's face smiling at her.

"A man who says he loves you wouldn't think of hurting his woman."

"Yeah, I guess you are right, but that nigger trying to make it with you was a dead man. Your return is the only thing that saved that motherfucker's life 'cause I was itching to kill his ass."

They sat staring at each other as Anna wiped at the tears that streamed down her face. Taking the purse Anna held Jake searched through it taking out the extra black gold hash she had inside. After a few puffs, the hardness in his face began to disappear.

"I ain't smoked grass this fine since I was overseas. Your lover man get this fire for you?" Anna didn't answer. "Hell, Anna baby, I know you ain't lost all that smart mouth you came back here with." She closed her eyes to the pain of what lay ahead for her. "You hear me? I asked you, did he get this fire for you?"

"Yes," Anna whispered feeling the spider move beneath her skin, knowing if Jake struck her he would be a dead man.

"I can't hear you, baby. Speak up!" he said, screaming in her face.

"Yes, damn it, yes!" Anna choked on the tears she could not control.

"You know, Anna . . . I'm glad this happened tonight . . . otherwise, I would never have been able to say for sure you had been with another man." Sucking hard on the joint, he inhaled and placed it between her lips. "My wife laying up somewhere with a man who can connect with fire this mellow . . . clothe her better than I can . . . diamonds, furs . . . didn't you say he had killed for you? Jake leaned back in his seat staring out the window. "That is one big nigger's ass I gotta meet. Did the motherfucker give you this too?" Anna's heart skipped a beat as Jake took hold of the chain around her neck, holding on to the black horse.

"Please, Jake, don't! Daddy gave this to me . . . said he had been saving it but thought I would never return so he could give it to me." Jake smiled finally, letting go of the black horse on the gold chain. She breathed in deep, shivering down to her toes. Again, fear engulfed Anna as she watched Jake take the gun from his pocket.

"Now, what was that shit you were handing me . . . oh yeah, no matter how many guns that lover of yours had on his ass, the motherfucker would stand and die like a man . . . maybe a god is a better word. Fearless—isn't that how you described him to me, Anna?" Jake's laughter started her head spinning.

"The motherfucker must be a god if he is that strong." Listening to his analysis of Raymond, she didn't breathe easier until he lowered the gun.

"Whoever the motherfucker is, you sho' nuff think a lot of his abilities. Have you ever seen a man before tonight who was about to die, Anna?" Anna shook her head no, not even wanting to think about what she had actually seen. "The motherfucker's ass sweats like that nigger's ass did tonight when he thought his life was about to go. Fearless you called the man you were with, my ass gotta meet a nigger tougher than this blue steel, baby." Lifting the gun, he pointed it so close to her face she could smell it. "I thought I was the only motherfucker around these parts that bad. How many men did you say he has killed for you, Anna?" Jake stared at the gun he still held in his hand and kissed the barrel as he looked over at her.

"None. I was lying about that part, honest to God I was," Anna whispered. Her mind went back to the men killed on the highway when Raymond's explosives took their lives. Those men had threatened to abduct her when they were in the motel in Kay, Massachusetts. She remembered Raymond killing the Red Devil and one of his men after the Red Devil reached for his gun to kill her when she told his secret after seeing his fiendish deeds in a vision the Old Widow's young placed in her mind. All of those killings crossed her mind as well as the killing of the men who had entered her room after she exposed the theft of Mix's money not to mention the others. She couldn't tell Jake the truth even if she wanted to. Her husband had no idea what killing really looked like—he simply thought he did.

"One of these old days, me and that lover man of yours are going to meet up." Anna's eyes widened as she shuddered at the thought.

"I will be looking at him to see how well he walks to his death like the goddamn fearless motherfucker you believe him to be, because Anna baby . . ." Jake said laughing, "that's exactly what he's going to do—die!" Listening to her father's words coming from her husband's lips, Anna felt her entire body not just tremble but shake as his lips brush her bare shoulder.

"You are mine, Anna, and no other motherfucker will have you until they carry you away in a box. And you know what else, baby?" Anna's eyes enlarged, seeing the strange look gathering in her husband's eyes as he stared her way. "If that nigger's lips had touched yours, he would already be in hell kissing the devil's ass because I would have blown his motherfucking head right off his body! Now, wife of mine, every time you think of that fearless tough lover of yours, you think of that!"

Jake pulled out of the parking lot, and no words were spoken until they reached the home Anna had left four years ago, thinking she would be back home that same evening. It had never occurred to her then that it would be four years later before she saw their home again. When he stopped and moved to get out, she looked at him.

"I am not going in there," she said, staring out the window with a stubbornness entering her heart.

"What do you mean you are not going in there? You promised me." He insisted getting back into the car.

"I promised I would come back to you as your wife, and I am back with you. But I am not going to set one foot in that damn house. The next thing you will want to do is to lay my ass on that bed where you slept with her. You take me to my parents' house; we can stay there. I'll live in a two-room shack with you, but you'll have to kill me first and then drag my dead body into that house where you laid up with Barb, Jake Bradley." Her eyes narrowed as she stared at him, her mouth puffed. "I'll help you blow it up so we can really start all over again. I can and will do that with you." Anna watched Jake shake his head as he started the car up.

When they arrived at her parents' home, he stopped in the living room to watch the late news with her father. She undressed and took a tub bath because her mother did not believe showers got you clean enough. Once in bed, she waited for him. When he finally came to bed, he turned over and went right to sleep, leaving Anna lying there wondering what the next shock would be.

Chapter Eight

—◊—

The next evening at dinner, Jake laid down his fork, turning to face Anna's father.

"Sir, if it is okay with you and Momma—Anna, the children, and I will be living here until I can find a new home for us. Anna refuses to go back to the old one, so I must look for one she is willing to live in with me." Anna watched the look of shock cover her parents' faces.

"What's wrong wit the ole' one, gal?" her mother questioned.

Her father spoke. "Annabelle, we both want the kids to get back together so they can raise these children. Where Anna chooses for them to live is of no concern of ours. Son, you are welcome here as long as you need to stay."

"Of course, I will pay just as I would if we were living anywhere else. My father taught us never to live off another man free. We can discuss later what that will be." Loud yells caused Anna to stare at her children, who had jumped up from the table and were hugging each other.

"Our prayers have been answered like you said they would, Grandma. We get to have our momma and daddy back! I want to pick out our new house," Sheri' insisted.

"No, me!" Jake Jr. said. "You know nothing about houses. I do." They grimaced at each other.

****

Several days later, Anna felt herself being shaken awake. Looking up into her mother's face, she wondered what problem needed her attention.

"Git yerself up, gal. I got a call dat dat house of yers done burnt' to the ground."

"House . . . what house, Momma? What house are you talking about?"

"Dat house ya lived in 'fore ya left hare. The one ya fused to live in with dat husband 'f yers. Now hurry!" Her mother was backing out of the driveway before Anna could close the door. Five miles off the highway, they drove by the sign that read Hill Side Park Way and saw smoke curling up into the sky. Fire trucks hurried past them. The area had been roped off, but people stood behind it and looked on. Anna and her mother slowly made their way toward what once had been Anna's home.

"Miss, please . . . it is too dangerous to go any further!" the policemen patrolling the area called out to Anna and her mother.

"It's hur home burnin', officer."

"Sorry, Mrs. Bradley, but it is too dangerous for anyone to try and enter." Anna saw Jake get out of his construction truck, his hard hat still on, hurrying toward the scene.

"Hello sir, I'm sorry about this but there was nothing the firemen could do to save it. It was out of control long before they arrived. We will investigate to make sure arson was not involved."

"Thank you, officer. I better console my wife. I can see this has her in shock, and I myself am taken aback." Anna watched Jake staring wide-eyed at the ruins that had been their home.

"Anna, Momma, you two okay?" he asked, walking them away from the fenced-off area and the officer posted there to keep onlookers back.

"Jake, it's burned to the ground—nothing's left of it," Anna whispered, standing in a daze as she stared at the smoke-filled sky.

"Yes, baby," he whispered, "it's all gone, just like you wanted. Now we can really start a new life. I made sure nothing was left of it to remind us of her ever being in our lives. In the new house I plan to buy for you, no other woman will ever enter to lie in my bed but you. You are my wife—the only woman I will ever love. This is to let you know I say what I mean and I mean what I say." He lifted Anna's left finger, placing his rings back on it as his lips pressed down on hers, holding Anna spellbound.

Driving back with her mother from the fire, Anna looked ahead, saying nothing.

"Gal, ya mean 't tell me ya had dat young fool burn down a half-million-dollar house to git ya back?" Anna, still dazed by it all, looked over at her mother.

"Momma, I had my husband do nothing of the kind. I don't know what you are talking about . . . the house caught fire. Who knows why?" Anna looked at her mother. The conversation they had just concluded she knew would never again be discussed.

****

In the weeks that followed, Anna waited for Jake to insist on his right to have her as his wife. But he never once attempted to touch her. It appeared he was happy just to know she was back with him. One morning, feeling herself being shaken out of her sleep, she opened her eyes to see him staring down at her, telling her she needed to get up and get dressed. "We have to go find you a new home, remember?" Anna slowly rose from the bed. They had been living with her parents for three weeks during that time Jake went to work, came home, took a tub bath without complaining, ate dinner, and watched the news and sports with her father if they were on. Coming to bed, he would gently kiss her cheek and fall right to sleep. Anna had no idea what Jake was up to.

In the car, they drove around looking at houses he apparently had viewed before bringing her to see them. Anna sat wondering why Jake had become so quiet. In fact, she and Jake had little to say to each other except when they were with the children and her parents. Laughter and fun with them brought the two closer in a way that started to warm Anna's heart for the man she had once loved. After two weeks of house hunting, Anna found one that looked to be the one—a four-bedroom, white, split-level trimmed in pink. It had just been built and it had just enough yard space to keep their children happy but not so much that she would be forced to hire a gardener. Anna turned to Jake with a smile on her face. The children then had to approve and, of course, her parents came to give their approval. No one talked about how Anna and Jake had reunited. Anna knew neither James nor Fred had talked freely about that night at the waterfront by the Mississippi River. The criminal implications were too serious to risk it. The man had not died. Anna made sure of it by having Jake take her to see him from a distance. His face looked terrible, but he was alive and moving about. She doubted he ever went back to the Top Hat Club. She sure did not want to think about that night ever again.

Their bedroom set had been the first furniture to arrive. Anna had no idea how Jake managed to speed things up. Her eyes widened seeing him sunk down on the flowing waterbed he said he bought to please her. What was coming next, she wondered. First the house and now this bed as a reminder of a promise made to change for her. She smiled and Jake smiled. Removing his clothing down to his underwear, he looked up at her as he lay back on the bed.

"Anna, you remember when I first asked you to marry me?" he asked as she watched him feel the water-filled mattress under him.

"It was more like a threat, as I recall," Anna replied, looking through the empty chest of drawers.

"I had been begging you for sex for six or seven months, and you'd come up with some lame excuse every time why you just couldn't be sure it was the right thing to do."

"A lady just doesn't give it up to every man asking for some. I had been raised to wait until you knew you had the man's heart. I never thought I had your heart, so I had to keep saying no. Then you threatened me." Anna sank down on the flowing bed next to him. Looking inside the empty drawer in the nightstand as the water made the bed bounce up and down; she felt her dress slip from her shoulders as he unzipped it. His lips moving over her bare back after he unhooked her bra.

"I didn't exactly threaten you. I simply opened up the box holding the rings you are now wearing and told you either you accept them and we'd get married or I would have to take me some from you because I wasn't waiting any longer except to go to the altar and see the preacher. You put out your left hand and allowed me to put my engagement ring on your finger." He touched the wedding rings on her hand and kissed her deeply. She lay back on the bed beside him.

"Since I knew it was coming, I waited—not that I think I should have had to wait."

"Why shouldn't you have waited? I was worth the wait wasn't I?" Anna asked. Running her fingers over his back, she felt his lips smother hers.

"After your mother told me you were an innocent virgin girl, you made sure I heard different, telling me you were already sleeping with a man," he said when their lips parted. "That stumped me so I had my guys watch to see when the dude came by. After three months, I knew if one was in your life, he was in jail, in the service, or you were lying to me."

"You waited, didn't you?" she asked, sighing at the touch of his tongue sliding over each nipple.

"I sure did. I will never forget our wedding night. You were always a woman to shock a man, Anna." His hand moved slowly over her body as if rekindling a lost relationship with it.

"What was the shock?" Anna asked, remembering him pursuing his rights as her husband that night. His foreplay had put her in the mood right from the start, but when he tried to penetrate her, it had hurt like hell.

"What the hell is wrong?" he had asked, moving away after attempting to enter her.

"You are too large—it hurts. I cannot take you inside of me." She remembered sobbing and thinking that this marriage would never work.

"I thought you told me you had been with a man before, woman," he had said, staring down at her.

"I have, but it was in my dreams, not for real," she had cried. Anna now realized how stupid it must have sounded to him at the time. Scared he would be mad at her lie, Anna remembered turning from him feeling ashamed and embarrassed. Instead, Jake had taken her in his arms, explaining to her what he thought her dreams meant.

"Baby, what you had were wet dreams. Your body needed to have a man so bad those wet dreams made you think they were real. You don't know anything about your sign."

"What sign do you mean?" Anna remembered asking Jake as her panic had subsided.

He had said, "You were born October 24th under the sign of the Scorpio. It's ruled by the sex goddess, baby. You have to have sex. All the time your body was saying it needed a man, you were saying no, not understanding Scorpios have to have sex or they will go crazy."

"Jake, you were lying," she said laughing. "I was just too dumb to know it." Anna was unable to believe she had once been that naive.

"Yes baby, but I took my time and brought that Scorpio goddess to the surface, didn't I? After that, all you wanted was the real deal, and whenever I reached for you, you were ready. All I had to do was to touch here." His finger slid over her clitoris, sending an electrical charge so strong throughout Anna's body that she almost called out her lover's name but caught herself as Jake sealed his lips on hers. Their lovemaking took Anna back in time as she remembered the man who first trained her body to sing his song, and for the first time since she had left Session and him, it sang the tune he had been waiting for.

"Please forgive me for hurting you, baby. I know I can never undo what I did, but I will spend the rest of my life trying to make it up to you," Jake whispered, holding her in his arms as their lovemaking simmered in its aftermath.

"You are the only man I have now; there is no other. I just hope there will be no other women you'll need to sooth your male ego."

"There won't be—I guarantee you that," Jake said, his lips brushing over her left nipple, once again wakening in her the need to make love. For Anna, making love in a brand new house in a brand new waterbed seemed like the right place for a brand new beginning. As she drifted off to sleep, she found herself in the rainforest.

"Daughter, soon you will feel the yearning to love the earth creature you first mated with, it will be natural—just as it was when he first sought and charmed you. You will always love the Young Chemist because his heart is sealed to yours, but the love you once had for your first mate is still where you left it. It will be up to him to rekindle it again. You will be with him until the twists and turns of your journey take you away once again."

Anna lay in the rainforest with the fragrance of wildflowers serenading her nostrils as she listened to the words of the Old Head and wondered what would be coming next. This, she realized, was also a part of her journey, unfolding and leading to some unknown place to keep a promise made before she was a thought on this planet.

****

Dee called later in the week, informing Anna that she had finally gotten tickets for the play *Dolls A Lay*, a romance–comedy they both wanted to see. All week, she and Dee went through the wardrobe her designer had sent her and the clothes Dee had packed away talking about the great reviews the play had received. The night of the play, Anna dropped Jake Jr. and Sheri' off at her parents' home and hurried home to dress.

The phone rang just as Jake stepped out of the shower. Handing it to him, she smoothed the silver floor-length gown. It shimmered against her body. Her Paris designer had it hugging her in just the right places. The splits showed her thighs as smooth as nylons. Hanging up the phone, Jake came up behind Anna and gave her a kiss behind her ear.

"Baby, a meeting has been called by the city councilmen to rezone the new shopping mall being built here in Session. It will mean a lot of jobs for people in Session. We've finalized the plans, but I would like to attend to make sure nothing goes wrong." Listening to him, Anna continued to apply her makeup, thinking she had heard those words before when they were about to dine out together. It was like she was revisiting her old life with him again.

"Honey, did you hear me?" Jake asked, placing his arms around her waist.

"Yes, I heard you, honey," she answered.

"Look, I promise I'll make it up to you. There'll only be men present. I'd look silly with my wife up under me," he stated, turning her to face him. "I guess it is all right for you to go with Fred and Dee."

"Jake, this is a couples' affair. You go right ahead to your meeting. I'll find somewhere else to spend the evening."

"Not by yourself . . . dressed like that," he insisted, looking down at the revealing evening gown she wore. She knew he did not want her to go anywhere without him by the way he gazed at the gown she wore.

"Jake, I'm a big girl now, remember? You don't have to be afraid for me. I can handle being around people of any race," Anna assured him remembering her trips abroad. It doesn't make sense for me to waste this beautiful gown I have gotten all dressed up in by sitting at home because your plans have changed. I will find some entertainment at one of the local clubs. You go right ahead and take care of your business, sweetheart."

"I'll tell you what . . . I'll call James; he owes me."

"How do I look, honey?" Anna asked, whirling around as she smiled at Jake while he talked to his brother on the phone.

"Let's get going before we are late," Jake said quickly hanging up the phone.

"But I thought . . ."

"James will cover for me . . . It's the same as my being there."

Anna reached for her coat just as the doorbell rang.

"Butler, what is it, man?" Jake asked. Anna gazed at the young black man standing in the doorway. He looked anxiously at them.

"Mr. Bradley, I'm sorry for barging in on you like this, but that job you sent me to, the guy said he didn't need no help. I don't understand it. I thought it was a sho' gig . . . got my old lady's jaws all tight . . . just had to come see you to find out what was going down."

"Hell, man, I don't know. The dude assured me he needed the help. Look, don't get down on it yet. I'll check it out and let you know the first thing in the morning."

"Yeah, well thanks! I'll be waiting on that call. This job means everything to me. I just . . ."

"Look, you're going to work. I'll go by there right now and see the man. And here is something to hang on to until your pay starts coming in." Anna watched the man's eyes light up at the two one-hundred-dollar bills Jake handed him. Though the man put his hand up to refuse the money, Jake pushed it into his hand anyway.

"Man, I know what it is to be down on your luck—been there myself. When your pockets are empty, your woman is bitching; now, get the hell on out of here and wait for my call tomorrow morning."

"You cool, man. I'll drop this back on you soon as I git this gig going strong, now I know why people call you *THE MAN*." Anna listened to Butler said then saw him smile at the money in his hand as Jake closed the door behind him."

Anna listened as Jake told Fred over the phone that they would meet them at the theater in Godfrey, Illinois, forty miles away from Session. Jake liked to tell his constituents that it was a city void of all but four black families.

"Let's hurry and get out of here, baby." Anna looked at the time as Jake rushed her out of the door.

"Where are we going?" Anna asked once they arrived in Godfrey. "This is not the way to the theater."

"I gotta go in and see this dude about the job he promised my man . . . I won't be a minute."

"I'll wait here in the car if you won't be but a minute."

"Hell no, fine as you are dressed, I would be scared some mother's son might come along and snatch you up out of here while I'm inside. I can't hear you out here screaming. Anyway, I like having you by my side, good as you're looking." Jake smiled as he opened the door for her.

A white maid admitted them into the house. The woman who greeted them was a dark skinned tall black woman, much to Anna's surprise. Her gray streaked hair was wrapped around her head in a high cone. Though formally dressed, she didn't appear to be going anywhere. Anna turned to look at the luxuries of the home and was fascinated by the beautiful African artifacts. An odd black statue of a nude man kissing a nude woman caught her eye.

"It's jade, would you believe? Picked it up in Hong Kong—goes to show everything there isn't junk." Anna smiled as she continued to look around the expensively furnished home.

A short stout bald headed light skinned man who appeared to be some years older than Jake entered the room. He looked surprised but delighted to see her husband.

"Hey Harry, I can't stay," Jake said, shaking hands with him and declining the seats he offered. "I've got to get out of here and take my wife to the play she's having a fit to see."

"*Dolls A Lay*, I'm sure," the woman said, speaking with pride at naming the play.

"Yes," Anna replied, smiling back at her, wondering where she picked up her white-sounding voice. Must be from Godfrey, she thought to herself, and then had to laugh as she remembered Dee's accusing her of sounding white. What damn difference did it make what ones voice sounded like as long as the listener got the message being delivered, she asked to herself? But in her heart, she knew it did make a difference to blacks who saw blacks speaking like whites as the spies that came into their world pretending to be one of them, only to laugh with whites later, telling them lies like the ones told to the priests who could never enter their world undetected. Well, Dee may never know it, but no matter how Anna's voice sounded to her, there was a scarf that told a different story about who she really was and what she thought of her people regardless of what station in life they held.

"Hon, someone called for the job. They should be arriving soon."

"Thanks, Martha," the man said, smiling over at this wife.

"Yeah, my man, that's why I'm here. The dude I sent over to do that job you said you needed a man for told me you told him you weren't hiring." Anna looked at the man, knowing Jake waited impatiently for an answer.

"You know how it is, Bradley. You get too many niggers off the street and they don't get the job done right." Anna bit her top lip at his choice of words. "He didn't look like he was the man to handle the job."

"What do you mean he didn't look like the man to handle the job? I handpicked him. He's a top wire man; fact is, he's got a family and he needs the work."

"Yeah, I know how that is, man, but you've got to understand . . ." His sentence trailed off at the sound of the doorbell.

"Hon, here are the men who called." Anna and Jake stared at each other as two white men entered and shook hands with Harry.

"Mr. Johnson, here's the man you wanted to do that wiring job. We pulled him off another job and put another one of our wire men on that job so he could do the work for you." The white men smiled at Mr. Johnson. Anna felt herself being pulled by the arm.

"Come on, Anna; let's get the hell out of this house!"

"Bradley!" Harry Johnson said, hurrying behind Jake and Anna.

"Johnson, we ain't got a damn thing to discuss; you're already talking to the men you want to discuss business with." Anna had to walk fast to keep up and her four-inch heels weren't giving her much help. The words she heard Jake whispering under his breath she knew were not for a public audience.

"Bradley, I have got to make you understand." The man somehow caught up with them before they reached their car.

"Look, Johnson, you have already made me understand."

"I got to be fair, man. I can't just hire my people."

"Fair, nigger? Don't you come talking to me about fair." Anna listened to hear how her husband would counter him.

"Was Rosen fair when he hired four white boys after telling your old man there was no work for him? At least that's the way your old man put it to my old man, causing him to lay my young ass off so that he could put a man with a family to work so he could put meals on your table. *'A way of helping another black man keep his self-respect,'* the old man told me. At the time it was money out of my pocket and I thought I got a shitty deal, but as I grew older I understood. You, man, you think only those white boys need that respect." Anna listened to the conversation learning things about her husband she never knew.

"Talking about he can't do the job just because his skin is black. All you white niggers are just alike when you get one foot up the ladder; you think that white man is not looking out for his own; first and foremost. Thanks to niggers like you wanting to be nice to white folks, we'll always be left hanging in the end. Come on, baby, let's get the hell outta this white nigger's yard."

"Goddamn you, Bradley! Tell the man to see me Monday morning . . . he's got the job. It's just that, well, man, sometimes you just forget."

"Yeah man, that's the reason I always make that trip back down Broadway, so I won't ever forget. It's like I always say, 'we're all in this together . . . especially for those at the bottom who can't make that climb alone.'"

"You chill out with that white nigger shit, man . . . my head is clear."

"Yeah good; keep it clear. It's all right to help them if they need it, but he didn't need it. I will never forget my old man's words to me before his death."

"What the hell were they?"

"'*Never forget to help your own.*' That's their way we need to learn to make it our way."

"Yes, I guess you are right, man," Harry Johnson said as he turned to go back into his home.

"Jake, you called him a white nigger. What does it mean?" Anna asked as Jake started the car up to drive out of the driveway.

"Baby, it's a black-ass nigger, man or woman, who sees another black person needing help and have the ability to help but refuse to—like Johnson wanted to help a white man who didn't even need the help that the job would have given a black man. They like to tell themselves they have no power to do anything unless the white man gives it to them—and even when they do, they fear placing themselves in harm's way with the white man if it is to help another brother.

"If I had not stopped by his house that is the way it would have gone down. He already had it explained in his mind, telling himself that is just the way it is. But no, that is just the way he accepts it. There are just times, baby, you must stand on principles, never forgetting if one of your own is hurting, so are you, even if it's no place but in your heart." His words made Anna recall walking into the café and seeing signs hanging above her head that took her back in time, reading a ledger that showed two different pay scales for blacks versus whites doing the same work, and even worse than that, the condition of the black southern women's clinic where they and their babies were forced to receive unclean medical care. She placed her arms around Jake, giving him a long seductive kiss as she realized he had explained why she did what she had done for those black people struggling in Kentucky in a way she had not even been able to explain to herself.

"We can always go back home," he whispered, pulling her closer.

"It would be months before Dee spoke to me again if I didn't show up," Anna said, regaining her composure.

****

Twenty minutes before the play began, Dee and Anna stood in Godfrey's theater playhouse where whites and blacks stood packed together in a theater that just four years before had held only whites. Anna realized Godfrey as well as Session had done some progressive changing since she had left and returned. There were far more interracial couples together than there had been before she left. Whites and blacks appeared to be on friendlier terms with each other socially now than they had ever been before she left.

"Anna, you look gorgeous in that silver gown—it's a knock out," Dee said, giving her the once over.

"Like you don't in your glittering golden gown showing off those hips of yours," Anna countered, looking her up and down.

"I see the new Anna is making some strong moves to be coming here to Godfrey, and Jake giving up a meeting. Girl, you have changed yourself and that man." Anna listened to Dee, who was showing all her pearly whites in her happiness at her return to Jake.

"I gave him no quarrel about giving up his meeting. He made that decision on his own. Of course, I didn't plan to sit around the house while he was gone—that he learned soon enough."

"You are insane, girl, but I love it . . . getting more like me every day." Fred and Jake rejoined them with drinks in their hands.

"You ladies all right?"

"Of course, why shouldn't we be?" Dee asked.

"That man walking this way has been staring at you or Dee. Haven't you noticed?" Fred asked as the man approached them with a broad smile on his face.

"If it isn't Jake Bradley taking time away from work to enjoy some entertainment tonight," the man said, Anna turned with Dee to see the man speaking to them.

"I see there is nothing better for the richest man in thoroughbred racing to be doing this fine evening. Anna, Fred, Dee, meet Nathan Forlorn," Jake said, turning their way after shaking hands with the white man who had walked up to him. Anna's purse fell to the floor. She stooped to pick it up, but not before the white man bent to help her retrieve her belongings.

Their eyes met as Anna hurried to place the last item inside her purse and rise from the floor. She saw a younger vision of Raymond but with no mustache and with blue instead of gray eyes smiling at her.

"Is this the little wife you were in such an upheaval about?" His southern drawl caused her heart to go crazy; he sounded so much like her former lover, Anna trembled lest he say something that indicated he knew her.

"Yes, my wife is home now," Jake, said, his arm going immediately around Anna's waist.

"We'll both have to thank God for her safe return," Nathan Forlorn said, smiling down at Anna. "Oh, let me not forget my manners. This is my secretary, Angela." The blonde hair attractive white woman had been looking hard at Jake, Anna realized, as she turned her attention to her. She could not utter a greeting to her; the shock of the man standing before her had her paralyzed. Nathan even smiled like Raymond—with that wicked grin she knew him to have when he was thinking of something to entice her.

"I remember your wife from the papers when she disappeared. I must say they did her no justice—none at all," he said, his penetrating eyes steadfast on Anna as her heart pounded and threatened to burst through the gown she wore.

"This dude owns the racetrack out on Highway 4. He is loaded, and I do mean loaded," Jake said.

"Nonsense," Nathan Forlorn replied, his eyes still on Anna. "I work perhaps longer hours than you do, Mr. Bradley."

"If this man is working, it is figuring out how to make more bread to add to those millions he has lost count of." Anna listened to their conversation while she searched her mind; she knew nothing about a racetrack that close to them. Yes, Ray had mentioned his brother was in charge of a racetrack in the Midwest, but it had never dawned on her where in the Midwest. She suddenly realized that the Old Head had made sure Ray had been close to her that night she fell down those stairs.

"Mrs. Bradley, I'm a hard-working man who has not had the pleasure of meeting Jake's beautiful wife before now," he said, reaching to shake hands with Anna. Anna saw the rise in his brow. She could not faint—not now—but she knew she was on the verge of dropping to the floor because her knees didn't seem to want to hold her. Yes, there was no doubt it was he; his southern drawl sounded as if it were an echo of his brother's. Anna saw his eyes drop down to the chain around her neck.

"Being a horseman, I'm always fascinated by trinkets such as that chain you are wearing around your neck, Mrs. Bradley. Would you part with it?"

"Ah, man, you can forget it. Her father gave that to her, and as much as he means to her, I know she'll never part with it," Jake quickly responded.

"One never knows; perhaps I can seduce Mrs. Bradley with a price that might make her change her mind." Their eyes locked, sending messages words could not causing Anna to feel a shock wave as though she had been touched by a live wire.

"I'm afraid my husband is correct; I have become too attached to it to ever part with it," she answered turning from the hand offered to her. Shaking hands with Fred and Dee, Nathan placed his arm around Angela.

"I guess, Mrs. Bradley, I can't blame you; it looks far better around your neck than it would around mine," he said as he bid them goodbye.

"Oh, Forlorn," Jake called after him, "I heard it was a smart black sister who found the cure for those dying horses of yours. I can't understand why there was no press coverage as to her identity." Anna held her breath as she stared hard into the eyes now turned back to them.

"Yes, Jake, she is a genius to have come up with that cure and so fast. Many of us would be in the unemployment line had it not been for her brilliance. However, it was her desire to remain anonymous. Thoroughbred owners honored her privacy." Anna blinked and turned from his knowing smile.

"Anna, my slip is falling—go to the ladies' room with me to see if we can get it back up," Dee announced, walking fast in that direction. Anna followed on legs so wobbly she was hardly able to keep up. Once inside, Dee turned around to face her.

"What the hell is going on with you Anna? You looked like you had seen a ghost. I thought you were going to break and run for a minute there." Anna stood staring at Dee, unable to speak after seeing her lover's brother. They looked so much alike that Nathan could have been Raymond.

"You told me you had gotten over your fear of whites. It didn't look that way out there, and I'm telling you it scared me." Anna blinked as if coming out of a trance.

"I'm fine, Dee. I'll admit I'm still not comfortable around whites I don't know. It's not like with Shirley—I know her. I promise you I'm not about to run out the door. I can handle myself. Let's go before we miss the play, girlfriend, and thank you for caring about me."

Seated in the dark theater, Anna wondered what had stopped her picture from being plastered over every newspaper in not only this country but the world because so many horses had received the cure. Rubbing the orange spot, she felt her mind expand, allowing her to see back in time. She watched May Lue ride bareback into the yard of the Main House in Kentucky were Anna had worked in the infirmary on a cure for the dying horses. Sliding from the back of the horse, she ran inside.

"'Mrs. Mike, they are all over the place trying to get in to see and interview Ms. Anna,' she breathlessly shared with Julia. '"I don't think she is aware of them yet. And Ted said she would leave if her presence became public. We need those tears, Mrs. Julia.' Anna saw the Old Widow hanging on Julia's window seal and knew the Old Head must have protected her identity.

"He's right, May Lue. She wants no public exposure. We better stop them Yankees from taking pictures or getting to her right now." In the next scene, Julia was standing before a group of ranch hands with a whip in her hand.

"Boys, those Yankee reporters have crawled onto this ranch with their Northern cameras to make light of us like they have always done in the past. If they take pictures for their Northern newspapers, you can about believe it will come to no good for the South. Get rid of them bastards, and be sure to destroy any cameras brought on this land. Don't let any near Ms. Anna. Our horses' lives depend on it." In the next scene, she saw May Lue and the other women ranchers standing at the gate turning away anyone who didn't have a horse in need of healing. The big young white rancher who loved Callie the black cook's cooking worked with the other ranchers to confiscate cameras and haul trespassers, as they were called, off Forlorn's property. Anna blinked in the next scene. There stood Julia talking with Raymond. It must have been after he had returned and had taken her back to the cabin.

"'We got rid of those bastards, but I think it's time you find another way to administer to those thoroughbreds people are bringing in from everywhere. She's working herself to death as it is.' She watched Julia start out of the room, and then turned back saying, "I must admit, Raymond, Arnold was right."

"'Right about what, Julia?'

"'You brought one phenomenal lady here to this ranch, boy.' The smile on his face brought one to Julia's.

Seated inside the dark theater, Anna's heart would not quiet down. It had been two months since they had split. Those four years seemed but a dream that might not have really happened. Nothing before tonight had come to challenge that it wasn't just a dream . . . and now this encounter so close to home. His brother lived too close and he undoubtedly knew her beyond what Jake, Dee or Fred could have imagined. He must have laughed to himself when Jake mentioned her father had given the chain to her. What had really shocked her was that he did not counter Jake's reason for her not giving up the chain. He would have had to expose his brother. He wouldn't do that, she thought, praying her heart would slow its pace before it burst through to expose her and the white man inside the theater. Her missing past had now been recovered, thanks to the Old Head and Raymond. He had gone back into his world as she had come back into hers. She needed nothing to connect her with him . . . not now—not ever.

Chapter Nine

—∿—

Anna woke with a start hearing the ringing telephone. She turned and looked at the clock beside their bed. It was two in the morning. It must be for Jake, she thought to herself, refusing to answer it. After the fifth ring, she heard him pick up the receiver from the floor after it fell. A few minutes later, Anna squeezed her eyes shut to keep out the light that Jake flipped on.

"Where have they got him?" she heard him ask. "When was it supposed to have happened? I'll be right down and see what the hell I can do. It's James, Anna. He is in jail!" Jake said after hanging up the phone.

"In jail!" Her eyes popped open. "What for?"

"I don't know for sure . . . Lois was crying so hard. The police evidently came to their home and picked him up. I'm going down there to try and make bail for him."

At six o'clock that morning, Jake returned home. The look on his face told Anna things had gone bad. She poured him a cup of coffee, and then sat down to her cup of hot tea as she watched Jake sip from his cup, waiting for him to tell her what had happened.

"Honey, I've gotta tell you something. I know we've been through our hell, but now you seem to have matured enough to understand more . . ."

"Jake, let's have it." Anna held her cup up to her lips as she waited for him to tell her what had gotten James in trouble. Of the three brothers, he was the quietest—never involved in anything unless Jake was instrumental in setting it up. Remembering the night with the man at the Top Hat Club, she wondered what Jake had him involved in that had gotten him arrested. Taking a deep breath, Jake took a seat across from her at the dining room table.

"James has been seeing this white chick. She lives over in Godfrey—some Senator's daughter. It seems she had wedding bells on her mind. He failed, of course, to tell her he was already married"

"She found out, of course," Anna said, shaking her head with a look of disgust on her face as she remembered her own discovery of Jake's deceit.

"Yes," Jake said, sighing as he ran his hand through his hair.

"And you knew about it, of course?" Anna asked, taking a sip of her tea and looking hard at him.

"Yes, but he is a grown ass man, Anna. How can I tell him what not to do? As you already know, I have not been preacher-clean myself. No one else knew about her. She's had him arrested for rape and assault. Who would believe me, his brother, saying he did not rape this woman—that she willingly consented to having sex with him? She said she had never seen him before in her life. It looks bad."

Anna looked beyond her husband, remembering her time with Raymond when they looked together and saw James through Raymond's binoculars with some white woman standing in front of the Holiday Inn.

"Anna, you are spilling your tea!" Anna jumped from the pain of the hot tea in her lap.

"What does the woman look like?" she asked, wanting to know if she was the same one.

"What damn difference does it make? She's white, about your size, black hair, wears really nice shit like that shit you wear now."

"How long?"

"How long? What do you mean, how long?" Jake asked anger in his voice.

"I mean, husband of mine, how long have they been in bed together? You know, having sex!"

"Long enough for her to have wedding bells on her mind,"

"Using a Senator's daughter . . . he had that little sense? That stupid bastard deserves whatever he gets!" Anna replied shaking her head in disgust.

"She maintains that she had never seen him before last night."

"What does James say?"

"What can he say but that he had never set eyes on her before in his life?"

"You black men just have to try out that new-found freedom . . . The white man's precious blessing. I may not be light enough for you according to your brother but that little white goddess has given him a gut full of her whiteness and now he's about to choke on it. I still say it serves him right. She trusted the bastard, listening to his lies. He trashed her—now he's getting trashed." Anna looked at the hateful expression on Jake's face.

Anna continued, "Don't get me wrong. It's wrong of her to screw him like this. She does not realize she is not only hurting him but so many others who had nothing to do with what he did to her. We don't deserve to share in his payback. That's why I left and didn't come back. Too many people get hurt when you seek revenge for a wrong done to you." Anna stared at her husband.

"Yes, but . . ."

"She's running back to sit on that throne, Jake, and let the great white father whip James's black ass. That's the name of the white woman's game. We have never as black women been able to get retribution for our tragic past. But oh boy, you better believe because she is a white woman, his day of reckoning is at hand." Anna almost laughed as she saw in her mind the two kissing passionately in front of the Holiday Inn.

"I believe he cares for her," Jake said.

"Yes, just like he cares for Lois," Anna replied, disgust in her voice. "Like you, he is such a handsome man that women just throw themselves at him just as you told me before I met him. As far as his loving or caring about anyone, I don't think his mind has ever been on anything but getting that head between his legs into any *body* that would open for him."

"Anna," Jake protested.

"Well, it hurts thinking about all that you damn men get away with . . . using and abusing women and then discarding us on a whim. One day you will realize women are not toys to be played with and then dumped when you feel the need to rid yourselves of us to go out and find another toy to play with and dump.

"Had it been me," she said, looking at her husband, "I would have killed his ass and been done with it. The same as you would have gotten if I had stayed here. As it was, you have paid your own price for the hurt you dumped on the women who loved you." They both looked at his leg with the limp that slowed his gait.

"I thought we promised each other not to bring past relationships up again. I'm not talking about that fearless lover of yours. What the hell happened to end that? Did he dump you?" Jake asked, setting his cup down as they stared at each other.

"You want to go there, Jake Bradley?" Anna asked, setting her cup of tea down as she rose from her chair.

"Look," he said, taking a deep breath, "there are no other women in my life but you, Anna." She could hear the tone in his voice calming down.

"So that there is no misunderstanding as to how I and my fearless lover—that you threw up in my face—parted, he didn't dump me. If there was any way he thought I would have him back, he would walk right through that front door and take me as we speak."

"Him and how many goddamn armies, woman?" Jake's voice never rose—just the tone of his voice hissed as he stared at her. "Anna, I would have gladly killed that nigger's ass if you had not agreed to come back to me. Don't think for one minute that I would hesitate to kill one trying to come here thinking he will take shit from me. His ass will be dead on short notice. Have no doubts about that shit. I love you, and now that you are back, there will be no man in your life but me until they nail you in a box. As for James, his ass can rot in prison for all I care if it means you and I have to fight over him and this situation he got his ass in."

"Jake, I think . . ."

"Don't think, Anna. I don't need his troubles to become ours." He pulled her into his arms. "I've learned from my mistakes. No woman or man will ever come between us again. You are mine forever."

****

Anna sat across from Lois. Before she had left Session, their relationship had been barely casual. Lois's white features caused her to have an uppity attitude, her mother liked to say. She enjoyed throwing her long dark brown hair out of her face the way Anna had seen many white women toss theirs. Though Lois could hardly be called white, she was white enough so that you knew some white man had been in the bed somewhere.

"Anna, I knew that sucker was fooling around with the white bitch. She wouldn't have just picked him out of a crowd of goddamn black men to accuse. It's just that I hate the looks of pity I see in the faces of the women around here. I know what they are thinking."

Anna tried to interrupt her. "Lois . . ."

"No, Anna. I know they are thinking he wasn't satisfied with the almost-white bitch he had; the nigger had to go get him some real white meat and got his ass caught up. If it had been a black bitch, hell, I would have cussed the nigger's ass out but held my head up."

"Lois, there is no woman around here who can stick her chest out saying she's got a perfect man. Even those who've never suspected their husbands know they are capable."

"Anna, when your man starts crossing the color line, it becomes funky shit—something I can't hang with."

"Lois, I'm sure things will work themselves out."

"Will they? Anna, my kids are being teased at school. You don't know how it feels being totally humiliated that way. You come tell me how it feels when you find your man has gone to jail for sleeping white."

Anna sat looking at Lois, remembering the white man who had been in her life. Jake would kill her dead body if he knew. Nothing she could say would stop the hurt Lois felt. They hugged and Anna left, wishing there was something more she could do to help.

****

In front of her parents' home, Anna stood and watched her daughter and son come running down the sidewalk toward her. Sheri' was crying. Anna frowned as she took her daughter into her arms.

"Jake Jr., I hope you have not been fighting again." At seven, his temper was such that Anna worried her son was becoming too much like her mother when he became angry. The boy would fight at the drop of a hat.

"They called Uncle James a jailbird . . . said he was trying to take white meat and got caught. Pat and James Jr. have to fight every day at school now because the kids make fun of them." Anna thought how hard it must be for James's children. Though they grudgingly accepted it when forced, many blacks in Session had no understanding of white–black relationships. This charge let everyone know Session's true feeling about it. It didn't help that James had none of Jake's qualities that made him likeable to many

112

people. He had a quick temper and didn't have a problem becoming physical. He had quiet a few enemies because of it.

"And you, Jake Jr., felt you must help defend them. I see your clothes are torn, as always, when you've been fighting." Anna sat with her children on her parents' swing on the front porch.

"They wanted to fight. I accommodated them. Grandma taught me to get some ass if anybody brings shit my way."

"Jake Jr.!" Anna said in a raised voice, realizing the influence her mother had had on her children was not what she wanted for them.

"Momma, I am not going to fight for no good reason, but they are my little cousins and they needed defending." He looked at her as if daring her to deny his reason was good enough.

"There are some people in this world who don't care who they hurt or how. There is just the pleasure they get out of hurting someone else," Anna said to her son, thinking of the trouble he might one day get into if he did not learn to control that temper of his.

"I guess it's because they are really hurting inside themselves. As the saying goes, 'misery loves company,' doesn't it, Momma?" Sheri', of course, put in her words of wisdom.

"What is misery, Momma?" Jake Jr. asked.

"It is hatefulness inside of you, boy," Sheri' hurried to answer. "Momma, they must have the devil in them like Grandma says when people do wrong."

"Yes, Sheri', I guess it would have to take a bit of the devil to make someone hurt another person for whatever reason. I'm afraid all we can do is to pray that God takes the devil out of her." Hugging her daughter, Anna thought of the woman and why she had accused James. She wondered if the woman knew or even cared how many people she was hurting.

Anna followed her children inside. After the children wandered off into their old rooms, Anna's mother turned to her and shook her head.

"Things are not going well, Momma."

"They are gonna hang that young nigger's ass, ya hare me?" Anna froze, hearing her mother's verdict.

"Momma, they don't hang people anymore, and I can't understand how you hate hearing the words coming from white people's lips and love saying it yourself about your own people."

"I still say thay gonna hang him. And fer yer information, thare's more'n one way to hang ya, gal." Anna frowned and turned away from her mother as she continued to talk. "White folks sly like a fox. They may say it's okay to bed one of thay women but b'lieve me, ya mess up and thay go git yer ass, gal."

"Come on, Sheri' and Jake Jr. It's time to go home," Anna called to her children, refusing to discuss the subject with her mother any longer.

At home, Anna listened to Jake and Fred figuring out how they could come up with the two million dollars needed to bail James out of jail. Fred figured on his house because Jake and Anna had just bought theirs and didn't have any equity. The construction company seemed to be their only out. They both would sell the shirts off their backs to get James out of jail and hopefully keep him from going to prison. They needed an attorney to take the case. That would take money and lots of it because the lawyers in Tora, Godfrey, and Session were refusing to touch the case. It seemed it was "too high profile."

Godfrey was essentially all white. The whites held all the high positions, and no one felt brave enough to tackle those powerful political forces—they had money and would be willing to use it to stop any help sought for James. Now they were demanding the stiffest possible penalty. It was already hurting Jake's business. His brother's arrest for the type of crime he had been charged with meant some whites had begun to question Jake's credibility. Those previously cordial to him became distant and avoided social contact with him.

"James's case . . . I don't think he is going to make it. He needs not only a lawyer but the best lawyer money can buy or they will railroad him for sure." Listening to her husband, Anna thought about her children fighting to defend their cousins at school when other students harassed them. The situation was getting out of hand. She had to do something quickly.

****

Anna gazed at the array of flowers blooming inside a white picket fence in the middle of the racetrack. Her dark glasses shaded the colors. A perfect carpet of green grass lay evenly around the field. Only the track itself lay barren and wet from being watered down just moments before. In the center of the green carpet, a large scoreboard displayed various numbers and dates; Anna knew they were numbers of horses and times of races. A tractor rolled around the long mile track, kicking up dust as it graded the grounds where evening racing would soon fill the bleachers behind her with hundreds, if not thousands, of racing fans.

Anna looked at her watch; they had agreed to meet at eight am that morning. She watched a chestnut thoroughbred trailed a brown-and-white horse with a rider down the field. She knew they would soon work out at five furloughs. The gate spread across the field. She and Raymond had watched his thoroughbreds work out at that distance.

Anna's feet felt like lead. She wanted to turn and walk away from Looper's racetrack. It had been a daring and foolish move on her part. Now she felt she had been wrong and needed to leave.

"Sorry I'm a little late—a problem came up that one of the judges needed to discuss with me and it took longer than I thought." Anna didn't turn to acknowledge the man who came up beside her. It had been hard enough coming here. A warm breeze blew her multicolored scarf into her face. She brushed it aside, remembering that she had worn it because it accented the navy blue two piece suit she had decided to wear at the last minute.

"I called because I believe we might be able to negotiate an exchange if you are agreeable." Her eyes still on the field in front of her, she could not bring herself to look at her former lover's brother—just being close to him unnerved her enough.

"Exchange?" Out of the corner of her eye, Anna saw him look over at her with a puzzled expression on his face.

"I'm sure you have read in the papers that my husband's brother is in jail on some trumped-up charge," Anna said, getting right to the point before her courage failed her.

"The incident has come to my attention. I can tell you do not believe it to be true." Anna watched the chestnut horse walk toward the starting gate.

"It's true that he slept with her, but he did not rape her as she has led everyone to believe." They would soon be off and running, thought Anna, at last gaining enough courage to turn and face him.

"How can I be of service?" he asked, smiling down at her. Anna still had trouble gazing his way and averted her eyes. He looked too much like his brother. Though his face was hairless, his mannerisms played out the same.

"I have something that belongs to your family, an heirloom that you appeared to have desired the night of the play." Anna fingered the chain around her neck. It had become the door to an otherwise closed chapter in her life—a chapter she knew she must forget. She dreaded letting go of it because it meant so much to her.

"I want you to know that it means a great deal to me, but under the circumstances I have no other choices." Anna sighed. "We must have lawyers who can at least get James a fair trial—lawyers who have not been prejudiced by public opinion—lawyers who can be paid enough so that we will not have to worry about them being bought off. If you will do this for me, I'll give you the chain in return."

They were off and running, racing as fast as the wind. Anna knew it would be the chestnut. He looked the healthiest, plus his legs appeared the strongest.

"Ms. Anna, you are the scientist who performed a miracle in saving hundreds of thousands of thoroughbreds from having to be destroyed, not to mention the end of thoroughbred racing itself. Your name is revered at the ranch by not only Julia, Ted, and Arnold but also by the hands they all still love and speak of you in awe. They say God brought you to them. I believe so," he said, handing Anna the white handkerchief in his hand and looking away as if in deep thought as she dabbed at the tears sliding from under her shades. "You refused to give your name as the one who developed the Healing Tree serum, even though it could have brought millions of dollars to you personally instead of to my brother. Understanding how things are in Session, I have no doubt you felt it to be the best decision.

"While I cannot promise you that the lawyers I send will perform the miracle you need, I will send those from our Pennsylvania firm. They can't be bought off. They are the best I know in this country."

"Thank you," Anna said, reaching to take the chain from around her neck.

"No, I cannot accept it," he said, stopping her. My brother would never forgive me. I would never use such a reason to take the chain from you. It connects you and him. Even if I had a mind to do so, my conscience would not allow it. It is too bad Jake cannot know the brilliant woman he has for a wife. You have given me my brother back—a brother I had no communication with for years. I am so thankful that he is alive and healthy. We have become devoted to each other, thanks to the miracle you performed in giving him his life back. If there is anything else you need, please don't hesitate to call on me." Anna felt the pressure of his lips on her cheek.

"I must go," she said, handing him back his handkerchief. As she turned to walk toward the parking lot, Anna stopped a yard away and turned back. He stood there looking after her. "Please," she said, "let this meeting remain between the two of us. Ray need not know."

"And that it shall, Ms. Anna," he said, raising his hand to wave goodbye.

Chapter Ten

—◦◦—

"I thought you had become liberated," Jake said, opening the car door for Anna now that she allowed him the privilege of doing so since her return to him.

"I am liberated. Now white women get to work like we black women have worked all our lives and I have decided to enjoy the pleasures they have been taking for granted for so long," Anna said, stepping inside his red Seville Cadillac as they prepared to drive to Godfrey where James's preliminary trial was to be held.

Soon after driving onto the highway, Jake put in a tape. Hearing Aretha's voice fill the car, Anna felt a cold chill spin her mind back in time. She saw herself standing in the apartment, looking out of the window as she listened to Aretha's *I've Got to Find Me an Angel* when she heard the apartment door open and close. She knew Raymond had walked inside. Aretha's voice was loud, and Anna wasn't talking.

"What have I done to upset you, Ms. Anna?"

"You couldn't call to tell me you would be a day late?" She said turning to face him.

"You missed me," she heard him say as she felt his arms wrap around her. The force of his weight caused her to catch him as he fell into her arms.

"Ray, what has happened to you?" she cried, pulling his coat open and gasping at his blood-soaked shirt.

"Ms. Anna, I promise I will love you until these eyes of mine close forever." It was all she could do to get him into their bed before he passed out. Minutes later, Mix was there with the doctor she remembered seeing when she had cut Ray.

In the car, the memory of that scene so overwhelmed her that she reached and turned off the stereo and the sound of Aretha's voice, killing the vision of that terrifying scene.

"I thought you loved Sister Franklin," Jake said, smiling as he looked over at her.

"I didn't want you to become upset with her message and tear up your console." Jake's laughter rang out inside the car, further turning Anna's mind away from the chilling scene.

"Every time you were upset about something I had done, you were always using her as your messenger, playing one record over and over again like I couldn't hear. I used to think the sister never had a good word for a brother, I know that."

"She had a good word for a brother when the brother deserved it. You just never wanted to be called on your wrongs. That is your problem—you men think women are your property, not human beings just like you with feelings that need respecting."

"You played her ass every goddamn day about some shit you were angry with me about. And when you really became upset, I would hear one record until I thought my eardrums would burst."

"Yes, I did that because you were always doing something to piss me off. I just didn't have the words to express my feelings so I had her sing it for me. Of course, you didn't like it so you destroyed my records of her."

"Yes, I remember coming home, snatching her record off the record player, and stomping it as I told her to shut up her goddamn mouth 'cause I don't want to hear her shit no damn more." Anna had to laugh, thinking back to the times Jake stomped on the records of Aretha asthough they were live people.

"I told you, '"Look, I'm not going to hear her shit no more today unless you want this stereo of yours to look like that record I just finished stomping to pieces.'

"Your problem was you didn't want to hear the truth. But I didn't care that you destroyed the record."

"Hell no, you didn't care because you would drive down to the record shop and buy three to take the place of that one."

"Yes, I did—told the record store owner I needed three of every record she ever made so that when the time came and you needed my message, her voice would be there to make sure you got it."

"I guess I stomped about a hundred of those motherfuckers to pieces just so I could infuriate you."

"I think you were really stomping on me, hating me as you must have during those times."

"No, it wasn't you I hated," he said, placing his arm around her and pulling her closer to him. "It was me I hated. I knew I was wrong as two left shoes. I just didn't care to be called on my shit as you liked to tell me. I thought the world revolved around my ass, I guess. I lay in that hospital, worrying about your fall down those stairs, knowing it was my fault.

"After your car was discovered, I waited scared to death you would be found inside. I couldn't sleep or eat. I just laid there listening to Aretha spell out life between a woman and her man, thinking what a fool I had been. Since your return to me, I have wondered how to tell you what was on my mind and figured what better way than the way you always used?" Anna watched him take a tape out of his pocket, eject the one inside the player, and replace it with the one in his hand. He drove in to a rest stop just as the voice of Aretha filled the car with its beautiful melody.

"Baby," he said, as he sang along with the song "I Can't Love You if You Won't Let Me." "I feel your rejection even though you live in the house with me. How can I love you when you freeze up as though I am a stranger you have never slept with?" Anna felt his hand move through her hair as he spoke the words Aretha sang, and she heard in her mind the voice of the Old Head.

"The love you had for your earth mate is still in your heart, Daughter. You must find it."

The Old Head's voice resonated as Anna accepted her husband's embrace, realizing that a supernatural force had taken charge of her life, and the hate that had once filled her heart against her husband was being replaced with her lost love for him. Something was coming, if only she knew what.

****

As they drove the forty miles from Session to Godfrey, Jake informed Anna that attorneys from the firm Nathan Forlorn owned had come forth to try James's case. It seems Nathan would like to talk to Jake about a business venture he thought would be good for Session, and this gave him an opportunity to show his good will.

"I don't know what he wants from me, but right now I need those lawyers. You understand, don't you, baby? You don't think I'm selling out to save James, do you?" Jake asked.

"Of course not, I understand you must have them to get James a fair trial—it's all he has going for him." Anna sensed that with the presence of the attorneys from Nathan's firm, some of the tension and stress the family was feeling was relieved. He talked hopefully now of his brother having a half-way fair trial. Anna thought back to her mother's words. From the looks of things, she had been right. Without the best lawyers, innocent or not, James's life would be doomed.

Inside the parking lot at the courthouse, they waited for a black couple to get into their car so they could get their parking space. With their windows down, they could not help but hear the heated conversation between the couple.

"Honey," Anna listened to the woman said to the man, "would you please open the door? I've got the baby and her diaper bag." The young man, Anna observed, carried nothing and was about to get in on the driver's side. Anna watched him look over the hood of the car at the woman, the infant, and the diaper bag she carried.

"Shit, put her ass down—she can walk," the young man said.

"But Mike, she's asleep."

"Look woman, put her ass down and open the goddamn door—hell, I ain't no fuckin' doorman." As the woman began to lower the baby down, Jake jumped out of the car and opened the door for her.

Saying loudly, "One day you will realize you are worth more than this puck. Find you a man who appreciates you and is willing to bring his ass around to open the door at least for his own sleeping baby. Get rid of this lazy-ass nigger and find you a man with some good sense" Anna sat stunned as she listened to Jake again tell the girl to find herself a man instead of a goddamn fool while the startled young man looked on in shock. She could tell the man's thoughts were on what he should do to Jake but they were in the courthouse parking lot and there were as many police cars as visitors' cars. Saying something under his breath, he got inside his car and almost hit Jake's Cadillac as he drove off.

"Jake, are you crazy getting in that man's business like that? He could have had a gun or something. What would you have done then?"

"I'd have whipped his ass and made him eat the motherfucker. As wild as I am, I never had you carrying our babies and a diaper bag while I strolled down the street carrying nothing but my black ass. Now that is a fool thinking he's all that, treating the woman who has carried his baby like shit. I wish he had made a bad move. I was never that rude—never . . . and if I was, I never want to see that side of me again."

****

"I must be getting an infection," Anna said to herself as she ran to the courthouse bathroom to empty her bladder a second time. As she was about to wash her hands, Anna realized she stood right beside the Senator's daughter. Her memory returned to the scene she and Ray had witnessed as she had looked through his binoculars in Taro. Yes, Anna thought to herself, there was no doubt it was this girl. Such a sweet, pretty, innocent-looking girl, Anna thought. James's darling light brown eyes must have been all it took to sweep her off her feet. He had been known to make even a road-wise woman's heart tremble. If it were not for Jake and her children fighting in defense of their cousins, Anna would not care what happened to him. After all, no woman deserved being taken advantage of by a man seeking nothing but his own pleasures.

"Missing the Holiday Inn these days and that fine black buck warming your bed?" Anna asked, turning to face the young white woman standing beside her. "You won't have that big black buck warming your bed anymore now that you are putting him away."

"I . . . beg your pardon . . . I have no idea what you are talking about." Anna watched the color rise in the cheeks of the woman James had been sleeping with.

"Wouldn't it be a shame for daddy to find out his baby girl has been sleeping in the arms of that black buck—the same one out there about to go on trial?"

"Is this some kind of joke or is it just your way of trying to get him off for what he has done to me?" she asked Anna, starting to walk out the door.

"Now when it comes my turn to testify, I am going to for sure say I saw the two of you coming out of the Holiday Inn motel in Taro together. You were wearing that light pink sundress with the low back. Not to mention the dates and times I have from the motel register. I saw you standing in front of that motel down in Tora kissing him like he was the only man on earth. Of course I was not alone," Anna, said, watching the young woman's eyes widen as her lips trembled.

"No one will believe you and another nigger saying you saw me doing any damn thing," she countered, staring Anna down.

"You're right about that," Anna said, blocking her exit as she took a well-hidden picture out of her wallet. They might, however, believe this man. Wouldn't you say he looks a lot less like the nigger you called him?" It was a picture of Anna and Ray in bathing suits about to kiss. One of his white hands covered her bare dark thigh. Looking at the picture, the woman's mouth fell open.

"Now you didn't think you white women had the edge on trading men, did you? I think perhaps the world has forgotten that we black women were the ones white men first fell into bed with, mixing the races. Read our history, darling. It was his desire for our black bodies that started this ball to rolling." Placing the picture back into her wallet, Anna said to the staring woman, "My sweet honey will do about anything his black baby wants, including telling the truth about you and James. And since his money is a bit heavier than the Senator's, when he and I both say we saw you, people are going to start to wonder what reason he would have to lie. The Senator will become the laughing stock of Godfrey, if not the country . . . it will probably lose him the election coming up this year." Anna looked with pity at the tears falling from the woman's eyes.

"He lied to me. I loved him so much . . . but he just wanted my body, and after that, I was nothing to him." Anna looked at her, realizing that just like all women dumped by men who used them, this young woman did not deserve what James had done to her. She hated what she had to do, but she could not allow everyone in her family to suffer because the woman had made a foolish mistake.

"Yes," Anna said to her, the harshness now out of her voice, "you white women come down off those pedestals thinking you are going to find heaven down here playing in bed with black men who hardly know how to treat their own women much less appreciate any others." Anna sighed. She hated having to say this to the young white woman who had been a victim of loving the wrong black man, but it had to be said.

"When you find out what hell it can be for you, you want to run back into the arms of your white men. It can't be done—not in your case. It won't be done.

"When you screamed rape, I don't think you realized your revenge went much further than hurting him. You hurt a woman and her six- and seven-year-old children who have done nothing to you. Because of what you have accused James of, his children and mine have to fight their way through school because they have become the victims of a man labeled as a rapist and a jailbird. Why? Because he was out looking for a thrill, just like you were."

"But he deserves" . . . The young white woman was about to argue until Anna interrupted her.

"What, that cowardly type of punishment you white women forever use? If you think the bastard deserves punishment, punish him, not the entire black race. Those poor innocent children never did a thing to you. What do they deserve?" Anna could tell the woman was thinking about what she was saying because she just stared at her without saying anything. "Sometimes you have to do what we black women have learned to do."

"And what the hell is that?"

"Walk away and chalk it up to experience in dealing with the next man that comes along."

****

The four attorneys Nathan Forlorn had sent to defend her brother-in-law were the best. The young woman agreed to take the stand. Anna saw the pain in the woman's eyes as she looked down at James, and Anna sensed the hurt she must have experienced to do what she had done. The bastard had hurt her bad. Anna knew white women, especially those of her caliber, were not accustomed to the hard knocks of life—not those given by men who would use any woman, no matter what race.

Listening to the attorneys cut away at the young white woman's testimony, Anna thought of a conversation she had had with Shirley, Dee's white friend, after she had returned to Session and had made it a point to treat her with the same respect she would give a black sister. Shirley had explained things to her and Dee after James had been taken to jail and the three of them had stood discussing what might happen to him.

"I was lucky. I've got a black guy who loves me and I love him. Not that we don't have problems, but he is there for me. Some of us aren't that lucky, so we get hurt. We get hurt a lot worse than if a white man hurts a black woman because we feel we are risking a lot more than if we were black women. So we hurt back the only way we know how—the only way a white woman knows she can really hurt a black man."

"How is that?" Anna remembered asking her as she looked out across in Dee's back yard at the woman's two biracial children swinging in the swings in Shirley's back yard.

"By turning him over to our men who want to see him destroyed anyway when he takes their women. What better way to punish him for crushing our lives?" Anna had looked down to see Shirley's baby tugging at her leg, and she remembered the first time she had held him, causing her to think again of the white man who had been in her life.

Anna listened to the young white woman break down in court, admitting she wasn't sure who the man was. The man might have been taller and heavier and that she could not remember his face.

James was freed, but as luck would have it, Lois and their children were long gone when he returned home. Jake told Anna the next door neighbor told James that Lois had packed all their clothes, gotten a U-Haul, and moved all of the furniture, leaving him high and dry in an empty house.

****

The pills Anna had gotten from Dee to regulate her period were making her sick to her stomach; in addition, they had her sleeping most of the time. Anna decided she needed to see a doctor . . . this had been the second appointment she had missed because Jake had insisted he needed her in court with him. Now that James was freed of the charges against him, she would be able to start a normal life again. In the process of taking a nap, Anna groaned at the sound of the ringing phone.

"Hello, Anna." It was Dee. Anna listened to her tell her she needed to see her. The sound of her voice said it was urgent. Anna did not feel like visiting. She turned over, wanting to go back to sleep.

"Dee, can you at least tell me what it is you need to see me about? I was in the middle of a much-needed nap. Can't it at least wait until I see you tonight at the china ware party?" The voice coming through the phone caused Anna to jump quickly out of her waterbed. Picking up the receiver from where she had dropped it on the floor, screaming into it, "I'm coming! I'm coming!"

"My God," she gasped, after taking seconds to dress. Soon she sped down the highway to her parents' house, which was where Dee said she would be waiting for her. She thought, the attaché case—I left it under my bed in my room at my parents' house. I had not even thought to look inside. I forgot all about it. Pictures . . . what pictures? If Momma has gotten her hands on those, I'm dead.

****

Anna sat on the edge of the bed in her bedroom at her parents' home beside Dee, looking at her face and Raymond's. There was a blown-up picture of them in New York near the Statue of Liberty and another of her in Morocco after her back surgery when they were out at Mix's villa. Pulling another picture out of an envelope Sheri' had not opened, Anna gazed at a print of the one she'd destroyed after showing it to the woman who had accused James of raping her. His lips were almost touching hers as his white hand lay on her dark thigh.

"Sheri' with her little nosy self found the attaché case under your bed, she told me. I made her admit she had searched your purse until she found a key that fit it." A sealed envelope with Anna's name written across the front fell to the floor. Anna reached down and picked up the envelope opening it she found a letter inside written to her from Raymond. Dee moved closer, and Anna knew she read along with her, but at this point it did not matter.

My dearest Anna,

If you are reading this letter, it means we are no longer together. At the time I am writing it, we are still in Paris. You are lying here in bed napping. I had a few things on my mind, and since you're the only person I can share them with, I thought it time I wrote you this letter just in case we get separated somehow—something I would regret with all my heart.

Things have been good for us since our return from the ranch. Too good I fear. How and why you came into my life has been a mysterious miracle for me.

I love you, sweetheart. You're one hell of a lady, one I've been proud to have by my side. And I guess right about now if you are no longer with me, I am one lonely man who sure as hell is missing my lady.

At this moment, I have that rot-gut feeling that something, God knows what, is about to happen. It's like a horse I've got running in a race that's supposed to be sound, but inside I know that something just AIN'T right. I don't know what the hell it is, but something is amiss. You know how Ray gets when he's busy keeping his eyes on you and bets the wrong horse. I'm putting this letter in here along with the money I want you to have because it's one thing I can give you I know you'll never allow anyone to take away. Take care, my love. I've got to run now; you're awake now beckoning me to come and do what I love doing best with no one but you.

To my beloved Ms. Anna,
Ray

Anna read the handwritten letter, hating that Dee saw the tears that dropped from her eyes. Her friend took it from her, placed it back inside the envelope along with the money, and put everything back inside the attaché case and relocked it.

"I told Sheri' that unless she wanted you dead . . . I mean dead and I do mean dead like in the grave dead, she's not to tell a living soul . . . especially not Jake or her grandmother what she found. Heaven forbid if she had seen the last picture! He really does exist! Damn, Anna! A real white man—he must be the one from your dreams. How did you find him?"

"Yes, Dee, he is. I didn't find him—he found me. When my car turned over, he pulled me from it, saving my life."

"Damn, coming just in the nick of time to save your life after your dreaming about him for so long. I'm trying to think who he looks like that I have seen before," she said, staring down at the picture in her hands. "Anna, this man looks a lot like that white dude we met at the play, for real."

"He's his brother, Dee."

"You are kidding me! For real? Anna watched her look with her at the letter again. You really were in Paris, France, and all those other countries you told me about? No wonder you were so scared that night at the play.

This is the deep dark secret the others couldn't get out of you—things you told me I thought were a part of your dreams. The new, different Anna—so changed no one could believe it was still the Anna we knew. Everything you were telling me was the gospel truth! Sister girl, I thought you were making all that shit up. The white man in your dreams is a real person. He is the man you have been living with all this time, for real." Anna watched Dee shake her head in wonderment. "This money . . . no wonder! If his brother is rich, he has to be rich too." Anna looked at the attaché case, thinking about the hundred thousand dollars inside of it.

"I never would have believed it if I had not looked and seen it with my own eyes. God, I'm so glad Mrs. Annabelle was not home. All along, I knew something had happened, but never, never, I mean never in a million years would I have believed this could have been it. You, Anna, a woman who hated whites as much as your mother. Now I understand why you hugged Shirley without a problem. Sleeping with a white man for four years made that shit easy. Why didn't you counter me when I told you what Fred believed about white men?" Anna looked her without speaking. "I know, it would have been a dead giveaway to a secret you couldn't share with anyone, not even me."

Anna bit her bottom lip as fear mounted in her heart. "Thank God Sheri' told you instead of Momma, Dee," she said, still wiping tears from her eyes. "I know you think it is shameful of me to say but I'll always love him, no matter what. I would have died in that car accident if he had not come along. He helped me become the woman I am today. I'm not ashamed of what we had together; there are nights I don't sleep, thinking of what we were to each other. No, I don't plan to ever go back to him. I am Jake's wife again. I'm beginning to find that love I once had for Jake. Looking away she sighed. Dee, this is where I belong. It is over, but I will always keep him here in my heart. You have got to understand that."

"Anna, please, don't even think those thoughts, much less say them," Dee pleaded, shaking her head as she stared at Anna, who looked away. "You are putting your life on the line, and it wouldn't be worth a plugged nickel if Jake or Mrs. Annabelle ever suspected that the man in your life those four years was a white man."

"You've got to destroy all of it—the money, the letter, all of it. I know it's a lot of bread to burn, but Anna, it could mean your life if you don't."

Both Dee and Anna looked up as her mother walked into the room, standing there with her hands on her hips as she stared down at them.

"What's wrong with ya two gals? Yer men actin' up?"

"No, Momma!" Anna answered, tossing her spread over the attaché case as she rose from the bed. "Dee and I were discussing the Chinaware party she is having tonight. There are some things she wants me to help her with."

"That's right, Mrs. Annabelle. I didn't realize how late it was getting. I have to get back home to get things ready for the party tonight. Anna, don't you forget what I told you," Dee said, looking back at the bed.

"Sure," Anna answered, making sure the spread covered the attaché case. When she heard Dee and her mother talking outside of her room, she turned her thoughts back to the contents of the attaché case and what she might do to protect it from rediscovery. Eventually she would be forced to destroy it, but there was no time to do it now, not that she wanted to let go of it yet. I must reread the letter, she thought to herself. Pushing the attaché case back under the bed, Anna watched the Old Widow crawl past and felt the sudden knowledge that something horrible was about to happen.

****

"Lie down here beside me, Sheri', so that we can talk together." Anna felt her daughter's body tremble.

"Momma, I didn't mean to be a snoop. I just thought there might be some more beautiful clothing in there for me to try on. I had no idea there'd be all that money or that you would be with . . ."

"Him . . ." Anna said, looking into her daughter's tearful eyes as she tried to think how and what she could tell her that would make sense.

"Momma, he . . . is he the guardian angel you were telling Jake Jr. and me about? He is, isn't he?" Anna closed her eyes, thinking to herself, "No, baby. He's the man your mother lived in adultery with these past four years." She might still be away from her babies had he still been in her life. Anna was kinder to her daughter than she was to herself.

"Yes, honey, he was something like that. He took care of me when I was sick. When I got well, he gave me this money so that I would be taken care of when he was no longer with me."

"I know why Grandma can't know, but why can't Daddy know? He worried about you all the while you were away," Sheri' asked with a puzzled look on her face.

"Because if either knew, just as Dee has told you, they would not understand, and it is also true that if you told them, I would be dead . . . gone forever out of your life. So please, I must ask you not to tell a living soul, not even Jake Jr. about the attaché case. It means my very life if you breathe one word of what you saw." Anna began to cry as she put her arms around her daughter; hating the secret she was forcing her to share.

"Momma, I will never tell a soul. I love you too much to want anything bad to happen to you." Anna hugged her closer; remembering when she had come home it was days before her children's birthday. She had asked them if they wanted a party because she had no idea who their friends were, and she had wanted to make sure she had time to round them up. Sheri' quickly told her and Jake Jr. agreed, "'When I woke up and Grandma told me you were home, I ran into Jake Jr.'s room and got him. You are the birthday present we have been praying so long for. With you home, we already have our birthday present. As long as we have been praying for this day, there is nothing else we want.'

Anna wondered where it would all end and what twisted, winding road she would travel next. Sheri' soon fell asleep nestled in her arms. Anna thought about what her daughter thought Raymond was to her. Her guardian angel, she had called him. Aretha's song, came back to her as her mind whirled back to when Ray had fallen into her arms. She had not seen so much blood spill from a person's body in her life. Just as she had gotten him into bed, there was a hard knock at her door. It had been Mix, and behind him was the doctor she remembered and a woman she had assumed to be a nurse.

"Where is he," The doctor had asked. They had hurried into her bedroom. She and Mix lived in the living room; a grave, silence filled the air so thick Anna could hardly breathe. She had hated Mix, knowing he was somehow responsible for what had happened to Ray.

"Mix," she had finally forced herself to say when it seemed his life would not last much longer, "He loves you like a son loves his father. This lifestyle you have led him into is killing him. One day you will look around and wonder whatever happened to that young man you could count on to risk his life for you."

"Don't you think I'm thinking about that? I told him not to take risks, but it is in his nature to do it dangerously. It's like the kiss of death is always his answer to life."

"Why can't you get involved with what he really enjoys doing?"

"What is that, Ms. Anna? Tell me—I'd like to know."

"Thoroughbred racing—it was his father's life's work. There are millions of dollars to be made legally there with a lot less danger. Some of those horses are worth millions of dollars if they are bred right. Anything is better than this," Anna had cried, walking away from him into the bathroom and then up into the clouds.

"Daughter, the Young Chemist will be forced to return to the energy of the universe if he continues to embrace life as he does."

Anna had shaken her head without answering as sobs racked her body. There was a question she wanted answered, but she feared asking. It was too hard, and she didn't want to know if there was nothing that could be done to save him. He had been in that bedroom for seven days with the doctor and his nurse working day and night trying to save him. Mix sat in the living room answering the knocks that brought what the doctor asked for. Anna had almost given up, her tears falling like rain.

"If he is to continue on this journey with you, he must find another way to spread his energy. It is about to deplete, and even I will not be able to give him back to you."

She had let go a sigh of relief that the Old Head had given him one last chance.

That week Raymond had lain unconscious, the doctor never talked to her about his condition. A week later Mix came and told her Raymond would live, but if he took a turn for the worse to call him at once. She watched them leave then turned her thoughts to Raymond's condition.

"'Anna,' she heard his voice calling from the bedroom three days later. His eyes finally opened; it was the hardest two weeks of her life. 'Baby, I know you are angry with me about all of this.' She listened to his labored breathing and knew one of his lungs had been damaged.

"No, I'm not angry. How can I be? I knew when I followed you to Las Vegas what your lifestyle was. And the kind of man I was with. I tried to blame what you do on Mix, but I realize now what you have become is not his fault."

"Anna, listen . . ."

"No, you listen, Raymond Forlorn," Anna hissed staring down at him. "I know you get a satanic thrill out of embracing death. The purpose you use those chemicals for is criminal. I have refrained from admitting it to myself, but now that I have said it, my head is clear. There will no longer be talk of our divorcing our mates, marrying and starting a family of our own. I'll be damned if I'll have children for a man and one day be forced to tell them why he has come home all shot up. Or listen to his daughter ask me why her father is not around to tell her how a lady conducts herself or if the boy who likes her is the right one.

I damn sure don't plan to have his son wonder what it would have been like to grow up with a father because the one he should have had is dead because he decided to go out and get himself killed blowing up the world. Damn your ass, you have been determined to kill yourself since your mother died. Well let me tell you, I lost my memory and I can't even remember why. My back is marred and I don't even know why. Do you see me trying to kill myself? Hell no! I'm here trying to keep you alive, but this time after you are able to fend for yourself, Anna will no longer be around to worry if you come home—or if and when you do show up, having you pull me into your arms as that heart of yours races so fast I know what you have been doing—I just don't know how many have died because of it. I am done, goddamn you! Do you understand me?" she had sobbed.

"'How many babies were you planning on us having?' Anna remembered how his question had caught her off guard.

"I thought ten would be a good starting number. Were you hoping for more?"

"'Damn, I had better get started real soon. With ten kids to raise, I won't have time to leave the house.' She knew she had his attention. Turning to see his smiling face, Anna buried her head in the pillow his head rested on as their laughter filled the room.

"'Baby, this bed has been cold without you in it with me. Come get under the covers with me.'

"I can't. The doctor says you need . . ."

"'You tell that damn doctor to spend one night in your arms and then come tell you what Ray needs,' he whispered as she moved closer to him. "'Ms. Anna, the pain of my mother's death has never left me. When I'm out there about to die, I feel her embrace me in a way I cannot explain even to myself. She calls me to come to her, but it never happens. I always survive. I'm willing to try to change my life. I just need you to ease the pain like you always do. Now put on Aretha's *Doctor Feel Good* so I know I'm in good standing with you again.'"

Everything had changed after that, Anna remembered. Sometimes he would come in smelling like horses, but she loved it, especially when he brought Mix with him and they talked for hours about where and when they would go to find that special thoroughbred that might make them millions. On the phone with his brother, he laughed about memories of their father—something Raymond had never before allowed in his brief conversations with him. Yes, and as Sheri' had said, he had played the part of her guardian angel. All of that was over for her now. There would be not even one baby for him by her, but his lifestyle change had made the idea of having his children worth it.

Who knows, she mused now, maybe it will be his wife who will give him those ten babies, keeping him too busy to think about that other lifestyle that would surely take him out. She kissed her daughter's bangs and soon fell asleep beside her.

Chapter Eleven

—w—

Anna woke up, finding Sheri' gone. She rose as she heard her mother telling her Jake was on the phone for her. Picking up the receiver, she took a deep breath, wondering what in the world he wanted.

"I've been trying to reach you. What are you doing at your parents' home in bed? Are you sick or something?" she heard him ask. Anna looked at the clock on the nightstand next to her bed. It was nearly six o'clock. She had been asleep four hours.

"I'm fine. I came over to help plan Dee's party with her. Is something wrong?" Anna asked, hopeful there was nothing to ruin the rest of the evening for her.

"I can see you are still planning to go to that hen's party?"

"Oh yes, it has already begun; let me get up and get dressed. What are your plans?"

"Well, I'm sure as hell not going home and wait for you to get back from some hen's party. I'll see you later." The phone clicked in Anna's ear. She took the attaché case and put it in the trunk of her car while her daughter watched. She would have to take the money and place it in a safety deposit box. Sighing, Anna kissed and hugged Sheri', glad it was she and not her mother who had found and opened the case.

Back in her old bedroom, Anna dressed and prepared to leave for Dee's Chinaware party.

"Anna, chile, I don't like yer looks." It was her mother coming into her old bedroom like she used to before Anna had married and left home. Anna sighed, knowing she would have to let her have her say. "Ya sho' everthang all right 'tweens ya and dat husband of yers?" Anna looked at her mother. Her hazel eyes and fair skin were to those of her race a sign of beauty—beauty her father must have been captivated by. It had always amazed Anna how strong her father's genes had to be to give her his dark color instead of her mother's light complexion. Of course, her mother loved telling her how proud she was to have a strong black man and a dark baby she knew was his to love. Smoothing a strand of her hair back, she held her mother close.

"I'm fine, Momma, and everything is perfect at home." She knew that was what her mother wanted to hear because she and her father seemed elated to have her and Jake back together again.

"I don't want ya to go back to bein' like Hattie Bradley was 'fore she died, lettin' Bradley run all over hur 'cause he was a fine-lookin' devil hisself. Folks tell me he done run over her til the day thay laid her in the ground, God rest hur soul." Anna gazed at the long pearl-handled razor her mother brought out from her bosom.

"If that Negro starts dat cheatin' stuff agin, dis 'll help ya. I don't thank I'll be needin' it agin," Annabelle Drake said, sticking the razor between Anna's breasts. She added, "Ya make sho' dat's whare it stays, always." Anna looked into her mother's eyes, seeing the horrid gleam in them that had caused her much distress at the ranch and at her apartment in Las Vegas. Thinking of what Sheri' had found she began to shiver.

"Momma, everything is fine, just as I said," Anna reassured her as she allowed her mother to place the razor inside her bra, much the same as Madria had done when she felt Anna had needed to have protection.

"Yeah, I know ya' done changed good . . . but," her mother said, after a moment's hesitation, "I don't want ya goin' back to the way ya was. A woman who can't stand for hurself is a waste of God's good earth."

****

Anna walked into Dee's home and was greeted by a house filled with female guests. "What did you do with it?" Dee asked, pulling her into her bedroom and quickly closing the door behind them.

"It's in the trunk of my car," whispered Anna.

"That's too dangerous, girl. Suppose Jake looks in there?"

"He won't. He still believes Ray sent the car to me and won't even ride in it. Don't worry, Dee. I'll take care of it the first thing in the morning after Jake goes to the office."

"I am worried, and there is no sense in you telling me not to worry. Anybody gets their hands on that shit you got, you are dead, my sister girl, and I mean dead as a doorknob. Have you forgotten about that young girl they found dead in the ditch? Remember her head. Hell, you know how folks 'round here feel about black women who fool around with white men. It would be one ugly scene, and we both know what would happen to you."

"Yes, I know." Anna turned with her hands on her hips. "And now that it is over for good, it will stay buried. Come, let's go in to the party and forget what you saw back there," Anna whispered as she turned to walk out of Dee's bedroom and into a room full of women, most of whom she did not know.

"Wait a minute, there is something I gotta tell you." Anna looked at Dee, wondering what now?"

"Barb is here . . . I didn't invite her; she just came. She said she needed some Chinaware. If you think her being here will make you too uncomfortable, I'll ask her to order what she wants and leave."

"Why would you do that, Dee? No way . . . let her stay. Why should you lose money because of our hatred for each other? I know you're thinking about what has happened between us, but I promise not to say one word to her, no matter what she says. This is your home, and I don't think even she could push me far enough not to respect that," Anna said, seeing a look of relief on Dee's face.

As it happened, she and Barb bumped into each other just as she entered the living room.

"Well, well, if it isn't Anna—nice having you back in town," Barb said, smiling at her. By the look Barb gave her Anna knew she somehow knew she would be there.

"It's nice being back," Anna said, moving away from the woman she had had so many nightmares about. The astonishing beauty of the larger, light-skinned black woman quickly brought the past rushing back to her.

"Well now, Anna, I heard you have changed since your return, but I had no idea how much," Barb said, catching up with her. Anna saw her staring at the fashionable blue silk designer dress she wore compared to the sweat shirt and blue jeans she had never seen Barb wear before. Anna knew she was baiting her and turned from her to speak to Shirley.

"You talk to whites now? You have changed," Barb said, finishing off a can of beer and laughing as the women looked on with frowns. Behind Barb, Anna watched the Old Widow crawl down her web.

"I can't believe you're finally dressing in style. God that shit you used to wear—those Mexican skirts made you look like a peasant." Anna felt its power as the Old Widow's web grew larger. She wasn't about to allow Barb's insults to bother her; those skirts had been loved by women much more important than Barb was Anna felt.

"You and Jake making it alright now?" Barb asked when they were seated in the living room looking at the china on display.

"He's a much better husband, thanks to you, Barb," Anna said, turning away from her.

"You have to admit he wasn't shit before you left his ass. Damn did we turn some flips in that heart-shaped bed of yours? Hasn't it been about four years since you left town?" Anna said nothing.

"I know that nigger's got his ass another woman somewhere. I had a hard enough time keeping his ass focused on me when I had him. They all wanted him, even Terri and Joy," Barb said, smiling as she opened up another can of beer.

"You just mad 'cause that woman is no longer you, Barb," one of the women Anna did not know said, staring hatefully Barb's way. Barb turned up her can of beer, ignoring the woman's remark. Anna sat shocked as she wondered what had happened to replace the sophisticated woman she'd met years back with this slum-talking, street whore, poorly dressed woman she was listening to now. Whatever work she was in, Anna thought, it sure was not keeping her in the lifestyle Anna once knew her to be accustomed to.

"That was a good-loving motherfucker though . . . Oh Lord, yes! Haven't found a better lay yet." Anna felt rage stirring inside of her. This woman, she thought to herself, could not let well enough alone. Anna watched the face of her mother whirl past her eyes. She reached in and touched the razor between her breasts. How many nights had she dreamed of this meeting? Too many, she thought to herself.

"I used to call that nigger the sizzler—his mouth worked such wonders on this body of mine," Barb said, smiling over at Anna, another can of beer up to her lips.

"Look, Barb, if that's what you came here for, you gotta go. I'm not having that shit in my home."

"No, Dee, let her have her say. I'd rather hear it coming from her lips than from someone saying she said it . . . not knowing how much of it is true," Anna replied, thinking to herself soon Barb would realize she was no threat to her.

"See, Dee, what I'm saying doesn't bother this new Anna at all," Barb assured her, smiling at Anna.

"Yes, that nigger was one of those men who had a long healthy handle and knew how to use it, right, Anna?" Madria's face suddenly appeared before Anna and she heard her voice resonating throughout the room: "She still thinks you are weak, Anna. That's why she's disrespecting you. Are you weak, Anna? Weeeaaakkk!"

"Anna, come help me fill out these order blanks . . . ain't nothing wrong with that heifer but wishing Jake would look her way again," Dee said, getting laughter from the other women in the room.

"You got that right . . . I sho' nuff miss that nigger's ass. She wasn't doing shit for him before she left here. I don't blame him for tripping. A hen could have laid an egg right in front of her nose and she wouldn't have been the wiser. Too busy hating white folks, huh Shirley?" Anna saw Shirley's face flush red as she turned away from Barb.

"If only I had that nigger's ass now. The motherfucker laid my apartment out with brand new shit." Anna decided to leave. Madria's voice whispered again to her.

"Kill that bitch! Cut her ass up! She is downright disrespecting you, Ms. Anna!" The rage filling her consciousness was much the same as when Ray had prevented her from killing her downstairs neighbor. She needed someone to stop her before it was too late.

"Shit," Barb said, "he told me if you didn't want to spend his money, he got pleasure out of seeing how much of it I could spend." As Barb's laughter filled the room, Anna's head began to spin. She knew she had to go and go quickly. She did not want to disrespect her friend's home.

"Here, Anna, add up these lists for me," Barb said, shelving a piece of paper in front of Anna. "Sitting behind a desk was one thing you were always good at, huh? I like that outfit you're wearing. Sho' nuff beats the bargain store shit you used to drag around in at the shelter. Makes me miss having his ass fill my closet like he used to." Barb popped open another can of beer. Anna looked at the paper without touching it as she turned away.

"Barb, I have told you—I'm not having that shit you came here to start. And if I were you I would watch my mouth Ms. Anna has changed sweetheart and I don't think you want to meet up with that change.," Dee said with her hands on her hips as she stared hard at Barb. Everyone in the room except Barb started laughing.

"You say Ms. Anna has changed, except for those clothes she is wearing she don't look changed to me" Barb swallowed some more of her beer. Anna saw the Old Widow head for the bathroom.

"She should be thanking me for helping put her through her first day of real school sister girl as you Session women like to call each other. Gave her a lesson she'll never forget. My friends and I tricked that son of a bitch in to coming up to my apartment right before we called you. I got worried you wouldn't show up. Terri and Joy hoped you wouldn't." Anna saw the other women look her way, shaking their heads. Her eyes begin to sting. I must let it go, Anna thought to herself, but then Barb spoke again.

"And the motherfucker had the nerve to admit to me that she were pregnant after he insisted I get rid of my baby. They told me she lost it falling down my stairs. Well, that's one damn baby the world will never get to see, right Anna? Tears fell from that nigger's eyes talking about how he didn't want her to lose his baby. 'That is one dead baby,' I told him before I shot his ass. He limps now from it. Don't let him send you back to the funny farm, sister girl. That's where they say you were all that time you were away." Barb's laughter filled the room as she drank more beer down.

Listening to Barb brag about how she had caused her to lose her baby, Anna thought back to that awful night. As she had fallen down those stairs, she remembered feeling something tear loose inside of her. Driving down the highway, blood had seeped from her body, causing her to push harder on the accelerator to hurry and get to the hospital so that they could stop the bleeding and save her baby's life.

"Hey, where in the hell is she going?" Anna heard Barb ask as she walked toward Dee's bathroom.

"Somewhere so you can stop laughing at her," she heard Shirley tell Barb.

"Bitches that dumb need to be laughed at," Anna heard Barb reply as she popped open the next can of beer in her hand. In the darkened bathroom, Anna waited. The Old Widow stood overhead, its orange back pulsating.

"Anna, ain't I done tole ya, gal . . . lettin' that hussy talk to ya like yer dirt . . . ya ain't a daughter of mine!" The voice of her mother rode her like a demon just as it had the day she struck out at the students tormenting her on the bus and at Raymond after encountering her downstairs neighbor. "In my day, Annabelle brought 'em down to hur size, gal!" Anna swallowed hard. A crazy excitement filled her as she saw the face of Madria.

"Ms. Anna, if I taught you anything, I taught you not to be weak. Use your wits when your enemies try to treat you like a sucker. Make them know you are nobody to be pushed around even if it means you must pay in some way. Promise Madria you will never again be caught weak." Suddenly, the bathroom door opened.

"What the hell are you doing in here hiding? That husband of yours fill your belly with another baby for him to limp down the stairs after?" Barb asked, pulling down her jeans and lowering her panties to take a seat on the toilet. Anna's hand went up into the air. The razor in it struck like a warrior's sword. They tussled and turned as Barb tried to pull her underwear up and get the razor away from Anna at the same time, a razor that had begun to lay open the skin on her body. Barb fell to the floor, with no escape from the deadly razor cutting away at her.

"Git hur neck, gal!" Anna could still hear her mother's voice. "Cut the whore's guzzle vein and let hur know ya's Annabelle's daughter!" she heard her mother say. Hearing loud screams from the other women at the party, Anna came to herself realizing that someone had opened the door and they had fallen out of the bathroom. Blood poured from Barb's body onto Anna. The bloody razor still in her hand, Anna continued cutting layer after layer of Barb's flesh open. Her underwear still halfway down her legs, Barb struggled to escape as blood ran across the floor like a river overflowing. Anna felt herself being pulled away from Barb. Looking down at Barb and the blood running from her body, Anna hissed in the midst of her rage,

"Today was your first day in my school whore. You no longer have to wonder have Ms. Anna changed—now you know it! I don't hear you laughing about my dead baby now, bitch!" Barb opened her mouth to speak, but only blood poured from her lips. Pulling away from a person she realized was Fred, Anna pushed her bloodstained body through the crowd as she looked for an escape from her raging madness.

****

"Oh my God!" Anna heard her mother cry and her children scream as she opened the door and fell into her arms. "Thank God yer Daddy is down at the pit." Anna knew her mother was referring to his barbecue restaurant. She listened to the running water in the bathtub and was glad to feel her bloody clothing being stripped from her.

Seated in the bath water, Anna felt her mother's hands move over her body as she examined it. "Thank God, ya ain't hurt none. Dee called and told me what happened. Lord have mercy! I hate to say it but the whore got hur just due at last," Anna glimpsed a wicked grin on her mother's face.

"Momma, I have got to get out of town. I killed her; I know it!" Anna cried. "I cut her to death with that razor you gave me. I couldn't stop myself." Anna began to laugh hysterically. "You were right—she laughed at me like I was nothing right in front of everyone there like what she had done to me was something she was proud of. Momma, she even laughed about my losing my baby."

"She won't be laughing none now, I bet ya. I'm tole ya cut hur ass a good minute," her mother hissed, helping her out of the bathtub.

"You would have been proud of your little girl." Anna's mind whirled back through the past to recall Barb and her two friends and how they had laughed at deceiving her. A quiet calm enveloped her. It had to be done. No longer would the women in Session look at her with pity in their eyes. Anna felt her mother's arms around her, rocking her as if she were a little girl again crying because of something she did not understand.

"Yer Momma loves ya, and she's proud of hur baby. I'm glad ya finally learnt dat in dis mean old world ya gotta stand up and fight yur own battles . . . don't let nobody thank thay can walk on ya. Yer Momma had to leave Oinston after hur killins, but she felt good. If my Momma woulda used a razor on dat white cracker's neck, done took her away she woulda come back to us like my grandma say she sposed to."

"Come, gal," her mother said, pushing her from her lap, "we gotta hurry!" Anna dressed and then kissed her children again and again. She hated leaving them, but she knew she must go before they came for her.

Anna stood with her suitcase packed, listening to her mother call her brother in Oinston, Louisiana. After hanging up the phone, quick as she could, her mother pushed her along with Sheri' and Jake Jr. out the door towards her Lincoln.

"Momma!" Sheri' screamed, pulling Anna back to her own car.

"Now what is it dat gal wants? Anna we gotta hurry," Her mother insisted, as Anna and Sheri' raced toward her car.

"You forgot your guardian angel," Sheri' whispered. Rushing back with her daughter, Anna hugged and kissed her as she took the key from her purse and bent to open the trunk of her car, taking the attaché case out of it she stopped to listen to the roar of thunder, seeing lightning dash across the sky. Rain began to pour down.

"Hurry, Anna, 'fore the storm comes," her mother called out to her as she placed the children in the back seat of the car. Her mother drove the forty miles into Godfrey where she bought a ticket for Anna. Kissing her children again, Anna boarded the bus.

"Anna, no one will know; I won't tell a soul not even Jake til I know for sho' she ain't dead—and if she is, thay ain't gonna find ya way down south. If they do come, ya gotta keep goin'."

"Momma, I love you!" Anna felt a hard kiss from her mother as she pushed her on board the bus.

With the few things her mother had thrown in a suitcase, Anna sat riding down the highway, holding the attaché case in her lap. Tears slipped down her face as the bus traveled southward. She looked out into the starless night. The pain of having to leave again moved her out of her consciousness into the outer world in the oblong capsule on the back of the Old Widow.

Everything around her whirled with such force that she thought at any minute the wild turbulence would have them both tumbling down one of the black holes the hairy legs of the spider crossed. Winds blew so hard that mountains could be seen falling to the ground some creating holes as large as cities. Her heart stopped when two volcanoes sent debris so high up into the sky that not even the red stars could be seen. Pain and suffering filled her heart as she realized this journey of her was far from over. She was apart of the quest that supernatural force was driven by and the promise it set out to keep. Her breasts throbbed as though filled with milk. She wanted to scream because they hurt so, as if needing to be sucked.

Fear continued to grip her sense of reality as she saw the outer world destroying itself as clouds of dust rose and fell. Beasts of all descriptions flew against each other; their dying howls terrifying her. Huge chucks of debris flew into the air. This journey she had embarked upon in order to fulfill a sacred promise had tossed her into a world gone mad. It seemed that this time the Old Widow would not survive to get her to the land of the Healing Tree before they were killed. As sounds of dying beasts blended with death calls, she watched their bodies being whirled into outer space, yet the Old Widow moved on steel-like threads as if guided by some unknown force. She would soon be dead, she feared, but as suddenly as her eyes had closed, they opened again, and Anna found herself still on the bus, riding down the highway, scared and shaken by the nightmare. She knew it meant something terrifying was about to happen; she just did not know what.

Chapter Twelve

—∿—

Anna spied a public pay phone while walking through the bus terminal in Arkansas.

Finding change in her purse, she picked up the receiver. Her heart wrenched as she placed the needed coins in then dialed Dee's number, hopeful she would answer and not Fred, which would cause her to have to hang up. Hearing her friend's voice, Anna's voice trembled.

"Please Dee, please forgive me for disrespecting your home the way I did." Anna said waiting to be severely reprimanded for using the razor on Barb in Dee's bathroom. It was the last thing she had wanted to happen. What she had done she believed was unforgiveable, and she had to let Dee know her deep regret about her actions.

"For what, Anna?" she heard Dee ask. "Didn't you see me moving all my breakables and getting that china out of the way? I warned that heifer that you had changed? That low-down dirty backstabbing two-faced bitch pretended to be your friend and brought her lowdown ass to my house bragging about how she crawled up in your bed with your husband. She better be glad it was you got her in that hospital. I would have had her in the morgue with them trying to figure out where to haul her ass off to. I thought I was going to have to kick that heifer's ass and throw her out of my house. We all saw how she was deliberately humiliating you." Anna suddenly felt a sense of relief.

"Anna where the hell are you sister girl." Anna listened to Dee whisper. "No, no don't tell me if I don't know I won't be lying when I tell anybody that asks, I don't know where the hell you are. Anyway, that sister got what she deserved."

"Dee, she didn't know when to stop talking. I think she came there to degrade me in front of everyone."

144

"Anna that sister was like the signifying monkey—all mouth with no ass to back it up."

"But why, Dee? Hadn't she done enough to me already?" Anna asked, still not feeling good about her actions but better that her friend understood.

"Anna, you can't reason with a mad dog—you gotta kill it. That bitch came here looking for trouble. She knew you would be here. She used my home to continue getting back at Jake by making you look bad in front of my friends whose husbands know Jake. Of course they would run back and tell them how pitiful she made you look." Anna knew she told the truth.

"She didn't realize you are no longer the Anna who fell down those stairs four years ago. When it came time for her to back up that tough ass fronting you off she was doing, she found her ass with her panties down below her knees lying in a puddle of blood and couldn't figure out how she got there. Now she can go back and tell her New York friends Session women may not be as sophisticated as they are, but we are not putting up with that kinda bullshit from nobody—that's for sure."

"I tried all I could not to have to go there with her, Dee, but you are right, I am not the Anna that fell down her stairs four years ago. Now she knows it." Anna remembered how that rage felt when it overtook her.

"She found that out soon enough didn't she? You cut that bitch from the top of her head to the bottom of her feet. She is cut up like meat in a slaughterhouse! Like I said, she is in that hospital trying to figure out where her face went to, you hear me! If you hadn't stepped up to the plate like we all were afraid you wouldn't, I would have. How could you have held up your head before the women here in Session the way she was stomping on you? They would have thought you were the same weak Anna you were before you left. Now when you walk the streets, they will sho' nuff know you are Mrs. Annabelle's daughter won't they?" Anna could here Dee laughing.

"Oh my God, Dee! Why did it have to come to that?" Anna asked, still feeling pains of despair.

"Anna, stop beating up on yourself! The bitch took it there. Now when she looks in the mirror, if she is ever able to again, she will think twice before pulling that shit on another woman here in Session. Anna, is that attaché case still in the back of your car, heaven forbid?"

"No, thanks to Sheri' I have it with me."

"Thank God! That's a problem I sure wouldn't want you to have to face. Get rid of it while you are away. Whatever you do, don't bring it back here.

"I won't, Dee. I gotta go." Anna's fear subsided and a smile spread across her face as she watched her tall dark skinny cousin hurrying toward her in the Arkansas bus station. "Dee, I have got to go."

"Look, you stay put til this shit clears 'cause I got your back. I won't tell Fred I talked to you. I know he would go back and tell Jake."

"Thanks, Dee. I love you, sister girl."

"Yeah, keep safe and stop tripping over this shit. I love you too, sister girl," Anna heard her friend say before the phone clicked in her ear. Her cousin Frankie Lee a year older than her, whistled loud enough to make Anna blush as she hurried his way.

"Don't you know women aren't to be whistled at any longer?" Anna asked as her cousin picked her up off the floor, hugging her so tight she stopped breathing.

"Nobody told me that. Damn it, woman, if ya wasn't a blood cousin, I'd have to git next to ya myself. Ya don't even look like the skinny little gurl I 'member. All those fine hips spreading out hare." Anna shook her head, as she looked at the tall, dark-skinned, thin, raw-boned man standing over her. A gold crown capped his left eyetooth. Frankie Lee just happened to be her favorite cousin, but when she thought of it, he was the only cousin she really knew. He would always have Jake in the streets when he drove his newest Chevy to Session to see her and her mom and dad. No other car for him but his two- to three-year-old Chevy.

Placing the one piece of luggage her mother had packed for her and her attaché case inside the back of his '76 Chevy, they took off for Oinston, Louisiana.

"Where are those cute little babies you sent Momma pictures of and that wife of yours, Frankie Lee?" Anna asked, noticing he still wore a fine thick natural instead of the fashionable shag curl so well loved by the men in Session. A frown crested his dark brows, making Anna think of how her mother frowned when something was asked of her that she had trouble answering.

"She's home taking care 'f the kids. We kinda separated right now."

"Separated? When did that happen?" Anna asked as they drove down the two-lane highway.

"We got along fine til she start thanking I'm out doin wrong . . . which ain't the truth. I just needed a little space sometimes," he said laughing as he pulled Anna closer to him. Anna listened carefully to his words. They came out a lot like the black rancher Ray baby in Kentucky. Always reminding Anna of where her ancestors' early language started.

"Never thought I'd be seeing ya, Cous. Not like dis. When the old man told me ya ware coming, I sho' nuff was glad, but surprised. What ya do back thare dis time . . . shot at dat husband of yers? He always did think he was one of those black power Tony Curtis dudes all rolled into one," Frankie Lee said as Anna continued to process the southern dialect that connected him to her mother's language. "Is he still wearin them fine threads?"

"No, Frankie Lee, I did not shoot Jake. I do, however, have to keep a low profile."

"Oh shit, I knew somebody caught hell. The old man said ya sho nuff just like his sister Aunt Annabelle. She was always fightin' and didn't like a soul til she met up with Uncle Jeff. He calmed hur down a lot the Old Man said."

"Frankie Lee, it was terrible. My kids saw me come home all bloody. I know it devastated them. I was not at all myself. It was as though I blanked out and became someone else. I know they are thinking the worst of me. Oh my God, how I hated having to leave them again—it is too much to bear.

"Don't worry, Anna. By now Aunt Annabelle got 'em wishing some of dat blood had gotten on 'em. Ya know she love 'commodatin' a body if thay comes hur way wrong. Use to tell me all the time, 'I'll accommodate 'em boy, send 'em my way.' Yer kids will be fine in dat world she done fixed up for 'em."

"But Frankie Lee, I cut a woman nearly to death last night. I don't feel good about that for me or my kids who have to reap the effects of my actions by losing their mother again."

"I knew it," Frankie Lee said, interrupting her. "I bet it was one of Jake's street honeys, huh?"

"Frankie Lee, she crashed the China ware party I had been invited to, coming uninvited as good as she felt and sat there like a storyteller telling everyone how she and two other women had Jake in bed."

"Did you say that husband of yers was in bed with three women? Damn, he is a man after my own heart. All three at the same time, Anna?" her cousin asked, his eyes enlarged.

"If you must know, yes, they all had him tied up in bed making out. His honey set it up so I would find them that way. Some friend, I thought she was over him and wanted to forget like I did, but oh no! She regurgitated everything they had ever done. Her tongue would not stop and with every word she put her feet in my business and stomped me into the ground. Let everyone there know how she had slept with him in my bed. I could see the pity in the eyes of the women listening to her." Anna watched her cousin raised an eye brow. "Frankie Lee, I tried hard to be cool about it and let her have her say. I thought she would figure out I didn't want to hear her shit and shut the hell up, but she wouldn't—she just got bolder and bolder."

"Those women looked at me like I was a two-year-old child being spanked by my momma. Still, I tried to ignore her. But she made one fatal mistake."

"What was dat?" Frankie Lee asked, taking his eyes off the road to glance Anna's way.

"She laughed about me losing my baby. It would have been four years old if I hadn't lost it falling down her stairs. That whore had the nerve to laugh at that—thought it was funny. When she confronted Jake with how he made her get rid of her baby, I felt bad for her. The death of mine baby she just laughed about it. I walked into that bathroom and waited for her ass," Anna said, reliving how it all happened as she and Frankie Lee continued traveling down the two lane highway.

"Ya waited for hur in the bathroom. How ya know she would come in thare?" Frankie Lee asked, staring over at her.

"There is no way anyone can pop four cans of beer and not have to make a trip to the bathroom, Frankie Lee. When she walked in, I already had Momma's pearl-handle razor out waiting for her."

"Whoa," Frankie Lee said, shaking his head.

"My plan was to cut that damn tongue out of her mouth, but she just wouldn't open it so I could get to it. I had to settle with cutting everywhere else I could reach."

"Aunt Annabelle's straight-edge razor! Oh shit, she's either dead or wishing she was. Jake always did thank he was God's gift to women. 'Course now the times I was with him, he didn't have to pull. Thay was thare for the takin'. All I had to do was to follow him 'round . . . damned women beggin to be had."

Anna ignored Frankie Lee's comment as she looked out of the window. It was as though she were once again traveling through Kentucky. The environment was so similar . . . though the road they now travelled was paved. Rows and rows of trees lined the highway like in Kentucky. Anna frowned at an armadillo on the roadside. In the south again—it was so different from the Northern and Midwestern city life where there was concrete buildings and little else.

At least she was free of the pollution that traps the air in the city. Breathing in a stream of fresh air, she at last felt glad about something. She really did need a retreat of some sort. If only, she thought, it hadn't been because of Barb that she had to leave again. Frankie Lee turned off the two-lane highway onto a dirt road. Anna noticed that a church stood to the right and a row of wood framed houses and a café stood on the left. Soon they turned onto another shorter road where a row of houses stood on both sides. The people on the porches waved to them Frankie Lee waved back naming each.

The car stopped in front of a white wood-framed house trimmed in green inside a wooden fenced in yard. When Frankie Lee opened the gate for her Anna walked inside the yard and up several steps to a short porch. The Inside of the house had the look of male living. Anna knew very few women visited this house. The furniture was made of crude unvarnished wood that appeared to have been hand carved. An old straw rocker sat in a far corner. From the front room you could see into the kitchen. The kitchen table must have been handmade—it was also made of wood and at least five feet long with long benches for seating on either side. A bedroom off to the left that was to be hers had an old-style feather bed mattress, or tick as Frankie Lee called it, which gave Anna a soft but uneven lay, as she later discovered. All of it brought back memories of Kentucky and southern living.

Her uncle who Frankie Lee looked a lot like, her mother's tall, raw-boned younger brother was a dark-skinned man named Jessie Bailey. Stepping out of another room, he stood a foot taller than her father's six two. He hugged and kissed Anna, then stood looking down at her, a big smile on his face as though he was glad to see her. Anna had always admired her uncle Jessie learning from her mother that he had raised Frankie Lee alone after the woman he had impregnated left them when Frankie Lee was two months old. She never returned.

"How's that big sister of mine? Sho' do miss hur." Anna smiled as she noticed how much he favored her mother though he was much darker and did not have the coldness in his keen cat eyes that her mother had in hers. She thought to herself that they sure did speak that southern drawl the same.

"She's fine," Anna assured him.

"Gotta see dat gal . . . she's ain't up thare passin agin is she? Kinda surprised to heer from hur wantin a place for ya. I'm over to Emma's now. Frankie Lee's been holding the house down now dat him and his old lady is spoutin'. Just make yerself at home long as ya need to," he said grinning as he rubbed his clean-shaven face while running his hands through his close-cropped graying hair. Anna glimpsed the gold cap on his left eyetooth, the same as in Frankie Lee's mouth.

"Old Man I gotta go sign up." He said signaling Anna they were leaving.

"Where are we going Frankie Lee," Anna asked as he pushed her out of the door. "What is it you have to sign up for?"

"Unemployment!"

"You are not working, Frankie Lee?" Anna asked, looking over at him.

"Hell no, and who the hell else hare is? Most of the factories have laid off men hare in Oinston . . . others sharecrop. I ain't no farmer . . . I'm a lover." He laughed as Anna frowned over at him.

"Been thankin about comin up yer way to see if I can get me somethin' goin' up thare."

"Come on up, Frankie Lee. It would be nice having you there to remind Jake what a good man looks like," Anna said as they both laughed at her joke.

"He would definitely find you something to do," Anna said, thinking back about the man who had come to their home and what Jake had gone through to assure him a job.

****

"Momma, I'm so glad you finally called me. I was thinking the worst, you know."

"Gal, you didn't kill hur but ya might as well. I went up thare and peeped in on hur. Looks like she been mauled by a bear. She still in 'tensive care up at dat hospital. Hur face looks worse than yer back when it was mauled."

"Momma, I might be going to jail. I am going to have to leave the country before they catch up with me," Anna replied as fear stole its way into her heart.

"Gal," her mother informed her, "not a woman at Dee's place owned up to knowin' who it was done the cuttin'. Thay all claimed to not seein a thang 'cause it happened in the bathroom. When yer name come up, Jake told the police ya was out of town—been gone fer several days so it couldn't a been ya."

"Oh my God, Momma. What does Daddy say about all this?"

"Well, he knowed it was me done give ya dat razor soon as he heerd what was used. 'Course I tole him I ain't done no more than he'd done if he knowed ya was going whare harm was. Dee come told him it was nothin ya could of done he wouldn't a done anyhow. Like I done tole ya, not one of 'em women tole thay knowd who done the cuttin'. Dee done tole me when thay ask hur, she tole 'em thare was so many women in hur home she couldn't give no name 'cause she didn't know 'em all. Said thay all was glad, ever one of 'em. Yer doin' was somethin' the whore brung on hurself."

"Momma, I hate that it had to come to that," Anna replied, unhappy at hearing the joy in her mother's voice.

"Ya cain't reason with no mad dog, gal, ya gotta kill it."

"I know, Momma, but I hated being the one that had to do it," Anna said, remembering hearing the same words come from Dee.

"Call dat husband of yers. He pretty well in a fit with me 'cause I didn't tell him first off whare ya went to, not dat I care a tall, ya know dat." Anna listened to her mother and knew she didn't care what Jake thought when she thought otherwise, especially when it was her daughter's life at stake.

That evening, she and Frankie Lee sat in a place that Anna could only describe as a large barn. The music was down-home blues. The people in it were strictly homegrown, a term Jake used for the black southern people they visited down in Louisiana. The women sat with their men, many with their heads wrapped in pretty colorful scarves, with large or small loop earrings dangling from their ears. When their mouths open the first thing she saw was gold somewhere inside. Anna listened to them talk about their babies and what they would be doing in church on Sunday. She could not help but think about the women in Kentucky at the Ranch, strictly homegrown but not as modern in their dress before she came as these women here.

One of Frankie Lee's friends, he introduced to her as Ned, had taken a seat at their wooden table. His muscles were so huge that Anna was sure he must be a professional weight lifter. Frankie Lee, however, assured her the only things the big dark man lifted were hogs and calves. Anna ran her hand over one arm as Frankie Lee sat there laughing.

"If'n I had a gal little as ya in my arms, I'd reckon I'd have to be careful I didn't crush hur." Both Anna and Frankie Lee laughed out loud along with the couple at the next table.

"Shit, man, this hare's a city woman; if ya git hur, it'd be like Tarzan gittin Jane." Anna covered her mouth as the entire barn roared with laughter.

"Anna," Frankie Lee said as they drove home from the Barn, "ya had better call Jake 'fore it 'curs to him ya have relatives living hare and he come to find ya like he done when ya left the last time. Stayed 'round 'bout a week thankin' ya would come through. I tole him I hadn't seen or heerd from ya, but he waited around to make sure. He was hoppin' on dat cane but he followed me everwhare thankin' I had ya hid, I guess. By the way, ya ain't tole me 'bout yer little take off yet, Cous. What gives with that?"

"Jake knows I'm down here, but you're right, Frankie Lee. Right now I'd better take your advice and call him."

Anna waited to call until she knew Jake should be home.

"Why haven't you called me before now?" Jake asked, sounding quite upset.

"I knew you would be angry. And if you're going to fuss and blame me, I'm going to hang up right now," Anna replied, about to set the receiver down.

"Anna, you better not—as worried as I have been about you. She's not dead, but you messed her up pretty bad."

"What do you mean by pretty bad, Jake?"

"The woman looks as though she's been run over by a freight train. All over her face and body she has cuts, and straightedge razors don't leave pretty scars. I guess I can count my blessings you didn't have your mother's razor when you caught me with her."

"I guess you can," Anna said, feeling raw rage stir between her breasts again.

"I'll be down after you this weekend. And you tell that goddamned cousin of yours not to be pushing men your way!"

"Bye, Jake," Anna said, thinking of Ned, the big hog and calf carrier Frankie Lee had already introduced her to.

"I'll be down there after you tomorrow evening." Anna listened to the click of the phone signaling that he was gone.

******

Her sleep ended a little after midnight with the sound of Frankie Lee calling her.

"Come on out of dat bedroom; ya done slept long enuf. The Old Man is gone back over to Emma's so ya can start by tellin' me 'bout dat vacation ya took 'fore Jake gits his ass down hare after ya." Anna took a seat at the table, watching Frankie Lee rolling some marijuana into a joint, something he had not done while his father was there.

"Where did you get this poison?" Anna asked, coughing after she sucked on the joint. Frankie Lee laughed.

"Let me get us some smooth fire before you kill us both with that poison." Going into her bedroom, Anna opened up the edge of the false bottom of the attaché case. More money lay beneath, as well as the black gold, the stash Raymond had kept. She had never disclosed this to Dee— what she had already seen had scared her enough.

After Frankie Lee looked at her smiling, Anna knew she had lit him up with fire they could float on without choking to death.

"Ya left Jake . . . it's hard to b'lieve. If it wasn't fer the fact dat he was hare with his men huntin ya down, I wouldn't a believed it myself. Ya loved dat cat, gal . . . thought he was the catch of yer life. I can't b'lieve ya left him fer four yeers. That's a long time, Cous."

"Four good long years," Anna said, smiling over at him.

"Very good yeers," Frankie Lee echoed, sucking down more of the potent smoke from the hash.

"All four seasons."

"I kept askin' Jake what happened to make ya leave, but he would never give me a straight answer."

"Like I told you, those women set me up back then."

"How?"

Anna related to him how she received a call from work telling her Barb needed to see her at her apartment. When she arrived at Barb's apartment she continued to share, she discovered, Barb and the two other counselors that worked at the women's shelter in bed with Jake working up a sweat."

She watched her cousin's eyes enlarge as a smile bubbled up on his lips.

"I'm gonna to ask him for his autograph the first I see him 'cause dat man is sho' nuff tuff."

"Yeah, tuff on that cane he has to use since she shot him."

"Don't thank I'll mention it . . . might have to fight. No man wants to be reminded of dat shit."

Anna shared with her cousin the incident of her accident and her trip to Las Vegas, but nothing about the Old Head, Raymond's race, or his condition that had kept her with him. She knew her cousin would never understand any of it.

"Was the dude ya got with slick like Jake or one of them country boys like what we got 'round hare?" Hearing Frankie's question, Anna thought about her former lover, so different from her husband kind of reminded her of how her daddy treated her mother. A rose found its way into her hair on more than one occasion. His smile reassured her when she frowned at some expensive gift she accepted only after complaining of its extravagance. Always, though, she remembered the Red Devil and her first encounter with Raymond's criminal life and his deadly violent nature so unlike her father. She thought of the men in their motel room and how they had lost their lives. And she thought of when he threw the explosives and pulled her down to the ground under him, taking her in his arms and kissing her in a way that let her know he planned to make love to her before long. She never imagined she would be flying in the air when it happened.

"Raymond was an exciting man. Just between us, Frankie Lee, this chain is really valuable. In fact, it's worth more money than you or I will ever see in our lifetimes. I told Jake it was from Daddy; otherwise, he would have destroyed it no matter what its value."

"How did ya talk dat dude outta dat much gold?" Frankie Lee asked after he blew out smoke, from the joint gazing at the chain with the black horse swing from it.

"A sex wager, fool. I'm sure with all your babies, you know what sex is? We took this trip to Kentucky and both agreed there would be no sex during our stay there."

"Kentucky? What the hell ya doin' in Kentucky?"

"Visiting his ranch," Anna replied, laughing as she felt the effects of the black gold hash.

"How the hell ya git talked into goin' south with some brother with so many white crackers walkin' 'round? Ya know I know how ya and my auntie hates whites."

"Frankie Lee, he needed me there."

"Did Aunt Annabelle know ya went thare?

"No Frankie Lee she did not. Anyway the bet was that there would be no sex as I stated

"Ya ain't never got the hots, of course."

"Frankie Lee, a woman's desires can equal and sometimes exceed a man's," Anna answered, thinking of Jake's explanation of her Scorpio nature as to why she must have sex. "One night, yes, I did look over at him lying next to me in bed asleep."

"He was lyin' in bed with ya and couldn't get nothin'? Goddamn!"

"No, of course not. I thought about just sneaking a kiss—even thought of saying to hell with the bet and let him have the two thousand dollars I bet him."

"Two thousand dollars? I needs 'bout half that much right now," Frankie Lee said, shaking his head.

"When I decided to allow him to have me, it suddenly occurred to me where I was."

"Down south whare dem redneck peckerwoods sho' nuff b'lieve in hangin us!" Frankie Lee said, laughing.

"I knew that no matter how much his chain was worth, cash money was the only thing that was going to get Anna out of Kentucky fast and in a hurry if and when things went bad. I got my hot tail up and went into the kitchen, filled a plastic bag with all the ice it could hold, and stuck it down inside my panties until I cooled down." Both she and Frankie Lee were holding their sides at her admission. Tears rolled down Anna's checks from her laughter.

"You think it's funny," Anna finally was able to say, looking at him laughing, "but I knew I could swing this damn chain all I wanted to, but it wasn't going to influence one cracker down there wanting to hang this neck of mine. And, shit, if you have some clansmen after your ass with white sheets over their heads trying to hang a rope around your neck, Kentucky is too damn long a state to try to run through. You can believe I found my way into that kitchen every time I thought I needed to make love."

Anna looked at Frankie Lee's gold tooth shining as he laughed. It was nice, she thought, to have had the opportunity to visit with her cousin. He was so much fun and so loose that she felt free and protected with him. She could at last talk about those four years without fear of reprisals.

"I can see who lost since ya're wearin the chain. What about Jake? Do ya love him anymore?" Anna searched her heart for the answer to Frankie Lee's question.

"Frankie Lee, when I returned to Session, my plans was to take my children and divorce Jake, but I found everyone there was set on our getting back together. They didn't care what had taken place between us. In their hearts, they felt he had paid dearly for what he did. I had been gone four years—time enough to have moved past that—forgive and forget and make family my priority, they felt. It was really my children that caused me to give my marriage another chance," Anna said, remembering their take on the situation.

"Do ya regret it?" Anna thought about her regrets and shook her head saying,

"Frankie Lee, he has been trying so hard since my return. I guess it'll take time to forget all the pain he put me through . . . the child I lost because of what I caught him doing. and all of my own inadequacies with my lost memory, not to mention my marred back that you now can see is perfectly smooth." Anna smiled exposing her back to her cousin who looked shocked to see it.

"Whoa Anna it is smooth. Granny really hated it happened."

"Who?"

"Dis weed got me buzzing. Let's turn in fore I fall asleep in dis chair."

****

That night in bed Anna felt the chain around her neck. Perhaps, she thought as she lay in her uncle's house, it had all been an illusion of her mind and only the chain remained. Even the Old Head seemed lost to her. Remembering the nightmarish dream she had experienced on the bus ride there, Anna opened her eyes as she suddenly heard the sound of thunder roaring in the distance. Fear engulfed her. Looking of out the window beside the bed where she slept, she saw lightning following a crooked path and envisioned the thirteen eyes of the Old Head and how the magic of it had wedged its way into her life, changing it forever.

Chapter Thirteen

—◊—

Early the next morning, Anna woke up smiling. Sitting up in bed, she looked at the orange pulsating light coming from the back of the Old Widow hanging on the wall just above the black-and-white picture of her mother. She had been meaning to ask Frankie Lee if he knew how old her mother was when the picture was taken. She had to have been in her twenties, if even that old. Her near-white-looking mother must have captivated her father, she thought, looking harder at the beautiful picture of her. Anna noticed she looked away instead of into the camera as though something more interesting had caught the attention of those hazel eyes that appeared almost clear in her fair face. Her long brown hair lay in an under flip around her shoulders.

"Momma," she said aloud to herself looking at the picture on the wall, "this is the very first time I've heard you speak proudly about something I have done. I hate that it had to be violence that got it out of you, but I was glad to hear it coming from your lips at long last. Never before this happened did you have a good word to say about your child. Thank God I can come back home now that I know Barb will live.

The sweat pants Anna pulled from her luggage once loose on her now felt tight on her. Even the top felt snug. Looking at the fullness that had begun to develop in her middle, she reprimanded herself for not exercising more to keep her body toned and in shape since she had returned home. She and Raymond had religiously gone to the gym and worked out at least four times a week when he was home, and if he was not, she went on her own.

Just look at me," she said to herself, exclaiming how her body had thickened up. I need to exercise this body before that husband of mine comes and finds he has a fat wife." Laughing to herself, Anna walked into the room where her cousin slept. Shaking him awake, she insisted he hurry and dress so they could go jogging in the nearby park. Slowly getting dressed Frankie Lee complained that he was not into all that damn running.

"Come on, Frankie Lee, we've got to run. I'm getting as fat as a pig sitting around doing nothing but eating all the time. Anna can't keep her husband if she's all out of shape." Slowly he made his way out of bed and into his pants taking her to the nearby park.

As they jogged around the park Anna saw that Frankie Lee was not participating, "Frankie Lee, running, is good for you. You don't have to run fast. Look at you, puffing like a drunk. I'll bet you can't keep up for two laps around this park."

"How much?"

"That thousand dollars you said you needed."

"A thousand dollars? Let's get goin, Cous!" Frankie Lee said, moving ahead of Anna as they continued to jog around the park. It wasn't long after they got their speed up that Anna began to see spots before her eyes. She shook her head and kept going.

All of a sudden she found herself sailing through the air. Before she realized what had happened to her, she was standing in the midst of the rainforest. Everywhere she looked plant life strained to move up through the ground as if searching for room to grow. Roped vines and green vegetation prevented any sight of the earth. Light rain soon had her soaked from head to toe.

In the distance, lightning flashed as if a storm had just passed. Before she could focus her mind to think, an odd black round cauldron appeared in the distance. White smoke churned along its edges.

"It contains the tears from the Healing Tree. Drink from it so that your body is made ready. You must prepare for the twists and turns of your next journey. It is near at hand, Daughter."

Anna gasped as she looked into the thirteen eyes of the Old Head. They revolved so fast she could not keep up with the different directions each took.

"Am I sick, Old Head? Why have you brought me here? I thought you had gone from my life forever."

"Daughter, your journey on this earth world is still unfolding to prepare you for your life's destiny. You have confronted challenge

after challenge, meeting each twist and turn fearlessly when it became
necessary. This new twist will challenge you in a different way. If you
confront it as you have all the others, the outcome will bring you closer
to the promise we must fulfill."

Listening to the words of the Old Head, Anna trembled as she once
again sat on the soft flower petals in the rainforest. The thirteen eyes
and the Old Head continued to whirl above her. She thought of the Old
Widow and looked down at her palm, feeling its young pulsating in it like
a heartbeat. The Old Head had warned of the unhappiness that would
follow if she fell into that pond.

"Old Head, on my word of honor, I never meant to ignore your
warning. It was that horrid image of my mother that caused me to fall
backward into the pond. The purple passion that filled my body overrode
my good senses. Please forgive me," she pleaded, absorbing into her nostrils
the lavender fragrance that scented the warm air.

"Your falling into the pool of passion was no fault of your own,
Daughter, just as you and the Young Chemist consuming the passion
of the red berries before and after boarding that aircraft was an
inevitable part of your journey still unfolding. You must confront
this new twist in your journey head-on as you have faced every other
challenge. I cannot redirect the direction it will take. You must endure
its twists and turns. Many untold secrets will be revealed as you move
toward your destiny."

When Anna finished drinking the contents of the cauldron, the mouth
of the Old Head opened up swooping her inside of it.

"Daughter, its contents will protect your young from harm."

Anna felt the power of its energy fill her and wondered what the Old
Head meant.

"From this moment forward, your life will change. You must
fulfill the promise made long before your conception. All suffering
has a reason and a purpose. The potion has prepared you for what is
to come. It cannot be altered."

"What change?" Anna whispered as she opened her eyes to see Frankie
Lee seated beside where she lay on a hospital bed.

"Frankie Lee, where am I?" Anna asked, looking around at her
unfamiliar surroundings.

"In the emergency room, Cous" he answered, a worried look on his face.

"What? Why?"

"Ya passed out in the park and I couldn't wake ya up . . . scared the shit outta me. Why didn't ya tell me ya had a baby in ya? No way I woulda been runnin' out thare with ya even for a thousand dollars."

"Me, pregnant? You have got to be kidding! I had no idea. Maybe that is why I've been gaining so much weight lately. Jake will be happy." Anna sighed to herself and said, "Damn it. I hadn't planned to get pregnant so soon." Well, she and Jake had lost one child; this would make up for it.

"Ya know how it is with us black dudes—we make babies fast."

Anna smiled at the elderly gray haired black doctor walking into the room introducing himself as Dr. Mason. He towered over her much the same as her father did except that he was wider around the waist. A much older man than her father, he looked down at her with a wide grin on his face. His large black hands covered her stomach, as he signaled Frankie Lee to leave the room. Anna smiled up at the doctor who seemed more like a grandfather figure than a doctor and waited to hear what he had to say.

Taking her pulse, he pressed down gently on her abdomen. "Mrs. Bradley, I'm afraid you are going to have to give jogging up until after this baby is born."

"Yes, I guess you're right. I had no idea or I wouldn't have been out there in the first place."

"You mean you had no knowledge you were pregnant?" Like Ray, the doctor's drawl was spoken in perfect English.

"Of course not. Why is that so strange? I couldn't be more than two months, if that far," Anna replied, staring up at him. His smile widened as he shook his head.

"It seems as though there would have been some signs before now because from my examination, it appears you are moving into your fifth month." Anna looked at the doctor and laughed.

"You mean fifth week, not fifth month, doctor," Anna said.

"No, my dear, I mean five months, not five weeks. This baby is already fully developed."

"Doctor, I know I am not almost five months. Four months ago, I was living in Las Vegas. Before I left there, I had a pregnancy test done; it was negative. Two months is all I could possibly be. You need to reevaluate your findings."

"Sometimes those tests are inaccurate," the doctor stated, a smile flickering across his face as he took a pencil and pad and drew a diagram of how a fetus develops. Anna listened impatiently as he pointed out the different stages of development.

"Mrs. Bradley, my findings tell me you are four and a half months into your pregnancy." When Anna still refused to believe him, he ordered an ultrasound. Anna remember the test that had confirmed she was having twins After two hours of having Frankie Lee peek in every fifteen minutes to ask if everything was all right, the ultrasound tech explained to her that the picture on the screen they were looking at was almost a five-month-old fetus as the doctor had stated. She had a fully developed baby growing inside of her, already moving even if she hadn't felt its quickening.

Stubborn in her belief that they were wrong, Anna insisted they call the clinic where her test had been performed. She sat listening to the nurse there tell her and the doctor there had been a mix-up. She had been pregnant since before she left Las Vegas. She looked at the doctor, feeling a sudden pounding begin to close off her breathing. Smiling at her and the doctor the tech left the room.

The Old Widow hanging above her mother's picture had been a warning she missed. The Old Head telling her to drink from the cauldron so that she could prepare for the next part of her journey was meant to protect the baby she carried. At that moment, Anna knew what the twists and turns of her journey it spoke of would be.

"It can't be. I've been home only three and half months. My God, it can't be. I'm dead! I'm dead!" she screamed. The doctor hurried to her bedside.

"Mrs. Bradley, babies are born every day. I saw this was not your first pregnancy. You're married," he said as Anna noticed him glance at her wedding rings. "There is no reason for you not to deliver a normal, healthy baby." The doctor continued to smile down at her.

"Where can I get an abortion?" Anna asked, slowly rising from where she lay.

"Even if you weren't but a month along, you could not get a legal abortion in this state. Anyway, the child is developed too far along to do something that drastic." Patting her abdomen again, the doctor added, "Must've wanted to get here pretty bad to have hidden its existence this long, and anyway, in all the thirty-eight years I've been in this business, I've only delivered God's blessings to this world, never destroyed even one." Anna grabbed the doctor's hand.

"Doctor, I can't have it. Please, please, all you have to do is to give me something or open me up. I swear to God I would never tell a soul. Please, doctor. I'll pay you to do it. This baby is not my husband's child. He'd kill me if he found out."

The doctor pulled away from her saying, "I'm sorry, Mrs. Bradley, but this baby will have to be born. For you to even think of aborting now would be downright taking a life."

"Doctor, I'll pay you thirty thousand dollars to do it. I have it now and it's all yours, I swear to God!" Anna replied, sobbing out of control.

"Mrs. Bradley, I'm sorry the child was not fathered by your husband; however, as far and as long as this child has struggled to come into the world, I wouldn't kill it even if you offered me fifty thousand dollars. It seems to me its living must be God's will or you would have discovered it long before now."

"Damn you, bastard! You men think all women are good for is having damn babies. It will come into this world over my dead body!"

"Mrs. Bradley, I'm as sad as you must be that men can't bring God's gifts into this world, but as for your dying, some babies are born after their mother's death." He walked from the room leaving Anna crying out of control.

"What's wrong, Anna?" Frankie Lee asked, hurrying into the room. Anna continued sobbing out of control. "Did the doctor say ya were goin to die or somethin'?" Anna placed her hands over her face, still crying nonstop. "Jake will be hare tomorrow. I'll go call him now. See if he can fly out hare today," Frankie Lee said, about to rise from where he was seated next to Anna. She saw the scared look on his face.

"No!" Anna screamed between sobs.

"Damn, Cous, I've gotta do somethin' 'cause right now the way yer actin' is scarin' the hell outta me. Aunt Annabelle will know what to do."

"Frankie Lee, you've got to get me out of here or I will be dead come tomorrow."

Leaving to get the release form, Frankie Lee came back with a prescription for Anna. They passed the doctor on the way out. He stopped them. Anna looked away still crying. He said to Frankie Lee, "I hope you will attempt to persuade Mrs. Bradley against having this abortion she is set on having. Her pregnancy is too far advanced for any licensed physician to legally perform for her. In this state, as I have already informed her, it is illegal—and if discovered will result in jail time. There are only one or two quacks I know of who would risk something that dangerous. If by some unlucky chance she ends up in here after taking that risk, I'll see to it that she goes to prison along with whoever performs it."

Once outside in the car, Frankie Lee shook his head and said to Anna while he looked straight ahead, "Anna, ya shouldn't 'f asked Ole' Doc. Mason to perform an abortion for ya. He b'lieves babies are sacred gifts from God."

"His old ass should have been retired years ago," Anna insisted between sobs.

"Gurl, old doc's been the only doctor colored folk had 'round hare for yeers. Still makes house calls. What he says can take ya to heaven or hell. Got a lot of clout, even with the white folks round hare. Thay never know when thay might need Ole' Doc"

"I don't need him. He is an old fool and I don't want to hear any more about him. Momma says white folk always have a house boy, and he must be one of them."

"No, it ain't dat way with him a'tall. Many des young bucks would've been in the pen if he hadn't stepped in and spoke up for 'em.

"I don't care what he has done for these young bucks—he's not willing to do shit for Anna," she insisted, still unable to stop crying while cursing herself for being so stupid. Once the test came back negative, she was so sure she had beaten the Old Head's warning. She should have known she could never outwit the supernatural force controlling her life. She thought she had gotten out without reprisals . . . running from him when all the time, unknown to her, she carried with her a part of him.

In her mind, Anna could hear her smart words to Linda that last night at the beauty salon: "If his fangs are in me, I don't know it nor can I feel them, Linda." You stupid fool. You felt them all right, she now thought to herself. They just felt so good, that's all you wanted to feel.

Anna's mind continued to roam. Damn it, the Madame must have known. She kept telling me that I needed to listen to what my body was telling me. But I thought I was smarter than her with her naive Middle Eastern ways. I felt sorry for her because she had her head wrapped tight and mine wasn't . . . thought I knew so much more and I didn't know shit. Boy, she must have laughed herself silly at my Western smarts. I thought myself way more sophisticated than that simple woman, or so I felt. What a fool! Anna almost laughed but she was too near tears.

Back at her uncle's home, she sat in the living room with Frankie Lee looking at her with a puzzled expression still on his face.

"Anna, ya were so happy when ya first came. It's like the time Aunt Annabelle brung ya hare to hide ya when ya was a young kid. At first we had lots of fun together, like ya were on vacation. When ya found out yer daddy was in prison and it would be a long time 'fore Aunt Annabelle would return, ya would hardly talk or eat. I felt so sorry for ya," he said, taking her hand in his.

Anna wanted it to be like it was before she knew about this baby she did not want. Oh God, how she wished it was all a dream and she would wake up laughing at how silly it sounded—her pregnant with Raymond's baby. She watched her cousin roll a black gold joint from her stash she had made available to him. Anna reached for it after he took a couple of draws from it.

"No Anna, ya carryin' a baby—ya shouldn't," Frankie Lee told her, refusing to give her the joint. "Ya carryin' this other dude's kid. Go on and have it. If ya tell Jake it's his, he'll b'lieve it."

"Frankie Lee, don't be ridiculous. The baby comes full term two months early . . . would you believe it? No, I've got to get rid of it somehow."

"I'll help ya. But under the circumstances, I b'lieve Jake could love this kid. After all, he made some mistakes hisself. If he don't 'cept it, just have it and leave him. Ya can go on with yer life 'cause ya still got yer other kids, Aunt Annabelle, and Uncle Jeff."

Anna's laughter filled the room. "Oh Frankie Lee, you are so funny. I wish it was that simple, God knows I do," Anna whispered, muffling more sobs.

"I don't thank it is such a bad idea. Yer my cousin and I love ya, gal. Ya know dat."

No matter what bad things I've done, you will still love me? After all, like you said, we are blood cousins, right?" She knew Frankie Lee was trying to make things better for her, not knowing it could never be made better. But what she didn't know was how he would receive the knowledge of a white man in her life.

"Anna, nothing ya could ever do would make me stop lovin' ya or stickin' by ya. Ya know dat."

"You are not lying just to get me to tell you my secrets and then hurt me after I've confessed my soul to you, are you?" Anna asked. She felt her tears spill down her cheeks as she looked at her cousin.

"Hell no, Anna, ya know better'n dat," Frankie Lee said, placing his arms around her. "Thare is nothin on earth ya could do that would make me stop lovin ya, Cous. Are ya crazy, woman? Hell, I know damn well thare ain't nothin ya've done no worse than some of the thangs I done. Got two babies Kate knows nothin 'bout—at lease the gal say they mine. Anyway, ya blood, and I don't give a shit what ya've done, I'll stick by ya, even fight dat damned husband of yers if I have to."

"I wish it were that simple," Anna said, sobbing again. "Go look under my bed and bring me that blue attaché case that's under there. I guess when Sheri' opened it, it was a sign that my life was about to fall apart."

Anna watched Frankie Lee's eyes stretched as his mouth dropped open just as she had seen Dee's do. She could not tell whether it was the money that excited him or the pictures of her and Raymond together that caused him to whistle.

"Ya couldn't fool a deaf-and-dumb blind black man dat dis man's baby was his. Anna ya always hated white folks as much as Aunt Annabelle. I 'member. How the hell did ya git with him?"

"Yes, Frankie Lee, I know all about how I hated white people."

Anna again remembered Linda from the beauty salon telling her how she used to think she was so smart and where had it gotten her—painting nails in a jive beauty salon. Anna realized she had been a fool, so wrapped up in the bliss of their lovemaking that she had forgotten the Old Head's warning and had thrown all caution to the wind. She was a thousand times worse off than working in a beauty salon. If Jake found out about this baby, he would sit and wait patiently for it to be born. When he discovered it was biracial, he'd go get her mother. He knew, just as everyone in Session knew, her mother had a deep-seated hatred of whites. She would ask first who the baby's father was. She would then insist upon meeting him. When she discovered he was white, she would kill Anna right there in the hospital.

"Tomorrow we'll git yer thangs together and find ya a place in the next parish. I'll thank of somethin' to tell Jake. Thare ain't no way I'll let him see ya in the shape ya're in. Hell, ya're liable to tell dat husband of yers just to die early." He put his arms around Anna, talking calmly and gently to her. "I'm yer blood kin no matter what the hell ya've done; I'll protect ya from any mother's son walkin' the earth, even Jake. Now ya stop cryin' and we'll put our heads together and keep this thang under wraps til we can figure out what the hell to do." Anna was so glad he was willing to help her that she stopped crying and began to believe they would figure out a way to get rid of the baby she carried.

The evening before Jake arrived, Frankie Lee found Anna a small apartment over in another parish. Before leaving Anna sat on the bench in the kitchen of her uncle's home looking up at her cousin. "Frankie Lee, when are you going to say it? I've been waiting to hear you say it."

"Hear me say what, Cous?" he asked as they prepared to leave his father's home.

"What the hell was I doing with this white man in the first place when I should have known better?"

"Anna, ya already tole me why ya was with the dude. Ya woulda been dead in dat car if it don't be for him pullin' ya out. Now as to him bein' what he is, well, I see it like dis. Generally speakin, every black man is the same, but specifically speaking, each and every one of us is different. Hell, I know thare are some thangs I see other black dudes trippin' off of dat I wouldn't thank 'f doin'. So dat makes me my own man. Now dis white dude ya was with helped ya through some heavy shit, and like every other white man, he is the same, but thare are those specifics I am speakin' of. Any man who can get a lady so hot she puts ice in her panties to keep from losin' a sex bet to him has to be one hell of a motherfucker, especially when the lady is my cousin. Now ya cut out all dat cryin' 'cause we gonna get dis problem taken care of so ya can head on back home."

Chapter Fourteen

—ᗰᗯ—

So overwhelmed was Anna by the sudden news of her pregnancy, she sat looking out of the window of the apartment Frankie Lee had rented for her to stay in, thinking that her entire life had been destroyed in that hospital room. She could still hear the doctor's voice vibrating in her mind: "Mrs. Bradley, you are almost five months along." Plagued with worries, she trembled lest by some strange twist of fate Jake happened to walk in on her. It would be up to Frankie Lee to convince him she was no longer in Oinston. Thoughts of Jake finding her pregnant were driving her crazy. She had been unable to think of anything else.

Tired of looking outside, she moved away from the window as she reached down to touch the quivering fetus in her womb, a quivering reminding her that a baby was growing inside of her. She had felt the movement before now but had not understood its meaning. The baby quivered again. As soon as she had discovered this pregnancy, her body seemed to balloon. Those hips she was jogging to tone down grew heavy with the weight of the child, as had her waist. She could not get enough sleep.

Tears fell down her cheeks as memories filled her mind of standing dripping wet at the edge of that pond just beyond the cabin. For months she had denied herself any intimacy with him. God, how she had tried to obey that warning, but the horror of her mother's hideous face came boring down on her so unexpectedly, pushing her where she had hoped death would take her. Raymond's preventing her from drowning had stopped the ending of her life and started the power of the purple liquid hidden inside the pond's water that would stir passion in them they could no longer resist. It took two months to abate the wanton desire inside of her. He welcomed the pleasure of having her because he had soaked up as much of the potion water as she had. The purple passion's water turned their minds to the forbidden intimacy so long denied. In that cabin and out of the country, they had compensated for lost months. Now she would pay dearly if she did not rid herself of the results.

The split between she and Raymond Forlorn happened so fast and unexpectedly that Anna had had no time to prepare for its coming. Thinking back on it now, she knew the forces of the Old Head must have willed it to happen. His wife had appeared out of nowhere—the call from the Madame—those occurrences didn't just happen. It was as though the Madame and the Old Head were somehow connected. She kept thinking about the Madame and the strange way their lives had come together. There was nothing about this woman she understood. How was it possible Anna wondered, she knew more about her body than she did?

Anna began to think hard and long on her stay with the Madame. She had never warned her of her uninvited guest. That Old Head needed her there for its own purpose. The baby could develop undetected in a place where the environment provided exercise, warm pool swims, and everything a mother-to-be needed. She kept trying to piece together how the Madame as well as the Old Head got that one over on her.

Bidding farewell to her three friends, she had boarded a flight out of the country. When she had landed at the airport, the Madame's limousine had been waiting for her.

Anna remembered falling into her arms once they reached the spa, spilling tears all over her hijab.

"He is gone, Madame. It's over," she had sobbed. Safe inside the Madame's private suite, Anna had asked, "Why can't I stop loving him? I feel him all over and inside my body."

"You have been with him four years, my dear, and years before that in the private world of your dreams where not one hater could destroy that love." Anna's mind continued to ramble on about her visit with the Madame as it all came back to her.

She had shared with the Madame that their split felt like something had been ripped out of her forever, even though it would have destroyed her had he attempted to have them both. Still, she felt as though she was dying inside without him. Why can't I forget him? I'm sure he has already forgotten me."

"How can he forget a woman who has saved his life as well as the lives of the animals he loves?" the Madame had asked, settling down on the sofa next to her. Anna's thoughts ran rampant as she began to think back to her life with him. On her latest visit with the Madame, the Madame had shared her own memories of him; Anna remembered her telling her when Raymond and Mix first came to arrange for her stay. "'He said he needed her assurance that when he left his lady in her care, she would receive the same treatment and respect as all her other clients.'

At the time she explained to Anna that she had had no idea what he meant. Her stay had already been planned and paid for before she went into surgery for her back. He had come himself to be assured Anna would have a place of solitude to rest without stress of any kind, stating to the Madame that his lady was very dear to him. He wanted the best for her. "'Ms. Anna,' he told her, "'is my lady, my heart, and my soul.' She believed those were his exact words. Anna listened to her tell her. "'She had left him, she shared, with no doubt as to what would be in store for her,' Anna's heart had grown sad thinking at the time of the warmth of their relationship.

The Madame continued to tell her that when she stepped from Mix's limousine with the two, her shock came from the race of woman she was. She knew he was an American Southern white man and had read of the turbulent backlash American blacks had encountered in her country with white Americans. In fact, she shared with Anna that she had overheard some harsh conversations from white females as to their non-acceptance of women of her race. She had never met a Western black woman before Anna she shared. Not one has since visited her spa. Her acknowledgement of that fact came as no surprise to Anna.

That sense of entitlement she had experienced when meeting most white Americans was missing in Mousieur Forlorn. She shared with Anna being impressed. His not mentioning her race said something special about him and left the Madame with an impression she reserved for few white Americans she had met. She admitted. She also admitted wondering what he thought she could do for Anna. Her ebony skin glowed as though she had just received a treatment. Her thick black hair needed no attention for it too felt and looked as though it had been touched by the hands of the gods."

Anna had thought at the time of the tears that had washed over her hair and body, leaving them as soft as velvet and her without a trace of the old wounds that had marred her back. Those tears mixed with his love had given her a new life. Just as he had introduced her to the Madame as Ms. Anna, she remembered his introduction of her to others, especially men—black men she was most aware of who would then say "nice to meet you, Anna." He would stare them down. "Did you not hear me? Her name is Ms. Anna." Their eyes would grow alert as they corrected their mistake. Anna remembered holding her breath, especially when the men were white, believing they would say something nasty, but they never did. The adjustment was always made, and she was addressed as Ms. Anna as she had been Ms. Anna to Julia and the employees at the ranch. The white students at Camelot Academy who had given her that title would never know how long it has lasted, she thought; still sadden at the loss of their friendships. They had loved and adored her, as she had them, until her mother's hatred of them destroyed it all. Anna sighed as her thoughts continued to roam.

She had returned to Session as a stranger whose changes had frightened the people she loved. She had not brought Raymond back to Session as her father feared, but his baby grew inside of her—a living testimony of those four years away from home. She just could not imagine having it without him. And now that Jake was once again in her life, it was unthinkable.

Frankie Lee had spoken of calling her mother. Anna knew her mother would have found Raymond's part in her life a despicable horror. As for his baby, she thought to herself as her hand moved over her stomach, her mother would want it dead no matter how much of a pro-lifer she claimed to be.

Her tears started flowing again as her thoughts continued to ramble. Nothing had turned out the way she had planned. Now this! She might as well bury herself and the baby with her. Those four years seemed to be just a dream she had finally awakened from. Ray had returned to his family and she had returned to hers. She wanted to no longer think of the man known as Raymond Forlorn—not now, not ever again—yet as a result of her discovery, her thoughts stayed every waking moment on him and the baby he had left inside of her.

Anna again thought of her first trip to the Repair Your Body Spa and the Madame. A gift, Raymond had informed her, had come from Mix

Miller because he wanted to show his appreciation for the many ways she had been instrumental in helping him. After the miracle of her back smoothing out beyond what anyone thought possible, Raymond had left her for two weeks in the hands of the Madame, where Mix had assured them she would find a place of solitude to rest while she recuperated.

Anna had also found a friend as well as a sanctuary of peace, harmony, and solitude. She loved the serenity she had experienced on her first visit but she also knew her lover never knew of the friendship that had developed between her and the Middle Eastern woman. Being invited again to her spa by the Madame after she and Raymond split had been a stroke of good luck thinking at the time going back home too soon meant that, Raymond would have come to Session in hopes of continuing their relationship. She knew he had no plans of ending it, even with his wife again in his life. In Session, that would have been deadly even if he divorced his wife. She could ill afford to have that happen. Once the unexpected call from the Madame came, she made a detour; one that she now knew the Old Head must have been instrumental in making happen.

Now to discover this baby inside of her—she felt the Madame had violated their friendship by not telling her what she knew. The Old Head knew only too well of their developing friendship, something that had ensued because of a slip of the tongue when Anna, on her first visit, had made a comment after seeing fifteen covered women being escorted out of the Madame's spa and discovered them to be the wives of one man.

"How" Anna had asked absently as she watched them leave, "can one man service fifteen women? He would collapse by the time he made love to half of them. What pleasure could he possibly give even the fifth wife?" She had asked this more of herself than of anyone else, except the Madame had overheard her comment.

"'You Western women are confusing our husband's role with the Western male's sexual appetite,' the Madame stated as they watched the wives depart in the two limousines that had come for them. The Madame then invited her into her private room.

"How so?" Anna remembered asking as they entered the small room that was bare of all but a table and two sofas. She loved listening to the melody of the Madame's broken English.

"We don't sleep with our husbands for the simple pleasure of enjoying sex as you Western women are so fond of exclaiming . . . you have become as masculine in your sexual desires as your men.

"If we attempted one-tenth of what you Western women take for granted, we would be killed instantly," the Madame said, smiling as her light brown eyes gazed intensely into Anna's. Anna listened to her and then allowed her thoughts their freedom.

"You think it's because you Mid Eastern women have no rights to speak of anyway?" Anna had asked, referring at the time to how only the Madame's eyes could be seen in the presence of males. She routinely sat fully veiled with her hijab in place. No male eyes could look upon on her except those of her husband. The Madame smiled, shaking her unwrapped long dark brown hair, something she exposed only in the privacy of the room. This room found them often sitting, sipping tea, and engaging in long conversations on women's issues across continents as a result of Anna's slip of the tongue. Anna knew the Madame loved evoking conversation from her on what she called the privileged customs of Western woman that were not allowed to the women of her own race and culture.

As soon as Anna had arrived on her last visit, the Madame had hurried Anna into her private sanctuary for tea.

"'Ms. Anna there is an unusual glow about you. Is there something you have not shared with me?' she had asked. Anna now remembered the guarded look that had been in her eyes as she gazed at her. Maybe she had been trying to tell her then, but Anna realized she had misunderstood her meaning.

"What more is there to share? We had a clean split. Once I confirmed I was not pregnant, my worst fear vanished." Anna remembered dismissing the look of shock on the Madame's face, not understanding why it had been there at the time.

"'What fear do you speak of, Ms. Anna?' the Madame had asked as a frown crested her brows. Anna sat in the small apartment and shook her head as she thought of how the Madame had quizzed her on a question she had already known the answer to.

Not picking up on the Madame's train of thought, Anna had explained that she wouldn't have to get that abortion she would have been forced to get had she been pregnant. She informed the Madame that she surely could not have had his baby with him out of her life. What on earth would she have done with it? She had jokingly added that it would be her luck to have it born white with blonde hair looking just like him. Anna remembered laughing at the thought—a baby she had believed at the time did not exist.

"Ms. Anna, you are just as prejudiced in your thoughts of race as white Americans are. I would not have thought it of you." Anna remembered smiling at the Madame.

"Madame, once again you don't understand the American way of thinking," Anna had countered, remembering how impossible it had been to make the Old Head understand the morals that the humans in her world lived by.

"Help me understand," Anna remembered her asking, "because you are right. I cannot understand why you would want to destroy a life because it is born with features of its father. That makes little sense to me."

"Madame, in America, people will ostracize you if you are black and your baby is by a white man. At least that's the way it is in the black culture where I'm from."

"But why, my dear?"

"White people are seen as having caused the horrors we have had to struggle with for at least three centuries. Even though we do not have the power to destroy their lives as they have often destroyed ours, we do have the power to vent our anger in other ways. Within our hearts we always live with the memory of what our fore parents lived through. I know my mother has never forgotten the horror of what she lived through, seeing those white people kill her father and her grandfather and then having her mother taken away by a white man as if she were property to be seized.

If I brought a half-white baby back to Session, talking about it being one I conceived by a white man, I would be worse than the woman wearing the scarlet letter, not to mention my mother would kill me and it, and I do mean literally." Anna had felt a chill pass through her as she thought about the horrible face of her mother that still haunted her in nightmares.

"Yet you say you love him still. How can a woman love a man and be willing to kill his child?"

"Madame, if he were still with me, I would not be happy about having a baby by him, but I would have no choice but to have it. He would not allow anything else. But he is not with me, so he has no say in the matter.

It is all up to me. I could never face my mother or anyone else with a white man's baby. I could not without him there to father it. I just couldn't."

"Sometimes, Ms. Anna, the very things we say we cannot do become the things we must do. Your mother's life is her own, just as your life is your own to live. Once you confront that fact, you will be able to face those haunting fears on your own terms. That being said, let's get on with my favorite topic, which is still the customs of the Western woman versus those of the Eastern woman.

"What new freedoms have been allowed the Western woman since your last visit, Ms. Anna?" Anna now knew she had shifted subjects after she gave her reasons not to tell her something to cause her to take an action against her beliefs.

"One thing for sure, we don't think of our bodies as vessels for men to pour babies into. We enjoy sex as much as they do, and they must see to it that we are pleased with their performance."

"Like your men, you Western women think of your bodies as pleasure tools, functioning simply to lure and entice."

"Lure and entice, Madame? Come on now, you mean to tell me you Eastern women are not allowed to enjoy what your men take for granted?"

"'Come, my dear. Let me show you what it is I am speaking of,' the Madame had said as Anna followed her into a room void of furniture. Thick black sponge mats lay on a white marble floor. Taking a seat on one of the mats next to the Madame, Anna remembered she had crossed her legs under her as she watched the Madame click a button on the wall next to them. Suddenly, they sat in complete darkness. Anna gazed up into what appeared to be the sky lit up by millions of stars and a blue planet.

"'It is Mother Earth, my dear, the most reverent female of all. See how generously she gives and receives life. As you must know, all of life comes through her and returns to her.' Anna looked as the blue ball turned into the earth. Plants of every description sprang up through her in the form of different varieties of vegetation that reminded her of the rainforest. Anna was overwhelmed as she took in the breathtaking scene.

"'It is so with the females of my culture. Those women you saw do not see their husband as a man there simply to give them sexual pleasures in the sense you Western women are so fond of. It is that he comes during their fertile period so that the egg in their bodies can be fertilized. That is the pleasure they are seeking. It is the ultimate goal so that they can accomplish what mother earth has been doing since the beginning of her existence. The husband of those fifteen women feels honored to be allowed to visit the temple of their bodies for a short period in hopes of fulfilling the sole purpose allowed him by the creator,' the Madame explained.

Anna looked wide-eyed as a mother's body stretched as she gave birth. It had stunned her senses, remembering she had been that woman when her twins sprang from her body. Seeing the creation of life unfolding before her seemed strange. She knew it would not be something women in her country would find attractive or something they sought after. In that sense the Madame's claims rang true.

Anna had responded to the Madame, "Once a child is born, the act of actual childbirth for the Western woman is not seen as a miraculous event. Nor is it ever played out as such in the minds of any woman I know. The entire ordeal is thought to be uncomfortable and soon forgotten. Nothing about it is sacred except the birth of the child, if the child is wanted. There is nothing special the mother will receive or feel from those around her—not really. She has a baby—so what?" Anna had paused as another thought had just occurred to her, causing a smile to flicker across her lips.

"Don't have too many or wait until you are thought of as having gotten too old. If you do, even if you are married, you are frowned upon as a foolish woman. In fact, the woman who has a career with one or no children is most respected." The Madame had received this information while shaking her head, as if not liking what she had heard.

Anna freely shared that childbirth was certainly not something she desired of her own body at that point. Listening to the Madame, Anna had to admit that the desirability of having children seemed to be dwindling in the hearts of Western women. She, like most women in her culture, thought only of her body in the sense that the Madame spoke of at certain times of the month, hoping no baby had gotten between her and the birth control pill. Childbirth was not something women celebrated these days, not like the Madame thought of celebrating it. For the Western women she knew, the body was something to be made beautiful and enticing to solicit the desire of the opposite sex and envy from other women.

Anna remembered the Madame's words, "'When a man in my culture touches the breasts of a woman, he kisses them, hopeful that they will supply enough nourishment for the child he is there to fertilize.' Remembering the scene when she was with the Madame, Anna watched the mother examine her breast and then place one nipple in the mouth of her newborn infant. Thoughts of her own babies taking nourishment from her breasts came to her mind, and of Raymond who had taken nourishment from them. Leave it up to the Old Head to take the body functions of the female to another level.

The Madame had said, the woman of her country is honored by the gift she will be given and the long months of preparation for that gift. She assured Anna that their females are not allowed to publicly display their bodies for they understand that they are sacred and are in waiting for a special purpose that is given them by the creator because they are female. Girls as early as twelve learn how their bodies are meant to perform, clearly understanding God's creation of childbirth and the special meaning in its beauty.'

"But that should be frightening to them. Childbirth is so painful if allowed naturally," Anna had exclaimed.

"'That occurs, Ms. Anna, only if it is taught that the pain is harmful or something to be feared. If it is taught to be respected as a part of the beauty she gives to the world from the creator, her thoughts of pain will be replaced with rejoicing, realizing that her special ability to create life is to be honored. You tell me, Ms. Anna, what time during the year are you Western women celebrated by your men? I mean all women—just because they are female?'

"Well . . ."

"'And I am surely not speaking of the time you are allowed to parade around half-naked on stage, looking like apple pies there to be tasted.'

Anna had thrown back her head and her laughter had rung out through the empty room, "Madame, why are you so negative when it comes to the Western woman?"

"'The word negative is incorrect, Ms. Anna. Saddened would be a better term.'

"Well, I think Mother's Day is the one day everyone thinks of the female, no matter what her status."

"'That is so ironic because it is the one thing you Western women hate about being female,' the Madame had replied, smiling at Anna as she turned on the light and stared over at her.

"I don't think we hate being mothers. I do think we hate having too many babies that will tie us down," Anna countered, realizing the Madame was seeking a deeper understand into the mind of the western woman.

"I am the mother of six children, my dear. The time my husband found me most beautiful was when my stomach here," she said, touching her smooth flat mid-ribs, "grew large and life kicked inside of it. The child is surely the most precious gift we could give each other."

Anna had looked at the Madame. She could not have been more than five feet tall. Her straight brown hair hung down her back. Her smooth, ageless skin gave Anna no clue as to how old she was. She had discovered that although she spoke French fluently, she was not French. Other women of her race there at the spa spoke a strange different dialect that had puzzled Anna. She had meant to ask, but the Madame had kept her off guard, asking the most outrageous questions and making the most outlandish statements about the Western woman.

"'All you Western women have,' the Madame had gone on to say, "'are your outer appearances and your sexy-looking bodies to depend on, and that's only from your men's point of view. Where is that beauty that is most valuable to this world?'

"'What beauty are you speaking of, Madame?' "Beauty that is eternal." Anna began to listen and realize the Madame's wisdom. "'For the women you saw, their husband knows he can never carry life inside his body. All he can do is fertilize their egg or eggs that may bring forth life, and after that, his usefulness has ended and he must wait while the women's bodies complete what they began if the women are fortunate enough when their visits are completed.' Listening to the Madame, Anna remembered the mother's look of joy as she gazed down at the infant she had just delivered to the world.

"'While you Western women run from the beauty of what your bodies were meant for, we run toward it knowing that the real beauty in a woman is everlasting.'

"And that is Madame?"

"'Years after our faces grow old and our bodies wrinkle our husbands will see our youth and theirs living in the bodies of our children and grandchildren.'

"No woman I know of these days wants a house filled with unwanted babies to clutter their lives. Later in life, one or two will do, and if no man has come into their lives by that time, they still have their careers that give them a sense of accomplishment," Anna told her with much conviction.

"'Yes, I must agree that too many children can be a burden in today's world," the Madame had thoughtfully admitted. "That's why the young girl is encouraged to marry as early as fifteen or sixteen—no later than seventeen. It is then that their bodies are young and their spirits are strong enough to handle managing a family,' the Madame had replied, smiling over at Anna.

"We'll have to agree to disagree because I would not want my daughter to have children that young. It would ruin her life and her future career," Anna had answered in reply to the Madame.

"'A career that lasts perhaps, twenty maybe thirty years, and then what? You wait until you have established your career to have your children, but your body in the meantime is constantly changing. Pollutants invade the cells, and foul air and other unnamed harmful toxics mother earth has been injected with have long since taken its toll on your bodies. No, Ms. Anna, while I agree that there should be some form of birth control, I must disagree with the Western woman's theory of her place on this earth. "'You women have giving up the one most important function no man can perform to try to do the things that have always killed men and is now killing you Western Women. By the time you do settle down to the important functions in life, your body and your minds will be too old to enjoy them.' Anna had listened intently as the Madame gave her take on the Western female and how they had robbed themselves and their bodies of their importance.

"'You have allowed your men to take from you your rightful place on this earth. It's too bad you have settled for their meager ideal of beauty and happiness— a five-minute bliss that satisfies but a short moment and the willingness to kill that, which is most precious. You are giving up your true purpose to possess a beauty that keeps changing depending on what your man's desires for you are. You will never understand that you are precious and are the creator's most important gift to the world. Even if your man misunderstands your role in life, you, my dear you, should never misunderstand it.' Anna could not help but think of Momma Lucy's theory of the woman being the cake and the man as simply the icing around her.

"What you say may be true; however, if we don't seek alternatives, a life awaits us of no more than that of a housewife without any rights to speak of, grappling for the crumbs our mates may or may not bring home. No, Madame, the Western woman may not be what she is meant to be according to your world's standards, but she knows only too well the way out of a desperate life is to demand that she be equal to her man, standing beside him and not behind him—something that is incomprehensible to you and the women of your culture," Anna countered, refusing to yield to her way of thinking.

The Madame, Anna knew, had been intrigued with their conversations. As she had said, Anna's visit was the first only by a black female from the Western world. Anna had realized the Madame had very little understanding of the Western culture and no real knowledge of the black Western culture. Listening to her questions and feelings about the freedom she felt Western women were privileged to she had wondered why the Madame had not had these conversations with her white Western female clients. Perhaps she had, unknown to her.

Anna had seen that the Madame wanted to absorb everything there was to know about the culture of the Western woman. It had also interested Anna that the Madame never referred to her as being a black female from America. She sensed that like the Old Head's thoughts about all humans, in the Madame's way of thinking, all Americans women thought the same and came from the same cultural background. Anna also knew that in the Madame's mind, all Western women were privileged with the same rights. Anna knew the white women rich enough to spend two weeks at Repair Your Body would hardly take the time for the kinds of conversations she and the Madame found interesting enough to discuss. Because women were her specialty, how the mind of the Western female worked intrigued her to no end.

"Anna, my dear, I am told most of your young girls have never seen childbirth and that they are encouraged to use birth control early so they freely give their bodies to males thinking not at all about their virtue." Anna found herself confronted with many such questions by the Madame. She assured her that most of what she had heard about Western women was fabricated. Like most foreigners who fantasized American life as being outside of the "normal" that they understood, the Madame chose to believe that which would be seen as most outlandish in her own culture.

****

Exercising beside the pregnant women, Anna had thought maybe one day she would have a child for the next man in her life, but that would have to wait a few years. She needed to get over this last man before another one entered the picture. She did not realize that the Madame had read the signs of her body better than she and was preparing her for a baby she knew Anna already carried. With a fair-sized ball between her legs, Anna lay with a row of twenty women squeezing then breathing, repeating the exercise until the Madame said to stop and rest and then began again.

Deep massages would awaken the senses of every cell in the female body to the purpose it was meant for she told the group of women. Diving into the warm pool invigorated Anna's body. Those weeks turned into a month as Anna worked her body into shape at the Madame's insistence. After the exercises were over, Anna and the Madame sat sipping tea while the Madame continued sharing her thoughts of the Western woman and what she thought were their strange ways of thinking.

"'You Western women are so fascinated with being equal to your men," the Madame shared in the privacy of her room where they often visited. "You have no time to listen to the needs of your body or to understand that it speaks to the female differently than it does the male." Anna had not understood her meaning until that moment. The Madame's olive-colored oval face held light brown eyes that shinned as though a star stood behind them, eyes that appeared to penetrate hers. When Anna had finally remembered to ask her nationality, she had simply answered, "More important than race or culture, Ms. Anna, is that we are females—the givers and the receivers of all human life. Soon, you Western women will create machines to make your babies, using your bodies only for the sexual act and the satisfaction derived from it. Next there will be no need for the female at all.'

"Madame," Anna replied, shaking her head, "when that happens, neither of us will be living to speak of it." The Madame had to laugh at that one. Anna continued, "I see no difference in American women and other women as far as the purpose of the female. All must perform the sexual act if life is to continue. Of course, there is always artificial insemination,"

"'See what I mean about the machine? How late in life is artificial insemination necessary?' she asked, an unsettling smile on her face. "In my culture, the young girl's body is ripe and ready to do what it was created to do by the time she is fifteen. By the time she is sixteen or seventeen, she has had at least one child or perhaps two if she is very fertile. In your culture, the woman waits until her body is filled with too many pollutants to have babies while using it only for sexual pleasure in her youth. By the time she seeks a mate, she so resembles the male that there is no need to seek motherhood. She is concerned with meeting the man as an equal losing sight of her own uniqueness that actually supersedes all he can ever give to the world."

"Thanks for repairing my body, Madame, but I plan to keep men and more babies out of my life. I will take care of the children I have. Anna needs no more men and surely no more babies ever, and since I must be fertilized by a man, I won't have that problem, now will I?" She had smiled at the Middle Eastern woman she so admired but hardly understood, thinking she had set the record straight with her as far as she was concerned. They both finally had agreed that each had been so indoctrinated in their own culture's beliefs that it would be next to impossible to change the other's views. That night, as Anna had curled up under the soft blankets in a firm bed, the Old Head had come to her in a dream. Its blue light circled the small room of the spa where she slept, with its thirteen eyes stared down at her.

"The time has come Daughter. You must return to the life you left behind. Bid this place good-bye. It is time to once again begin your journey."

Rising early the next morning, Anna had packed and let the Madame know the time had come for her journey to continue.

"Yours is a saga I will look forward to hearing more about. A ticket will be waiting for you when it is time for you to come again."

"Madame, how is it you know I will come again?" Anna asked after they entered the airport. The Madame had smiled, taking her hands into hers.

"You will come to see me again someday. Yours is now a perfect body already prepared for your next journey, one which I hope turns out well for you." Anna remembered smiling, feeling a sense of sadness having to leave such a wise and simple woman, one she never understood. "'Ms. Anna, please hear the words of this foolish woman when she tells you that you must learn to listen to that body of yours when it speaks to you. Of course, that is another problem. You Western women have never understood how to connect with the voice within that is whispering to you things you must know. One day I hope you will understand that not all things should be changed by the hands of man but should rather be left to the will of the god spirit that guides us all.'

"I'll have time to learn to listen to that voice now that I have no man in my life disrupting it. Good bye, my friend, until we meet again." With that, Anna had embraced the woman wearing a hooded veil one last time before she hurried out of the limousine to catch her flight home.

****

She sure as hell was listening now she thought to herself as she sat in the apartment thinking about how the Madame must have laughed herself silly. It's a wonder, she thought as she continued to piece together this new crisis in her life that she didn't have a miscarriage fighting with Barb. Anna sighed. It would have been a blessing—another baby gone because of her. Between the blessings of the Madame's spa and the Old Head's Healing Tree tears, she knew she could have jumped into a concrete hole and the baby would have stayed intact. Once she had fallen into that pond, she was doomed, just like the Old Head had first warned her.

From Kentucky, Ray had flown them to New York and introduced her to his love of opera and the spell of ballet dancers whirling around in the air. They hypnotized Anna as they created a beautiful love story out of song and dance. Anna cheered with the rest of the audience enjoying an art form completely new to her.

In Brazil, it had been the excitement of the bullfights and the dazzling colorful culture of the Spanish people he had wanted her to enjoy. To her surprise, many had skin as dark as her skin. In Paris, looking up at the Eiffel Tower at night, she felt mesmerized. Time had stopped for Ms. Anna as she had entered worlds so unknown to her that she felt as disoriented as she had felt in the land of the Healing Tree. They had flown to New Zealand to enjoy the sport of rugby—an aggressive football game played without the benefit of any protection, she could see. At halftime, Anna had found herself closed-mouthed, wondering how many brutal injuries would take place before they stopped the game. Of course, Raymond she noticed had sat enthralled the entire time.

"Rugby is a vigorous, rugged sport that requires its players to be in superior physical condition. It is not for the sick or weak-at-heart, honey," he had explained to her.

She had replied, "Those men are built like prize fighters. Look at their muscles. It must be the reason you are always in the gym tightening up yours."

"You seem to have no problem cuddling up in these arms of mine," he had said, wrapping one arm around her as a smile grew on his face.

The highlight of their trip found them seated in the bleachers in London as they watched a soccer game. A sport the Europeans she was informed called football because it is a game played using the feet. For Anna, it was special because it took her back to Camelot Academy where she had played the game with her classmates. They had taught her soccer and she had taught them in the classroom.

Anna had realized she had missed too many doctor's appointments and needed to replace the missing pills. Thinking of nothing but the magic of the moment, she had found herself high on a cloud—a cloud that had filled her with an unexpected guest—one who was determined to stay if at all possible.

Chapter Fifteen

——⟋⟍——

Frankie Lee came to assure her Jake had believed him when he had him listen to the police radio in a friend's car that was rigged to ask about an Anna Bradley and her connection with a possible homicide. Frankie Lee told her that Jake had been so shocked at the mention of her name associated with a possible murder that he believed Anna would run for sure.

"Frankie Lee, I must get an abortion. It's the only way out for me. The five thousand dollars I gave you was just to find someone to do it. I will pay whatever money they ask. Just get them quick so I can get this baby out of me. It is the only way I can return home," Anna insisted after he told her how he had gotten Jake to believe she had left Winston on the run.

"I must get back home as soon as possible or Jake will believe I have returned to Ray. That would not be good for this marriage we have just gotten back together. Even if I wanted to, I cannot tell Ray about this baby or expect him to do anything for it since he is now with his wife."

"Alright, Cous. I'll see if I can arrange somethin' soon. Thare's this dude I know . . . he knows somebody."

"Good! Go see him today. I don't care what it costs as long as he gets it done."

Anna failed to keep her promise to call her children or her mother. If she called, her children would want to know where she was. She would have to lie about no longer being in Oinston. Then she would have to answer more questions she had no answers for and would not have answers for until she was free of the baby inside of her. She did not want them to find out that for whatever reason Frankie Lee had lied to Jake about her being gone. The worst of it would be for her mother to come looking for her only to find her pregnant and insisting on the evils of baby killing. If she were to bear the child, the hatred in her mother's heart and the knowledge that the baby's father had to be a white man meant she would be done for.

****

Frankie Lee came to see Anna as much as possible. She kept insisting that he hurry and find someone to do the abortion. The movements of the fetus were increasing daily. She would soon enter her fifth month. When he came by saying he had finally lucked up on the right person, she seemed overjoyed. They had to wait another week, but at least now she could smile, feeling in better spirits.

When the time came, Frankie Lee was forced to tell her that the person performing the abortion was not a licensed physician, and all he could guarantee was that she knew how to get rid of the child. He had no idea as to how safe it would be.

"Let's just get it done and over with. Right now, I'd just as soon die with it."

"Cous, hell, I know the fix ya're in, but I can't help feelin down on this. Ya're so far gone. I don't want nothin to happen to ya."

"Don't worry about me unless I don't get this baby out of me," Anna insisted. Her eyes closed as she felt the fetus moving stronger than ever. The movements were constant now. She knew this had to be done quickly or it would be taking a life. Frankie Lee squeezed her to him, kissing her head. Looking down at her palm, she saw the bright orange light of the spider buried in it illuminating in the darkness. Her fear increased.

"What am I goin to do with ya? Ya was always the one to do the damndest thangs," he said, drawing her into his arms as tears slipped down her cheeks.

The next night he came for her, and they drove down a dark dirt country back road up into the woods. She was reminded of the first time she and Raymond had traveled to his Ranch. Only the lights of Frankie Lee's car penetrated the night. She looked to see if shiny eyes pierced the darkness, indicating that deer stood nearby. Soon they came to a house hidden from view. Dim lights from the interior were the only indicators that it existed. Frankie Lee stopped the car and got out. He opened the door for Anna. Touching her enlarged abdomen, he shook his head asking, "Cous, are ya sure ya wanta go through with dis? I can feel it moving."

"Frankie Lee, it has to be done now. Let's get it over with. I'm not far enough along for it to live even if it does come out alive," Anna insisted, walking ahead of him to the house.

Just as they got to the door, two people came out carrying someone on a stretcher to a white and red ambulance Anna had not seen until that moment.

"What happened to Ms. Moss?" Frankie Lee asked, running up to the two men carrying the woman lying on the stretcher.

"She just up and had a heart attack while she was standing at the table getting ready for her next customer. Can't figure it out. One minute she was gathering the things she needed, and the next minute she was clutching her chest. Just can't figure it out." Anna looked at Frankie Lee and then at the pulsating light in her palm. She shook her head, thinking how messed up her life was becoming. What would she do now? This had seemed to be her only hope out of this fix she was in, and now it was gone.

****

A few nights later they started out again. Frankie Lee informed Anna that he had offered the butcher five thousand dollars. The butcher, as he called the man who had agreed to perform the abortion, had insisted he needed ten thousand dollars for all the risks he had to take in ridding a woman of a five-month pregnancy. Frankie Lee was angry about the fee for something the butcher usually got a hundred dollars, if that much, for doing. Anna insisted that they give the man the money and be done with it. Frankie Lee parked the car. Anna watched him pat his pockets to assure the needed money was there. Helping Anna out of the car, he put his arm around her and led her down the street and into a dark side alley.

"Ya're not afraid, are ya cous?" Frankie Lee whispered.

"Yes, Frankie Lee, I'm scared to death, but it has to be done and that's all there is to it," Anna insisted, following him and not wanting to think about what she was about to do or the baby kicking inside of her.

"Damn it!" Frankie Lee whispered through clenched teeth stopping. He pulled Anna back from a speeding police car entering the alley its lights blasting. Anna moved away, in shock, her mouth opened seeing about ten police cars parked behind the building all their lights blasting.

Oh my God, she thought, we walked right into a police raid. Anna and Frankie Lee stood watching the policemen bringing out a white man and an older white woman. Both were wearing handcuffs. Next, a black man who looked to be in his late twenties came out in handcuffs, followed by three black and two white teenage girls. All were placed in a large police van. Red, white, and blue lights flashed everywhere.

Two ambulance drivers carried out a young girl on a stretcher. Anna walked up closer to see what was going on. The girl on the stretcher looked so young. She heard the doctor urge the attendants to hurry because they were losing her. Anna's hand went up against her mouth as she came face-to-face with the doctor from the hospital—the one who had refused to abort the baby she had begged him to get rid of. He sneered at Frankie Lee through clenched teeth as he shook his gray head in anger. "You were bringing her here for the same butchering that may cause the death of that thirteen-year old child. The only thing I hate is that we didn't wait long enough so that you two could have been arrested along with the others."

Anna shivered; so glad they had arrived too late to be a part of the raid. She stared at the doctor's back when he turned and followed the ambulance attendant to the flashing lights of the ambulance.

"Frankie Lee, what will we do now?" Anna asked, falling on the bed sobbing when they returned to her apartment.

"Don't worry. I'll thank of somethin'," he said. Anna noticed the frightened look on his face and feared all was lost for her.

Weeks turned into another month, and her stomach had grown so large that there was no doubt she carried a child. Not only was her stomach growing faster, the baby was kicking harder, making Anna more and more aware of its existence and its determined will to live. Eating very little did nothing to stop its growth. Her stomach grew as large as when she had carried her twins. She remembered the Old Head had her drink from the black cauldron and knew it had given her enough nourishment to last a year, just as she had nourished Raymond while he lay unconscious.

As time passed, Frankie Lee expressed his fear that aborting the baby now could possibly cost Anna her life—something he could not be a part of.

"It's too dangerous. Ya're gonna have to have it then give it away, Cous, that's all thare is to it. I can't help ya kill a livin' baby already kickin' inside ya. I just can't, Cous."

Sobbing, Anna turned from his pleading eyes, realizing there was nothing to do but wait it out. Kissing her cheek, he left. Trapped in the two-room apartment, she felt jailed in her own prison. Anna now realized the power of that pond had her imprisoned in a crisis she had no way of escaping except by death. There was no telling how extensive her loss might still be because of this baby she carried.

Anna drifted off to sleep thinking of the baby she carried. In the middle of a dream, she heard herself cry out as though the baby was coming. Drums could be heard beating in the distance. Long-skirted black women huddled close by looking on to witness the pending birth. Suddenly, her mother appeared and stared down at her just as the baby emerged.

"Ah, ah!" she screamed. "It's another white devil comin' into dis world. We must kill it." Anna heard herself scream out in horror as she saw her mother reach in to snatch the baby out of her body, the pearl-handled razor in her hand. Anna woke up in bed with beads of sweat pouring from her face as she snatched rapid breaths to calm her heartbeat.

When sleep overcame her again, she dreamed her stomach had grown so large that she could see nothing else. The baby kicked as she moved her hand over her enlarged body. Soon, there was another hand moving over it.

"Anna is this my baby you are carrying or is it that nigger's you just left?" Anna's fear intensified as she stared into Jake's face, seeing a look of anger on it. "Perhaps we should wait until it's born to see. If it is his, we'll send his bastard back to him. You already know I'm not one to take on another man's responsibility," he whispered, staring down at her. Anna felt her heart began to palpitate and sweat poured from her body as her fear mounted. "He might refuse to take it, Anna." Jake's sinister smile evoked terror in Anna's heart. "I have a better idea for his baby." Anna felt chills run down her spine as she watched him move from the bed beside her and walk into the tiny kitchen next to her bedroom. He returned carrying a large knife, causing her eyes to widen as she tried to leap from the bed as she remembered Dee reminding her of the young woman found in a ditch behead after been warned to stop dating a white man.

"I'm going to cut his bastard out of you right now, baby, so he'll have nothing to return for." When Jake drew back to push the knife inside of her, Anna woke up screaming.

Frankie Lee's job called him back to work weeks after Anna realized she would not be able to get the abortion she so desperately needed. Without his coming over to keep her company, the loneliness of the apartment sunk her into a deep depression. The child growing inside of her was now her only companion. Anna's tears came and went. A hollow emptiness filled her. What Jake might do to her no longer mattered anymore to Anna; bitterness took the place of the love she had once had for Raymond Forlorn.

"Daughter, even in the darkest night, the light of dawn awaits you."

Anna sat up in bed semi-alert as she listened to the voice of the Old Head she had not heard since before she discovered her pregnancy. It was the last voice she wanted to hear, feeling it was responsible for her tragic condition.

"Have you come to further destroy my life more than it already is, Old Head?" Anna asked bitterness in her voice.

"Why Daughter, now you have a child to share with the earth creature that once again mates with you as your husband. He mourned the loss of the embryo that escaped your body when you fell down the flight of stairs. He now has you and a child to replace the lost one. Go back to him so that the two of you can share the child you now carry."

Anna almost laughed at what the Old Head wanted her to do—it sounded so utterly ridiculous. Had she not realized the seriousness of the implication of what the Old Head had suggested, she might have seen the humor in it.

"Daughter, the form is the same. My eyes and I now understand strange forms are repulsive to the human mind. Your young will not be disfigured as the Young Chemist once was but will be a perfect human form for your earth mate and you to embrace as the human heart desires."

"Old Head, you still don't get it, do you? This white man's baby will not be a human form my husband or anyone in my family will want to embrace. This baby is by another man, as you well know. One that is white. How many times have I counseled you on matters of race, Old Head? Once my husband sees it, he will probably kill it and me," Anna sobbed thinking about the nightmare that had awakened her a few nights before. The eyes began to circle the room, causing her to somehow sense their thoughts.

"It must be as you say, Daughter. I do not understand your human morals."

"Old Head, you must send this baby back to the universe as you did the one before it. It is the only way I can return home to my family."

"I cannot send it back. Long before your conception, it was destined to enter this earth world. Its human form must become a part of your journey, Daughter, so that it can fulfill a part of your destiny that is still unfolding. When you drank the contents of the cauldron, you were preparing for its coming."

Anna began to sob as she gazed at the eyes darting back and forth around the pulsating brain. In them, she sensed her doom. The Old Head planned for her to have this baby, not understanding it would destroy her life. "No, I can't have it! I just cannot on this earth world, Old Head, have this white man's baby!"

"Daughter, on this journey of yours, its life will bring you back to that which has been lost to you. It will be no different than the form of the earth young you already have."

"Damn you! You and your thirteen eyes understand nothing about this earth world," Anna screamed getting up from the bed taking a seat in a chair as she, became even more frustrated with the Old Head. "You have done this to me, thinking in ways that will not work on this world of mine. It will not!" she screamed again as she rose from the chair where she was seated and threw it. Electric sparks flew around the room as the Old Head and its eyes began to shrink. When the chair bounced back at Anna, everything around her turned a bright orange as the eyes and the brain disappeared. She looked to see the Old Widow standing in the corner, hideous in its gruesome form. It reminded her of the nightmarish dream she had had while traveling down to Louisiana after her fight with Barb—seeing the outer world fall apart right before her eyes as she rode the spider's back. She knew that dream of her lying in the capsule whirling through that place of self-destruction meant something. She now lived in her own outer world, realizing there would be no dawn ever waiting to rescue her.

"Old Widow, I've destroyed the Old Head and its eyes. You must come poison my blood and end this horrible life of mine." The Old Widow flashed its light on Anna's swollen stomach. The baby kicked, and Anna began to cry.

Desperate in her desire to end her life in the days that followed, Anna allowed thoughts of suicide to enter her mind. As time went on, the thoughts became a plan. All she needed to do was to turn the oven on, suck in the fumes, and wait for death to overtake her. Or maybe she could hang herself as she had heard her mother say white folks used to do to coloreds. Could she do it to herself? The thought hung in the air. It came to her that chemicals would do it quick and painless—chemicals much the same as Ray had planned before she came and destroyed the chemicals he planned to use on himself. But who would get the needed chemicals? Frankie Lee would question her need for raw acid. She surely was not going out of the apartment in case someone who knew Frankie Lee might see her and tell Jake or her mother if either of them wandered down there looking for her.

Anna had never before contemplated taking her life, but now she felt she had no life. It had ended that day in the hospital as sure as if she had been struck by lightning.

"Daughter, you must learn to think not of your own life but of that life which will guide your destiny. It is the fulfilling of a promise that will soon be revealed to you."

In her heart, Anna thanked God that the Old Head and its eyes had not been harmed by her anger when she threw the chair. But she had no reason to want them back in her life. Enough had already been done to her.

"I thought I told you to go away, Old Head, and not inflict more damage to my life than you already have," she insisted, wanting no one around her.

"Daughter, you have faced much greater challenges and succeeded. Soon the young growing inside you, who you believe has your life in peril, will lead you to a place that will open a door that has been closed to you."

"To see what, Old Head? To see this baby born so everyone will know my sins? There is nothing and no one in this world who can make me want to keep it in me. It's going to die even if I must die with it. No one, do you hear me? Not even God himself, if there is a God. He does not give a damn about the fool I have made of myself." Anna laughed through her tears. "Didn't I tell you I never wanted to see you in my life again?" Her sobbing continued nonstop.

"Our coming has always brought you to a good end, Daughter."

"What good end Old Head? All I need is for that husband of mine to walk through the door and find me in this condition, or heaven forbid, my mother. That's the end you have brought me to. You have shattered my life, dragging me into this dream world you made for me and destroying any common sense I might have had." Anna turned away from the Old Head as her tears spilled down her face. "Fooling me into a relationship that you knew would end in disaster. It's over for me, can't you see that?" She turned back, looking up at the thirteen eyes, hating how they changed directions. The odd-looking brain pulsating inside of the magnetic field allowed Anna to sense its confusion.

"Go, Old Head—you and your thirteen eyes that see nothing. Like you, they are blind to the ways of this earth world. This baby will never be born into it—never! Even if I have to die with it. How many times do I have to tell you that?" Anna screamed. "Get out of my life! You have ruined it, do you hear me?" Anna felt her body knot up as she pulled her arms around herself. "If you think I am going to have this white man's baby and bring disgrace to myself and it, you have another thing coming. It will be born over my dead body. What will you do with it then Old Head?" Anna's laughter filled the room. "You knew all the time this baby was in me. You've known everything about my life from the moment you struck lightning into my teacher and me that day down in that lab." Anna stared up at the eyes staring down at her, hoping they sensed the hate she felt for them and herself.

"I've not had control of this life of mine since I was fourteen year old after my teacher opened that door and you killed him," Anna sobbed, falling to her knees. "My life has been controlled by you and god knows what else. Well it is over now. I'm going to be dead soon!" Anna closed her eyes, wanting to not ever again see that hideous supernatural force she felt had betrayed her.

****

When Anna finally allowed her eyes to open again, she found herself alone. Even the Old Widow had vanished. The baby kicked hard, causing her to realize she was not alone. Moving inside of her as if attempting to find a good resting place, the baby seemed to be telling her something. Anna touched her stomach as she began to talk to the baby.

"I want you to know that I don't blame you, baby," Anna said, touching her enlarged stomach. "It's not your fault that I was a stupid fool. I hate having to make you die along with me. It is not fair to you, but there is nothing else I can do. Please forgive me, but I know no other way out of this madness."

Hearing her front door open the next day, Anna rose. She knew it was Frankie Lee bringing her food supplies she had called and asked him to bring her. She heard him talking to her but paid little attention to his conversation.

"Ray . . . I mean, Frankie Lee, did you bring the razors like I asked? My legs are getting hairy and need shaving."

"I got them, Cous," he said, taking the food from the bags he had carried in. "I brought a safety razor and some blades for ya to insert. Don't want ya to hurt yerself. I heerd who ya just called me. Yer momma's thanking about dat daddy of yers, little man." Anna turned from the smile he gave her as he touched her enlarged stomach. He had told Anna that the baby would be born a boy when it became evident that an abortion was not possible.

"Frankie Lee, I need to get some rest. You go on home to Kate and your children now that you and she are back together again. I don't want her to think you are out cheating."

"Cous, all ya been doin is restin'. I tole ya to at least let me take ya out to the barn so ya can be aroun' other folks."

"Are you crazy, boy? I'm not taking this big body of mine nowhere until I get this baby out of it."

"Ya need anythang else? I know I haven't been 'round much lately, but by the time I git off work, I'm dog tired." Anna shook her head no. Frankie Lee rubbed her stomach and smiled as he walked out of the door.

Listening to the door shut behind her cousin, Anna took out the razor blades she had asked Frankie Lee to bring her. Taking a seat on the bed, she unwrapped one of the sharp blades. Contemplating how she would go about it, when suddenly the voice of Julia Mike Raymond's cousin spoke to her as though she stood in the room with her: 'Damn you, Ms. Anna! You should never say never! I'm old enough to be your mother, and I know from experience that you have just made a damnable statement. One day you'll learn that never means until death, and some of the cruel twists of life can make even you break if the pressures are strong enough.' When the voice could no longer be heard, the baby kicked.

"Goddamn it, white woman, I am broken," she hissed as the blade came down, slicing into one wrist then the other. Her eyes became fixated on the blood flowing from them. Suddenly, the door opened again and Frankie Lee stood there.

"Any more of your stash left, Cous?" he asked. Anna quickly hid her wrists under the towel she was holding, but it soon became saturated with blood.

"Did ya hurt yerself?"

"It's nothing, Frankie Lee. Go on home. I can take care of it," Anna replied, placing her hand under her bed sheet in an attempt to hide the blood. He walked toward her with a look of shock on his face. She pulled her sleeves down, but he pushed them back up.

"Frankie Lee, I will be all right. Now go. You'll be late getting home and Kate will worry about you." He pulled the bloodstained towel away. Blood gushed from her wrists. She saw him staring over at the bloody razor lying on the bed next to her.

"Frankie Lee, leave me alone!" she screamed, trying to push him away. "This is a hell I can no longer endure. It is my only way out. When they find me, you can pretend you didn't know I was still here," she pleaded as he tore part of a sheet to tie her wrists to stop the bleeding.

Somewhere in the distance she could hear him begging her not to die on him—that there had to be another way out without killing herself.

"You can't stop me from dying—if not this time, there'll be another!" she screamed as they took her out on a stretcher and placed her into an ambulance. As she continued to scream, she realized Frankie Lee had somehow called for an ambulance, but she thought one must have been waiting around the corner.

Chapter Sixteen

—✺—

Anna lost so much blood that she had to have a transfusion to save her life. The child in her kicked as hard as ever under the pressing hand of the old black doctor who was humming some spiritual hymn that made her think of what she had done and how he planned to stop her.

"Mrs. Bradley, you are a very determined woman. I can see that now, but as I told you before, this little fellow is as determined to be born as you are to kill it and yourself, it seems." Anna turned away from the doctor, but that did not stop him from adding, "That alone tells me God is in the plan somehow and He is going to work it out for this baby to be born with or without your help, young lady. With me giving him a little help, we're going to try and see that he succeeds." Humming louder, he pressed her abdomen again, causing the baby to kick hard and swift. Anna never looked his way.

After the doctor left, she turned as Frankie Lee entered the room. He sank down in the chair next to her bed, his head down.

"Anna, thangs is gittin' pretty bad. Jake and Aunt Annabelle are gonna blame me for everthang if ya kill yerself like ya are tryin' to do. Shit, Jake—ya know he's gonna know I deliberately lied to him." Lying there listening to her cousin, Anna realized she was getting him in more trouble than he deserved trying to help her do something that would cause Jake and her mother to want to hurt him if she turned up dead there in Oinston. "Cous, ya ain't thanking straight. I need ya to come out of this thang alive for both our sakes, not to mention dat poor little baby dat can't be blamed for nothin' dat's happenin' to ya." Anna felt tears seep from the corners of her eyes as she felt the baby kick again. "Ole' doc is talkin' 'bout puttin' ya away. Down hare dat means with every crazy nut in the state. Ya'd be tied down til dat baby comes. He says for them to do that means I gotta contact Jake 'cause he's technically your next of kin. He knows the Old

Man, and if he has to, he will call him in. I sho' nuff don't need dat kinda heat!" Anna heard him sigh deeply as she felt his hands squeeze hers. "Jake is gonna be mad as hell."

Anna watched him scoot further down in the chair he was seated in. "He might wanta to do somethin' crazy, and I don't wanna git hurt . . . sho' hate to hurt him, but I couldn't blame him 'cause if it was my wife I would feel 'bout the same. If ya don't come 'round soon, I'm gonna be catchin' hell from all sides when all I was tryin to do was help ya the best way I knowd how." Laying his head in her hand, Anna heard him say to himself. "Damn ya, Frankie Lee, thangs is reilly a mess now, and man, it's all yer fault." His tears wet the hand that held his head. She moved her hand over his cheek as tears fell from her eyes.

"Frankie Lee, I really fucked up my life, didn't I?"

"No, but ya sure as hell is tryin' to, Cous," he answered, shaking his head as his wet eyes stared over at her.

****

Anna gave the doctor all the signs that she had recovered from her mental depression. She was released to Frankie Lee's care and advised she was not to be left alone for long periods of time. The doctor believed her depression would return, and there could be a repeated attempt of suicide with no one to stop her. Anna listened to Frankie Lee assure the doctor he would see to it that she was never left by herself again.

Anna still believed her life was a total loss, but she knew it was wrong for her to include her cousin in her problems. As he had stated, all he had tried to do was help her the best way he knew how. She would have to go away somewhere and do this thing—whatever it was she felt driven to do—all alone because there was no one she could talk to who would understand the pain of what she was going through. Her anger at the Old Head and Raymond for what she felt they had done to destroy her life filled her every thought. The sight of the Old Widow with its back pulsating hanging at the top of the door as they walked out of the hospital, caused Anna to pause, wondering what new disaster awaited her.

She noticed as they drove back to the apartment where she had lived the last two months that nothing looked familiar. Red dust flew everywhere on this country dirt road they were traveling. Frankie Lee twisted and turned the car in so many directions she could not tell where they would end up back in those woods. It seemed as though they were traveling back into the swamps. No one would ever be able to find a way out of this maze, she thought to herself.

"Where are we going, Frankie Lee?" she asked, a frown forming on her brows.

"I'm takin ya to whare ya will be safe, Cous."

"Safe from what? What are you talking about, Frankie Lee?" Her mind went back to the Old Widow hanging at the door. She knew something was amiss—something terrible.

"Anna, ya know I love ya and dat anythang I do for ya it's 'cause I b'lieve it's the best thang for ya."

"Where are you taking me, Frankie Lee?" Anna asked staring over at him as the car bumped along the dirt road. She saw him looking down at her bandaged wrists and knew something serious was up.

"I'm not takin' ya back to dat apartment. I'd be damn scared to death ya would try killin' yerself agin. And dis time, ya probably would succeed." Anna opened her mouth, but he raised his hand to halt her protest.

"No, Cous, I know better . . . the same as ya. Yer neighbor tole me how she come knockin' on yer door times she heard ya screamin', thankin' somethin was the matter." Anna frowned, remembering her next-door neighbor had come asking if there was something wrong. Without opening her door, she had said that she was fine and needed no help.

"Ya need someone stronger and wiser than me, Cous, to protect ya from yerself. The person I am taking ya to is the only one I b'lieve can help ya."

"Did you tell Kate what happened and she has you taking me to someone she knows?"

"No Kate don't know nothing. She thanks ya gone back. The person I'm taking you to is, the same person Aunt Annabelle brung ya to yeers ago when she had to hide ya from the law dat was lookin' to take ya away."

"What are you talking about, Frankie Lee?" Anna asked, feeling her pulsating palm vibrating under her bandaged wrist.

"Ya 'member when Uncle Jeff went to prison?"

"Do I have to be reminded of that?" Anna asked, blinking back tears.

"Aunt Annabelle called the Old Man just 'fore she come down with ya. She tole him she needed to talk to Granny, insistin' it was a matter of life and death. 'Course when he told me I was shocked. I had to take a seat 'cause I knowd she had never forgave Granny for not killin' Grandpa Porter and comin' back to hur and my daddy. Granny knowd how Aunt Annabelle felt about hur and came just to see if the Old Man was talkin' out of his head. I sat thare as shocked when Aunt Annabelle walked in the house with ya. We all looked at hur and I was thankin' somethin' awful bad had to have happened to make this miracle come about. Both of ya looked like somethin' bad had happened. She tole Granny dat some white chilen at the school ya attended was fightin' ya. Dat everday ya come home with yer clothes torn. One day she said she gave ya a stick to fight back 'cause thare was so many. Now the white folks was after ya, sayin' ya hurt some of 'em. Dat she and Uncle Jeff had refused to tell 'em whare ya was. She needed a place to hide ya so ya couldn't be found. Granny just sat thare lookin at hur, still in shock like me and the Old Man, I spose. When Granny didn't respond Aunt Annabelle fell on her knees, telling Granny ya was the only chile she had and it would kill hur to see those white devils harm ya. Granny asked what yer name was. Aunt Annabelle tole hur it was Anna—dat she named ya after hur daddy's momma."

"What! Frankie Lee, I'm named after Momma. Who are all these people you are telling me about? Momma never told me anything like what you are saying!"

"At the time, Cous, I reckon Aunt Annabelle was desperate 'cause she tole Granny she would pay hur all the money she had. She didn't want to lose ya like she had lost everythang else in hur life. Granny looked at her cryin' like it was the end of the world for hur. Turning to you, Granny smiled, sayin' she would be takin' ya to a safe place til yer Momma could back for ya. The Old Man and I sat thare with our mouths hung open. 'Course, the Old Man couldn't keep ya in Oinston. The law would've found ya thare." Anna shook her head, still not understanding anything her cousin was telling her.

"When Aunt Annabelle started for the door to leave, ya jumped up callin' hur. She came back and hugged ya. Ya asked her for the cream for yer back. Aunt Annabelle got a strange look on hur face and then took a small jar from hur purse and pushed it into yur hands then left.

"Anna ya turned to me like ya was my little sister—fell in my arms cryin' dat ya had destroyed yer momma and daddy's life. I tole ya everythang was gonna to be alright and asked ya what happened. Ya tole me 'bout the white school yer daddy put ya in and how yer momma hated ya bein' thare. Ya showed me dat cream and had me look at yer back. Ya explained dat ya had gotten too friendly with one of the white kids and Aunt Annabelle had beat ya good. The Old Man and Granny just sat starin' with me at the switch marks. Thay looked healed, but ya could still see the long scratch marks down yer back. The cream must have been workin' 'cause thay had started to fade away. Is it true what ya tole me 'bout breakin' a white kid's glasses and makin' all them kids mad?"

Anna listened to her cousin's summary of her life after her mother beat her and the bus incident something she never remembered telling him.

"After that, ya and the white kids come to be enemies. Ya said Aunt Annabelle seemed happy because finally all she had tole you 'bout how thay would treat ya come true. Ya tole me in the back of the old man's car on the way to Granny's house dat thare was fights ever day on the bus comin' home. Tole me how it was 'fore Aunt Annabelle give ya that stick as an equalizer 'cause thare was so many and ya was by yerself. Anna listened to him tell her more about her life she never remembered sharing with him.

"Momma never told me anyone other than Uncle Jessie took care of me. Was it out there at that place where I lost my memory?"

"Most likely, Cous. 'Cause the next time Uncle Jeff and Aunt Annabelle brung ya down, ya never mentioned ever livin' with Granny. Fact be tole, ya never acted like ya had been livin' anywhare but with the Old Man and me. Aunt Annabelle swore us to secrecy after tellin' us bout yer lost memory. She didn't want ya or Uncle Jeff to know 'bout Granny."

"You are telling me I have a living grandmother, Frankie Lee? Why haven't you mentioned her before now? I don't remember staying with anyone but you and Uncle Jessie." Anna began to panic. "You're straight-up lying, Frankie Lee! You are taking me to some state hospital, aren't you?" A thousand questions crowded Anna's mind. He was giving her too much information at once, information she did not understand. "I don't want to stay with anyone, especially someone I don't even know or remember anything about. And if you are taking me to a state mental institution, I will find a way out and kill myself and this baby anyway, so you might as well take me back to that damn apartment you set me up in." Anna stared at Frankie Lee as he continued to take them deeper into the woods.

"Like I tole ya, the reason I never said anythang about hur is 'cause Aunt Annabelle begged me and the Old Man not to ever mention hur to ya. She always hated Grandpa Porter for killin' hur daddy. Dat's why the Old Man and me was shocked when she called him to git in touch with Granny."

"None of what you are telling me makes any sense."

"Thare's a lot Aunt Annabelle missed tellin' ya 'bout, Cous. Thangs I would not be talking to ya 'bout 'cept the guilt eating away in ya for bein' with the white dude forced my hand when ya tricked me into brangin' ya those blades when ya knowd what yer real intantions was."

"I didn't trick you, Frankie Lee," Anna countered, closing her eyes while trying hard not to think about what she had almost succeeded in doing. "Now—Grandpa Porter—who the hell is he?" Anna asked, noticing that Frankie Lee was become evasive in answering her questions.

"He is the white man who took our grandmother after killin' our grandfather. He kept her nearly forty years, gurl. I know Aunt Annabelle tole ya dat." Hearing him speak of the white man who had taken her mother's mother caused a picture of Ray to enter her mind. She had promised herself never to think of him again. It was a promise she had not been able to keep. He had been on her mind every second since she discovered her pregnancy. How could he not? It was his baby growing inside her body.

"Who is this person? And why are you calling him grandpa if he killed our black grandfather?" Anna asked again, frightened that Frankie Lee was taking her to some kind of institution but was not telling her.

"'Cause dat's what I was taught to call him since I was a little kid, Anna. Dat's all I knowd of him 'fore I got grown and the Old Man tole me what reilly went down.

"My God, I'm all twisted up inside. I don't know what to believe anymore."

"Anna, Granny is our grandmother—yers and mine. It was the only way ole doc would 'llow ya to leave the hospital. She had to come tell him she would take ya into hur home as long as ya needed to stay."

"Are you telling me the truth, Frankie Lee, or is this some kind of trick you are playing on me to take me somewhere I don't want to go?" Anna asked, staring over at him as though he were telling her something that certainly was not funny. "Both Daddy's parents are dead, and Momma already told me her mother is dead—and we both know her and Uncle Jessie's father was killed, Frankie Lee," Anna said with fear in her voice. "Tell me, Frankie Lee, who this person really is or I'm getting out of this car!" Anna threatened with her hand on the handle of the car door.

"Anna, ya looked at hur every time ya went into yer bedroom at the Old Man's house."

"I looked at her? Where did I look at her?"

"Her picture is on the wall in the room whare you been sleepin'. 'Course it's a picture of when she was young, but it's our grandmother, Mabel Porter."

"Who the hell is Mabel Porter? I have never heard that name before. Damn you, Frankie Lee, if she exists, you would have told me before now. That picture in Uncle Jessie's bedroom is of Momma," Anna replied, searching her mind for the face that would connect with the name Mabel Porter. Frankie Lee was drawing her into a part of her mother's past she had never heard before. Looking back, it seemed strange that her mother had never told her the name of her own mother.

"No, Anna—that's Aunt Annabelle's mother ya was lookin' at. Aunt Annabelle begged us not to tell ya nothin' 'bout our grandmother or what happened when ya stayed down hare with hur, 'specially not about Granny's part in yer life. She was not tellin' ya the truth when she tole ya hur mother was dead. I know she did it 'cause of hur hatred for Granny, but our grandmother is very much alive. She's probly the only person who could possibly know and understand what ya goin' through now 'cause her life has been no picnic.

"Harold Porter was the white man who took hur after killin our grandfather, Jessie Bailey. Ya already know yer Momma's last name was Bailey 'fore she married Uncle Jeff. Granny and Mr. Porter been together over forty yeers. After the birth of their four chilen, she married him to give them legal rights to his name and estate. He died five yeers ago, leavin' hur a home and a farm. She's Aunt Annabelle's and the Old Man's mother, Anna, and dat's the gospel truth." Anna held her temples, listening in shock as her cousin informed her of the grandmother she thought had died long ago.

Frankie Lee had known of her all this time, and she had never once thought to ask him about her. The place her mother had taken her—she did not remember it at all, and her mother had never mentioned it.

"Frankie Lee, I don't believe you. Where the hell are you taking me?" Anna asked her hand once again on the handle of the car door. She could not make herself believe her mother would not have told her she had a living grandmother—her own mother's mother. How was it possible? How could her mother keep something that important from both her husband and her daughter?

"Why ya thank Aunt Annabelle never mentioned who ya stayed with? Never talked about what happened to ya down hare dat caused ya to lose yer memory? It was 'cause she and Granny fell out about somethin' dat happened to ya while ya lived with Granny. "Frankie Lee, why would Momma be angry with this grandmother you say we have when she helped her out by taking me in, a woman I don't even remember?"

"Ya just don't know nothin' and ain't no use in me tryin' to tell ya when ya're not receivin' it, gurl!"

"Tell me what, Frankie Lee? What, godamnit am I not receiving!"

"No sense in me tellin' ya somethin' ya ain't gonna b'lieve no how."

"Oh my God, Frankie Lee! This is too much . . . too much! First that damn doctor tells me I'm carrying a baby I thought did not exist, and now you are telling me I have a living grandmother I thought was dead. A grandmother who fell out with my mother because of what happened to me while living with her something I don't even remember. It's too much, Frankie Lee! I am about to lose my mind." Her cousin slowed the car to a stop, turning to face Anna.

"Yer Momma never mentioned Granny's name since I've known hur 'cept when she brung ya to stay with Granny. It was as if she didn't have a momma, Cous. The Old Man says Aunt Annabelle never forgave hur for livin' with the white man. Said one day 'fore she left for good, him and hur come upon Granny comin' out of the dry goods store. He grabbed Granny and hugged her, callin' to Aunt Annabelle that she was their mother. He said she kept walkin' and tole him later her mother was in hell. He warned her then that she might need her mother one day, but she tole him 'Not livin' on this earth she won't need a white man's whore.' If it wasn't for what happened to ya with the law, she wouldn't have threw spit Granny's way if it would save hur life, gurl.

We knew Aunt Annabelle had to be desperate when she asked the Old Man to ask Granny to come see hur 'bout taking care of ya. Tellin' him of the white folks who was lookin' to hurt ya. Aunt Annabelle came back several times while you was down hare, but ya and I thought she was a white woman. The Old Man would go get ya and brang ya to see hur, but ya acted as if ya didn't know hur. Nobody couldn't blame ya cause she looked nothin' like she looks now. I don't thank Aunt Annabelle ever wanted ya to know dat she passed for white or dat hur mother still lived." Anna knew if her father had not already told her about her mother passing for white, she would have fainted right there in the car. It suddenly came to her how her mother quizzed her about getting her memory back.

"'Yer daddy done tole me ya got yer memory back, gal,' she remembered her saying. And Anna had answered, "Yes, Momma, I remember how you tried to beat me to death for touching a white boy's lips." Anna remembered the frown that had crested her mother's brows as she had turned away from her. Anna had continued, "Not to mention that stick filled with nails that caused me to hurt those children on the bus, Momma."

"'I never regretted the pain I caused those white devils,' she had hissed, turning back to face her, "'but it was the hurt I caused ya and your Daddy that grieved my heart somethin' awful. I thought he was lost to me forever and ya as well," she had shared, pausing in mid-sentence. "'What else ya 'member, gal?'

"Wasn't living up in Kay, Massachusetts, attending that white school enough, Momma?" Suddenly, her mother had started crying—something Anna had never seen her do in her life. Anna knew she had touched something horrible in her to get that reaction. She had rushed over, taking her mother in her arms and holding her trembling body against hers.

"Momma, it's over and I'm well now. Let's not dwell on that part of my life any longer." She had heard a deep sigh escape her mother's lips and the conversation had ended with her mother never divulging that she had a mother living or that Anna had lived with her grandmother while her father was in prison. All this time she had thought her memory had completely returned. Now she sat listening to her cousin tell her about a grandmother her mother never told her of. Neither she nor her father knew the woman lived. Her life was turning so many corners Anna did not know whether to laugh or cry.

"Cous, nobody knows better'n Granny how much Aunt Annabelle hates and despises hur, 'specially Grandpa Porter. But I guess lookin' at hur grandchile sittin' thare cryin' as hard as hur Momma, Granny couldn't say no after bein' tole white folks was wanta harm ya. Even livin' with a white man, she knew what dat meant," Frankie Lee explained to Anna that their grandmother lived with the white man, having his children because she couldn't leave. Where would she go that he couldn't find her? They had been together longer than he could remember. Back then, down in the South, there was no place to run from a white man wanting his way with a colored woman. "Even today, he explained, in some parts of the South it's still that way." Anna closed her eyes, cringing at the thought of what her grandmother's life must have been like. Frankie Lee further explained that his father had told him Annabelle never forgave their mother for not killing the white man and coming back home to them, not thinking about how the white southern people would have burned Granny in the electric chair for killing a white man no matter what he had done to her. Anna reflected back on Raymond and the night she had stabbed him. If he had died, she probably would be waiting on death row herself.

Frankie Lee told her how the Old Man told him that he had had to keep it a secret that he found out where Grandpa Porter kept Granny. Annabelle would not work in white folks' homes. The three of them were starving, but if his sister and his daddy's momma had known that the food and money he brought home had come from the white man who had killed their father and son, they would have starved to death rather than accept it. It was the Old Man who kept them living by working for Harold Porter.

"My father and your mother's daddy's grandmother is who ya named after, gurl," he shared, continuing to give Anna details of her mother's life.

"Momma and Uncle Jessie's father must be who Uncle Jessie is named after then."

"Sho' is." Frankie Lee shared and that his father had only been six and not home at the time his father and grandfather was murdered, so he never saw the horror of his father's death like Aunt Annabelle had. He managed to get over it, especially since he had to find a way to keep them from starving to death. His father, he told Anna was only ten at the time, two years younger than Annabelle, when Granny found him on the streets bare-footed with no shirt to speak of hangin' off of him. All those years they lived from pillow to post, taking handouts from other black families that knew his grandmother was unable to work."

Anna listened to Frankie Lee share that after Granny and Mr. Porter found his father out begging for food, Mr. Porter would wait for him at the edge of the woods to take him to his farm where he would work for him, taking food and the money he earned back to his sister and grandmother. Frankie Lee admitted learning this after he was a man himself and his father took to telling him how life was for him as a boy coming up with a grandmother and older sister to care for. Anna stared at Frankie Lee in disbelief. But seeing his tears, Anna knew he was speaking from his heart.

She asked no more questions and soon he drove them up into a country farmyard. Chickens and ducks flew everywhere. Corn stood growing in a garden off from other vegetables Anna had no name for. A large black and white house stood in the middle of the yard. Two brown and white terriers ran back and forth, barking at the car. Gazing out of the window, Anna remembered her time in Kentucky and knew she had stepped back in time. Beautiful potted flowers adored the edge of the porch where an older woman stood.

Her cousin was introducing her to a part of her mother's past she was unprepared to enter. Frankie Lee stopped the car and turned to her. "Anna I thank ya thought she was Aunt Annabelle 'cause ya always called hur Momma like the rest of hur kids did at dat time. She and Aunt Annabelle do favor a lot. She looked more like yer Momma looks now— 'fore she begin passing for white dat yeer Uncle Jeff was in prison." Stunned, Anna was unable to move. When Frankie Lee got out and opened the door for her, she sat there trying her best to digest all he had told her.

"Anna, yer grandma is standing on that porch up thare waiting to meet hur granddaughter agin after all dese yeers. I hope ya wouldn't want me to take ya away without even sayin' hello to hur." Looking at the woman standing on the porch of the house in front of them, Anna squeezed back tears as she slowly made her way out of the car. Following behind Frankie Lee, she stopped in the middle of the yard, looking at a large black round belly pot standing off to the side. Smoke curled out of it, and it came to her that she was entering a time zone unknown to her just as she had when she had entered Raymond's ranch in Kentucky. Time zones that reminded her of her trips to the land of the Healing Tree; the same feeling of awe swept over her.

They neared the porch where the older woman, small in stature and not quite as tall as her mother but with striking similarities of facial features stood staring at them. Even their hair color gave away the genes that made them mother and daughter; just like her mother's, the woman's hair lay rolled in a bun tucked neatly under a hairnet. Anna's heart quickened, thinking how much she reminded her of her mother. A pleated apron covered a floor-length brown dress with deep pockets. Though she hardly looked it, Anna believed she had to be in her seventies from what little history she had heard from her mother. She watched Mabel Porter's small hands move out of her pockets as she looked at Anna with light hazel catlike eyes so much like her mother's it caused Anna to quiver. Seeing the handkerchief in her grandmother's hand as she dabbed tears from her eyes, Anna felt her knees go weak.

"Hello, Granny," Frankie Lee called out as he rushed up onto the porch, hugging and kissing the older woman as she reached out to him. Anna felt like sinking into the ground having to meet her grandmother in her condition. Tears streamed down her face but she slowly made her way up the walk and onto the porch to stand before her. The fullness of her body clearly showed a baby was growing inside of it. She looked at the woman Frankie Lee said had cared for her after the nightmare on the bus in Kay, Massachusetts. Except that her skin tone was slightly darker and she was older, it was like standing before her own mother. Yes, she was truly her mother's mother—the likeness was uncanny. The woman her cousin called Granny reached out her hands as tears fell from her eyes the same as Anna's. Anna's body trembled as she moved into her outstretched arms, weeping as she clung to her, trying to find in her memory this grandmother who might have been lost to her forever had it not been for this baby she carried.

My chile's baby done come back to Granny, were the first words she heard her grandmother speak. They walked into Granny's home; taking the seats she offered them at her kitchen table, something her mother would have done to someone dear to her. Anna inhaled a lemony smell that filled the quaint house with its fragrance. Yes, she thought to herself, she had indeed stepped back into a distant era of her own people. Even the old-fashioned handmade furniture spoke of the past.

"Anna, I have explained to Granny how thangs went down for ya and Jake, and how ya came to be with yer baby's daddy. She understands yer situation but not why ya thought ya had to do what ya did." Her tears still falling, Anna looked at her grandmother as she listened to Frankie Lee, still trying to place Granny in her mind. Looking around her, the furniture reminded her of some of the old furniture her mother kept that she said had belonged to Anna's great-grandmother on her father's side of the family. Pictures of unknown people covered the walls. An oil lamp next to her reminded her of the antique shops in Las Vegas she had gone to with Momma Lucy. Listening to Frankie Lee, she watched to see if her grandmother really understood what he wanted of her.

"For now it's best Anna stay hare with ya til the baby comes. Adder dat, we can figure out what to do with it. I will go and get hur stuff from the apartment while the two of ya gits reacquainted," he said as he rose to leave.

"No, Frankie Lee!" Anna cried, attempting to get up from where she sat. "You are not going to pawn me off on her. She doesn't need me as a burden," Anna sobbed, hating that she had not succeeded in her suicide attempt. Now she sat there humiliated in front of this woman she did not even remember. Her grandmother came quickly to her side. Pulling a chair up beside her, she took Anna's hands in hers and kissed them.

"Sometimes chile, God is blessing ya, and ya don't even know it," Anna listened to her grandmother say as tears streamed from her eyes. "He done brung my baby's chile back home to me—somethin' I been prayin' for a long time. Not to leave this world with my grandchile-thanking Granny would do somethin' to harm hur. Granny ain't got much, but she got love if ya want some. Don't go 'cause ya thank ya gonna be a burden on me. I need the company out hare all alone in dese old woods," she whispered barely audibly, kissing Anna's hands again as her hand moved across her swollen stomach. "I now got de chile of dat gal of mine hare 'bout to have me another great-grandbaby soon. I got to git ready for God's blessing," she said as she reached over to kiss Anna's swollen stomach, causing the baby to move around slowly as if welcoming the embrace.

"Look at dat—it knows Granny a'ready."

"I don't want you to get too happy about this baby," Anna said through tears. "Since I couldn't kill it or myself, I'm going to give it away to anyone who wants it as soon as it is born." Anna noticed a frown gathering in Granny's brows that suddenly disappeared. She smiled.

"Chile, God gonna do what's right by ya and dis blessin' what's comin'. First Granny gotta know, Daughter. Please tell dis old woman," she said, staring at Anna who sat startled as she heard Granny address her in the same fashion as the Old Head. She waited for Granny to tell her what she meant.

"Surely ya wouldn't put misery in dis old heart 'f mine finding ya done kilted yerself while hare with me, would ya?" Granny asked, never taking her eyes from Anna's. Again Anna felt embarrassed that she had to face that question from her own grandmother who, like her mother, got right to the point.

"No, Granny, I would never dishonor your home by killing myself here." Anna paused as she looked at Frankie Lee who took a deep breath then smiled.

As if in deep thought as she gestured with outstretched hands, Anna concluded, "It seems I will be having this baby here with you no matter what my prior plans were." Anna could see that it pleased not only Frankie Lee but her grandmother by the smile spreading across her lips.

"Let Granny stop all dis foolish cryin'. There's dinner waitin' hare for ya two—now come let me fix some plates, chile." Her small hands touched Anna's full stomach.

"Why that youngun must be starvin' . . . ya look so thin and frail. Granny railly gonna fatten ya up while ya hare, chile." Anna had not planned to eat much, but she found herself eating the greens, yams, ham hocks, and potato pie with relish.

As Frankie Lee prepared to leave, Granny caught his hand. "Thank ya, boy, for brangin' yer Granny hur chile's baby back. Ya don't stop comin' roun', ya hare me, boy?" Anna caught the gleam of her gold eyetooth as she smiled at him.

"Now Granny, ya know I gotta come by and check on two of my three best ladies." Anna watched Granny's thin fingers slide down his face. As her tears started again, she shooed him away and reached pulling out the handkerchief in her pocket.

After Frankie Lee left, Granny showed Anna what would be her bedroom. A pretty pink flowered spread lay on top of a queen size bed in the small bedroom. Two handmade white chest of drawers stood on either side of the bed polished and varnished with wooden knobs to open and close the drawers. Two handmade nightstands painted white stood on the either side the one on the right with a clock that stood on three legs. The tan linoleum floor was covered with a long, wide, white rug. Anna sank down on the firm bed. She suddenly felt exhausted.

"Dis room b'longed to my gurls, 'course thay both grown and up North now. Come home once a yeer to see 'bout Granny. Both so near-white a soul wouldn't know thare's a lick 'f black blood in 'em. Neither of 'em gals I had by Mr. Porter ain't had not one single chile. Maybe thay thank Granny's black blood will show through." She shook her head as she removed Anna's shoes, leaving to bring back a pan of water for Anna to soak her feet in. The ointment Granny applied to her legs and feet had the same lemony scent she had smelled when she first entered the house feeling the soothing effect of it, Anna didn't know what to say to her, or how she, should thank her, or if she should even be there. Nothing came to her until her grandmother lifted her head and stared at her with those same catlike eyes her mother always looked at her with. But her eyes were soft and had a gentle look in them. "Sometimes chile, the Lord blesses us and we don't even know it's comin'. God sho' done sent a blessin' my way I didn't know was comin'." She smiled, and Anna was relieved to know her grandmother believed her coming had been a blessing to her.

"It seems this baby will be born no matter what my former plans for it were," Anna responded, feeling tears slide down her cheeks as she hugged her grandmother. "Thank you for loving me enough to want me and this baby that's bound to be born." Granny continued to smile as she stooped down to dry Anna's feet.

When Frankie Lee came later with her luggage and the attaché case tucked under his arm, Anna noticed his grin as Granny and she wrapped their arms around each other. He sat her luggage in the room that Granny had offered her. Last of all, he gave her the attaché case when they were alone in the room that would be hers. Opening the case, Anna counted out twenty thousand dollars and gave it to Frankie Lee. He stopped her, saying, "No Anna, ya done give me enough. Ya got a kid comin' . . . ya gonna need ever cent. I can't take it. It may be all his daddy'll ever give him." Placing her arms around her cousin, Anna found herself crying again.

"Damn you, Frankie Lee! When I thought nothing could save me, you saved my life and this baby's by bringing me here. You always told me it is blood that counts and that one must always take care of their own. The things you have done for me no one else would have placed their lives on the line to do. The things you put up with when just the wrong word could have sent me over the edge never came from your lips to hurt me. When I needed you, you were there for me every step of the way even when I foolishly endangered your life. If you won't accept it from me, accept it from this baby who's bound to live no matter what I do to stop it." Tightening her grip on his hand, she placed the money in his pocket. Then she exclaimed, "Oh Frankie Lee, she is such a beautiful person. If only Momma were willing to see that. Using her only when she needed her and then discarding her was awful. All these wasted years we could have all been together. I love her already."

"That old lady done been though hur own hell in her lifetime, Cous. If ya will ever learn anythang, it will come from hur. Don't judge hur too harsh—she has suffered a thousand times worse'n either of us, no matter what we been through. And to thank ya would never have met hur if ya hadn't found out ya was pregnant with dat white man's baby." Anna shook her head, thinking back to her grandmother's words: "Sometimes the Lord is blessing ya and ya don't even know it." The Old Head knew all along what was coming—telling her that the dawn awaited her. She now had to admit that in her darkest night, dawn had come.

Chapter Seventeen

There were no artificial lights outside her bedroom window Anna discovered her first night in her grandmother's home. The sound of insects was her only clue that life existed; everything else remained as silent as a graveyard. Looking out of the window beside her bed, she gazed out at stars piercing holes in a black sky. The baby flowed around in her body, seemingly content as though it felt safe now. For the first time, it didn't kick but moved as though swimming inside of her. It reminded her of her time in the apartment when Ray lay unconscious.

Looking out from the twenty-third floor, Anna had used his binoculars to look up at the black sky where billions of stars glittered like diamonds, just as they glittered in the dark from the bedroom window of her grandmother's home as she lay looking outside. She tried to imagine what shocker would occur next. From her office at the shelter to Barb's apartment, her life had changed taking her into many different directions.

The supernatural forces controlling her life had her standing in the apartment of a man she had known only in her dreams as a boy—a man who could suddenly wake up and ask why she was there. Somehow, just as she had known back then that those strange forces would protect her, she felt no fear now. She had stayed and cared for him until his eyes opened and a smile lit up his face, letting her know he, too, was a part of this mysterious journey of hers and had been a part of it through dreams for nine years of her lost memory. This baby moving inside of her brought her face-to-face with the reality of this continuing mysterious journey. It was a journey that had brought her to her grandmother.

Did these supernatural forces have her living a dream, she wondered as she found herself continuing the journey that had opened the door to another part of her lost past. She knew her mother would be devastated to learn she now lived with her grandmother, a woman she hated. Still she did not understand the reason behind it all.

What a joke her mother had played on not only her but also her father, hiding the knowledge that her mother was alive—a woman she had asked to care for Anna while she posed as white during Anna's father's incarceration. It was for sure a way to prevent the authorities from looking for her. As dark as I am, Anna thought to herself, no one in this country would have guessed a white woman had birthed me.

All that time, Annabelle had kept her living mother a secret. But why, after she came begging her to give refuge to her child? Remembering the winding, twisting roads they had traveled to get there, her mother had to have known no one would find her up in those woods. She wondered what had happened to make her mother's hatred of her mother resurface and again turn her against her grandmother.

The baby began to move through her body, causing her to think of it swimming around in her. The last time she had swum was with the Madame during her stay with her. Anna soon found herself soaking up the mist of the rainforest while her nostrils inhaled the sweet fragrance of lavender. High above her, the Old Head and its thirteen eyes surrounded her with their presence. Somehow she knew this dream she was living was apart of some mysterious quest she must embark upon.

The Old Head pulsating inside the magnetic blue ring could hardly be seen it was so encased in the blue light surrounding the thirteen eyes whirling around it. There appeared to be no harm done from the chair she had thrown at it. Anna knew she had also said some hurtful things to it. She lowered her head to look at the wounds she had cut into her wrists when suddenly she found herself thrown into the outer world, falling down into one of its deep crevasses. Sounds of growling beasts caused her to shiver as she remembered the creatures imprisoned there. Anna wanted to cry out to the Old Head for help, but her memory of their last encounter caused her to resolve herself to the fate before her.

"Daughter, let us look back into the past when you pleaded time and time again for the life of the Young Chemist to be saved, disavowing all my warnings of what would follow. Yet, you feel I and my eyes are responsible for your outcome."

Anna deep inside the black hole listened to the voice of the Old Head she could no longer see.

"Help me and my eyes see what you say we can not see. We are always confused by your meanings. They are so different from what you tell us you want. You say we are blind. Help us so that we may see what you see."

Her mind expanded and guided by the eyes of the Old Head, Anna heard herself gasp. She could see the Old Widow hurrying toward the blood dripping from Raymond's wound. "Nooo!" she heard herself scream, catching its leg. Its energy pulled her into a dark place where her voice sounded like a thousand echoes. "Old Head, have you forgotten it was your eye and the tears from the Healing Tree that gave him back his life? My heart still connects to his. If he dies, I must die also. I want him to live. My love is in his heart as his is in mine." Anna's heart filled with sadness, remembering how she had beseeched the Old Head for her lover's life and hearing its reply.

"So it shall be, Old Widow. Let the Young Chemist live as our Daughter wills it! We cannot go against her wishes after giving him to her. The veil hiding the secrets to your past, Daughter, is now dissolved. Through visions and ghosts, your memory will return to you. Go back to him, but know that your life shall be as the outer world, in turmoil with pain and anguish. Your mother will never allow you to live in peace as long as the Young Chemist exists in your life. The pleasures of love are filled with bittersweet lessons, my Daughter. Pray that your tears do not fill the rivers of Mother Earth as did those of your female ancestors."

"Yes, Old Head, what you say is true," Anna whispered, hearing her words echoed back to her. She remembered when the Old Head had sent the Old Widow to take the life of her lover after their physical encounter when she had cut him in a fit of anger. In alarm over her swollen face caused by Raymond's striking her, the Old Head had sent the Old Widow to take his life, but Anna had disallowed it, wanting no harm to come to him.

"Now the fear that you will be discovered carrying the Young Chemist's young holds you in its grip. This is a fear that has controlled your life since the day the earth creature that formed your energy into

matter spoke hate into your heart against all who exist in the white spectrum of color on your earth world. You have lived with that fear all your life. Yet, time and time again, you have conquered your fears as you did when you pleaded for his life, knowing how it might one day hurt yours, even going with him to the land of your ancestors conquering many fears"

Anna took a deep breath. The baby kicked as thoughts of Ray pummeled her mind.

"When and where was it that you confronted your fear of water and it became a friend to you, Daughter?"

Anna thought back on her many fears especially her fear of water. It was at Camelot Academy that she confronted her fear of the water. Having never learned to swim, she sat with the pink bathing suit on her father had bought—the one she had not allowed her mother to see. Seated near the pool, she refused to go in, pretending she had studies she had to work on. It was Peter who had come to her as she sat peering over her book as the others splashed around in the water. Some dived off boards into it while others danced around in it, something she wanted so much to learn. From time to time, swimmers would call out to her to come join them, to which she would pretend she had an important assignment she had to complete.

"'Ms. Anna,' Peter whispered as he climbed out of the water coming up to where she lay beside the pool. "'If you don't participate in our swim classes, you are going to get a big fat F on your report card for your gym grade. The gym instructor will surely give it to you.'

"An F! Why, I've never had an F in my life," Anna had whispered aloud. She thought to herself of the humiliation of taking an F home for her parents to see.

"'A red F! For sure, Ms. Anna!' Anna looked to see the seriousness in his bifocal lenses that made her white classmate's eyes larger than they really were.

"But I don't know how to swim, Peter. I'll drown if I jump in that water."

"'Don't worry! I have the solution for that problem," he had told her swimming away. Soon he returned with the swimming instructor and Anna received her first of many swimming lessons. She became as avid a swimmer as the best of the students realizing swimming was as much fun as Peter had assured her it was. In fact, as her memory cleared, she thought of how she and Peter soon had become inseparable. Riding the same school bus, they sat together while going over assignments from the previous day. Because they both excelled in calculus and chemistry, they were always busy working together on some project the other students shied away from, complaining that the projects appeared too complicated.

In the bottom of the black hole, it came to her that Peter had been for a time the boy who consumed much of her time. Their interests were the same, and she didn't mind that he was white or that he wore horn-rimmed glasses. She told him he looked like an intellectual in them after they fell from his face into the water, and she proudly dived down to retrieve them for him. When new happenings occurred in school, he was the one to inform her of them.

It was he who insisted she join him in summer school, assuring her it would be so much fun. But summer school changed them both she now realized. He spent more time with the seven boys attending summer school, and she spent her time with the only two girls attending. Soon he began teasing her about the teacher liking her smarts, and she denied any such thing.

After the lab accident, it never dawned on her that they no longer sat together on the bus. Their conversations became brief. No longer did they laugh over matters going on around them. So involved with what was happening to her in her dream world and the promise she had given her word to keep, she ignored Peter as much as he distanced himself from her. The intimate nature of their relationship before summer school came to her as clearly as if she were seeing in daylight for the first time, even though she could not see her hands before her face in that deep black hole. It was the seeing the Old Head spoke of, looking with eyes that stained the heart with undying truths about oneself. The same seeing the Madame spoke of. It was seeing that had nothing to do with the eyes in ones head.

Before summer school, she had had the same feelings for Peter that young girls bestow on a favorite boy who warms their hearts. She now realized she had looked forward to their time lying on the mats studying together while smiling as the others teased them about always being together. Not until that moment did she realize her feelings for Peter before summer school—something he must have felt long after that day when he watched her and Ray kissing down in the lab. Summer school and the boy who had come to teach them chemistry and math had changed it all. She now realized Peter saw the change in her long before she knew the change had come.

Down where there was no light to see with, Anna's eyes finally opened confronting her with the fact that had there been no summer school, she and Peter might still be together both working as nuclear scientists. She shook her head as tears fell from her eyes. Here she sat in a black hole with nothing to show for her life but a white man's baby she could not get rid of. And Peter was already a nuclear scientist; doing great things she wished she could do. Anna heard the sound of her own weeping as she listened to the horrid cries of the creatures with no escape from the deep hole she had fallen into.

"How can I release the energy of life from the young you carry, Daughter, when it is a part of your eternal journey unfolding? Already it is revealing lost secrets you never understood until you fell into darkness so that you could open the eyes of your heart and looked deep inside."

Listening to the voice within was what the Madame had spoken of, something she had not understood until that very moment.

"The dawn that was waiting has come. Because of the child you carry, you have now reunited with the earth mother you had long since forgotten. Your time with her will teach you much wisdom about this earth world that has no answers to the twists and turns of human life and its collective thinking. The Young Chemist has never left you. You still carry him with you as the new life from him forms inside your body."

"Old Head, I don't know why you didn't let me die. I have been such a disappointment. You now see the person I become when my fears gets the best of me. Please forgive me for throwing that chair at you, but I could not see any way but death out of the hell I found myself in. I blamed you for something I am to blame for. When my plans didn't turn out the way I wanted, fear held me in its grip. I thought dying was the only solution to my problem. This hole seems a fitting place for me to finish out this horrible life of mine."

"**Daughter, even now fear holds you in its grip. Still you understand no more than what the eyes can see. Fear will be with you always until you open up the eyes of your heart and allow it to show you your true destiny on this earth world.**"

"This life of mine has turned into one huge jigsaw puzzle, Old Head. Every way I turn, something unexpected throws me off balance, and I have no clue what will come next. Thinking I had regained all my memory, nothing prepared me for these last turn of events. What's next, Old Head? Is there more? How will I handle it all? Is there another part of my journey taking me somewhere to teach me more lessons? What? I don't know if I'm able to handle it all. These new challenges are too much for me!"

"**Daughter, all of life's journey is unknown before you enter its path—a path all humans must face or die. Your life journey on this earth world is one that has been waiting for you, one that ends only when the matter that formed you turns back to the energy of the universe.**"

"Finding my grandmother alive shakes the very foundation of my world, Old Head. She is a part of my life that has been kept from me. I feel cheated. Though she reminds me of Momma, she is so different. With her I feel safe, not fearful as I do with Momma. I now realize that although I regret falling into that pond, it drew me to this moment. Do you think it was meant to be, Old Head?"

"**Daughter, the pond of passion has been awaiting your arrival since before your birth. My warning was just to postpone the inevitable. The image of your mother was destined to take you there. You allowed your fears to determine your outcome adding more twists and turns to a journey that is still evolving. The child growing in you will unleash more lessons yet to unfold. Learning of your grandmother is only part of your journey unwinding. When the human mind relies only on those senses known to it, fear of the unknown causes it to want to destroy that which cannot be controlled or explained.**"

"I was afraid of what would happen to me if the knowledge of my pregnancy became known to my mother and husband, Old Head. I believed I knew the outcome. I would have preferred to die rather than face that ordeal."

"When life's journey does not follow the course outlined in the human mind as you believe it should, it is perceived as too intolerable. Like a storm that comes without warning—you run from it, finding no place to hide because the storm is in you, Daughter. How does one hide from oneself?"

Anna bowed her head, having no answer.

"You must travel the twisted road to find the answers that await you. Bless the unknown for it will take you places few ever tread. It is what sets you apart. You have attempted to solve a riddle that needs no solving. Your child will become a part of this world, and there is nothing you can do to stop its coming.

Anna suddenly felt her body moving. Looking upward her heartbeat eased as she saw a bright light filter into the black hole. Soon she found herself standing in the land of the Healing Tree. The half man and woman forms hurried right through her, their jeweled eyes reflecting the light of the color in them. Flowers whirled through the air clinging to the huge tree leaves that always reminded her of elephant ears. She stood up to her ankles in blue water. Looking down into it, she saw a young version of herself standing in her grandmother's yard beside an older teenage boy who must have been Frankie Lee. He had his arm around her shoulder. An older white man stood outside a cage thrusting meat inside. A wild cat of some kind growled, striking out at the cage door. Anna moved backwards in fear. Just as she was about to turn and run her eyes opened.

The morning sunlight beamed through the bedroom window of her grandmother's home. Roosters were crowing. She looked out to see chickens pecking at the ground, and she heard dogs barking. The orange light glowing in the palm of her hand reminded her that she had no control over this journey she had embarked upon when she made a promise, not realizing the extent of its outcome.

Chapter Eighteen

—⟋⟍⟍—

Anna found comfort in the home her grandmother had lived in for some fifty-odd years with the white man who had killed her husband and taken her away from her children. She sat before the woman she came to know as Granny, and Granny kept reminding her she was her granddaughter, her oldest daughter's only child, and her only granddaughter—blood of her blood, flesh of her flesh, about to give her another great-grandbaby. Anna looked in awe at the hardy food her grandmother had prepared, while ignoring her protests that she could not eat all of it. Smiling as Anna sat eating the old gray-headed lady sat in an old-fashioned rocking chair and stared at her, shaking her head back and forth with fresh tears flowing from her eyes.

"Lawdy me . . . it be a dream I scared to dream. A hope done 'bout faded with the passin' of the yeers of prayin' and askin' the Lord All Mighty to give me back my daughter as he done give me back my boy. Thank ya, Lord," Granny said, giving praise to God. It was something Anna would hear daily. Her grandmother's daily thanksgiving in prayer to the one she believed was responsible for all her blessings. Anna felt embarrassed for herself and her mother as she gazed at her grandmother's upturned head, her face illuminated by a faith she could not understand.

"Ya may not come when I call, but ya wouldn't see an old woman die fore givin' hur some parts of hur baby back," she cried, rejoicing. Anna knew in her heart that had Frankie Lee not returned for the black gold hash Raymond had placed in the attaché case, her baby would be dead and she would be in hell by now. Watching the tears stream down Granny's cheeks, Anna felt shame for all the suffering three generations had endured because of the desires of a dead white man she still could not remember.

For the first time since the discovery of her pregnancy, Anna felt sympathy for someone other than herself. Fingering the flowered cushions of the ancient couch, she looked around at the antique furniture her grandmother must have had since the time she first stepped into the home she had been brought to. She looked on the wall at all the pictures covering it—pictures of five white children and one darker one Anna knew to be her uncle Jessie. There was a picture of Frankie Lee when he was a teenager, standing next to a girl as dark as he was. Anna blushed, realizing she was the girl in the picture. She pressed her hand against it, wanting to remember the time it had been taken. She remembered Frankie Lee saying there were four children by the white man. When she asked her who the third young girl was, Granny smiled at her and said, "Why Chile, dat's yer Momma." Anna stared at the young white-looking girl with long brown hair crowning the top of her head. She stared back at her. The girl looked to be about seven as she stood smiling into the camera. The old black-and-white picture must have been taken before the tragedy.

The other four children appeared as white as their father. Frankie Lee had told her that although they were older, they had lived at home during the time she had lived with Granny. A large framed picture in the center of the wall was of her grandmother as she posed with Harold Porter when she was younger. His eyes were sky blue and set deep in his chalk-white face, leaving no doubt to the observer as to his race. It had been in her heart in past years that the man might have been biracial and had possibly passed for white. Looking at his picture, she now knew better. His razor-thin mustache curled at the ends. There was a look of passion in his eyes as he gazed down at her grandmother. Anna could not help but notice the look of servitude in her grandmother's eyes that were cast downward, unlike in the picture at her uncle Jessie's home in which she had a look of pride on them. Her hair, then brown like Anna's mother's had been pulled back behind her head in a bun. Her eyes were then as gray as Raymond's. Anna reminded herself to ask Granny about her lineage.

Granny spoke proudly of all of her children, even the ones she had borne for the white man. Anna sat listening as she rocked in the rocking chair Granny insisted she sit in so that the baby had room to stretch.

"Mr. Porter," she said, "was a learned man. While I's a fussin' dat my babies should be plowin' in the fields, he would have all dem books teachin' 'em readin', rithmatic, and writin'—foolish stuff I called it. Said it won't gonna help 'em no how. He won't lissen and just set 'em down and teach 'em chilen anyhow even taught my Jessie, paying no mind atall to what I be sayin'. Caused me to learn some adder lookin' after 'em and thay books thay kept askin' questions of me from. He insisted I must learn fer 'em."

"He really loved them; even knowing they were not pure white?" Anna asked. "I can't see how he could have been happy not having any pure white children."

"Loved 'em for a while more'n me 'cause I hated the white in 'em. Mr. Porter loved 'em just 'cause they be his. Chilen loved him too. Loved him so they soffen my own heart to him."

"You actually learned to love that white man after what he'd done to you and the black family he took you from after killing your husband?" Anna hated herself for asking, but the words came out before she had time to think about what she was asking.

"After 'em babies starta comin' and the yeers pass, it soffen any Godfearin' heart . . . but it don't mean I forget, Chile. I just learnt God is in control of ever livin' being on this earth. He be the paymaster of all his chilen, not Mabel. It's only for me to give him my faith dat all will be made right in the end. When I seed my babies a comin', I knowd God had 'is own plan." Anna felt sadness consume her as she watched Granny stare at the portrait of herself and the white man she called Mr. Porter.

"Mr. Porter was like most white men in his day. Use to havin' what thay thought thay had a right to. He always had a likin' for me way 'fore I was a grown woman. Don't know why. I never gave him cause to. He found me. I's workin' in dat white café up town. White folks tip big money so's us colors thought." The golden eyetooth glittered as a keen look appeared in her eyes. "Dems sharecroppin' times back in the thirties and dat café work put food on the table."

"Didn't your husband mind you working in a place where Mr. Porter frequented? I guess you know that Momma always blamed you for not killing the white man and coming back to them. Hearing only her side of how things happened, even I could not understand the reason for your staying with him." Her grandmother looked over at her shaking her head.

"Mabel knowd mean times for us colored back in them days. If'n white folks said thay would kill a colored, they done it and no law made it wrong. Dead for a colored is just dead. Mabel had two black babies woulda hung if she tried to kill him or herself like my gal thought I should do and ya been tryin' to do." Anna lowered her head, embarrassed now about having tried to take her own life.

"How ya git a baby for a white man?" Granny asked, a frown forming on her face. "Granny ain't yet understood how ya come to be with the white man if yer man is colored? Ya with him for money, honey?" Anna's face burned like fire. Her embarrassment about her own past relationship with a white man surpassed any her grandmother could have imagined, yet she felt an ever-growing love and kinship to this old black woman seated across from her.

"I caught my husband in bed having sex with three women, Granny," Anna said, watching her grandmother's eyes open wide as her brows grew closer. "One of the women was supposed to have been a good friend of mine. My husband brought her to our home and introduced her to me. They had been lovers prior to our introduction. She made me aware of that when I was forced to confront them."

"With three women . . . I do say dat's some man," Granny, said, shaking her head.

"He had gotten my so call friend pregnant and then made her get an abortion. She was determined to make him pay for that deed. She did so by calling me to her home to catch them with him and then telling me everything they had done behind my back. Of course she had a gun on both of us at the time. I fell down her stairs backwards and lost the baby I was carrying. She shot my husband—that's why he limps today. When I left there, I must have been driving recklessly. My car slid down a ravine. Ray, this baby's father, pulled me from my burning car before it exploded. He took care of me until I was well again. It was all so strange because we knew each other from when I was fourteen. I couldn't remember anything before the time I came to live with you. Because of him, my memory came back—at least part of it—and I guess you could say we became lovers and I ended up with his baby in me and him gone back to his wife. We were together four years before then. I returned home not knowing I was carrying his baby." Anna watched Granny's eyes grow, but not a word came from her lips.

"When I returned home, I found nothing the same. Everyone thought I had become too different. My husband wanted me back. He knew everyone in town so I wasn't about to find a new husband there even if I wanted one. My children were too young to know anything about why we separated. They loved their father and wanted us to get back together, as did everyone else in Session it seemed. So I guess I was sort of like you in that respect. Sometimes what one thinks should happen doesn't always turn out that way."

"What about ya, Anna? What ya want?" Granny asked.

"Granny, I wanted to take my children and leave there, but I soon discovered it wasn't about what I wanted but what was good for my family. My children knew nothing about what caused me to leave their father, and they wanted both of us in their lives.

"My husband vowed to kill the man I was with if he ever saw him. He sent a man to threaten my attorney, who then dropped my divorce case without telling me why. It just got crazy, Granny." Anna did not go into details about the night at the river or those thirteen eyes and the Old Head spinning around inside of them. She knew it would take days to tell and longer than that for Granny to understand.

"Anyway, I went to a friend's party and the woman I caught him in bed with was there. You would think after shooting him she would have been over him, but she must have still been upset with my husband for making her have the abortion. She couldn't keep her mouth shut about what they did in my home, and she began telling all the women at the party how she tricked me into coming to her house and all the things she had done with my husband behind my back—even having sex with him in my house in my bed. Granny, I know there is rage in me I can not control when I'm angry. If I can get away before my anger gets the best of me, it will pass, but I think I have a lot of Momma in me because if I don't get away from it, there is hell to pay. I couldn't get away from that mouth of hers; I lost it. I couldn't hear or see anything but red. I zoned in on killing her with Momma's straight edge razor she had given me, blocking out everything else. I ended up cutting her up something awful. It's the reason I'm down here. I'm running from incarceration in case she told the authorities that I was the one who cut her up so badly she had to be hospitalized." Anna looked at her grandmother, hating having to tell her how she had done harm to another human being. "I know," Anna said, seeing the startled look on Granny's face. "Granny, I tried hard not to be like that, but when she laughed about causing me to lose my baby, it pushed me over the edge."

"Yeah, dat jus might push Granny, too, hearin' such as dat comin' from the mouf of the one what caused it."

"Anyway, Granny, if it had not been for my having to come to Oinston and discovering this baby in me, I would never have reunited with you. For that I am thankful," Anna, said, seeing a smile light up Granny's face.

After Anna undressed for the night, Granny bathed her feet in something she said had healing powers. She then rubbed some ointment that smelled like almonds on Anna's stomach. She told Anna it was to prevent stretch marks. Tucking her in bed, Granny reached down and kissed Anna on the forehead. "Granny gonna help ya baby; now don't ya go thankin 'bout killin' ya self no more "cause ain't no need; God takes care of his own and ya sho' be his 'cause ya mine." Anna smiled up at her, feeling safe at last.

****

A week after Anna had come to live with her grandmother, there was knock on her bedroom door. "Anna, thare's somebody hare to see 'bout ya. Ya 'wake?" It was her grandmother, but Anna wondered who would be there to visit her. Fear stole into her heart. Before she could answer, the door opened, and there behind her grandmother stood the doctor who had taken care of her in the hospital. He was running his hand through the thin white hair on his head, and a smile lit up his face as he called out her name in his thick baritone voice that he used to hum spiritual hymns when he was not lecturing her. A stereoscope hung around his neck. He walked right in.

"Well, how is my patient?" He took her hand and felt her pulse, and then he placed the stereoscope in his ears to listen to the baby's heartbeat as Granny stood by smiling. Anna felt her baby kick and then move as if trying to escape the hands disturbing it.

"Yes, God is sure in the plans for this one. Its heartbeat is stronger than mine, and it moves like it owns the place." Anna took a deep breath but said nothing. She knew this man had the ability to remove her from her grandmother's home even now. She did not want him to think she was still of a mind to kill herself or the baby. He would not want her there with her grandmother if that were the case.

225

"Doctor, how much longer do you think it will be before it makes its arrival?"

"Two months give or take a week or two. How are you, young lady?" he asked, examining the scars on her arms.

"I'm fine, doctor. We are fine. As you can see, this baby is alive and well, and I am enjoying my grandmother with no thoughts of anything else."

His smile grew. "Good! That is what I need to hear. The Master knows when, why, and if not. You must be the vessel he is using to deliver his message. If that be the case, everything will turn out fine," he said, placing the sheet back over her as he and Granny left the room.

A little while later, she came out to find them drinking coffee and talking about other patients of his Granny must have known. She could tell they had been out to the hothouse where all her plants grew. He had a couple of jars of something Anna knew had come from her grandmother. It shocked her to listen to how knowledgeable her grandmother was about what a plant could do for or against the body. Granny was telling him what plant she had grown that took care of an ailment of a visitor she was expecting. Anna had answered the knocks at the door when people came to ask Granny for herbs or to ask what root would be good for whatever was ailing them.

Once, a young white girl knocked but was seated on the top step of Granny's porch when Anna opened the door. Anna saw from the looks of it that she would give birth about the same time Anna would. She wondered why she had come to see her grandmother when the woman smiled and said, "I see ya 'bout ready to give up yur load, too. Me and my man was married 'bout three yeers 'fore I could git with a baby. Thanks to Granny, I got me five younguns. Whatever it was she gim me, boy did it work!" She smiled as she rubbed her stomach. Anna smiled back, thinking she did not want to see anything that helped make babies. When her grandmother appeared at the door, she left them alone to talk.

Anna soon discovered that Granny was a midwife and cared for many of the women living in those woods bearing children. In the rear of her land, another smaller house had been built with windows at the top to let in the sun. Plants and herbs of every description stood in pots, jars, and cans with labels not much different than a pharmacist would have in a drug store. Anna inquired as to the purpose of the herbs and plants—they reminded her of the chemicals that had been labeled in the lab down in Kentucky. Granny smiled and told her it would take quite a while to learn the use of all the plants she had crossbred or even those that grew naturally. When the doctor came, he sometimes took back with him some of her plants and herbs. Anna wondered how they worked and what chemicals they possessed that might be extracted.

As it happened, every week the doctor was there to examine her. Afterwards, he sat talking to Granny, and Anna figured he really came to see Granny. Then again, she thought, perhaps he came to make sure she did not do anything drastic to cause Granny any problems. Anyway, she began to like his fatherly talks and felt comfortable enough to share with him some of her problems that had led to the situation she was in. He, of course, knew Granny's history. She could tell he adored her. It felt good to feel safe in a place she did not have to worry about being exposed.

Realizing she would bear Raymond Forlorn a child, Anna settled down to life with her grandmother. The old lady, just as Raymond had done during her time with him, petted and pampered her. She teased and humored her into doing things Anna knew were best for her and the child she carried. Anna sometimes caught Granny staring at her and felt a growing sadness for all the wasted years of not knowing this wonderful woman. Stopping whatever she was doing, Anna would go over and give her a hug, holding her so tightly that the baby would kick them both. Laughing, they would go back to wherever it was they had been doing.

Anna thought it was strange indeed to find herself seated next to her grandmother learning how to milk a cow. She also knew it would be the talk of Session to see her pour slop to squealing pigs out behind the house. She mentioned to Granny that she had seen a snake, and Granny informed her she must be careful of snakes because they could smell the milk from her breasts and would follow after her. Anna wondered about the truth of her grandmother's warning but was watchful to keep away from snakes after that. Rabbit cages stood empty at the back of the house. Granny informed her that there were many rabbits born in them while her husband lived. Next to it stood a larger cage. Looking at it caused Anna's palm to pulsate. In a vision, she saw a large cat inside the cage the same as when she was in the Land Of the Healing Tree looking down into its blue tears.

She and Frankie Lee poked a stick at it. An older white man she knew now to be her grandmother's husband walked up and told them the animal was dangerous and not to play around with it. The vision left her fearful. She wondered what had happened to that big cat.

Two weeks after she had settled in, Anna watched from her grandmother's window as a tall white man closed the door to a brown Volkswagen then walked toward the house. She called to her grandmother to let her know she had a visitor. The man walked into the house without knocking. She stood looking into the light brown eyes of a white man with shoulder-length straight brown hair. He stood and looked at her with intense eyes as though he was attempting to place her. Anna became perplexed as she watched him hug and kiss Granny and then speak in a southern drawl similar to Raymond's in perfect English. Anna turned to go into her room when she heard him ask in French if she was his niece that had lived with them some years ago.

"If the niece was fourteen at the time, it must have been me," Anna answered, her French as fluent as his.

"We had so much fun speaking the language no one understood but us. I am glad to see you have not forgotten it," he replied, staring at her in a way that alerted her he was surprised to see her.

"How are you doing, mother? I heard my niece is back." Anna stood there more puzzled than ever, staring at the strange white man claiming her as his niece.

He extended his hand as he told her in French that his name was Paul Porter. His eyes searched Anna's for some sign of recognition. Anna answered him in French, saying that her name was Anna and inquiring if they had met before.

"Hur past of us is buried inside," Granny said. Anna noticed the man looking from her enlarged stomach to the rings on her left ring finger. Jake had placed the rings back on her finger the day of the fire to seal the promises made for their new beginning. Seeing this uncle, she was thankful they were there.

During dinner, Anna remained silent as she listened to Granny's youngest son by the white man discuss the repairs needed on her home. Granny asked about his patients. He smiled, stating he had more patients than he had time. Her mind ran a mile a minute as she wondered about the white-looking man who was her uncle. She wondered what he thought about how his father had taken Granny. The genes in that white man had been strong. One had to look closely to see that he might have something else in him. Without prior knowledge, she never would have guessed. Even his mannerisms were those of a white man. Anna thought perhaps this might have been because his father had not dumped his sperm in her grandmother and left without looking back, but had been there with Granny, caring for the babies he had impregnated her with.

Paul had gone to school and become a dentist. She heard them discuss his oldest brother, now a neurosurgeon somewhere in Europe, and her aunts who were both registered nurses up North. She mused that they owed their professions to a father who understood the value of a good education.

"I'd like to meet your mother, my sister," he said to Anna in French as Granny stepped out to answer the phone.

"My mother is a reclusive woman. She rarely visits or accepts visitors." He must not know about the strained relationship between her mother and Granny, Anna thought as Granny reappeared to interrupt their conversation.

Anna would later learn from Frankie Lee that Granny's and Mr. Porter's youngest son had received the most information about his parents' past. As a dentist in Oinston, talk was cheap, especially coming from the lips of those wanting to hurt. He had absorbed it while accepting that only black patients would visit his office when it first opened.

According to Frankie Lee, Paul's professional services excelled, causing whites to become patients of the young biracial dentist after a while. After all, in a small town like Oinston, it was hard finding excellent health professionals willing to settle there. Frankie Lee further shared that Paul's love for Granny kept him not too far from her opening his office in Oinston. She was getting up in age, and he did not want to go north with her out in the woods and he not be able to at least come look in on her once in a while. Frankie Lee told her that it had been due to the constant pressure of her children by Mr. Porter that Granny had been persuaded to marry him, assuring their children legitimacy and the right to be his legal heirs.

However, it was Granny, as the days turned into weeks and then months, who shared in-depth with Anna about her tragic past. Though Granny told the story to her in bits and pieces, Anna kept every word of it embedded in her heart.

It seems that Granny had been a cook in an all-white café visited frequently by Mr. Porter in Oinston, Louisiana. With the money she made cooking, she helped her husband support their two children and his elderly parents.

Anna remembered how Granny's eyes glowed as she traveled back in the past telling her of a part of her life that was gone forever.

Back in the thirties, she had worked in a café where white folks frequent because they liked her cooking. Anna listened to how pleased her grandmother seemed to be at having been able to cook so well that white folks asked for her. It was doing that time Granny shared with Anna that Mr. Porter began to frequent the café asking for her cooking as well. He told her he had been watching her, her grandomother shared with Anna. Though she did not like him there was nothing she could say or do about his attention given her.

One of the cooks, she shared with Anna named Lilly Mary came and told her Mr. Porter had taken a liking to her. Her grandmother however reminded her she was already married and had no interest in anyone but her husband and that she sure did not need a white man.

"'Mabel had her Jessie and him be the only man in hur heart.' Anna knew her grandmother was no longer with her but reliving history long before her birth.

"'Lilly Mary done come to me agin with talk of thangs Mr. Porter done said to tell me. 'Ya go and git him for yerself. I got a man. Mabel don't want no man but hur own,' I done tole hur.'

Granny continued her story, telling Anna that one day, Josephine, an older black cook she worked with, had told her the boss wanted her to go back to the storageroom and fetch some flour. She saw there was plenty, but back in those times, you didn't question it if the white man said to go do something. She did as she was told. Once she got in the storageroom, there sat Mr. Porter on a cot that had never been there before. Granny told Anna that she must have looked scared, and she repeated his words to her as though they were just being said. "'Now Mabel, don't you go being afraid. I'm not about to hurt you, you know that. Come sit with me; I want to talk to you.' Granny admitted she had been scared but hadn't wanted to show it. Taking a seat next to him on the cot, she had listened to what he had to tell her.

"'Mabel, you know it's you I want, you know that. I've come here to take you away with me.'

Granny spoke the words she said to Mr. Porter, "'No, Mr. Porter! What ya want will make my name a disgrace in dis town. Anyhow I got my own man. Lillie Mary, she's alikin ya. Ya take up with hur. She'll be happy.'

"'Mabel, you know I am not interested in Lilly Mary or any other woman; he kissed her cheek. Anna watched her grandmother touch the cheek he must have kissed.

Granny continued. "Chile, ya bet Mabel kept hurself a razor hid in her bosom to use on anyone who give hur a mess of trouble." Anna thought about her mother and wondered if Granny had given her the idea.

"'Please,' I done tole him, 'Mr. Porter, I done tole ya I got a man and what ya want will brang nothin' but shame on me. Mabel gotta cut ya throat if'n ya a mine to touch hur.' The razor in my hand stood just at his guzzle pipe.' Boy did that piece of news send Anna back into the past and thoughts of her downstairs neighbor at the nightclub.

Mr. Porter had said, "What about your husband's old folks needing you, Mabel? Yes, and your man, too. What about him? Once my throat is cut, the other whites here will take them and you and hang all of you for everyone to see."

Granny sighed deeply as tears gathered in her eyes telling Anna, She knew he spoke the truth. After she slit his throat the whites would have come and killed her entire family even her two children if they had a mind to. The razor had slipped from her hand as he took her. The colored cook, Josephine had come later to help her in her misery. Josephine, she shared, had straightened her clothes as best she could and said how sorry she was but there was nothin' she could do."

After a long silence, Granny continued the story. Once he had started, Mr. Porter had been there often to rape her whether she liked it or not. She had become the white man's wench to use whenever he had a mind to, and both coloreds as well as whites very soon knew of her situation. There was no one she could turn to for help. It was accepted as a white man's right.

Her grandmother continued to tell Anna that when her husband had discovered what was happening at the cafe, he had blamed her and refused to touch her; he was shamed by the laughter of his friends about his wife becoming a white man's wench. Josephine had gone to her husband and explained to him how it had all happened. Granny and her husband had then made plans to take the family and leave Oinston.

The night they made ready, there had been a knock at the door. Thinking it was their family coming to help pack up the truck, her husband opened the door.

Mr. Porter, she said had barged in walking past her husband telling her he had come for her. A fight started between her husband Jessie and Mr. Porter with him knocking Mr. Porter to the floor. The door suddenly flew open and other white men began to beat her husband then dragged him outside. She had been forced to stand with Anna's mother, her grandmother shared with her as tears spattered her face, watching them shot her husband then hung him . . . Her mother was only eight at the time begged and cried for them not to kill her father. Her son Jessie was away down the country with some friends they planned to stay with until they could get out of the state." Anna rushed to her grandmother's side, seeing her tears running down her face.

"Granny, all that's in the past. Please don't talk about it anymore. It hurts me to hear you relive that awful horror again." Anna realized the tears of the Healing Tree that had drenched her body had showed her a vision while she was lying on its trunk when she was preparing for Raymond's healing and for the Old Head to get back its eye. It had been a vision of her grandmother, unknown to her at the time, being taken by the white man.

"Ya b'lieve I shoulda taken the lives of my babies by Mr. Porter 'cause of dat horrible night my Jessie was killed and hung?" Anna fell to the floor and held her grandmother's knees.

"Granny, that sin is mine, not yours—wanting to kill my baby because of my own selfish fears. You did nothing wrong. You were a victim, just as my grandfather was a victim. I willingly gave my body to my baby's white father. I'm the one who should be ashamed for trying to kill myself and this baby just because my plans didn't work the way I planned. You think God will ever forgive me, Granny?" Anna sobbed.

"He already forgave ya, Chile. It's ya who must forgive yerself. Just as it took yeers for me to find my peace in God, knowing his ways is not man's ways atall. Ya must look and find forgiveness for yer own life and the baby that bears no fault for its life."

****

It was the big black pot that restored Anna's memory of having lived with her grandmother as a child. Granny still insisted that the lye in the big old pot was the only way to clean the clothing she went by and picked up from Paul and Jessie when she was taken to town. She always managed to bring back a bundle to be washed.

Anna stood stirring the pot, her thoughts on what she planned to do after her baby was born. The heat caused smoke to rise up around the black pot. Bubbles rose and caused the clothes inside to rise inside. The strong lye stung her eyes. As Anna continued to stir, it occurred to her how much Granny and her mother were alike. Neither believed there was a better way than the old way they had learned to live by. As a matter of fact, they were so much alike in some ways that Anna found herself forgetting the difference and often calling Granny "Momma."

Another piece of clothing bubbled up. A frown appeared on Anna's face as her memory came back to her in this strange way. She remembered how happy she had been staying with her white uncles and aunts. Though older, they treated her the same way her classmates had treated her when she had first attended school in Massachusetts.

An older white man had lived in the house with them. Anna recalled that the white children had called him Papa. Her much older aunts and uncles had welcomed her into the household—even babied her so much so that she felt a part of the new family she had been taken to. She remembered the older white man never said much; he wore that thin curved mustache just as in the picture of him and Granny. He worked outside most of the day, coming in just at dinnertime when they all gathered to eat.

A white woman came to the house one evening and talked to her mother. At the time, Anna called Granny the same name as the other children in the house. Later on, Uncle Jessie would take her to his house to see the white woman. The woman talked to her, Anna now remembered, but she didn't recognize her so she never responded. The smoke from the pot circled her. Paul Porter appeared as a young boy in her mind—several years older than she—yes, now she remembered him. Anna's eyes widened. At the time, he had been learning to speak French in high school. Every day he would come home repeating in French what they had learned at school. Anna remembered teaching him the language she had learned so fluently. She and Paul spent months talking in French to each other until the language came as easily to him as it did to her.

Her grandmother had become the mother Anna had lost during that year she stayed with them. When her real mother came to take her away, she no longer looked white and actually resembled Granny. She remembered only that they talked and her mother offered Granny money; what was said after that she could not remember. Upon seeing her father, her memory of him was intact, and Anna reclaimed her parents. Why her memory of her stay with Granny had faded she did not know. She had never realized she had a grandmother out there somewhere. Her mother never discussed her stay with Granny. It seemed as though she would have appreciated all Granny had done in allowing Anna to stay that long a time, but her mother to that day talked with a harsh tongue about her own mother, leaving Anna and her father to believe she was dead

Chapter Nineteen

The spring months brought with them stormy weather in Oinston, Louisiana. A sudden change in the temperature could occur without warning, Granny informed her. The hot May breeze turned cool the day Anna sat alone on the porch watching Granny's chickens pecking in the dirt. She was glad for the unexpected cool breeze. It felt good to her large, heavy body. She hoped to have the baby any time now. The change in the weather at least gave her comfort for a while. She knew it soon would be so hot that she would have to talk Granny into turning on the air conditioning her children had long ago bought for her but that she insisted she did not need.

Her uncles had come and painted the outside of the house the same white trimmed in black. Its seven rooms had been built by Mr. Porter way off in the woods far from prying eyes to protect his family from those who would hurt them. Her grandmother shared that he taught his children at home until they were old enough to attend high school. They were teenagers before they knew what it was to interact with other children.

Anna tried to explain to Granny as her time draw near that the child she now carried had to be given away. It was her plan never to see the baby after its birth. She hoped that Frankie Lee was finding a family to take it. Anna knew she needed to return home and attempt to renew her relationship with Jake and her children if at all possible. This child she was carrying had kept her away so long it might be impossible to patch things up between her and her husband. The child's father, already a married man, could do nothing for the child even if he wanted to. This she told Granny to explain why it would have been best if the child were never born. But since God, the doctor, Granny, and the Old Head not to mention the Madame had defeated her in that effort, she would have to do the next best thing, which was to give it birth and then try to forget it had ever existed. Granny listened, making no comment . . . something Anna was glad of.

Now Anna felt more air, cooling her body. Looking up, she noticed dark green clouds covering the bright sun. Her uncle Jessie had come down with a cold he could not get rid of. Granny had gone over with her bag of herbs. There was no doubt he would be well before long.

A flash of lightning illuminated the sky as it darkened causing Anna to wish for Granny's presence as she hurried inside. The first window she reached up to close gave her a surprise. The Old Widow hung just at the windowsill. Its back was vibrating that orange light she was so familiar with. A strong pull in her lower back caused pressure in the bottom of her stomach. Anna winced, feeling her first contraction. The baby moved downward. She made an attempt to reach up again but felt another heavy tug at the bottom of her stomach.

As the storm turned the midday dark, Anna stumbled over a chair and fell to her knees. Her pains grew stronger. She screamed out, gasping for breath as she struggled to make a quick call to the doctor to say Granny was not there and she did not want to have the baby alone. He told her to go to bed—he was coming. Suddenly everything turned blue. Thirteen eyes whirled through the air. In the dead silence, the voice of the Old Head filled the room with its presence.

"Daughter, look into the mirror of life to see all there is to know. With the coming of this new life, answers will manifest themselves in the glory of its birth. Look, Daughter, and see all that is missing in your past."

Anna looked into the eyes surrounding the Old Head and saw herself as a teenage girl in Granny's yard following behind the older white man she had learned to call Papa.

"Be careful! Don't get too close to that cage. I got a pretty mean cougar in there," he said as she looked to see the animal inside circling it. Anna saw herself scattering the chickens and the geese as they chattered amongst themselves, flying in every direction trying to get away from her. The man placed food in the rabbit cage. He then lifted the top of the cougar's cage and put one part of a rabbit inside. Anna saw herself turn her back to the cage. The cougar became aggressive in his effort to get the rabbit part and begin to growl. She stepped back against the cage door as the two dogs began barking at her. Anna's mouth flew open in horror as she saw the cougar catch her hair in his paws then clawed her back. Her screams caused the old man to hurry over and beat the cougar off, but not before her back was badly mauled. She fell to the ground, screaming. Anna saw her grandmother running from the house. "She got too close to the cage and he mauled her, Mabel. God, I'm sorry."

"I done tole ya to git rid of dat damn animal!" Anna's eyes grew wide, seeing her grandmother take a double-barrel shotgun from a rack on the porch and shoot the cougar right in his cage. "Damn ya, ya won't hurt another soul on this earth!" Anna stared at herself lying in Granny's yard her back bleeding.

"Daughter, look. See the hate in your mother's and her mother's parting ways."

Anna struggled to lift herself from the floor again as the contractions grew stronger. The eyes of the Old Head moved just above her as she looked again into them. A violent argument between her mother and Granny caught her eyes as Anna lifted herself up to the chair in front of her.

In the vision she saw that her uncle had come to Granny's home earlier to tell her he was bringing Annabelle to take Anna home. Everyone had gone to town except her and Granny by the time they arrived. Anna saw her mother thank Granny and offered her payment for having taken care of Anna. Refusing the money Anna looked to see Granny pull up her blouse and showed Annabelle her back. When her grandmother pointed to the scars the cougar had caused, her mother screamed and asked what had happened to her baby. Anna listened as Granny explained the accident.

"'He tried to kill my baby just as he and those clan bastards killed my father and grandfather, the white bastard. I'll kill him!' she heard her mother scream.

"'He didn't mean for the cougar to hurt Anna, gal.' Anna listened to Granny tell her mother.

"'Goddamn ya,' Anna then listened to her mother yell, "'I should of knowd not to trust my baby with ya and dat damned white-ass devil!'

"'If ya thank I would hurt my own grandchile, ya take hur and go!' Anna forgot her labor pains as she stared in shock as her mother reached into her bosom and brought out her pearl-handled straight edge razor, striking out at Granny as she screamed, "'My husband will kill me if I take hur home with them horrible scars on hur back!' Her mother's eyes turned to slits. "'I will kill dat bastard. He done this to my chile to hurt me!'

"'I tole ya, he didn't mean for the cougar to hurt hur, gal.'

"'Ya takin' up for that dirty white devil—the white bastard! I'll kill ya!'" Anna watched Granny grab her mother's wrist, twisting the razor out of her hand.

"'Ya take 'em and go, Jessie. I don't want to have to kill my own daughter and have hur blood on my hands.'

"'Ya no good bitch—ya left us for dat white devil bastard! I hate ya! I've always hated ya!'

"'Damn ya, git out of my home! Jessie, take hur and go!' Anna watched her uncle push her mother and her out of the door as Granny locked it behind them weeping as she stood calling out to God asking why it had to happen. It all came back to Anna. Papa Porter had taken everyone to town but she and Granny.

"My God, Old Head, I now understand why no one mentioned her to me—why my mother hated her more than ever. Poor Granny! All she was trying to do was help her and that had to happen." The mauling was no one's fault—an accident that could have happened to any of her children. Anna wondered if Granny had felt something might happen with her and her mother because of the accident and made sure no one was home but her. And all this time, she had thought it was her mother's switches that had caused the disfiguring of her back. No wonder Granny hesitated in taking her in Anna thought as she view the scene being enacted before her. Her mother must have been terrified that her father would not take her back seeing the mauling after all she had put them through. Anna cried seeing her grandmother facing more misery, having forgotten about her labor pains until her body began expanding just as she had seen in the scene the Madame had shown her of the mother about to give birth.

"The hate in the heart of the one who gave birth to you still lives there, Daughter."

"Old Head, why did it have to happen? I loved them both, not knowing any of their past. How could I hate them like Momma wants me to?"

"Anna! My Lord, come let me get ya to bed!" Anna looked up from the thirteen eyes to see her grandmother entering the house dropping her bundle as she bent to help her up.

"Granny, I'll never make it back to my bed. I'll just have to have it here on this floor," Anna screamed as her grandmother pulled her up from the floor and into her own bedroom which was closer.

"Granny, I don't want to ruin your bed having this baby."

"You hush, Chile. Let me git washed up right quick," she said, helping Anna into her bed. Anna watched her grandmother move around the room lightning fast, laying things out she had never seen before. Granny soon placed a bowl of hot water by the bed and tossed all the instruments she had inside of it. Swiftly, she ripped Anna's clothing away from her. The doctor arrived soon after and hurried into the room after washing up. He began helping Granny prepare Anna for the birth of her child.

"Granny, I feel it coming; I can't stop it. Complete darkness filled the room. Anna's mind expanded and she saw herself in the hands of African women. She heard their words, and although they were foreign to her, she knew they meant for her to bear down. She screamed and screamed, hearing drums beating in the distance. It was the same sound she had heard when the tears from the Healing Tree brought forth her vision of the mother giving birth to the white infant, allowing it to drop from her body as she ran away. Light from an oil lamp soon lit up the room.

In the fury of the storm, the baby came out screaming. An image of Raymond appeared before Anna as though he were there in the room with her, smiling down at her with tears in his eyes. Anna watched the doctor lift the naked screaming baby up out of her body, saying to Granny, "It's a girl and I do believe her father must be mighty light, Granny—look how white she is!"

"Yes, Doc, she born as white as hur papa."

"God bless you, you made it here at last!" Anna heard the doctor say.

"Why Anna, God done give ya a fine baby gurl!" Granny exclaimed, smiling down at her. Lightning struck, bringing light to the dimly lit room. The naked baby in Granny's arms looked to Anna to be as white as her father. Raymond's image appeared again, smiling. His gentle gray eyes saying things to her she had pushed far into the recesses of her mind. Taking the baby from Granny, the doctor lifted the tiny infant up near Anna's face for her to see. Anna gazed at the white man's creation. She was a product of their love, a love that had not died but had just been born again.

****

"When Anna opened her eyes later that evening, Granny stood smiling down at her. The baby pulled vigorously at her nipple. To Anna's disappointment, she realized her and her grandmother had plans different for this baby.

"Poe little thang, sucking on hur fist. Granny oiled up them nipples and got that little gal sucking." Anna thought about the baby's father and how he had loved sucking her nipples. She shook her head, thinking this was just the beginning of more twists and turns in this journey of hers she would have to confront.

The next day she found her cousin peering down at her baby. "Heerd I had a little gurl cousin." Anna looked up at him, thinking how she had again failed in her plans. After Granny left the room, Frankie Lee grinned down at the baby sucking her breast.

"Cous, ya were right to hide. From the looks of hur, ya' gonna be in big trouble. What are ya gonna to do with hur if we don't find somebody to take hur?"

"Oh my God, Frankie Lee! I had not planned to look at her at all. Now I hate putting her up for adoption because her image will forever be with me," Anna sighed, still gazing down at the baby. "Tell me, Frankie Lee, where can I take a baby this white talking about she is mine? Surely not home. As white as Momma looks she would be in front of the line running me out of town once she found out who the baby's father was." She watched Frankie Lee nod his head in agreement.

"What did you name hur, Cous?"

"I didn't name her anything. The people who get her can name her whatever they want," Anna answered, again looking down with Frankie Lee at the baby who had stopped sucking as if listening.

"Anna, it don't make sense not to call hur somethin'," Frankie Lee insisted. Anna looked again at the baby and sighed.

"I could name her Raspy, after her father's mother. Her name was Rasp. What do you think?" Anna asked.

"Strange name, Anna, but without a name, she ain't nothin a'tall."

"Yeah, I guess you are right. She should be named something. Frankie Lee," Anna said, looking up at him again, "I need to ask you . . . no, tell you . . . something."

"Whatever it is, I didn't do it," Frankie Lee insisted, holding his hands up in the air.

"I know why Momma hates Granny so much." Anna watched her cousin's eyes widen. "She tried to cut Granny with a razor when Granny showed her how Papa's cougar mauled my back."

"Anna, ya 'member everythang about what happened if ya 'member Grandpa Porter!"

"I do, Frankie Lee! Momma must have been devastated seeing my back mauled like it was and then having to take me back to Daddy and explain to him what happened. I'm glad you told me you saw my back before the cougar mauled me."

"Anna, ain't no switches gonna put the scars on your back that cougar's claws did, gurl. Younguns git switched whipped around hare ever day and thay sho' don't leave no scars like ya had."

"Thank God Daddy took it better than Momma thought he would. He probably was so glad to get out of jail and have a place to start all over that he forgave her—and decided that since I had lost my memory of everything, they wouldn't have to explain my back or his time in jail to me. One thing for sure, Momma never told him it was her mother I stayed with. To this day, he thinks it was Uncle Jessie who kept me. How she explained the mauling to him I don't know."

"The Old Man said he thought he was gonna to have to knock her out she got so riled up. Blamed Grandpa Porter fer the accident and Granny fer stickin' up for him."

"Frankie Lee, when Momma brought out her pearl-handled razor she always kept tucked inside her bra, I thought she was going to kill Granny for sure."

"Yeah, Aunt Annabelle and the Old Man fell out 'bout dat. Granny never again mentioned ya or Aunt Annabelle adder dat day. I'm just glad Grandpa Porter and hur other kids was gone. If'n hur gurls had been thare, it would 'f been a fight. Ruth Ann and Jenny got a lot of Aunt Annabelle in 'em, too. I don't thank Granny ever told 'em 'bout the incident 'cause thare was never any talk of it dat I heerd.

"When Aunt Annabelle brought hur husband down to meet the Old Man, thay kinda made up, but he always said his sister was crazy in the head fer blamin' hur mother fer something dat was not hur fault adder askin' for hur help. She wouldn't let the Old Man or me tell him nothin' about hur. The Old Man thought it best adder what happened between hur and Granny."

"It's a wonder Granny allowed me to come here and stay with her, Frankie Lee."

"After I found out what old Doc planned to do with ya, Cous," Frankie Lee said, taking a seat next to her bed, "I jumped in my car and came out hare to see dat Granny of mine." Listening to him tell her of the visit, Anna rubbed her palm, which allowed her vision to expand beyond her mind. She saw Frankie Lee take a seat on the steps. His tear-stained eyes looked up at Granny.

"'Boy, what's ailin' ya?' Anna listened her ask.

"'Big problems, Granny.'

"'Son, ain't no problems so big God ain't got the answer fer 'em. Granny sho' knows dat."
,

"'My problem's bigger than God, Granny.'

"'Boy, don't ya be comin' hare with no talk such as dat.'

"'Ya 'member Aunt Annabelle's daughter ya kept dat time?'

"'Sho, ya knowd I ain't forgot I kept hur. She alright, boy?' Anna saw her eyes widen at the mention of her.

"'Granny, she down hare in the hospital. Maybe dyin' for all I know.'

"'What ya say, boy? How dat come to be?'

"'What's so killin', Granny is she tried to kill hurself.'

"'I do say. Why?' Anna watched Frankie Lee move up to sit on the porch in a chair beside Granny.

"'Granny, she's about six and half months pregnant with a white man's baby. Hur husband don't know it. When she found out, she tried to get old doc to get rid of it for hur, but he wouldn't, of course. I ain't gonna lie—I tried to help hur git rid of it, but somethin' always happened to stop it. If somethin' happens to hur, me and hur husband will have one of the worst fights. One of us might die. But Granny, Anna knows Aunt Annabelle would kill hur hurself if she discovers the baby is by a white man. Dat's why she did it, I b'lieve.' Anna listened to her cousin tell her grandmother.

"'Ya say she's in the hospital up yonder in Oinston?'

"'Yes ma'am, she is. Thay talkin about puttin' her in Shoot Hill. Granny, ya know dat's the place whare all those crazy folks live. Ole' Doc won't sign her out to me 'cause he said he don't trust me to see dat she won't try killin' hurself again.' Tears fell from Anna's eyes as she listened to their conversation about her.

"'Sho' hate hearin' that poe chile tried to kill hurself. It's a sin b'fore God, somethin' like dat.' Anna saw her grandmother's legs stetch out from under her.

"'Doc says he'd consider lettin' ya have hur. He'd trust ya more'n me. Ya maybe the only hope she got, Granny.'

"'Frankie Lee, hur thoughts may be the same as hur Momma's 'bout what happened back then. Adder all, it was hur back dat cougar mauled.' Anna watched her grandmother fold her hands under her arms as if in deep thought. "'No, I bet not.' Even though Anna knew it had not turned out that way, her heart sank to think that it might very well have turned out that her grandmother refused to take her in.

"'No, Granny, she don't even 'member none of it. She don't even 'member who ya is.'

"'What you say boy?'

"'When I casually mentioned yer name one day, she connected nothin' and asked who I was talkin' 'bout. Her back is completely well now. No one would ever know it had been mauled—it is so smooth and pretty now." She watched her grandmother sit up in her chair, staring at him in disbelief. "She needs ya, Granny. I need ya."

"'What you say, boy? Hur back ain't scarred up bad like it was when she left?'

"'Not a scratch, Granny. Her back is as smooth as a newborn baby's butt. I swear to God it is.'

"'Come take me to hur, son, so I can see for myself that hur back is straightened out. I can't b'lieve hur back is healed—those scars went deep. Once we thare, we'll see what she 'members.; As her vision faded, Anna listened to Frankie Lee tell her how he was finally able to convince her grandmother to take her in.

Granny and the doctor talked he shared with Anna saying grandmother confirmed that Anna was her granddaughter and that she didn't want her go to no crazy place when she had a home to take her to. By the time

Frankie Lee finished telling Anna what had happened, she was crying so hard that the baby started crying.

"What did she say when she saw my back? I know you, Frankie Lee. You showed her for sure."

"She just shook hur head and kept saying, 'Ain't God wonderful! He ain't never failed me yet.' "Anna, did ya tell hur ya know everything?" Frankie Lee asked, wiping the tears from Anna's eyes as he took the baby from her.

"No, Frankie Lee. I just couldn't hurt her by bringing it up when I know it was an accident—something she could not have prevented. She was kind enough to keep me when Momma needed her to. I know Momma was scared, thinking about what Daddy might say, but it was foolish not to listen and be thankful I had a place to come to that was safe from the authorities and that I was at least alive and well. This will be the second time she has saved my life Frankie Lee,"

"I'm glad you feel that way, Anna. Everythang she done has always been to help. She is an amazing woman. I'm glad ya got a chance to meet hur even if it had to happen like it did. The Old Man and Paul say thay ain't seen hur dis happy since before Mr. Porter died and her three children left going north. Ya've been good for her, Anna, and I know she has been good for ya."

"I'll never tell, Frankie Lee, especially not Momma," Anna said, reaching for the baby she planned to give up for adoption.

Chapter Twenty

In the next three months, Anna regained her strength while nursing a fast-growing baby. Her breasts had finally toughened to the sucking, and she sat in Granny's rocker, gaining a warm sensation from the pull of the baby's mouth. Offering her a finger, Anna felt the grasp of the baby's hand tighten around hers as she gazed up at her. Looking down at the child and then up at the portrait of Granny and Mr. Porter, and all their children a feeling of sadness suddenly overwhelmed her. The women in Granny's day could no more harm a baby as tiny and helpless as the one she held any more than they could have stopped the men putting them there. But she had thought no more about doing away with this baby than if she had been a nuisance bug needing swatting. Hugging Raspy to her, Anna squeezed back the tears smarting in her eyes. Love for her baby was developing inside of her, something she had tried hard to not let happen. Anna realized it would be hard letting her go, but she knew no other way out of the fix she was in.

Anna wondered what had happened to that willow branch. With the passing of each generation, had it become too brittle, giving way with the mere coming of a gentle breeze? She sighed, wondering what would be her next challenge.

One Sunday morning, Granny woke Anna and asked her to prepare for Sunday service. Showing her a small pink outfit she had made for little Raspy, she told Anna she planned to have her blessed in it that Sunday. Anna looked up in surprise at her grandmother. The last place she wanted to be was in a church, especially with her baby. She was reminded that Granny held Raspy on her shoulders, her hip, or her lap, grinning and talking to her all day long when she wasn't making sure Anna nursed her when she felt the baby was hungry. Anna wondered how she would tell her the baby was going away when she found a family that would take her.

"Granny, do you think I would be crazy enough to show my face with this white-looking baby in a church filled with black people? Even with these rings on my finger, they would know no white man married me. I don't know even now why I didn't kill her when I had the chance." The look Granny gave Anna caused her to turn her head away.

"May God have mercy on yer soul, Chile. My people laughed and taunted me. I dragged my babies to God's house even though they stoned me." Anna gazed at her in shock at this new information. "Yes, Chile, no mommas stopped thay chilen from throwin' stones at Mabel. A woman scorned . . . white man's whore, they called me. Only with Mr. Porter at my side did they leave Mabel be. If Granny had the hankies, she wiped slime the colored folk spit hur way, she could run a line all the way cross this big ole' country. White folks said nothin' 'cause thay knowd Mabel couldn't go back. My people knowd too . . . thay just needed someone to blame for thay own misery." It was hard listening to her grandmother's past life.

"Thay made Mabel pay even in God's house for somethin' she innocent of as the day she come outta her momma's womb. One morning, Mabel sat in back of the church with hur chilen ready to leave just b'fore the sermon ended" her grandmother told Anna. "Pastor called Mabel up front. Thought maybe he tell me I can't come back no more." Anna sat up in bed, seeing the faraway look in her grandmother's teary eyes.

"Pastor said to them colored folks that Mabel and hur younguns has suffered long enough said he wanted Mabel up front ever Sunday with the mothers of the church." Anna shook her head, realizing there would be nothing she could tell her grandmother to get out of going to church with her that Sunday, as much as she hated the thought of it.

"Anna, ya my chile's only chile. Granny wants ya to learn to take ya troubles to the Lord and leave 'em thare. He knows why this chile come into dis hare world. Hur life is not yers to take but his to save."

"Granny, I cursed God . . . asked him to take my life because I hated him. I told him this before I came to live with you. He has never given me happiness—just let me fool myself into believing I had happiness."

"Chile, the Lord is in ever plan. What'er yer sufferin', it ain't much as it could be. Granny can tell ya a heap about sufferin'. Dress Raspy. Granny's great-grandbaby needs hur blessin'," Granny said, smiling down at the baby in the bassinet next to Anna's bed as she pinned the white cap on her head indicating she was a member of the church's mother's board.

****

Anna sat in the large country church filled with all black people dressed so unlike the sophistication she was accustomed to in Session's All Saint's Baptist Church where they dressed in the best they could and sometimes could not afford. The minister of the church dressed up, too, and drove his Mercedes when his Lincoln was not feeling well Jake had often informed Anna. She remembered Jake telling her his take on the pastor of the All Saint's Baptist Church was that his threads were so fine that people went to church just to see what his attire would be that Sunday. Her husband referred to the high-fashion pastor as the preaching pimp, tougher by far than any street hustler. His prostitutes, according to Jake, included men, women, and children who gladly came paying their way to heaven through him.

"Where Anna sat now men wore blue jeans and white shirts or overalls that at had been starched and ironed. Most of the women dressed in simple dresses, their heads tied up in multicolored scarves such as the women had worn in the big barn Frankie Lee had taken her to. Children ran in bare feet across the floor.

Granny told Anna the black station wagon in the churchyard was the only car she would see, it was driven by their pastor. It looked so familiar to Anna somehow. The rhythm of the pianist and the organist filled the church with a spirit of pure southern gospel music. Voices sang the praises of a past generation of colored people as unfamiliar to her as the people singing them. She heard for the first time the old-time hymns her parents used to tell her about as she listened to the deacons praying prayers it was said made the hair rise at the nape of your neck.

Anna's eyes grew large as she looked over at Granny holding her blanketed baby. She wondered why Frankie Lee had not been able to find a family that wanted her. She had become so desperate that she had even offered to pay someone, but Frankie Lee insisted no one wanted a baby as white as hers. She could not blame them but wondered how they knew how light the baby was when they had not even seen her. Looking at the baby's white skin, she knew she was in big trouble if she didn't get rid of her soon.

Everyone in the church stood as a door in back of the pulpit opened. A man entered the room and walked up to the pulpit, his hand extended as if asking that they be seated. Anna's eyes stretched in disbelief—the pastor was the doctor she had cursed and scorned when he refused to give her the abortion she begged for. The same doctor who had visited Granny's caring for her every week even after he and Granny delivered Raspy. That station wagon outside was the same station wagon that stood outside her grandmother's house when he came to visit. She had been so busy trying to keep people from gazing at her that she had glanced at the station wagon without actually looking at it. Anna could not move.

"Oh my God," she whispered and then covered her mouth.

Granny placed her arm around Anna and whispered to her, "God still loves my grandchile, ya know it." She smiled at Anna, giving her Raspy to hold.

When the pastor called for Anna's baby to be brought forth she could not get it out of her head he was the doctor and, Granny had to push Anna to get her up. Among these humble people, she felt so out of place dressed as though she had just stepped out of Hollywood, as her father had said when she returned home. The deacons hummed a hymn so stirring it brought her to tears.

With the baby in his arms, the pastor prayed a prayer that caused Anna to want to run and never stop. "A poor helpless baby," he said, "has no one but her mother to love her, and if she forsakes her, what chance does she have in this world of so many miseries? Anna knew his message was meant for her. It came to her that if the child had been by a black man, she would have never thought of killing herself or harming it. She wondered what Raymond would think of her if he knew?

****

"Granny, I care what happens to her," Anna said when they returned to the house from having Raspy blessed in church. "I just don't know anything else to do but give her away. It is, I believe, the best for everyone. You know what it would mean for both of us if I took her back with me to Session."

"Let Granny keep hur, Chile." Anna took a seat in the first available chair, staring up at her grandmother, not believing she had heard correctly.

"You! But why would you want the responsibility of a baby this young?"

"Raspy ain't the first baby I done raised, Chile. I thank I did a well enough job caring for ya since ya been hare with Granny. Just having ya hare with me, knowin' ya be part of my own baby I'm carin' foe' done made many mo years come foe' old Granny. When Frankie Lee come tellin' Granny 'bout ya, it was like the Master done give me another chance to make it right wit my own chile I come into disfavor wit." Taking the baby from Anna, she hugged the infant and kissed her.

"Granny will love and care for hur. This chile is of the flesh I always loved. Even though my gal never forgave me fer what happened, I always loved hur. Granny understands about hatin'--she just don't want it in her life no mo. Hate kept God way from Granny til she learnt she needs him ever day of hur life. Nobody gonna take Granny's great-grandbaby unless thay know I don't want hur." Anna hardly knew what to say.

"But Granny, she has no resemblance to any member of our family except maybe Momma and you." Anna looked in her grandmother's eyes and saw pain she could not even start to understand. Anna thought Raspy must remind Granny of her own daughter by Jessie—the father Annabelle had loved and always talked about. Raspy, unlike Granny's children by Mr. Porter, would be that husband's grandchild by the daughter they had had together. Jessie's blood is in her somewhere. Anna knew if Raspy were to have a grandmother, it would never be her own mother because she would hate the baby just because a white man was her father.

"My boy never lived with hate in his heart, God bless him. I love him so much. Mr. Porter never stopped him from comin' to see me or payin' him to work. With little Raspy, I will have part of both my chilen." Anna looked at her grandmother, not knowing what to say.

"Granny will always tell her of her Momma. Maybe one day ya come back for hur. If it be so ya and yer colored man don't work out, ya can let hur father know of hur and see for yerself if he was worth yer time." Anna again did not know how to respond. The answer to her problem had come in such an unexpected way. She had been away from home almost a year. It was possible she no longer had a home to return to. But to leave her baby with her aging grandmother seemed a bit much--too much to ask for. Late in the night she pondered what Granny wanted to do for her. Wrestling with the pros and cons of such a decision, she was still stunned over her discovery that the doctor was also the pastor of the church. What a revelation. No wonder he refused to abort her baby. She couldn't wait to consult with Frankie Lee on the matter. He seemed to have all the answers.

It was the next weekend before Frankie Lee arrived. Two young boys beat Frankie Lee out of the car. They must be his sons she had not seen yet. At five and seven years old, they scurried into the yard with their hands waving in the air. Anna smiled as the chickens flew up to avoid their assaults, which caused the children to hurry after them.

The first thing Frankie Lee did was give Granny a kiss, telling her that her great-grandsons were out there scaring her chickens.

"Lardy a mercy," she said, hurrying outside.

"What ya got that serious look on ya fer, gurl." he asked, looking down at the baby asleep in the bassinet that had been pulled from her room.

Anna looked out the window at Granny and the boys talking as they all pointed to the farm animals. Turning back to him, she took a deep breath.

"Frankie Lee, Granny wants me to let her keep Raspy. Can you imagine that? What would she do with a baby this young?"

"The same thang every other family round hare do when thay gals go North and leave thay younguns behind. If ya gave Raspy away to somebody 'round hare, folks would know she's Granny's great-grandbaby and would wonder why she let it go to somebody not in the family."

"But Frankie Lee."

"Anna, we already done discussed it. The Old Man, Paul, and me— we already knowd Granny would git the kid. Dis ain't the North whare everbody is out for thayselves. Family is family. Ya need to be worryin' bout gittin' back home. Raspy's already at home."

"Frankie Lee, I can't! It would be wrong."

"Wrong, Cous, would be if ya give the kid to somebody don't love hur. Dat would be wrong. Ya need to git on up outta hare and find someone to make ya look like ya looked when ya first come to Oinston all pretty lookin'. If I was a man whose wife run off, if she come back lookin' like you lookin' now, I would send hur packin'. Ya already got a lot of 'plaining to do. I'm hoping ya do it lookin' better'n ya lookin' now, Cous. We got Raspy for ya. Ya best git on back and take care of dat business ya left waitin' on ya."

After Frankie Lee left, Anna sat alone in her room while Granny and Raspy had their evening time together before she came to bed. Anna thought about everything Frankie Lee had told her. Her baby was already loved by Granny. She knew that. And if Frankie Lee believed it was best, who was she to argue? He had brought her this far. She had needed to listen to him after all with no one wanting a baby as white as she it would be the best solution. Who else could she give her to but someone she knew loved her?

****

Anna began preparation for her journey back to Session, kissing Raspy over and over again; thinking how glad she was that Raspy would be with people she knew loved her. In her heart she felt she still would probably have to give her up but at least not now when she needed to return home. Getting the baby adjusted to sucking a bottle instand of her breasts proved to be a difficult task. One morning, Anna took a seat at Granny's feet so she could brush through her hair. The baby finally accepted the bottle after Granny put a little corn syrup on the nipple freeing her from breast-feeding. Anna sat with her on her lap feeling the pull of the brush as it moved through her hair. After a while, Anna laid her head on Granny's lap and said to her, "Granny, I long to be like you. You are such a strong woman, so sure of yourself. You know all the right things to do and you do them without even thinking about it. I'm so proud to have you as my grandmother." Anna listened to her grandmother's quiet laughter. "I mean it," Anna said, and before she knew it, what she had remembered slipped from her lips. "That day you took that shotgun and killed that cougar, I thought Mr. Porter would just about beat you to…" She stopped as her grandmother stopped brushing. "But he wasn't mad at you at all, Granny. He just said, 'Let's get this child to the hospital before she bleeds to death.' I got so much attention from the two of you it was like I was special somehow. When you were not kissing and petting on me, he was telling me Brer Rabbit stories I had never heard before; making me laugh all the while I was in the hospital. Even when I came home, I felt everybody's love especially Papa because he kept saying how he hated it happened. Even though we all hated what had happened, I got so much attention from my uncles and aunts I guess I was glad it happened in a way." Anna felt the brush move again through her hair.

"Mr. Porter done got that old cougar when it was just a pup. I done tole him time an agin dat animal need to be let loose. 'Course he kept it caged up til he had a mind to tend it. He knowd I was pretty well fit when I come up with that shotgun. I hated how it happened—my gal trustin' me to care for hur only chile and dat hadda come up. I prayed on how I would tell hur what happened and dat ya come out alright. I never figured she'd take a razor to hur own momma," Granny said, continuing to brush through Anna's hair. Taking a deep breath, Anna kissed the baby in her lap and looked up at Granny.

"It hurt me when Momma pulled that razor out. I remember it just like it happened a moment ago. As scared as I was, Granny, you made me so proud when you told Momma what you did. All of my memory is coming back to me Granny." Anna lowered her head as she looked at the orange pulsating light in the palm of her hand and then gazed beyond Granny. "On the way home we stopped at a little country grocery store. I remember now that I kept telling her that Papa was a nice man and that the mauling was an accident. He didn't mean for it to happen. I know now that I said the one thing she never wanted to hear or believe. A strange look appeared in Momma's eyes I now realize I didn't how bad I had upset her. There was a flowerbed just beyond that country store we were walking past. As soon as my words came out, she picked up one of the bricks that circled it and hit me so hard I didn't remember a thing when I came to. Feeling the lump on my head, I asked what had happened to me and where we were going and where had we been. She said she had picked me up from her brother's house and that we were going to meet Daddy in Illinois. After that, everything was erased from my mind. When I asked her to tell me about my past and the things I didn't remember, she said I had been ill and it was nothing for me to dwell on. I remembered nothing about Daddy's jail time. When I asked about my lost memory he agreed that it all should be left in the past."

Anna kissed her baby, saying to her, "Raspy, even if it took us almost dying to get our Granny back, it sure was worth it!" She looked up to see tears falling from her grandmother's eyes as she shook her head back and forth. Anna reached up, hugging and kissing her grandmother telling her everything was all right. As bad as it had seemed, her prayers were answered and the dawn had come.

"Anna, how did yer back come as to be healed chile? Dat pain stuck in my heart all dese yeers how I let my gal's baby git hurt."

"Granny, it was not your fault. Anyway, it was Raspy's father who took me out of the country to doctors who made my back as smooth as it is now. You see how God works, Granny. Sometimes he is blessing you and you don't even know it," Anna said, smiling seeing light filtering into her grandmother's eyes showed that she remembered her words to her.

"I promise Granny won't let nothin' happen to hurt dis baby like what happened to ya. I'd die first." Her apron went up to the corner of her eyes as her tears fell.

"Granny, no matter what happens—even to Raspy—I will never blame or stop loving you. Just do your best and let God do the rest." Granny's laughter filled the room as Anna squeezed Raspy closer, knowing she had just said something her grandmother could relate to.

****

Anna consented to the plan only after making both Granny and Frankie Lee promise they would get in touch with her if anything went wrong and insisting that Granny take thirty thousand dollars of the money in the attaché' case. Anna felt that even though Granny insisted she did not need it. since money was given to her by all her children gone and at home, Raspy's father had to take some responsibility for his baby's care. The money came from him, and he would want her to have it. Laying out the three pictures of Raymond and her, she taped them up in her room for the child to see, so that no matter what happened, she would know who her parents were.

****

Before leaving Granny's home, Anna had Frankie Lee take her to town so that she could make an international phone call to the Madame from a pay phone. Frankie Lee was right about the impression she would have to make. According to him, she looked like she had just had a baby. She needed to get herself ready for meeting her family, and she could never do it looking like a homely matron.

"The Madame, please. Tell her Anna Bradley is on the line." Seconds later, she heard the Madame's voice beaming through the receiver.

"Your money is no good here. To which airline do you want the Madame to send your ticket?"

The day Frankie Lee, Granny, and Raspy saw her off at the airport Anna kissed her daughter and grandmother again and again as she prepared to fly out of the country. Thanking Granny over and over for what she was doing for her, she looked at the baby wondering if she would ever-sat eyes on her again.

"Anna, ya are gonna to miss your flight," Frankie Lee told her, giving her a big hug.

"Have you spent all of your money?" she asked him of the money she had given him months before.

"Not one red cent. Got it rolled up with a rubber band hid away sos I can count and kiss it ever day." Anna laughed, as she was reminded of the dirt poor farmer in Kentucky Raymond's father had sent twenty thousand dollars to.

****

"You know, Madame," Anna said, looking at her Mid-Eastern friend taking hold of her hands after they arrived at the spa from the airport, "it helps when you have someone teaching you about life and things you are not up on. I did not want to go home physically and mentally broken. I had to get my mind and my body ready to return. I know you took a great deal of verbal abuse from me when I called you after discovering my pregnancy." Anna remembered that awful call she had made to the Madame in anger because she hadn't warned her she was carrying a baby. "I needed to come and apologize for that."

"If I had warned you, would you have been better off knowing, Ms. Anna?" Anna thought of all she had shared with the Madame.

"No, Madame. I would have destroyed a life without ever knowing what was waiting for me because of her. Me trying to kill myself then having my grandmother enter into my life again has been worth it all. Just knowing my grandmother loved me enough to risk taking me into her home after what she went through with my mother. Yes, now I am glad you withheld that information from me, even though at time I was furious."

"Ms. Anna, I took nothing you said to heart. You were struggling with a crisis you had no idea how to handle. As I have often informed you, it's you Western women who must have the answers right before your eyes or you think there is no answer. Once you got out of the way, the spirit brought order and revealed things to you that you would have otherwise never known. That Old Head you have in your energy takes excellent care of you while forcing you to face life's realities, my dear. Of course, your decision to allow your grandmother to care for your baby keeps her safe as she kept you safe when your mother left you with her. The cougar's mauling your back was an awful accident—something your grandmother regretted. Your mother's desperation in having her mother care for you went far beyond what she ever thought she would have to do. The incident with your back sent her back to that dark place she had lived in for so long. Thank the holyspirit for this Old Head that guides your life's journey, Ms. Anna. It is a phantasmagoria this life of yours."

Anna looked at the Madame, thinking about the Old Head she had unintentionally mentioned to her during one of their periods of meditation. The Madame had absorbed her information, assuring her the God spirit in her life had sent it to take care of her.

There was something about the Mid-Eastern woman that let Anna know she would understand that part of her life. As Anna explained to her, it was the Old Head that had brought her through hell and allowed her to see heaven. She knew this last ordeal had tested her in a way that had almost destroyed her. Thinking of the recent birth of her baby, she knew that from the day she agreed to allow her grandmother to keep her baby, she, Anna Drake Bradley, would live in two different worlds— one with her parents, her children, and her husband, and the other with her grandmother and her biracial baby she must keep a secret. Anna remembered seeing the tears in her grandmother's eyes as she hugged her before leaving while telling her how she was so happy to have the baby stay with her. Granny said she would pray that the Master would fix things so that Anna could come to know Him as she knew Him. His mercy and grace were things she wanted her granddaughter to seek and find in her life. Without it, Granny had warned her, she would always roam lost in a sad world. Anna had been glad to finally board the plane so that her tears could not be seen by those she was forced to leave behind.

She would need the Madame to work her miracles on her body. Granny had made sure her milk had completely dried up with special herbs from the plants she grew in her hothouse out back. Anna remembered having to hold her nose because of its horrible smell, but true to Granny's word, the milk in her breasts had dried up in days.

Once Anna had settled down and had given the Madame a full account of her recent journey, the Madame threw her hands up, exclaiming, "Ms. Anna, yours is a saga I keep trying to write the ending to, but my endings are always too tame and surely unworthy of a life as exciting and dangerous as a mountain climber in the Himalayas," she whispered, shaking her head. "Imagine being reacquainted with a grandmother you have known in an earlier life and being guided by an Old Head and a spider only you can see. What a journey the universe has bestowed on you! If only it were my life we were speaking of!" the Madame exclaimed, her fascination apparent in her voice.

"Madame, I wouldn't wish this journey on my worst enemy. All this time, I thought it was those switches that had scarred my back, only to learn it was not. I see now why my father did not tell me the truth about what happened. I doubt my mother told him. I know now why I lost my memory. It was that brick Momma hit me with. Her anger knows no boundaries. Of course, Momma is not a woman to be reasoned with once she makes up her mind of something good or bad. When I arrived home with no memory of what had happened, both of my parents were glad they didn't have to explain why my father had been in prison for a year. It relieved Momma of the burden of explaining her mother to us and the reason why she stayed away from me so long."

After a month, the Madame finally assured her that her body was fit as that of a young maiden. When the time came, Anna bid her goodbye, telling her it was time to continue her journey. She promised it would not be the last time they would see each other and promised that she would keep her abreast of whatever twists and turns her journey took.

Chapter Twenty-One

Hands clutched together, temperature elevated Anna felt her heart race as she walked into her husband's office. She had climbed the ten steps one at a time, dreading this day as she had many others since the discovery of her pregnancy. She made her way inside glancing at a vase of red roses that sat on the secretary's desk and of course hers when she had worked there. Thick brown carpet covered his office floor, replacing the green carpet she remembered. Sites of construction work with Jake and the men who worked for him hung around the wall.

"Is Mr. Bradley in?" she asked the unknown brown skinned woman seated at Jake's regular secretary's desk. Gazing at the madronly woman who looked up at her, Anna wondered where Mrs. Cory, his regular secretary was?

"Mrs. Bradley, he's not in, but you are welcome to wait in his office. He should be in from the construction site shortly." A puzzled look appeared on Anna's face as she wondered how the woman knew her.

"Oh, I'm just here until Mrs. Cory returns from vacation. There's the family picture on his desk, and I remembered you from the papers . . . when you were missing all that time."

"Oh," Anna replied realizing the woman must have read in her facial expression her concern. She turned and stepped into Jake's office as the secretary prepared to leave for the day.

A deep sigh escaped Anna's lips as she realized she was always coming or going. She looked around her husband's office as her hands slid over the three file cabinets of important documents he often reached for to give him information on some new or old project under construction. Anna picked up the picture of herself, their children, and Jake from his desk. She pressed the picture next to her breasts as she thought of her children she had left behind again, another unkept promise.

There were so many promises she had made and not kept, she couldn't keep up. Placing the picture back on the desk she prayed a silent prayer that they could at least be civil to each other even in if the marriage was over. A glance out of the window brought her attention to a jogger running along the sidewalk. That could be me, she thought. Always running, each time her life became more complex than before. Where and when would it all end she wondered?

Her heart skipped a beat seeing Jake drive up outside and get out of the company truck. A smile flashed across his face as he waved goodbye to the driver. She had not wanted to face him but knew it was something she could not avoid. He would tell her if it was over; if so, it would be easier to hear it from him in his office and get out of his life than it would be to feel his rejection in their home.

Anna trembled in anticipation when he entered his office. "How may I help you?" he asked, giving no indication that he knew her as he looked over mail he carried in his hand.

"I've come back to face my punishment, whatever the hell it might be." This had been her first stop; she felt she owed him that much after having been away so long. She watched the mail slip from his hands to the floor.

"Anna, my God! I'd given you up!" Taking her into his arms, he crushed her to him. "Where the hell have you been?"

"I've been in hell! A hell I thought I'd never live through," she whispered, her arms drawing him closer to her.

"Some way and somehow, I knew you would return. I knew it . . . if not for me, at least for our children. When Momma called and asked if I had found you or heard something. I knew then that you were really in hiding. Figured it might be a long time . . . but I had to wait it out."

"Barb—did she . . .?" Anna could not say the words that stood on the tip of her tongue.

"I don't know which is the worst, my limp or Barb's scarred face. Anna, that affair with Barb is something I will regret the rest of my life. It has left scars my fingers are forever crossing. She totally destroyed my life that night she set me up. It was a damnable payback."

"How bad is she, Jake?" Anna asked, easing out of his arms.

"The nurse I talked to in the hospital told me she was scarred all over most of her body. Her face is scarred almost beyond recognition. Rumor had it that my wife returned to take vengeance on Barb because of her betrayal. Barb insisted it was you, but no one at the party admitted seeing you there. I told the authorities you had been out of town for several weeks. With no witnesses and Barb half out of her mind, the case was finally dropped. Let's not stand here talking about her." Jake insisted, pushing Anna toward the door as he turned the lights out in his office.

Anna sucked in her breath as they drove into her parents' driveway. She was glad Jake knew this was where she would want to come. She needed to see her children and parents. She had been away from them too long. Jake unlocked the door allowing her to walk inside ahead of him. Her parents and children stood up from the dinner table and shouted her name. Anna's entire body warmed. It was as though she had journeyed from one world into another.

Sheri' wanted to know where she had been all that time. Jake Jr. quickly informed his sister that their mother had been in a secret place where the police couldn't go get her. He wanted to know why his sister didn't remember their grandmother telling them that. A deep frown formed in his brows as it always did when he had to clarify facts for his sister. The hugs and kisses she received from them let her know how much they had missed her. However, it was her father who captured the moment. He stood up from the table saying as he pulled her into his arms,

"Baby Girl never let dark catch you away from home without your family knowing your whereabouts. Your disappearance almost killed me." With his arms holding her ever so close, Anna wept, promising never to allow that to happen again.

Of course, her mother took control when the children scrambled to get their things to go home with their parents. She stated that they had to go to school from her home, something they wouldn't be missing just because their mother was back.

Anna let her mother do what she loved doing . . . taking charge of everyone's life. It occurred to Anna that she and her grandmother were certainly similar in their way of taking control of matters needing tending to. As a matter of fact, except for age, they still looked a lot alike. Now that she knew what had happened to her after the bus incident she hated her mother's bitterness against her grandmother for things she had no control over. When it appeared they might heal from the past of how her mother's father had died, an unfortunate accident rekindled the hate because of her fear of what her father would do when he discover how terrible her back had be marred. It caused the hate in her mother's heart towards her grandmother to rekindle. It seemed to Anna a sad thing to hate your own mother, especially someone who had been through the hell Granny had been through. She almost mentioned her grandmother on impulse, but something stopped her, and she filed it away with the rest of her past that she now remembered.

"Why ain't I heard from ya all the while ya been gone, gal? Lease when ya was gone b'fore, ya let yer Momma knowd how ya was. Nearly worried me and yer daddy outta our minds."

"Momma, I thought I had killed Barb. How could I call or write? If I had called and let you know where I was, the authorities would have forced a God-fearing woman to lie. It was important to protect you as well as Daddy; Momma wasn't it you who told me to keep on going?" Anna breathed a sigh of relief as her mother nodded that she did.

"My kids have grown like weeds. I never want to have to leave them again," Anna whispered, turning the subject away from her long absence.

"Chile, dem babies of yers sho' special now," her mother said, smiling.

"What are you talking about, Momma?"

"Everbody all over town knowed bout ya and dat whore ya used dat razor on. Even at the chilen's school, thay talked on it. And Jake Jr. come home a braggin'."

"Momma, that's horrible! Did it hurt them?" Anna asked, not wanting to believe they found joy in something that tragic.

"'Course not. Folks been tellin' thay chilen Sheri' and Jake Jr.'s momma—Mrs. Annabelle's daughter—almost kilted dat shelter woman 'bout her husband. They kinda special now up thare at dat school." Anna listened to her mother's laughter.

"Momma, that's nothing I want them to be proud of when they think of their mother."

"Say chilen askin' dem what weapon ya used. How many times the whore done been cut? Some says it was over a hundred times and some folks even claimed the angry Mrs. Bradley cut the woman under her feet she was so mad. Annabelle Drake's daughter, they says—yes, that's hur."

Seeing the pride her mother felt as her smile deepened, she turned, shaking her head feeling sadness for them all.

Anna wished she could have talked her mother into allowing the children to come home with her and Jake. She didn't know how things between them would turn out. That year must have taken a toll on their renewed marriage. Riding home she wondered would he ask where she had been? Who she had been with? There were too many questions he might ask that she had no true answers for.

Anna ran her fingers over the furniture in the home she had left and had intended to return to in a few hours after responding to Dee's call about discovering the contents of the attaché case Sheri' had found. It was a home that seemed foreign to her now. The gown she had tossed across the chair by the bed still lay there. She wondered why Jake had not moved it.

Later, lying in bed beside Jake that night, Anna noticed that he looked at her as if something was wrong.

"What is wrong, Jake? Why are you staring at me like that?" Anna asked, nervous about what he could possibly know.

"Have you been with him again? I've gotta know!" Jake asked his hand on his head as he looked down at her she sensed fear in his eyes.

"There has been no man in my life or bed since I last slept with you. As God is my witness, I swear on my own mother's grave that she might die this very minute." Tears slipped from his eyes as he pulled her to him.

"My God, I'm glad to hear that!" His hand moved across her breasts, causing Anna to freeze. Granny had assured her the herbs given her would rid her of all traces of milk and firm her nipples up again. As Granny had said to her, she would be going home to a husband who would want to have her if he wanted her at all. Her trip home had been postponed twice. Granny made sure her breasts were firm and dry, and the Madame made sure her body had no signs of childbirth.

Her nipples hardened at his touch. He sucked hard as the baby had done at times. A warm glow spread throughout Anna's body. "I've waited too long to have you," he whispered as his body covered hers.

****

Seated at the dinner table with Jake and the children later that week, Anna listened to Jake speak of James.

"Did he and Lois ever get back together?" she asked.

"You have been back almost week and I haven't gotten a chance to take you to see James. No, Lois never did return. They are divorced. Lois now lives in Springfield. James has a new wife. She's five months pregnant."

"You've got to be kidding!" Anna exclaimed as she listened to the latest family news. When she had called Dee, she had informed her that Barb had not been seen since she left the hospital and that she would tell her the details on everyone else when they got together.

"Well, Anna, its not every man who loves his wife as deeply as I love you. You don't realize how hard it was waiting for you."

"I love you too, Jake. When you get time, please take me by to see James's new wife. I sure want to meet her," Anna said, steering the conversation away from her long absence.

****

Anna stood waiting several days later for Jake to get home from work. They would be going to visit James and his new wife. It was James who greeted them at the door when they arrived. Reaching out to Anna, he gave her a hug and kiss. Nothing inside reminded her of Lois. The walls were now Beige instead of white, shorter red sofas with round glass end tables replaced Lois' long black sectional sofa.

"After seeing the damage you did to that woman, I told that brother of mine he sure as hell had better be glad it was Barb's ass and not his ass you were cutting on. Damn, you sho nuff a mean woman, Anna Bradley. You should have known we were not going to allow you to go down the river on that case. Here in Session we protect our own, and you certainly are Jake Bradley's wife. Bring your ass on out here, woman, so I can do some shocking myself," he shouted into the next room as the three of them took seats.

"Hey man," James said to Jake, "you know we have our council meeting next month. I hope now that you have Anna back, you can focus on what lies ahead for us in Session. You are coming to the next meeting, aren't you?"

"Yes, I'll be there," Jake, said as his arms went around Anna's shoulders. "With my wife by my side, I'm ready for anything. You know we'll be meeting some brothers from the West Coast. They want to bring in some new development they say is good for the city."

"Jake, I still think brother man Mike Smith is our best out. Even though he has that ofay dude with him, he is not talking about moving in on us so fast."

"You might be right. You can never tell about a brother. The ofay will tell you quick, 'I know I am the best because I am white.'"

Anna looked from Jake to James as James spoke again. "The brother will tell you, 'I am the best in spite of being black.'"

Anna turned back to Jake as he replied, "I can't stand that weakness in some black men. I think just like that ofay thinks: I'm the best because I am black. We might have to deal with these brothers carefully because if they think they are coming in here taking over for the man, there is nothing they can offer the people in Session."

A woman walked into the living room; Anna sucked in her breath. She was reminded of when her own stomach just months ago had stood out the same as this woman's. She smiled and spoke to Anna. "So you are the wife Jake has been so worried about. Now I know where your children get their good looks. I'm so glad we are finally meeting. I've heard so much about you." Anna could have dropped straight through the floor. There standing before her was the young white woman who had charged James with raping her. She was now his legal wife. Their eyes locked. Anna had no doubt that Tammy remembered her and the picture she had shown her. Why had she not said anything to James? From the look on her face, Anna knew Tammy was conscious of their awkward situation. The evening went along pleasantly enough, but Anna was glad when it was time to go.

It occurred to Anna that Tammy might be planning to wait until the appropriate time to expose her. The encounter had been anything but comfortable.

"You have the same look I had when I first discovered they were together," Jake said laughing as he looked over at Anna as they drove home.

"How did you find out?" Anna still felt the shock that must show in her face.

"James and I walked into Forals and there she sat with Bo Pee. That look you have now ain't nothing compared to how James looked when he saw her sitting there with Bo Pee's arm wrapped around her".

"What was she doing in Session, especially after what happened between her and James?" Anna asked, still stunned over her discovery.

"James went over to Godfrey and brought her back to Session. Had her hid away. He didn't want us to know he had taken the woman back, so he wouldn't take her anywhere or let her go anywhere. Didn't even tell me he had her," Jake said, laughing.

"James is too much," Anna replied, shaking her head.

"He couldn't stand seeing her about to be snatched up by Bo Pee, right? So he called her out, and she blew his cover. Told him if he thought she was going to stay hidden away because he was ashamed for people in Session to know they were together, he was mistaken. The woman told everything."

"I know James was embarrassed," Anna said.

"Yeah, but not enough to let Bo Pee have her, fool apologized to her right in front of everyone and told Bo Pee she was his woman. He walked out of Forals with her under his arm. Fool forgot I came with him—didn't even look back. Married the woman soon after Lois divorced him." Anna sat listening to Jake, fearing more than ever that the white woman would expose her.

****

I'm here because . . ." Anna said, taking the seat Tammy Bradley offered her.

"You're here to find out when I plan to divulge your secret."

"Yes. Of course, I can't blame you . . . not after everything that has happened. I can't, however, have you holding this matter over my head without knowing when you plan to bring it up. Tell whatever it is you feel you must and be done with it," Anna challenged her.

"To accomplish what, may I ask? You did me a favor, whether you realize it or not. I didn't want to hurt anyone but James. It was you who made me realize I was hurting innocent people, especially children who had nothing to do with our affair. My accusations hurt every other white woman desiring to have a relationship with a black man. No, Anna, you did me no evil deed. I was selfishly screwing up too many lives because of my own pain. You put yourself on Front Street, as James likes to say, because you knew how deep the pain was for your own children and others who didn't deserve being hurt something that didn't occur to me at the time. I don't know if I could have done that and anyway no one would have believed me." She spoke with her hands on her enlarged stomach. "You were right in doing what you did. It was you and you alone who made me agree to take the stand and change my story. I'm glad now because I at last have the man I have loved for so long." A smile lightened Tammy's face. But for Anna, a sudden sadness filled her heart.

"You know, Anna, the woman in the picture you showed me had something in her eyes that said she was a woman in love." Anna turned her head and looked away.

Tammy continued, saying, "It may be true that you black women and white men started the ball to rolling, but it may also be true that it will have to be white women and the black men that keep it rolling."

"Maybe you're right," Anna said as she thought of the white man who had been in her life and his child she had given birth to who was now in hiding. A feeling of inadequacy filled Anna's heart, and she again felt the need to flee.

Chapter Twenty-Two

$\sim\!\!\text{m}\!\!\sim$

Anna had her children scrambling around in an effort to get to church on time. She had promised Granny one of the first things she would do when she returned home was to attend a church. It had been too many years since she had attended any church services before she had gone with Granny. It was not her thing. As soon as she had gotten married to Jake, she had slowed down and then completely stopped going. For her it was like belonging to a country club. Once a week, the blacks in Session met, talked about God and how they needed to help those in need, and returned home, still distancing themselves from the poor souls in need. There was none of the pure form she had discovered in that country black church down in Louisiana.

She knew in Session's Southern Saints Baptist Church, the members came every Sunday dressed to the hilt in all their finery. All that godliness Granny kept telling her she would get going to church had not surfaced for her there. Anyway it was easy to blame Jake for not going.

"Momma, why can't we stay here with Daddy?" Sheri' asked, stalling. Anna knew her daughter did not want to go to church with her. Sheri' had hoped she would get out of going to church by spending the weekend with her parents instead of her grandparents.

"Because I said you can't. Hurry up before I call and tell your grandmother you are trying to play hooky from church. You go to church every Sunday when you're living with your grandmother and grandfather; now hurry! I don't want to walk in late like a lot of people do who have children who make them late by trying to get out of going. Jake Jr., are you ready, boy?"

"Yes ma'am. I've been ready." He smiled at Anna while throwing a quick glance at his sister who frowned furiously at him.

"Where's my family going dressed so fine?" Jake asked, coming out of the bedroom in his pajamas.

"We are on our way to church, Jake, and I don't want us to be late."

"When did you become interested in church?" Anna threw him a look of annoyance.

"Come to think about it—I think I need a little church. Give me a minute or two and I will come along, too," Jake said as Sheri' ran into his arms.

"Daddy, if you are willing to go 'cause Momma is making us, I will be happy to go, too," Sheri' said, sticking her tongue out at her brother.

"Sheri', it's a man's place to be there for and with his family. Just give me a minute and I'll be right along," Jake said, smiling at Anna as Sheri' and Jake Jr. now gave more enthusiasm to going to church with their parents.

****

If Anna had not realized before how important her husband was to the black community of Session, she soon discovered it as heads turned and smiles enveloped the members when they saw him walk into the church with his family. Even the pastor raised a brow upon seeing them enter. She watched the surprised smile appear on her mother's face as she sat on the deaconess bench opposite her father, who was a deacon on the board. Both had been members in the church for as long as they had lived in Session. Anna caught her father's gaze as he smiled and shook his head. To Anna's surprise, she saw Dee, Fred, and their three children. And, of course, James sat with Tammy. Anna knew they were all glad to see Jake there. Here, Anna sat in her comfort zone, for all of the members dressed in the style suited for upper-middle-class progressive blacks. Hats, suits, and all sorts of fancy hairstyles made the congregation a picturesque scene. The sermon, typical of most upper-class churches, was not geared to raise the emotions but a slitter; there was no sweating caused by shouting or dancing around the church. After the sermon, a woman rose and sang "Sweet Home," a gospel song Anna had not heard since she had lived with her parents and had listened to her father sing it around the house. He had said his mother had loved the song. He use to listen to her sing it when he was a boy. She looked at her father and saw tears falling from his eyes. Her mother pulled out her handkerchief and wiped tears from her eyes. Anna felt her own tears fall as her mind wandered back to that tiny country church down in Louisiana, and to her grandmother and the child Anna was unable to acknowledge.

Getting out of church took over an hour with people hugging and kissing Jake, the kids, and even Anna, though she hardly knew any of them. A woman walked up to Anna just as she and the children were about to step out of the door.

"Do you remember me?" the brown-skinned woman asked. She was wearing a sweeping beige hat with a dark brown feather across it that matched the beige and tan suit she wore. Taller though thinner than Anna she stood in the doorway, preventing her from passing.

"I can't say that I ever recall meeting you," Anna replied, staring hard at the woman, trying to remember her.

"I came in needing shelter for me and my daughter who was sick at the time. I told you we were living on the streets. You told me there was room and sent me to see Barb to get registered in. She refused to allow me to have the room, telling me she was holding it for someone else who would need it in a couple of days. I begged her to allow me to stay at least for the night because my baby was so sick. She refused even when you informed her there was one bed open. I lost my six-month-old baby to pneumonia." She lifted Anna's hands and kissed them. "I was there at Dee's that night you cut that heifer almost to death and left her bloody ass laying on the floor with her drawers around her ankles. Pay back is a bitch!"

A frown filled her face as she looked beyond Anna. Anna saw in it the kind of hate she had seen only in the face of her mother when she talked about her tragic past. "I went to that hospital to see that heifer and laughed as I stared down at her reminding her of all that big talk she was doing that night at the Chinaware Party. She turned her horrible looking face away from me."

A far away look appeared in the woman's eyes. "I then told her what happened to my baby after she turned us away." I can go on with my life now, knowing she will have to live with her own pain." Kissing Anna's hands again, she turned and walked back down the steps.

"Who was that woman?" Sheri' asked, looking up at her mother.

"A woman who lives with grief," Anna answered. The Old Head and its thirteen eyes appeared in her mind as she looked at her pulsating palm, thinking of the tragic lives that filled the earth world.

"Hey girl, you are the last person I expected to find here!" Dee said, looking with Anna at the woman leaving the church. "Oh, she hasn't been right since her baby died about six years ago. It was such a tragedy. She was living in her car at the time." Shaking her head, Dee turned back to Anna.

"Girl, you and Jake looked so good coming in here with the kids. I had to shed a tear myself when I saw you walk through that door. Fred was about floored. He looked over at James and said that only the new Anna could have gotten that fool in here." Anna hunched her shoulders in response. Of course, every man, woman, and child in town wanted to shake Jake's hand or talk to him about the upcoming town meeting in the next month.

By the time they arrived at her father's restaurant, all of the family had gathered. Tables were placed together so they could all be seated. Anna overheard her father discussing something with her mother. Walking over, she realized her mother was stalling about taking a seat. She was already annoyed that she had had to sit in church with Tammy.

"Momma the tables are far enough apart so that you won't have to sit anywhere near Tammy. Don't embarrass Daddy for goodness sake," Anna, whispered, a frown forming in her brows as she stared her mother down. Finally Annabelle agreed to sit at the far end of the table so she would not have to look at Tammy at all. Of course, neither Tammy nor James had any knowledge of the problem.

"Only Momma can get away with behaving like this. We just have to realize why and look over it," Jake said, laughing.

After everyone was seated, the table was filled with food. Anna listened to her father bless the food they were about to eat and thought of the doctor/pastor down in Louisiana.

"Dad, this is a feast fit for a king, but I must tell you that your daughter has been keeping a secret. It shocked the socks off my feet." Anna stared at Jake, not knowing if she should try to stop him from saying something that might destroy her in the eyes of everyone there or if she should leave to escape being exposed. Everyone's eyes fell on her as Jake wrapped his arm around her shoulders. "My wife has been cooking me some of the most delicious meals I have ever eaten in my life since she has returned," he said, smiling as his lips lightly touched Anna's. A smile lit up Anna's face as she let out a breath of air. "She fills this stomach of mine full of the lightest biscuits I have ever eaten, right kids?" Anna thought about her grandmother's cooking and how anxious she had been to learn from her how to cook, something that had never interested her before.

"Daddy's telling the truth. Jake Jr. said they tasted better than Grandma's," Sheri' told them all.

Jake Jr. spoke up. "Shut up, bitch. You talk too much. I like both Grandma's and Momma's biscuits!" Anna saw the shocked looks on everyone's faces as they looked up and stared in Jake Jr.'s direction.

"Son, did I just hear you call your sister a bitch?" Anna watched Jake's eyes narrow as he released his hold on her shoulder and rose from his seat as he stared over at his son.

"Daddy, I didn't mean nothing by it—it's just a word dudes use to refer to girls these days."

"Son, you have been hanging around the wrong dudes. Only a fool or a coward addresses a female as though she were a dog. Didn't you just come out of church?"

"Yes sir," Jake Jr. answered as he lowered his head.

"Well you didn't learn a thing because if you had, you would know that women and girls are God's most precious gift to man, son. Your mother is my queen and your sister is my princess. A prince would never refer to his princess sister in such a degrading manner. Do you understand what I'm trying to teach you, boy?"

"Yes sir," Jake Jr. answered as Anna watched her son look down in embarrassment.

"Good. Now apologize to your sister, and then apologize to the family members who heard that degrading, filthy word come out of your mouth," Jake told him sternly.

Jake Jr. turned to his sister. "I apologize to you Sheri' and everyone here for that rude comment I just made." He then looked down at the floor. "A prince should never address a princess or any female in such a manner. Jake Jr. looked over at his sister and said, "Sheri' please don't quote me incorrectly next time. Is that better, Daddy?" he asked, again looking down at the floor. Anna knew he was embarrassed by the attention his rude statement had caused. She realized that he was being exposed too early to the kind of teenage influence that would become a part of his language as a man if he was not taught better soon.

"Yes son, that is better. A man who has no control over what come out of his mouth will not amount to much in this world," Jake replied, as everyone at the table nodded in agreement. Soon, they gave the food before them their attention. Anna felt her heartbeat slowing down as she realized her fear of being exposed was unfounded and was glad that her son had been soundly reprimanded. Everyone she noticed relaxed and began to enjoy the barbecue her father was famous for along with the rest of the meal served for their enjoyment. Of course, as they filed out of the restaurant to return home, her mother pulled her to the side.

"Gal, whare ya been to lern how to cook? Ya never found interest in cookin' hot water as long as I've knowd ya." Anna gazed into the knowing eyes of her mother, remembering her ability to confront matters that left her victim unprepared with a quick answer.

"New York, Momma. You know they have some of the best chefs in the country." Anna knew better than to look away, so she stared her mother in the face locking eyes with her. Her mother smiled.

"I knowed I'd find out whare ya being hidin'. New York—well, I do say. Hope ya didn't pick up no bad habits. Cookin' for that husband of yers. I'm glad ya finally realize what a wife's job is gal." Anna turned to get in the car when Jake opened the door for her realizing the era her mother was from demanded a place for its women that no longer existed for all women.

****

Standing outside her home, she chatted with Sheri' while she waited for her school bus, something they both enjoyed doing every morning. The school was located near her parents' home. That was where both children had attended until Anna had noticed her son's aptitude test scores were high enough for him to enter into the gifted program offered. Of course, it was a problem that the school he would have to attend was in Godfrey. Annabelle had stood firm against his going to the school with white students. With Anna's insistence, Jake for once went against Annabelle's wishes and allowed Jake Jr. to be bused to the gifted school. He now was off to Godfrey, attending school with students embracing higher academic studies than his sister. Anna noticed that Sheri' seemed glad to be relieved of the competition because she was unable to make the grades her brother achieved.

Returning inside, she noticed the black widow hanging from her light fixture. Her heart skipped a beat as she reached to answer the ringing phone and heard Frankie Lee's voice on the other end. Anna took a seat as her heart speed increased, wondering what had happened down in Louisiana. He wanted to know when she was coming down to see Raspy. Two years seemed a long time to him for her not to have come to see about her baby at least once.

"Don't you think I know that, Frankie Lee?" she replied, near tears at hearing the seriousness of his voice. She could still feel the soft touch of her baby's body lying across her chest as she slept. Her heart warmed as she remembered the pull of her tiny lips on her nipples. Whenever she could get to a phone booth and call, she had asked Granny to place Raspy's ear to the telephone and she had promised that she would soon be coming to see about her. Tears filled her eyes as she thought about how fast time passed. Missed opportunities came and went. First there was school and having to help the kids with schoolwork. Then, she thought she would be able to take a weekend and drive down for a short visit, but when she mentioned driving down, Jake had assured her he would take off and accompany her. Finding an excuse not to go, she missed that year. Now another year was nearly gone. Raspy would be two years old. She had not laid eyes on her since she was three months old. Anna broke down crying.

"By the time ya git down hare, the kid'll be grown, Anna." Anna squeezed the phone, listening to her cousin reprimand her about something that lay heavy on her heart every minute of the day.

"Frankie Lee, what do you want me to do? Tell you to bring her here?"

"Nah Anna, I couldn't do dat. She looks too much like dat pappy of hurs." Anna's heart sank; hearing news that she hoped had changed.

"I have not been able to get away, Frankie Lee. Jake keeps on insisting on coming with me whenever I mention coming. I cannot let that happen. Suppose someone says something and blows everything. I wish I could just adopt her out to someone." She heard his grunt and hated that she had said it.

"Granny ain't lettin' nobody have dat chile. Aunt Jenny asked fer dat baby several times. Granny wouldn't allow hur to call ya to see if it was okay. Aunt Nancy even offered to take hur off hur hands. Granny keeps telling 'em hur momma is comin' fer hur. That ole woman has got 'tached to dat kid, and she ain't lettin' hur go with nobody but ya, Anna."

"I don't know what to do short of bringing her here, Frankie Lee. If I leave with her and go somewhere else, I'd have to leave my other children here. I cannot do that, I just can't. We are just now getting reacquainted, and I don't want to lose my relationship with them again. You should understand that."

"Anna, this baby needs ya, too. I don't know what to tell ya. It seems to me ya done dumped her for Jake and yer other kids. Raspy needs to see hur mother at least once a yeer. Somehow ya gotta make it happen." Anna realized that Frankie Lee must have become attached to the baby just as he said her grandmother had.

"I'll try, Frankie Lee. I swear to God, I'm going to find a way to get down there even if it means bringing Jake with me."

"Cous, I know the fix ya're in. I'll figure somethin' out even if I have to brang Granny and Raspy to see ya. We could get a place to stay in a nearby town, and ya could come thare and visit with the baby. How's dat?"

"Yes, Frankie Lee, if it has to happen like that, I am all for it."

"Yeah Cous, if it comes to dat, dat's what we'll do." She heard a deep sigh before the phone clicked in her ear. The Old Widow crawled along the windowsill and was soon out of sight. Anna hung up the phone realizing her two worlds were about to collide.

****

That evening when Jake came home, Anna lay in their bedroom crying nonstop.

"What's wrong, baby?" he asked, taking a seat on the bed beside her.

"Jake, my life is so messed up. I'd just as soon take a gun and end it all right now."

"What the hell has happened to you, Anna?"

Not able to tell him what had happened, Anna drew him into her arms, allowing him to make love to her.

Frankie Lee's call caused guilt to eat away at Anna for not going to see about her baby. Jumping at the sound of the ringing phone, she felt as imprisoned as she had felt when she was in the two-room apartment down in Louisiana, carrying the baby she desperately wanted to rid herself of. Now she couldn't even go see her. At dinner, Anna had to be asked the same question several times before she answered. The puzzled looks on Jake's face and her children's faces let her know it was not the answer they expected.

Jake came home one evening and commented that the house was clean enough to eat off the floor. Anna had begun unconscious cleaning to try to keep her mind off the problem she had no way of solving. She welcomed the time Jake made sure to spend with her. Soon, however, Jake's construction business and the needs of the city council took more and more of his time. Anna's tears came and went as the days dragged into weeks and the weeks melted away into months. Two years she knew was far too long not to have come back to see her baby. When she had left her twins, she had returned to see them—in and out—but she had always come back to Sheri' and Jake Jr. Not like this. Now a stranger to the child she had left, Anna knew soon she would have to think of some way to get back down to Louisiana somehow.

One night, Anna woke up. Jake was nowhere to be found. The clock read four o'clock in the morning. Anna shivered, seeing the Old Widow hanging high above the foot of the bed. Her mind on Frankie Lee's telephone call, she lay in the dark room thinking back to her time with him, Granny, and her newborn infant. Frankie Lee had come by Granny's to see them when the baby was a month old.

"Damn, Anna," he had said looking down at the nursing baby, "the older Raspy gits the whiter she gits. Looks like ya woulda gave that white man a little help. All she got is yer dimples."

"Frankie Lee, shut your mouth. Granny, she is getting whiter. There must be some white man in your mother's past who caused your color and Momma's, because it seems as though this baby has all white genes and I know she came out of my black body." A smile formed on her grandmother's lips.

"No baby . . . thare ain't been no white man coused my light color." Anna and Frankie Lee looked at each other and then back at Granny.

"'Thare's a bit on one side corse my Papa was a fair-skinned man but it was on my own momma's deathbed that she whispered to Mabel, 'Gal, all this time I done fool dese white folks into thinkin' I be a light-skinned colored. Truth be tole I's as white as any of "em ole crackers. Vinegar and salt water coarse my hair.'" Frankie Lee and Anna's mouths gapped open in shock. "Whispered it so's no one heard hur. My papa said it be so. My momma be a pure white woman. My papa be a man light in color so Mabel come hare a fair chile."

"Dat ole woman laughed 'bout dat til death took hur from us. Dem white folk woulda hung my papa and hur if they'd knowd," Granny shared, laughing. Anna remembered shaking her head, looking again at the white-looking baby she had borne. Both she and Frankie Lee looked down at the baby when Granny said to no one in particular, "I'd like to know what dat white man done gave his seed to my granddaughter would feel knowin' he got a prutty little gurl needing hur Papa."

"Granny, I told him I wasn't pregnant. He might not believe she is his," Anna remembered replying, feeling downhearted that the baby had no father to speak of. Having already posted her picture and Raymond's in the bedroom where she had slept, Anna admitted to both Frankie Lee and Granny that if no one took her, she wanted the baby to at least know what her parents looked like. At the time, Granny had looked up at Raymond Forlorn's picture and had said to Anna, "Surely my granddaughter didn't just pick any ole white man to lay up wit."

Embarrassed, Anna had blushed as Frankie Lee cleared his throat saying, "I am with ya, Granny. I'd like to know if my cousin gave hurself to any ole' white man. Who knows," he said, sounding serious for once, "the cat might be a decent dude who would wanna know 'bout his daughter even if she is bald as an eagle with gray eyes."

"Shut up, Frankie Lee. She will have hair soon enough, won't she, Granny?" Anna had asked, worried as she thought about all the hair her twins had been born with.

"Sho', gal. Dis baby gonna git pleny hair. All Mr. Porter's babies come without a lick of hair."

Frankie Lee spoke up. "Just don't let it come blonde like his hair. Anna will be too shamed to walk down the street carrying hur. Folks will be lookin' so hard wonderin' whose baby she done got hold 'f."

"Frankie Lee, I don't want to hear another word out of you about my baby," Anna remembered insisting while mean mugging him as he grabbed and hugged the baby.

"Cous, I'm just teasin'. I love hur just cause she yers. Ya know dat, huh Granny?" Nothing else had been said as Granny took her great grandchild from him and carried her out of the room.

Anna sighed as she continued to look out into the dead, silent room, wondering where her husband was this time of night. Slowly she moved out of her body and willed herself up into the clouds. In the wink of an eye, she found herself dripping wet and standing in the rain forest where everything smelled of fresh flowers in bloom.

"Old Head, you must tell me where this journey is leading me. My grandmother is not a young woman. Sooner or later, I will receive a call to come for the child I left with her. What will I do when that happens? I must know something. It is driving me crazy having thoughts of being discovered crowd my mind every waking minute. I am constantly jumping at the ringing of the phone. Even when the doorbell rings, I am afraid I'll open it and it will be someone with her telling me I have to take her. Since you gave her to me you must know something."

"Daughter, all will be revealed in your earth time."

"In my earth time? It has been two years, Old Head. That is too much earth time for anything to be revealed."

"What is this time you speak of but a blink? There is no time, Daughter. What will come shall seek you out and embrace you unexpectedly. As long as you carry the Old Widow's young one in your palm, you will be safe. Just as with your last violent encounter, those who would perpetrate harm toward you will themselves be whirled into madness."

Anna looked into the eyes surrounding the Old Head, thinking nothing made sense. This journey, wherever it was taking her, seemed to be going in a direction that had to lead to disaster. She knew the Old Widow's coming was a bad omen. What she did not know was what destruction would come crashing down on her head and when.

Several nights after her encounter with the Old Head, she woke suddenly out of a disturbing sleep to again find Jake still not home at five o'clock in the morning. This was the third time he had been out all night long. She had been thinking about Granny and Frankie Lee's words about what Raymond would do if he knew of the child. There was no one except Raymond she wanted to have the child, if he wanted her.

The thought came to her that she could go to the apartment and write him a letter telling him that she had a daughter who was his. She racked her brain thinking of how she should word the letter. What if she said that there was a package waiting for him and to get it, he would have to contact Frankie Lee Bailey in Oinston, Louisiana. That way, he would at least get a chance to see the baby before he denied she was his. Anna hesitated, wondering if he would think it was a hoax. If he went there, once Frankie Lee and Granny showed him the pictures and the attaché case, he would know it wasn't a hoax. She got out of bed.

If Jake came back before she returned, she would tell him she was out looking for him. Anna did not like the idea of calling the baby a package. It sounded a bit cold. She must, she thought, refer to her as person however she planned to tell him about her. What could Jake say if she ran into him? Whose bed had he fallen asleep in? She wondered. Could she stand finding out there was another Barb in his life? There had to be; she had been away so long this last time, and few women were willing to give up a good bed partner just because the wife returned.

Lifting her coat from the closet she realized she was not angry, just sad. She had wanted it to work, but as with everything in her life, nothing good lasted very long. Just as she turned out the lights and opened the door to leave, Jake hurried in and attempted to pull her into his arms. She pushed him away.

"I know what you are thinking, but it is not that way. We had this card game going down at Forals. I lost track of time drinking and arguing about the federal funds we received and how the mayor would insist on spending them." Anna turned away from him.

"It was you, Jake, who told me that at three o'clock in the morning, a man is either in the hospital, in jail, or in some woman's bed. I know I deserve no better, but I've been trying to make up for the time I was away. If there is another woman, I will understand—I swear to God, I will. Just say so and let me go. Please don't keep me here if you have another woman hidden away somewhere." Anna looked at him as tears slipped from her eyes.

"Anna, baby," Jake said, taking her coat from her, "I swear to God I haven't been with another woman."

"How do you swear it?" Anna asked, staring at her husband.

"On my dead mother's grave, I swear it. My God, woman, don't you realize how much I love you?"

"No . . . sometimes, I guess . . . I guess I feel as though I don't deserve to be loved," Anna sobbed, taking a seat on the sofa trying hard to stop crying.

"I love you, Anna . . . more than you will ever know. You are mine until death."

"Yes, until death," she sighed as she allowed herself to receive his embrace.

Chapter Twenty-Three

T here were no more late night card games. Jake arrived home right after work for dinner. Sometimes he would call to tell Anna they would be going out. She soon realized that after dinner and watching the news, there was not much else to do in the evenings at home. The children opted most of the time to have their grandparents' company. While sex was great, Anna dreaded going to bed. Her dreams turned into nightmares, causing her to wake up screaming during the night. It was the same dream over and over again. She would go to sleep clutching her pillow, hoping she could sleep through the night. As always, the drums sounded the coming of a new life. She became the African mother large with the child she carried. Lying on a dirt floor, her body expanded to expel the new life. As soon as she heard the baby cry, there stood her mother with the baby lifted up by its heels.

"What is this white demon ya being carrying?" Annabelle sneered while Anna screamed as she saw her baby being dropped from her mother's hands.

"Anna, what the hell is going on with you and these nightmares? This is the fifth one this week, baby. Something is happening to you and I want to know what and why." Anna pulled Jake closer, squeezing him as she cried out of control.

"Jake, help me die. I don't deserve to live after what I've done."

"Anna, you have to stop thinking about cutting up Barb. That shit is driving you crazy. It has already kept us apart nearly a year," he said, messaging his lame leg. "The woman deserved what she got. I, too, had nightmares about her shooting me and you falling down those stairs. Thank God I don't wake up screaming anymore. You are back with me. I don't let myself think about that shit now. I've got to get help for you, baby. Dying is not what my wife needs to have on her mind." Anna allowed him to hold her in his arms, wondering what his thoughts would be if he knew her true fears.

****

After driving forty-five minutes, Anna looked out the window and wondered where Jake was taking her. He had called just before leaving work, asking her to dress in one of her nice outfits. He would be taking her out—where he did not say. Going out was the last thing on her mind these days, but after waking him up the last few nights, she knew he was trying to get her mind off of whatever was bothering her. There was no way out of it—she had to go. Just as she stepped into her bedroom, she spied the Old Widow, her bright orange back glowing as if telling her something important. Moving her fingers through her wardrobe, she felt her body trembling. She wondered what hell was she about to fall into this time. Thinking Jake would be home soon, she hurried to dress.

When Jake turned off highway 4 onto exit 157, she noticed he followed the sign that read "Looper's Race Track—Next Turn." The orange light in her palm turned from orange to bright red. Closing her hand, she trembled as she thought back to the time Jake, James, Fred and the man called Jay Man had come to the High Top Club taking her and the man at her table down under the bridge on the river front. What reason would her husband have to bring her out to Looper's? Somehow, she reasoned, he had found out something to associate her with this racetrack. Why else would they be going there when black jack and poker were his choices of entertainment? What had he discovered? He sure was not a racing fan, Anna thought, clutching the purse she held in her hand.

No matter what, it came to her that her sins always caught up with her. There was no way she could talk her way out of not knowing Raymond when the baby she had left down in Louisiana placed him in her thoughts during her every waking moment. Fear engulfed her as she watched Fred approaching their car; the next person she expected to see was that scar-faced Jay Man. A hideous sight he was for sure. She hated the scornful way he looked at her. He had to hate women. She already knew he didn't have a lady in his life—not that it would be easy picking for him. Her thoughts turned back to her situation as Jake stopped the car and got out at a rest stop, hurrying over to the passenger side.

280

"Get out, Anna," he said to her. Anna froze, wondering what was coming next.

"Come on, Anna. I don't want to have to pull you out." Slowly, she made her way out, thinking at any minute she would look up to see Nathan or, heaven forbid, Raymond himself standing before her. Once outside the car, Jake placed his arm around her shoulder. Her mind turned upside down wondering what bomb shell was about to explode as he slowly walked her toward Dee's burnt orange car. Suddenly, he stopped and turned her to face him.

"Anna," he whispered so low she could hardly hear his words, "you are becoming the Anna you were when you had no memory of your past. Though I loved you even then, you have gotten me accustomed to the Anna who waltzed in here looking and acting as though she owned the world. You still have my heart throbbing trying to get a little of your attention. This thing with you cutting up Barb has got you going off the deep end like her shooting me had me four years ago. I've decided to help you get your mind on something else besides those nightmares and talking about killing yourself." Before Anna could reply, a head popped out of the window of the car ahead of them.

"Hurry, Anna, or we will be late for the first race!" She heard Dee say. The smile on her friend's face eased the pounding in her heart.

Opening her purse, Jake dropped some folded bills inside. "Its long past time you stopped sitting at home . . . like I once told you, sitting at home doing nothing will make an old woman out of you long before your time. Go on, have some fun, baby," he said kissing her in a way that eased her fears.

"Hey, Anna!" Anna looked in the back seat to see Shirley smiling at her as Jake pushed her into the car beside Dee.

"All right," Jake said, his head inside the window, "Greenhorn, bring me some money home." Giving her a quick kiss, he hurried to his car where Fred waited for him.

"Let's go win some money, sister girls!" Dee shouted as she sped toward Looper's. Once there, Dee had to almost push Anna inside the gate after paying for them to enter. Handing her a folding chair, she guided Anna to where they would be seated.

Slowly unfolding her chair, Anna knew coming anywhere near a racetrack where she could be spotted had her on a downward spiral. This place was too close to him. What if Nathan walked past and saw her there? He might think she was there for all the wrong reasons. Looking around, she noticed Looper's was small compared to the large tracks Raymond had taken her to in Europe, California, Kentucky, or even Suffolk Downs in Massachusetts.

People were all over the place just as though it was Santa Anita or any of the other larger tracks—betting, talking, and buying racing forms of some sort. She could not afford to have Jake worried about her or to get the idea she wanted to leave and go somewhere without him. The morning she opened the door to leave, he had stood there looking stunned to see her with her coat on about to walk out the door. Since then, there had been no more late-night-early-morning arrivals home. She looked in surprise to see him coming home during work hours or right after work, and if he had to stay out for any length of time, she received a call telling her what he was doing, even if he was doing something else. Holding her in his arms in bed, he continued to assure her that their marriage was until death. It seemed he could sense when her dreams turned to nightmares, and he woke her before they woke her.

He promised never to give her a reason to leave him ever again. Still, she pondered as to how she would find a way to see her baby without his discovering why she needed to go to Louisiana alone. When she left home and returned; he wanted to know her whereabouts, even when she went to the store. He seemed worried that she might leave again and not return. Guilt soaked her thoughts. She knew this new surprise was leading her somewhere. It was where that frightened her.

Glad they had made it there before the first race, she could tell Dee did not like being late. After they made their first race bets, Shirley informed Anna that the daily double included two races, and Dee never missed the first. When Shirley went to make her bet, Anna turned to her friend.

"Dee, I hope this was not your idea. You know my being here is the worst possible thing that could happen."

"Of course I know, but it wasn't my idea. Jake insisted, and I couldn't come out and tell him I didn't want you with us. Fred would have wanted to know why, and all I need is him thinking we are out here for reasons other than betting on horses. Anyway, you don't have nothing to worry about. You told me his brother always had box seats for the two of you when you were with him. This is the poor folks section. Ain't no rich white men coming through here. Hell, it beats sitting at home looking at four walls day in and day out and then trying to leave him at five in the morning when he is out having fun with the boys." Dee shook her head and frowned at Anna as she turned to watch the horses parading around the track.

"Jake told you . . ."

"Yes, Anna. He told me. Next thing you know you'll be in the funny farm where Barb told everyone you were, worrying about shit you can do nothing about. She got what she deserved, end of story. Now it's time you start living again, sister girl. Jake is right, we want to see the woman who came waltzing into Session like she owned the place." Anna sighed, thinking how funny it was that everyone except her knew what was on her mind.

****

Three nights later Dee honked the horn for her as Jake was just leaving for a council meeting. Kissing her lightly on the lips, he led her outside to Dee's car.

"Take care of my wife, and don't let no damn men look her way," he said, smiling as he peeked at Dee and Shirley looking at him and Anna out of their windows.

"I can't get her to look up. If a man wanted to hit on her, he would have get on his knees."

"Good," Jake said, kissing Anna as he opened Dee's car door and then closed it for her.

Seated in Looper's Racetrack general section, Anna's curiosity kicked in. She watched two women purchasing single slips of paper.

"What are those papers for?" she asked Dee.

"They are tout sheets, written by so-called track experts," Shirley answered. "They are supposed to have the winning horses, but they don't usually come in. When they do come in, they don't always come in as winners, so you are still hoping to win even with them."

"She means," Dee, said, "there are no for-sure winning horses, Anna." Seeing a vendor waving the American Turf Daily Racing Form that

Raymond as well as everyone else on the ranch in Kentucky had studied like the Bible, Anna walked over and bought a copy. The other two women looked scornfully at her, asking why in the world she would waste her money on a paper it took years of schooling to decipher. Anna gave no reply as she tucked the racing form under her arm.

Shirley walked up and got herself a tout sheet, explaining to Anna that not all the top-named horses the experts picked on her tout sheet came in winners, but she liked to read what they had to say about the thoroughbreds—good or bad. It was up to the readers to figure out from the information they were given which thoroughbred had a chance of winning.

Dee played by betting on jockeys she thought had a good chance of winning the race. It did not matter what condition the horse was in; Dee stood steadfast on the jockey she picked to bring in the winner. Anna discovered that Dee also had a habit of waiting right until the last minute before placing her bet. It was her belief that her jockey's horse might be scratched. Where would that leave her? If there were changes, her choice of what to play automatically changed, especially if it was a jockey she favored. Long lines sometimes caused her to miss a bet she wanted to change at the last minute.

Anna watched her friends cheer and boo the horses crossing the finish line. Having learned in Kentucky what long fingernails could do, she moved far away when she saw Dee's nails go up in the air while she screamed as one of her favorite jockeys brought in a winner for her.

Unfortunately, Shirley chose a loser. Dee's lips spread into a big grin as she wiped perspiration from her face after waving a colorful handkerchief she said brought her luck as she shouted in her winner. "Shirley and Anna, you ladies are looking at a liberated winning woman!" Her hands went down to hug her shapely hips as she wiggled them and then marched down to get her money. Anna and Shirley laughed and shook their heads.

Dee talked Anna into going again the next two nights, telling her, "Anna, you got to relax and enjoy yourself! You haven't made a bet yet. I told you nobody down here will know or care who you are. They are too busy try to make a winning bet. Jake was right about you."

"Right about what?" Anna asked, frowning Dee's way.

"You've been in the house way too long. What happened between you and that white dude is history. Jake and Barb are history, especially since you damn near killed her ass. Barb knows damn well she provoked you and got damn well what she deserved, so there is no sense in feeling guilty about cutting her ass up for the rest of your life. Anyway, I started to sue the whore for bloodying up my house the way she did. You sure put locks on her lips for a long time to come."

"Please, Dee. I don't even want to be reminded of that night or her ever again. I cannot understand why Jake thought it was necessary to pawn me off on you and Shirley."

"He had to do something about you talking about killing yourself."

"Damn! Jake can't keep his mouth shut about anything."

"Anna, you scared him to death with that kinda talk. Anyway, he has been missing all his poker nights to be home with you. He knew you would be waiting up for him. He missed having fun with his friends and decided to find some help for you so he wouldn't have to feel guilty about leaving you home alone."

"Help for me? Oh my God! Okay, Dee, go place a bet on seven in the next race," Anna said, taking money from her purse as she realized she was stuck with them whether she wanted to be or not.

"That's my girl! Let's have some fun—at least we are together at long last," Dee said, smiling as she took the money Anna gave her to make her bet.

After Dee left, Anna sighed, unable to tell her friend her real problems. She unfolded the pages of a paper, a part of a past she hoped she could forget. Looking up at the top of the page, she read in big bold black letters that Nathan Forlorn was chairman of the Illinois racing association. His face flashed before her. She had never thanked him for the attorneys he had sent.

Anna's fingers trembled as she traced the past performances of the first thoroughbred listed. As hard as she tried not to, her thoughts traveled back to the past as the paper in her hand led her back to Raymond and his teachings about the horses he called thoroughbreds. The Daily Racing Form, he shared, provided information a seasoned player needed to inform him or her of the conditions a horse raced under, the dates, times and speed of the horse, and where the horse placed at the end of the race.

Soon, her frequent visits to the racetrack caused Anna to become familiar with the social order practiced there. There were events occurring there that once in a while visitors seldom noticed. The same people visited the fifty-dollar betting windows and came as often as the regulars who visited the two-dollar betting windows. Dee pointed out to Anna the addicts who spent their entire earnings not realizing their winnings could never exceed their losses.

Anna grew accustomed to looking for the regulars like Dee, Shirley, and now herself. One such player was pointed out to her as the Candy Man, an older black fellow who always chewed on bits of candy as he walked and talked to himself. He was known for the obvious habit of changing windows in the middle of a bet, looking back over his shoulders to see if the person behind him stood too close. The tickets he purchased he kept close to his chest as if afraid someone might see them.

"Look Anna, there they are." Anna knew Shirley spoke of the self-made bookies—men and women carrying small note pads with dozens of wagers made for people unable to come to the racetrack to make their own bets. These bookies received ten percent of the money won by their clients. After going with Dee and Shirley for two months, three times a week, Anna felt like a regular herself, handicapped successfully enough to keep herself and her friends ahead. Handicapping was what Ray had taught her to do. She prided herself at being good at it.

Once, Anna talked her mother into driving her out to meet them. It amazed her how her mother only noticed the number of elderly and handicapped people wheeling and hobbling their way to the track. As Annabelle put it, "Thay was throwing thay money away to them devils in the windows. Such a pity." Anna gave up trying to convince her that those people were as normal as anyone else. They had chosen the type of entertainment that best suited them. Thoroughbred racing happened to be the entertainment they had chosen, just like anyone would choose their choice of entertainment.

As always, Anna and Dee were at odds on what horses could possibly win the race. Anna's winning percentage averaged higher than Dee's, yet Dee insisted her method of betting on jockeys was the best. No matter how much Anna won and told Dee she needed to be aware of the condition or form of the horse ridden by the jockey, Dee still chose jockeys she liked, switching off if a change affected her choice. Anna did have to admit that Dee sometimes won large sums of money when the jockeys won on sudden changes and long odds. Dee lost, however, when the regular jockeys she picked failed to bring in a thoroughbred that was a favorite to win.

Seated in front of her vanity applying her makeup, Anna smiled as she thought of the fun she had been having visiting Looper's racetrack. By the time she got home after the last race, she slept through the night. There had been no farther calls from her cousin, so she assumed everything was all right. She needed a little time to think of some way to get down to Granny's and see about her baby. She realized it was impossible at the moment. Anna soon allowed the problem to slip from her mind.

At Looper's, thoughts of Ray filled her heart as though he were right there beside her telling her what horse to pick and why. Jake had no idea how close she was to the man he wanted her farthest away from. Two well-known lovers Shirley and Dee pointed out to her met there. Both were married to other people. Anna shuddered to think what might happen if all four met up. Rising from her vanity, she looked admiringly at herself in the mirror. The new powder blue, two-piece suit she wore complimented her four-inch blue-and-white heels. Anna hurried out of her bedroom, running into Jake as he was coming in. Her racing form tucked under her arm, she gave him a slight kiss and headed for the door.

"Hey, wait a second," he said, as he grabbed her wrist. "Why not go with me tonight?" Anna saw how his eyes gave her sleek designer two-piece suit the once over. "I've got a meeting with the council. There will be lots of people there. We can go out afterward," he suggested, kissing her cheek.

"I can't," Anna replied, thinking to herself that a dull council meeting was the last place she wanted to go.

"What do you mean, you can't?" Jake asked, his voice sounding serious.

"I'm driving Dee and Shirley to the racetrack tonight," Anna answered, working her way closer to the door.

"Again tonight?" She saw the questioning look in Jake's eyes. "You women haven't by any chance found male escorts out there to keep you company, have you?"

"Wasn't it you who sent me out there?" Anna asked, becoming irritated by his probing questions that detained her. She needed to hurry and pick up Dee and Shirley before the first race started, and she knew she would not have time if he kept talking. "If you are worried, come along with me, but you must hurry," Anna said as she turned her back to him.

"I want you with me tonight." Anna heard in his voice that he was determined to have his way.

"But I already have plans to go with Dee and Shirley, plus it is my night to drive," Anna insisted as her last-ditch effort to escape having to attend the dull council meeting with him.

"So call them and tell them one or the other will have to drive," Jake insisted.

"They are my sister girls and I don't want to disappoint them," Anna countered.

"Look who is more important to you, your sister girls or your husband?"

"Jake, are you kidding me?" Anna answered, determined to have her way.

"For the last three months, the only way I get to see you is coming in or going out. I miss you. Tonight I want you with me. Call and tell Dee and Shirley you're going out with your husband. They will understand."

****

The meeting at the city hall must have been important—about five hundred people stood inside and outside the building. The mayor, aldermen, and other city officials sat around a long oval table. Several other elected members of the citizens' council sat in front-row seats. Anna waved at Fred and James seated among them. Jake found her a seat between her parents who sat on the front row also.

"I see you still in them designer clothes, gal," Annabelle said, smiling as Anna bent and kissed her parents before taking a seat next to her father. Anna smiled looking around thinking that she had not seen this many black people together in Session except at sporting events when there were competitions against white teams.

"Momma, you are looking pretty sharp yourself in that expensive maroon tailored suit you're wearing. Daddy sure seems pleased to be sitting next to you," Anna replied, looking at how close his arm held her mother to him. In the background she could hear people screaming at each other across the room, calling each other nigger this and nigger that.

"As far as we come, gal, we still gotta call ourselves dat name the white crackers give us." Anna listened to her mother as the noise level in the hall continued to rise. "Dese colored folk don't know no better than to keep 'dressing each other as niggers? Can't ya hear 'em, Anna? Every other word is nigger dis or nigger dat."

"Momma, as long as white people are not calling them nigger, they don't have a problem with calling themselves the word," her father informed her mother.

"I wouldn't let the women at the shelter use that word," Anna put in. Her mother shook her head as they listened to two young black men say, "Them niggers gonna get down tonight."

"That nigger Jake Bradley's ass looks good enough to eat." Anna turned around in shock to see two young girls behind them commenting.

"How old are you girls?"

"Thirteen," the girls shyly admitted.

"That's not a conversation thirteen-year-old girls should be having about my husband. He is old enough to be your father or at least your older brother. Your parents should teach you better. It's unbecoming to any girl, especially ones as young as you two."

"Yes, ma'am," they both said, as one whispered that she didn't know that she was Jake's wife but that she was sho' dressed to kill, adding, "My nigger needs to be getting' me an outfit like that."

Anna shook her head as she looked again back at the two girls. She knew by the plastic rings on their fingers and the old cut-up jeans they wore that the boys those girls were dating worked out of some fast-food place—if they really had boyfriends and were not just saying they did to make themselves seem grown. Using the N-word was something that had been passed down to them from some adult who had no understanding of the real history in this country, Anna thought to herself thinking back to one of the few times she had spoken to the group of women in the shelter.

She had talked to them much like she had spoken to the black women on the ranch in Kentucky after she discovered the awful condition of the colored clinic they had to receive care from. Shirley had just been allowed into Session's first black women's shelter and had come and sat among the women during on of Anna's rare sessions with them. She remembered telling them she did not know if God had brought man or woman on this planet first, but women must have all been sisters at one time because women in history depended on each other just like sisters—sharing and helping each other.

Then saying to them that she had never understood why women coined the term "bitch" for themselves when they don't have to come into heat to have sex and they never travel very far on four legs, causing laughter among the women. The term demeans them as females, and as long as they were in the shelter, she told them she would like for them to think of themselves as sisters who were sharing and helping other sisters. Of course, they had all glanced at Shirley, the only white woman in the room. Anna had mentally digested their glance, understanding what they were asking. "Shirley," she had asked, "what color is your blood when you have your period?"

"Red," Shirley had replied, looking nervously at the black women who were staring her way.

"Do you have C-sections or natural birth when delivering your babies?"

Staring down at her body, Shirley exclaimed that they came straight outta her coushy. All the women had laughed.

"And when your babies are born, how are they fed?"

"From these little old titties," Shirley responded. "Actually, they get a little bigger when the baby comes." That again brought laughter from the other women, who were now smiling her way instead of staring her down like they had at the start of the meeting.

"It's a no-brainer—as far as I am concerned, while she is here, she is a sister, too. They had all smiled along with Shirley, who seemed to relax. Anna then took a deep breath because she knew she could make the point she needed to make but not before a young black girl with a swollen face who had just come into the shelter after a fight with her girlfriend she had been trying to leave hit her, stating that while she believed Anna was right in her assessment of how sisters should treat each other if a sister came at her wrong she will be called a bitch even if she stood on her ass. Anna could not counter the amens coming from the group of women. An assessment she had revisited over the following years.

"Before I depart from your company, I would like to point out that the word "nigger" that you ladies love to throw out to make your point was coined by the slave masters who had to find a term that would make the wrongs done to our ancestors okay. Our ancestors, of course, used it to refer to each other because the slave masters would have killed them if they had referred to themselves as men and women. While you are in this shelter, that word is off limits. Shirley is not allowed to use it because it cannot be thought of as a word of endearment when it comes from her lips. We should never use a word we know is a racial slur meant to hurt us because it means the same when we degrade our own race by using it. So sisters, using it will get you outta here quick and in a hurry." They had all applauded, but it had taken time for them to understand her meaning.

"Did I just hare you two use that nigger word again? Who's yer folks?" Annabelle turned and asked, gazing hard at the two young girls behind them. Anna was quickly brought back to the present as she watched the young girls rush away. She realized those girls were just showing out a term used by adults in her culture to refer to children who mimic adult behavior.

"Momma, you scared them away," Anna said, laughing.

"Somebody come tole me thay heard ya using dat dirty word, much less talkin' such womanish talk 'bout men at that age, I would have whipped your ass, gal, and ya know it."

"I do believe Baby Girl knows it," her father said, smiling as they listened to several men ask when them niggers was going to get started. Anna shook her head, realizing this was going to be one of those evenings when her mother was on a roll.

"Chile, long as dese Negras don't hear dat word comin' out of a cracker's lips, thay thank it's cute to say, not realizin' if I make a dress, it don't mater atall who weers it it's still the dress I made."

"Baby Girl, you do understand the parable your mother is making, I hope," her father said, kissing her forehead as he smiled down at her.

"Yes Daddy, I just can't for the life of me understand why it is so hard for the people wearing the dress to understand it, too." There were no further comments as the meeting got started.

Minutes from the previous meeting took up every bit of an hour while Anna thought about how much fun Dee and Shirley were having at the racetrack. Dee, of course, had cursed Jake out over the phone, telling him he better fill her tank up because it was Anna's night to drive. Laughing, he had agreed to do so as he hung up and hurried Anna out of the house.

Soon talk began about the verdict from the council as to how the money from the federal government would be spent for the city. The need for public housing improvements stood foremost on the list of concerns. Because of so many muggings of the elderly, many wanted more police protection and better street lighting after dark. Parks and training programs were needed for teens so they would not have to stand on the street corners involving themselves in illegal activities. Anna thought of the shelter; she knew too many in Session were suffering from lack of food as well as shelter. She was not surprised to see the stern look on her mother's face, which meant that she was ready to do battle on behalf of the Women's League that worked so hard to help families in need.

Anna watched the mayor, Jake, and several other men discussing papers on the table before them. She knew Jake had deliberated long and hard before deciding to back Mike Gage, the present mayor, feeling him to be the better of two bad candidates. Anna sighed, wishing she had left before Jake had arrived home. Her friends were having fun picking winners, she thought to herself. She was already bored, listening to the old minutes that seemed to be an indication of what the rest of the evening would be like.

When the new proposal was read, Anna saw her mother grip her purse and knew trouble was ahead. She concluded that an enormous amount of the money would be going to the affluent sections of the city where they lived. It didn't seem that things were going to get any better for the poor and elderly people of Session. She watched Jake lean back in his chair. Anna knew that many of the proposed plans to help the poor and elderly listed in the first proposal were missing from this new proposal she was listening to.

"Gage, what the hell is going on here? This is not the proposal we drew up."

"Well, Bradley, we thought it best to change some things," Gage answered, looking around at the other men seated at the table with them. James jumped up, a frown on his face as he glared down at Gage.

"You dirty son of a bitch! You know damn well this is not what we agreed on. Jake, he has sold us out."

"You made some changes to benefit whom, may I ask?" Jake asked, waving James back in his seat.

"Bradley . . . I thought . . ."

"You thought after these poor black souls voted your ass into office that you didn't really owe them anything, right? Anna saw the mayor roll his eyes Jake's way. "Gage, they voted your ass into office because I backed you for mayor, believing you had the best interest of all the citizens of Session at heart."

"Now Bradley, you're missing the . . ."

"I'm not missing a damn thing, Gage. I'm on to your ass is what I am." Anna watched her mother's jaws tighten as Jake's face faded from a smile to a frown. "You white men's boys go back and tell your white bosses who chose not to show their faces that the meeting has been adjourned. This proposal is null and void."

"What?" Gage shouted, rising six feet four inches into the air. He commanded his space as he towered over Jake.

"Yes, my man, you know I know. This proposal would only benefit me and people like you and the white men running the county who I see had a hand in redesigning this proposal to benefit their own interests, Gage," Jake said, still seated, his eyes on the papers before him. We don't live downtown, but what about all these blacks that do? Jake said his eyes leveled at Gage. "I know I can do without improvements in Hillside but not our senior citizens living on unprotected streets or our kids who can't or won't attend schools because they are so overcrowded, run down, and filled with hardened thugs? The proposal you have here will never help them shake loose their desperate lives."

An uproar sounded throughout the room as the citizens rose shouting, "Go, Jake, go! You are our man! Don't let Gage and his white hounds dog us this time!"

"I know what is best for the people in Session, Bradley."

Screams of "Bullshit, nigger!" could be heard throughout the angry crowd. Anna saw that her mother held her purse tighter. Gage had not been the candidate she wanted Jake to back.

"Gage is one of 'em coloreds dat uses other coloreds to ride on, thankin' white devils gonna to 'spect and 'cept him in thay circle 'cause he's mayor and can wage power over us coloreds," Annabelle whispered as they sat listening to the crowd jeer at Gage.

"Of course he does, Momma," Anna heard her father say.

"Ain't no crackers I knowd of ever had no use for one of us 'ceptin' to use us. Dat Negra been cursed with a little color thankin' some of 'em white devils gonna treat him better. Far as thay concern, if ya ain't pure white they ain't got no use for ya atall. Wouldn't shake a leaf yer way to save a dying colored 'fore they would a dog lyin' in the road." Anna took a deep breath as she listened to her mother's beliefs about what all whites won't do for any black person. Her mind flashed back a few years. She could hear Raymond tell the two white men in their motel room who had wanted to take her that they would have to go through him to get to her. The vial he had thrown in the air let her know he meant it when it blew up and caused a deep impression in the ground a short distance from them after the men ran off with the money they were after.

"Momma," she said, eyeing her mother.

"Momma nothin'. All we been hearin' since we walked through dat door is NIGGER, gal. To a white cracker," her mother said, looking at her near-white hands, "we all NIGGERS. Never trust nar one of 'em devils tellin' ya lies 'bout how thay like ya. Thay'll cut ya down somewhares remindin' ya what thay true thoughts of ya is. Somebody needs to remind Gage 'bout dat. None of 'em is worth the time to throw 'em away to a colored nowhares on this earth. Ya hear me, gal?"

"Annabelle . . ." Anna's father said as Anna's look told him things she could never reveal to her mother. "You don't know every white person in the world to be making such a broad statement like that. How many times has someone asked me if my wife is white?"

"I hope ya tole 'em dese hare blood of mine is colored, so no matter what I look to be, I'm a colored woman, ain't no doubt bout dat."

"Which means, Momma," Anna informed her, color has nothing to do with race. You are a living testimony of that."

"If'n it ain't color, what is it?"

"It's the genetic makeup of your DNA, Momma. Any person can tell you they are of a certain race. If their DNA says something different, they are not what they say or think they are. The test for that is so expensive that few if any want to go through the trouble of finding out, therefore few of us will ever for sure know what our exact race is just by looking at skin color, Momma."

"Didn't I tell you we made us up a smart little girl, Annabelle?" her father said, switching seats with Anna and surprising his wife with a kiss. Smiling down at her he said, "You made me an awesome baby." A man and a woman in front of them turned around to stare at Annabelle. That embarrassed her and, of course, shut her up. Anna was then able to refocus her attention on the conversation the mayor and Jake were having.

"Gage, are you telling me you know better than these people who are out rioting in the streets their suffering is so desperate?" Anna watched Gage frown over at Jake and then take his seat again.

"Of course I know! Anyway, I'm the mayor, not you, Bradley. You should have run for the office if you wanted my job."

"I could have, but I didn't. Now that that's understood, let's get back to the business at hand. You know what is best for you and those white men pushing you Gage. But from the looks of this new proposal, let me remind you again, you haven't shown that you know what is best for my black people." Amens could be heard throughout the room. "The reason nothing has changed for black people is because we get blacks like you in office with the White Man Syndrome Gage which is, if you have not heard, believing no way is right but his way, trashing our lives worst than the white man now that you have power over your own people. All you think about is what you can take from us just as he has done. We are sick and tired of that kind of bullshit, especially coming from our own black leadership with no one to complain to."

Screams of "Right on, Jake baby!" echoed throughout the room.

"Just what are you getting at, Bradley?"

"Gage, you don't give a damn about the poor black people who voted you into office now that you're in. Their lives don't mean shit to you. We both know damned well you and I can live another ten years without having these improvements in Hillside. But the people downtown cannot last another year without the help they need. I think, Gage, you had better go back to the drawing board and next time come closer—much closer— to the plans we first drew up."

"I'm mayor of this damn city, not you, Bradley. I think I know what's best for the city and the people in it." Gage ran his hand over his slightly balding head as his light complexion reddened. "We were up half the night drawing up these plans." Anna sat tense as she waited for Jake's reply. The room was so quiet a pin could have been heard had one dropped to the floor.

"For whom, Gage?" Anna listened to her husband's voice rise though he never rose from his seat as he looked into the face of the bigger and taller man.

"The people downtown can wait . . . ."

"Here's where the White Man's Syndrome again plays against us Gage. Wait has always been his goal for the black man in this country since he enslaved then supposingly freed us? How long do you and the white man plan to have us wait this time, Gage? Until all the money is spent in Hillside?" Jake shouted. His voice was now louder than Gage's. "How long do blacks downtown have to wait to live like people? It's a shame to say Gage but you're a white man painted black." Laughter filled the room, causing Gage's face to turn a darker shade of red than it already was Anna noticed. She could tell that he was angry to the point of becoming physical, something that did not appear to upset her husband.

"You could make a good mayor, but because you were raised as a southern boy, you think the white man's way of treating black people in this country has to be accepted. You also believe that you are powerless when it comes to telling that white motherfucker 'hell no!' You'd rather fuck over and lie to your own people the same way he fucks over and lies to his own people. He's ruthless in his malicious belief that if he can throw his people's attention off what their real problems are he can always keep them oppressed along with the rest. It must be something you learned from him Gage."

"You are out of line, Bradley," Gage insisted as the people began to chant Jake's name.

"Yeah, I guess I am out of line for those blacks like you, Gage, who think the white man has to be pleased. I've always told you, man, if chitterlings and greens ain't good enough for the white man's belly, that's all well and good, but I'll not eat caviar because he says it is the proper thing to do." Anna watched Jake stick a toothpick in his mouth and leaned back in his chair his eyes on Gage. "White men can't hang black men and nothing is done any more, Gage, at least not here in Session they can't. They will get their own asses hung coming up in here thinking they are dealing with niggers of the past." The crowd roared. Anna listened to her mother chuckle as she took a deep breath and said, "Yes, son, I love ya telling 'em like it is now!"

"I know that as the white man's boy, you will have to report back to him, so tell him this: We, the true blacks of Session, refuse to accept this proposal, and we won't be accepting that which will profit only the whites and blacks already living the good life up on Hillside like you and me! Anna saw disbelief in the mayor's face as he stared back at Jake.

"As mayor, you cannot gulp down every damn penny sent in to help the poor for your own selfish ends, Gage—at least not here in Session you won't. This meeting is adjourned until next week." Jake slapped the minute's book closed and stood staring down at the mayor. Screams and shouts filled the room. Jake's name became a roar. Anna's mouth opened in shock as she looked at Jake smile over at the mayor. The mayor at that moment seemed two feet tall. Within seconds, Jake was surrounded.

"I don't know why that husband of yours does not become mayor himself, the people of Session love him so much," her father said, smiling at Anna.

"'Cause, baby, dat rascal don't wanta be in the hot seat. He wants to be the one dat keeps dat seat in check," Annabelle said, smiling back at her husband as they walked toward the door.

It was a good two hours before Anna and Jake drove way from city hall. She realized that night how much the people in Session loved her husband. She also knew that later he and Gage would talk and settle things right. If Gage ran again and Jake thought him to be the better candidate, he would help him get into office again. But, as he always told her, the people should always keep tabs on the man in office, never allowing him to forget those who put him there.

****

"You made Gage so angry that I thought surely he would reach down and box you in the mouth," Anna said as they sat in the restaurant waiting to be served.

"Yeah, well the nigger would have gotten his fist bitten off, not to mention all those angry people waiting to see him flinch the wrong way."

"Why did you vote for him if you didn't believe he took office to help the people?"

"The man is a good guy at heart, but as I stated, he was southern-born and reared to believe white men have to be pleased first and foremost. He probably told them what we wanted, only to have them tell him what they wanted, which is what he thought he had to do."

"And . . ." Anna insisted on knowing.

"Back in Gage's bringing-up days, black men couldn't even keep white men out of their women's beds for Christ's sake Anna. How do you expect a man like that to fight white men for poor niggers just because they voted for him? He doesn't realize the white man bleeds just like he bleeds, and his tears can be made to fall just as hard as ours. Niggers like Gage never learned that."

"Oh my God, I have heard that word so much tonight, I think I'll go nuts if I hear it again, Jake Bradley," Anna sighed.

"As long as it's not said in front of white folks, Anna, I see nothing wrong with calling ourselves that word."

"And I keep telling you that you can't fool yourself into believing shit smells like anything but shit. Any way you put it, shit stinks, baby."

"What are you talking about?"

"Nigger, Jake. No matter how you say it, it is not okay for you as a black man to call another black man nigger. I'm telling you it is not okay. Demeaning is demeaning whether it comes from your lips or the white man's lips. When he coined the word nigger, there was no doubt he intended for it to demean us. For you to tell yourself it is not demeaning when you call yourself or another black man nigger is like telling yourself shit doesn't stink when it comes from the black man's body. It is the same as what you are saying about Gage.

"Even though you don't realize it you also have the White Man's Syndrome. Anyone who knows American history will know you are attempting to make a fact something it isn't simply because you want it to be different. You know, like telling someone night is day and thinking it's going to make them see night as if it were day. It is what it is, Jake Bradley. You should not be calling another black man a nigger. It's a fool's fallacy. Momma says that you can wear the dress anyway you want to, but in the end it is how she designed it to be worn that really matters. Anyway I told you how I felt about that word when I first met you."

"Yeah, I know you are right. I guess I have been brainwashed to believe what I hear from other black men and choose to believe it is okay. I will be checking myself in the future. The respect I require from any other man I should give to myself." Anna felt his lips smother hers. "One of the many reasons I love you, baby, is because you always know what's real even when I don't want to hear it. My black people—they need my support, Anna."

"Getting back to that subject, I don't know about these blacks you believe in so much. They sway too easily when the weather gets stormy."

"Who wouldn't rush out of the rain? These people have so many segments of the government controlling their lives that they can only guess for the next four years what hole they are going to be pitched into."

"Yeah, I guess the lower you are on the totem pole, the more people use you for a footstool, not caring one bit what happens to you," Anna mused.

"You're right, and that women's lib you black women have bought into is not helping one damn bit. It's just a means of kicking the black man when he is already down."

"You black men don't appreciate what good women you have. You are always trying to keep us buried under your feet."

"How the hell is that?" Jake asked as the waitress set their dinners on the table.

"You forget that I ran a shelter for women once upon a time. Most of the women coming there were women who had insecure men who couldn't stand not being lord and master, even when the woman was the one putting the food on the table. The men still wanted to mistreat the women, thinking it was okay because they were male. It was as though the women trying to help them survive were the enemy their men had to abuse, while scared as hell of the white bosses walking on their black asses."

"That's bullshit."

"Bullshit? Oh, it's bullshit all right! I can't tell you how many times I have listened to victims tell me how they had to pick themselves up off the floor because they refused to agree with their men about something they knew was wrong."

"You black women have a knack of bringing out insecurities in your men. You threaten us with all that power you have." Anna watched his right eyebrow rise as he stared her way. "Don't sit there looking like you don't know what I am talking about," Jake said as Anna stared over at him with her mouth open. "You can make me feel like I am worth less than two cents when you open that mouth of yours sometimes." Anna took in a breath as she listened to her husband's account of how he felt being verbally reprimanded by her. She remembered only too well Raymond telling her much the same thing.

"We have enough problems trying to survive in this damned white man's world," Jake continued. "He's not bothered with insecurities. Everything is peaches and cream for him, especially for those who have all the money and own every damned thing in the first place." Anna sucked in another breath as she listened to Jake account of the white man's good life. She knew that at least for one white man, everything was not always peaches and cream and there were always those insecurities money could not buy off.

"What I hate about you black men," Anna responded, "is that you believe you have to threaten and knock a woman on her butt and curse her to high heaven. You think that will ease your insecurities instead of understanding that your behavior only creates more problems.

"There is, of course, no reasoning with you when you lose your cool." Anna watched her husband cut into the bloody prime rib he had ordered. "We can't console or try to cushion your pains. You blame us for all of your downfalls, even though you know we couldn't possibly be the blame for all of the problems you are having out on the streets. For some reason you believe that if you come home and beat the hell out of your women it will make you feel more like men." Anna turned from Jake's eyes as he rolled them at her.

"The only person you think makes you stand tall is that precious white woman out there you finally got your hands on. Anything she tells you is right, no questions asked." Anna tasted a bite of her chicken salad and then pushed it away.

"Let's get the hell out of here. The more you open that mouth of yours the deeper in trouble I get."

"See what I mean? You black men just can't stand hearing the truth, can you?"

****

Later that night, Anna lay in bed beside her husband after some intense lovemaking. She could tell he was up for conversation. If he wanted to sleep, he would lay on his stomach. When he really wanted the night to end, he would pull her into his arms and soon she would hear the sound of his breathing.

"Baby, I look at my home," Jake said, his arm around her, "and see all the things I've been blessed to do for my family. You can't imagine how it makes me feel seeing other black men I've known all my life growing old before their time as they struggle just to survive. Men who see their families starving to death and are shaken with fear. Whether work is there for them or not, it's such that they can barely live off the bread they are bringing home." Anna felt his lips as he kissed her bare shoulders. "Now here comes that white nigger—oh, I'm sorry, baby, there goes that word again—my brother Gage, letting white men tell him that the black man isn't ready to be helped. 'He needs to wait it's their favorite solution for all the black man's problems . . . calling him a fool because he lives in a shack and drives a nice car when men like Gages knows damned well in that black man's world—a world Gage has been lucky enough to escape—he'll never have the down payment to buy a home. What bank will loan him the money on a minimum wage job? He knows to other black males around him, he's someone to pity if he's a walking man—someone no other man respects. He'd just as soon be a bum on the street—a man who leaves his woman and kids rather than sit and watch them starving to death because he can't feed them."

"What hope is there, Jake?" Anna asked, thinking of those poor blacks living in shacks down in Kentucky. Thinking that they did not even know they should have been fighting for better health care and against those racist signs demeaning them, not to mention the discrepancy in pay.

"Baby, this is not just a race problem as so many of us seem to think. It's one of economics . . . and poor whites are facing it as well as nonwhites."

"Do you believe it's not as hard for them as it is for us?" Anna asked, remembering the poor white families without roofs over their heads and money in the bank who thought her black skin made her beneath them simply because their skin was white.

"You would be shocked at the white families catching as much hell as many black families." Anna gave him a menacing look. "I've known families—yes, white families—wiped out because they could not pay medical bills or the cost of the drugs that would prolong their lives or maybe save them. Think about how many of them would tell you to quickly paint them black and healthy." Anna laughed at Jake's humor.

"You are insane, Jake. It seems to me they'd rather die sick and white than be painted anything but white."

"I'm serious, honey. Dead serious."

"As a heart attack, huh?"

"Baby, poor white people are as vulnerable to white hate groups as we are to black ones. Look what your mother's hatred did to your life before you left me." Anna shivered, thinking about the horrid image of her mother's hate.

"Baby, I'm so sorry. We promised never to bring up the past. I am glad, though, that you can be by my side now and not allow the presence of whites terrify you."

Anna listened to him glad to hear him tell her that all whites were not bad people, as her mother believed they all were. He believed that it was only those whites wanting to have all the power blacks needed to be aware of. Sharing that the only way for them to accomplish it was by keeping blacks and poor whites separated while using the feeble conditions of poor whites as weapons for recruitment, making them believe that black people were responsible for their dire plights in life and that they should be hung and killed.

Any fool, he shared, knows no man came to this country begging to be another man's slave yet they claim anger at the black man. For what? He reminded her of those she had called brainwashed manipulators at the gala affair in Toro, agreeing that they are the real profiteers of all of this division. She thought on his words that they must continue to exploit a separate-unequal balance in a class of people who could better their plights in life if they stood as one regardless of race equating his beliefs with those he felt were Dr. King's beliefs to remedy the country's problems before he was murdered."

"Well, you can forget that and go to sleep because that will never happen," Anna warned her husband. "Whites would prefer death, starvation, and any other catastrophe to befall them before they give up their belief that their white skin makes them superior over every other race.

I know, not all of them, but enough that it matters," Anna assured him, remembering Julia's son and the cross tossed under the stable door where she stood, not to mention the thoughts of councilman Will and the white southern women she had met while in town with Julia Mike Raymond's cousin.

"Equality for every human on this earth was the essence of Martin Luther King, Jr.'s life's work but where have we ended up?"

"You are telling me what, my husband?" He smiled over at her shaking his head.

"Baby the toughest pimps on this planet are those who control our ability to live free only if they sanction it. Like Gage, politicians are pimping con arts." Anna's eyes widen as she listened to her husband beliefs about those who led the country. "They win their whores over, who by the way are the citizens, who pay taxes, making promises they seldom keep. But I'll be damn if I whore for a government that believes all a poor man is worth is a goddamned box of cheese and a can of tomato paste." Anna kissed Jake's lips; he kissed her back as his hands moved up to caress her most sacred place. Much later, they fell asleep in each other's arms.

Chapter Twenty-Four

—m—

Dee, Shirley, and Anna stood at the fence in Looper's racetrack trying to decide if they should play the first race; Anna shook her head in disbelief stating that she thought the thoroughbreds in it looked as if they needed to be put out to pasture.

"Anything might win among those nags," Anna moaned, getting an Amen from both Shirley and Dee.

"Where are you going, Dee?" Shirley asked as she and Anna watched Dee walk off to where the jockeys paraded their horses around the field ten minutes before post time her colorful handkerchief dangling in her hand. When Dee returned, she had a smug look on her face.

"Anna, I know you and Shirley will not believe this, but they've got David De Paul riding in all ten races tonight." Anna examined her program.

"You are right, Dee."

"Why are you looking at me with that silly grin on your face, Dee?" Shirley asked.

"Girl, didn't you read the papers this morning? He's only nine races away from having a thousand wins," Dee said, flipping through her program to make sure he was riding in all ten races. Anna knew of all the jockeys racing he was her favorite

"He can get that in a couple of days of winning two or three races a night," Anna replied, glancing at her racing form.

"I know damn well you ladies are going to say I am crazy, but I believe he'll win them all tonight."

"You are right, Dee. I can't speak for Shirley, but I certainly know you are crazy."

Shirley then added, "These horses are driving her nuts, Anna. I have to be careful because Tony has already told me that if I have to start dipping into the family budget, there will be no more horse racing for me."

"Oh Shirley, you're not going to lose your money. Tell you what—if you bet him and he loses, I'll replace your bread."

"You would do that for Shirley, Dee?" Anna asked, counting her own money.

"You heard me, Anna. I will cover these bets. I'm telling you, I've been studying these jockeys for the past six years. He is set to win tonight."

"I didn't know you had been coming out here that long." Anna cut her words short at the look Dee threw her way. "Oh all right. I'll fold my form. Let's pool our money together and bet on him until he loses. If and when he loses, we'll go to bingo for a month," Anna told her, laughing at the frown on Dee's face at the thought of bingo. "Well, is it a bet or not? All of our money pooled together? I don't want you covering my bet, Dee. If we lose, I want you out of this racetrack and on your way home when the jockey doesn't come in, okay?" Anna stared at her.

"Damn it, okay."

"I've got three hundred dollars to play with," Anna said.

"I've got a hundred," Shirley shared, counting her bankroll.

"I've got two hundred. Give me your money, girls. Let's put it all together like Anna has suggested. "That's the best idea she's come up with all night." Anna heard Dee's sarcasm and knew she was referring to her remark about leaving if and when the jockey lost.

I'll get two hundred dollars worth of two-dollar tickets. Anna and Shirley, you two do the same—then we won't have to worry about taxes."

Anna and her two friends stood watching to see if David De Paul would bring in the first half of the daily double. Their anticipation grew, as they all clutched the tickets they had purchased in their hands. Anna held her breath as they watched the jockey use his expertise to maneuver his horse around the others, holding him until just the right moment and then letting him fly across the finish line after coming in from far behind to win the race. Dee was screaming so loudly that Anna thought they were going to have to take her home. She remembered Ray speaking of the excitement of seeing thousands of fans screaming as the winner crossed the finish line. Dee was definitely a good example of that. When he won the second race, Shirley said, "We had better change now that we each have two thousand dollars."

"Like hell! You promised to play him until he loses. Anyway, you can still bet on another horse since you have no faith, Shirley," Dee said, rolling her eyes her way.

"Oh all right, Dee. We'll play him until he loses. But remember, Shirley will not be able to come again if she loses."

"I said I would replace her hundred dollars, didn't I? Good grief, I got to deal with no-faith women jinxing my jockey. What the hell is that?"

"Dee, when did you become so rich?" Shirley asked as they waited anxiously for the next race.

"You don't need to be rich when you have mother wit."

"Mother what? Come on, Anna. This woman is something else." Anna knew Shirley was thinking about the six thousand dollars they had placed on the next race. David De Paul led the race wire-to-wire in the next three races. Anna, Dee, and Shirley stood with the rest of crowd, mouths agape. They all ran to the window and placed the winnings they had parlayed from the previous race on the jockey again. Anna laughed with Shirley as they watched several men tearing up their losing tickets, cursing their bad luck.

"Anna, if he loses the next race, do you realize how much money we will have lost?"

"I know, Shirley. But Dee will never speak to us again if we break our promise and take our winnings now."

"I know," Shirley said, sighing.

Anna overheard one man complaining that if he bet on David De Paul, the jockey lost the race but if he didn't bet on him he won the race. "How in the hell can a man win?" he asked as Anna laughed and turned back to see what the plan was for the thousands they had already won.

In the seventh race, an inquiry showed that David De Paul had nosed out another jockey by lifting his horse's head right at the wire. Anna had to give the superior rider his respect. Never even with Raymond had she seen one jockey win that many races or heard one man cursed or blessed so many times by so many people. "You have to watch him, Shirley. He is going to win again. When that happens—and it will—you won't have to worry about Tony complaining no more this year—or next year for that matter."

"How do you know he is going to win, Mrs. Mother Wit?" Anna asked.

"By the star count in his eyes," Dee said, gazing at all the money they were about to take up to the window to bet. "What I mean, ladies, is that the gods have cast a spell on him. They are guiding him tonight."

"What the hell have you been drinking, Dee?" Anna asked, knowing Shirley was thinking the same thing by the look she was giving her. It would be best if they just placed half their winnings on the next three races. After all, win or lose, they would have plenty to take home. She thought about suggesting it because she saw that Shirley was afraid to.

"Dee!" She received no answer as Dee held on to all the money, now in the thousands. Shaking her head, she knew Dee would have none of what she and Shirley wanted, so she said nothing else as they hurried up to the ticket window and parlayed their winnings on the next race.

After the ninth race, even Anna stood in a trance-like state, not able to believe one jockey could win that many races.

"Do you think the races are fixed so that he will win?" Shirley asked Anna after Dee left to play the next race.

"I don't think so. Some of these trainers have two or three horses on tonight's card. They could not afford to purposely lose that many races. No, Shirley, no jockey or trainer could afford fixes like what's happening here tonight," Anna answered; beginning to feel the aura of what everyone was caught up in.

"People always think the worst when they are losing," Dee said when she returned with her handkerchief up in the air as she danced around shaking her hips and the fist that held the tickets to the last race.

After David De Paul came in to win the tenth and final race the roar was deafening. Someone began chanting his name just as Anna remembered them doing for Jake at the council meeting. Before long, his name was all you could hear—louder and louder the chant grew. Standing in the crowd with Dee and Shirley, Anna looked up at the tiny man seated on the winning horse; he looked as small as a child. But in his black eyes, she saw the wear and tear of too many years. As Ray had once told her of his jockey, Webb, this rider was of a special breed. His name would go down in history with the rest of the thousand-win legends in thoroughbred racing.

A mystic glow spread throughout her body when she looked at him gazing back at the crowd that was cheering him on. Anna believed the other jockeys had somehow fallen under the same spell they were all under. Was it possible they had unintentionally slowed their horses, allowing the rider to make his way into the pages of history as he brought in the last and final horse to win the entire program for that night?

Twenty guards could not keep the fans from the rider as they pulled him from his horse and lifted him up into the air, still chanting his name. This night was his, and as with all great heroes, he graciously accepted the praise and glory belonging to him alone. Anna had to admit that David De Paul had ridden his way to fame, proving himself to be among the greatest jockeys riding in thoroughbred racing. She and Shirley looked at the winning tickets in their hands and then hurried with Dee to the ticket window to cash them all in.

****

"Damn, I'm going to have to change my game!" Anna jumped up in bed as she heard Jake whistle. "You won all this money at the racetrack, baby?" Anna placed her hand over her heart to slow its pace. She remembered going to bed after pouring most of her twenty thousand dollars over the bed. The women had equally split the winnings. Dee kept reminding them all the way home that had it not been for her, they would be penniless along with the rest of the faithless players who had been too scared to put their money on the line for what they believed in. And, of course, she reminded Anna it was not the horse but the jockey who won races. Without the jockey's expertise, the horse's form was not worth jumping on his back," Dee insisted. Anna laughed while assuring Dee that no matter how good a jockey is a lame horse will always come in last at the finish line.

"Yes, we won the money at the racetrack. You told me you wanted me to bring some money home," Anna answered falling back against the pillow where she had been asleep.

"There is over twenty grand here!" Anna listened to Jake counting the money she had carelessly tossed over the bed and the floor as she once again thought of the jockey's spectacular rides. It had been a great night—a memory never to be forgotten. In the darkness, smiling grey eyes in a handsome white face stared down at her. In the next vision, a baby nursed at her breast, her gray eyes staring into hers. Anna pulled the covers over her head, remembering it had been months since she had called to check on her daughter.

****

On Christmas morning, Anna sat in her parents' living room with Jake and their children. Her mother and father were thrilled to have them all together for dinner and to exchange gifts at Christmas. Jake and her father had gone out and bought the largest tree they could find it seemed to Anna. Gifts filled the floor. Anna and her mother had prepared Christmas dinner with all the trimmings. Her parents' decorated home gave the Christmas spirit to everyone except Anna, who, although she smiled and acted quite cheerful, was anxious to get to the phone to call and find out if her package to Granny had arrived by Christmas. The opportunity came when it was discovered batteries were needed for one of Jake Jr.'s games. Anna offered to go out for them.

A public phone stood at the entrance of the almost-empty store. When she got her grandmother on the phone, she found that all the Porter children were there with their mother. Even her son who lived in Europe had arrived for Christmas. She spoke with her Uncle Jessie, who raved about how big Raspy was getting. Frankie Lee mentioned to her that both of Raspy's aunts had fallen in love with her baby and wanted to adopt her.

Frankie Lee had already informed her that Granny had told them she was having no part of that and it was time they gave her some grandbabies. The child would stay with her until her mother or father came for her. The subject was dropped after that because Granny had spoken. Since he was spending Christmas with Kate's parents Frankie Lee was not there to help persuade Granny and Anna knew she would never be able to talk Granny into letting one of her daughters adopt her daughter. It tore into Anna's heart to listen to the baby babbling as she attempted to put words together over the phone. To talk to one of them about adopting the baby would be going against Granny's word and she was not about to do that.

"Granny," Anna asked her grandmother once she was back on the phone again, "has she gotten any darker?"

"Much as I can see, she's more of hur Papa everday she lives. Walkin' now and into most ever thang hur little hands can git into. Granny's havin' trouble keepin' step with hur."

"Granny if she's giving you problems I'll come and try to figure out something to do with her." Anna choked on her words, trying to keep the desperation out of her voice.

"Granny can see adder hur great grandbaby, don't ya study none. Ya just see to dem babies ya got up yonder. The master go fix it, don't ya fret none, Chile. We got all dem nice gifts ya sent. Now ya send this youngun a kiss and stop yur frettin'. We prayin' and God's got his own way and time 'bout fixin' thangs."

What is God's time and when will that time come? Anna asked herself as tears spilled from her eyes. She was the mother of three children, none of whom she really felt belonged to her. Staring at the phone now in its cradle, Anna said out loud to herself, "Surely she must have gotten a little darker."

Chapter Twenty-Five

—m—

When Fred turned into Looper's racetrack on New Year's Day, both Anna and Dee sat with stunned looks on their faces.

"I thought you said we were going somewhere special," Anna said to Jake, thinking that if this was some kind of joke, it was not funny.

"What is the meaning of this, Fred?" Dee asked. Anna could see she looked as shocked as she was

"This is somewhere special," Fred replied smiling, his arms circling Dee's shoulder as he drove up into the valet parking area.

We thought we'd allow you ladies to teach us how to win some of that bread you've been bringing home," Fred said. Jake smiled over at Anna as they got out of the car.

"Thoroughbred racing has ended for the season," Dee insisted.

"Dee is right, Jake. That's why we haven't been going to the racetrack. Thoroughbred racing won't start again until April sometime. If you had asked, we would have told you. We don't know anything about harness racing."

"I don't wanta hear that shit, Dee," Fred said as they all emerged from the car and Fred handed the valet attendant the keys to their car. "You been bringing more money home than I make on my job in five months coming out here, woman."

Anna thought about all the money they had won and how freely they had shared that knowledge and the money with their husbands. They hadn't realized that their bragging had piqued their husbands' interest.

"What I don't understand is how you guys have the energy to bring us out here after being up all night playing poker. What time did we come in from partying last night, Dee? I think it was about two o'clock in the morning, and then the men went out to a poker game after that."

"Poker!" Dee shouted at Fred, snatching the valet parking ticket from his hand. "Fred Bradley, we will be getting some shit straight when I get your ass home." Anna said not another word, feeling that her question had opened up something she had not intended. She sure hoped Fred wasn't doing any cheating. Dee seemed upset about something.

Anna and Dee looked at each other as Fred and Jake led them into an unfamiliar gate. This was not the area of Looper's that Anna remembered coming to. Stepping off an elevator, she frowned, seeing the Old Widow crawling around a corner next to the door they were about to enter. She did not want to enter the room Dee pushed her into while they all looked around at the splendor of the surroundings. Glittering chandeliers hung over the gold-and-black-trimmed tablecloths covering the tables. The waitress and waiters were dressed in gold and black and escorted them to a reserved table. She remembered that these were the colors of the Forlorn Ranch. They warmed her heart, bringing Raymond to her thoughts.

Anna, after taking the seat offered her, had to think hard as to where she had seen the white woman now approaching their table.

"Ain't that the white woman we met at the play? Yeah, that sure is her," Dee said, answering her own question. "I know it's her skinny ass with all that long blonde hair flying. Look how she is looking at Jake, Anna. Girl, she might snatch him up if you ain't careful."

"Dee, Jake is going home with me when we leave here, so she can look all she wants," Anna whispered, noticing that the woman stared at him as though she knew him.

"Jake, ain't that the woman that Nathan dude brought to the play?" Fred asked as they all observed the woman approaching them. "What the hell is she doing here?"

"She's Nathan's personal secretary, Fred. Hello, Angela," Jake said, rising with Fred to shake hands with her. Although she extended her hand to Anna and Dee, her eyes stayed on Jake as he asked, "Where is your boss?"

"Mr. Forlorn is pleased that you wanted to spend New Year's here, especially because today is his birthday. Your coming is an unexpected pleasant surprise. He will be joining us shortly." Smiling at all of them, she announced, "You have the pleasure of dining in Mr. Forlorn's private dining room clubhouse. There's a full view of the racing field. The betting area is next door unless you wish a waitress to take your wagers from the table for you."

"Nah," Jake answered, "we'll be doing our own betting. I've discovered my wife and her friend have become good at it. They think it's more fun than poker."

"Is that right?" Angela asked as she locked eyes with Anna. The look Angela gave her was a look she had seen before. She remembered how her downstairs neighbor had gazed with envy at her when she had walked out of the apartment to give Raymond his forgotten keys. She somehow had known that her downstairs neighbor wanted her lover. This woman wanted her husband if she didn't already have him, Anna thought, remembering seeing the Old Widow as she came in. Developing that same sense of uneasiness she had experienced at that time, Anna held her gaze until Angela turned back to look at Jake. "Let's hope you are not disappointed, Mr. Bradley."

Anna turned her attention to the splendor of the room, not at all happy with the turn of events. Seeing the black widow had elevated her heart rate as had meeting Nathan's secretary. As it was, she had no desire to spend the evening looking at the image of her former lover. It unnerved her that she was even this close to him. Too many memories invaded her mind. She struggled to forget and not think about anything connected to Raymond Forlorn and the baby hidden away down in Louisiana. She hoped Nathan realized coming there was none of her doing.

"Oh God, Dee. What are Fred and Jake arguing about?" Anna asked, seeing Fred's lips moving fast as Jake spoke to him with outstretched hands and shook his head.

"Anna I'm sitting here just like you are. I can't hear what is being said, but I bet it has something to do with that damn poker game. If it does, you can bet we'll find out before the night is over." Anna let the subject drop, feeling to that her question about the poker game the night before had something to do with the argument—something she shouldn't have mentioned or maybe she should have.

As Fred and Jake returned to the table, Fred insisted that Dee tell him what horse would win the upcoming race. Dee responded, "This is my first time seeing these damn horses run, I told you. I don't know what the hell they're going to do, Fred."

"All the money you and Anna been bringing home and you're telling me 'cause I'm with you, you don't know shit?"

"Anna, will you explain to this fool what I'm trying to tell him?" The argument between Fred and Dee caused Anna's mind to stop wandering.

"Fred, Dee is right. There is a difference between thoroughbred racing and harness racing."

"What the hell is harness racing?" he asked, looking puzzled as he gazed at the program in front of him.

"When the drivers are seated in buggies pulled by horses, it's called harness racing. Riders called jockeys ride on the backs of thoroughbred horses, not in buggies as they will be riding this evening."

"How do you know so much about what the difference is, Anna?" Jake asked, a frown growing on his face. "I thought you were a greenhorn, baby," he said, taking the program from her and reading it.

"I'm afraid your wife is correct. There is a big difference between thoroughbred racing and harness racing. If you will permit me, I will explain," Nathan said, smiling down at them as he reached for the program in Jake's hand. Her mind raced as she looked up into the sky-blue eyes staring down into hers. The pounding in her chest continued to increase as her eyes looked behind him and saw the Old Widow parked on the ledge outside the window. The orange spot pulsating on its back turned a bright red-orange. Looking at her palm, she not only saw but also felt the pulsating of the Old Widow's young as the spot became brighter and brighter.

"How are you, Nathan?" Jake asked as he and Fred stood and shook hands with him. "You remember my wife. Fred and Dee, of course, accompanied us to the play."

"Certainly, it came as a delightful surprise when Angela informed me you had called wanting to visit the track. Mrs. Bradley, I must say this is the second beautiful hat I've seen you wear. It simply adds to the beauty of you and your attire. I must say the same of your friend. I am an admirer of ladies wearing hats, of course." The twinkle in his eyes as he gazed at her caused Anna's heart to step up its beat.

"Yes, I thought I'd surprise my wife with a different celebration to start out the New Year." Anna looked away from Nathan Forlorn as if to avoid seeming to know him more than she should. It felt as though needles were piercing her skull. Her mind kept spinning. She ached to escape from this place, at least go down below was where she, Dee, and Shirley had enjoyed handicapping.

"This is harness racing season here at the track. The drivers are pulled in buggies by trotters or pacers instead of thoroughbreds, Jake."

"Look my man, we're here to enjoy ourselves and we are going to win regardless . . . who couldn't enjoy this luxury we are surrounded by? Isn't that right, honey?" Jake asked, placing his arm around Anna's shoulder. She did not answer. It had become impossible for Anna to concentrate.

The Old Widow crawled up her web along the outside windowsill, giving her a sense of serious danger. Something was amiss. She had had the same feeling right before discovering Mix's accounts were off. At least Nathan had heard from Jake how she came to be there and understood her predicament. All she needed to do was to act as if she were enjoying herself. In a few hours, she would be home free. Once she got home, she would take a sleeping pill to help her forget the horror of this nightmare—one she planned never to revisit.

The storm inside her mind began as it always did when she realized trouble was on its way. Seeing how Angela looked at her husband, Anna reached down and rubbed her palm allowing her mind to expand.

"'So you're here to see Mr. Forlorn.' It was Angela, Nathan's secretary, talking to Jake while he sat waiting in Nathan's office. Anna could see in the vision that Angela was taken by not only his handsome face but; the distinguished way Jake carried himself. Her eyes traveled over him. Anna could see his polished look of a businessman impressed Angela as she gazed at him with eyes that said she would love to be his next woman.

"'Yes, we have business to discuss,' Jake said as he smiled back at Angela.

"'Your wife—has she been found yet? I mean, has she returned home?'

"'No, she hasn't. It's been two years now. It's hard being alone, but I'm sure she will return one day. Until then, I guess I must remain alone.' Anna saw the smile playing on Jake's lips, a look in his eyes that said she is mine for the taking as Angela took a seat, crossing her legs.

"It's sad when you are alone. Too many thoughts invade your mind that can drive you insane. A man like you needs the warmth of a woman to salve your pain her eyes on the cane lying across his lap." Frankie Lee was right, Anna thought to herself as she gazed at the two in the vision. All her husband had to do was show up and the women were willing to give him anything he asked for. All except her, as he reminded her time and time again. Before they were married, it had been "No Jake, not yet. I'm not sure of you. I was told you had twenty women waiting in line just to get a chance to bed you. Go sleep with one of them." Of course, he had denied any such thing.

"'Yes, it has been hard,' she listened to him tell Angela. "I need the phone number of such a woman who might be able to ease this pain I'm feeling right now." Anna watched her husband smile as he took the offered number, watching Nathan's secretary stroll out of Nathan's office as Nathan walked in.

In the next scene, Anna sat shocked to see them naked in her heart-shaped bed. Jake's hands moved over her white body in the aftermath of some vigorous lovemaking. "'As much as I want you, if my wife returns, this relationship has to end. It has to.'

"'If she returns,' she listened to Angela whispered, moving down and sucking in that which Anna knew would give her husband pleasure beyond the sexual act.

"'Ohhhhh, babyyyy,' he moaned, receiving something Anna had refused to give him. The vision ended when Dee shook Anna back to the present.

"Anna, what is wrong with you? You look all spaced out. I know that after being downstairs, this is not where either of us wants to be."

"My committee and I have worked out those plans to hire more employees from Session that I talked to you about, Jake," Nathan said as he and Jake rose from the table and walked toward the betting window. The Old Widow had warned her; what would she do now?

"You like it up here?" Anna heard Fred ask Dee, looking around with a smile on his face as he lit a cigarette.

"Too siddiddy for me. I prefer being downstairs where all the home folks are," Dee replied, seemingly struck by all the luxury surrounding them.

Anna forced a smile as she and Fred watched Dee gaze when her mouth opened as she looked at a woman in the betting room wearing a full-length black mink coat and sporting huge diamonds on all of her fingers.

"She could loan me two of those rocks." Anna and Fred laughed, looking with Dee at a scene Anna had marveled over many times before when she had been out nightclubbing with Raymond.

With Angela's help, everyone proved to be winners as they clinched the daily double. The six hundred ninety dollars won by Anna and Jake put him in high spirits as he and Fred drank champagne after ordering New York steak dinners.

"You got things going, brother! Now if my wife can get her nose in that book right, we are going to get our thang going." Everyone laughed at Dee as she insisted Fred was out of his mind.

"Dee and Fred won the third race exacta for three hundred and forty dollars, putting everyone in high spirits. At that point, no one except Anna was ready to leave; she hated having to look at Nathan seated across from her.

A waitress dressed in a short black and gold outfit came up to their table, gaining Nathan's attention. "Mr. Forlorn, other guests have arrived. Do you want to see them in the Luxor Room?"

"I was not expecting more guests," Nathan answered as he rose to go greet them. "I will have them join us—that is, if more guests wouldn't be a problem?" Nathan asked, hesitating.

"Nathan, have them come in," Jake insisted, rising. "We have plenty room." They all stood as Angela proceeded to push tables together for the new arrivals. Angela shared with them that this was a surprise for her boss, one she knew he would be pleased with. Smiling over at Jake, she left the room to attend to the newly arrived guests with Nathan.

"Why the hell did you bring me here, knowing you were having an affair with her?"

"Her, who? What the hell are you talking about? I couldn't be having an affair with anyone because I'm sitting here having an affair with you."

Anna stared over at Angela, who stood talking to Nathan about something she could not hear.

"All right, I've had my transgressions, but all of that was over once you returned. Fred wanted us to come here because of the money you guys won. What could I say? I'm no angel, but I have bared my soul to you. I'm here with you, so any woman wanting me knows you are my wife. I must want to be with you because I am not with them. She knows it's over. You want me to call her ass over here and tell her in front of you? Better still . . ." Jake said, taking a knife from his pocket.

"This is the switchblade you stabbed me with when you first returned home and I made advances toward you." Anna looked at Madria's switchblade knife she had placed in her bra after giving her a parting warning not to take any disrespect. She wanted no part of it after Jake pushed it into his chest with her hand holding it to make a point. "Yeah, I kept it to remind me how much you have changed. If you see me doing anything out of line, cut my ass like you cut Barb." When Anna refused to take it, he placed it inside her bra. "You're your Momma now, baby." With that, he kissed her rings.

"Don't be ridiculous, Jake."

"Look, after you were gone two years, yes—I stepped out with her a time or two. You were not here. I'm not asking about your time away from me and the man you were with. Have there ever been things in your life you have regretted and did not want to be reminded of, hopefully not? You know I have been doing everything in my power to let you know how much I love you."

Listening to him, Anna could not help but think of her own transgressions. The baby girl she had given birth to and who was now a toddler stayed on her mind, a testimony of her past transgressions with a man now out of her life forever. There was nothing she could do with the baby. Granny would have to allow her to have her adopted out. She had waited on God long enough. It was time she took matters into her own hands. Anna realized she needed to soften her heart. That heart shaped bed had been blown up along with the house it sat in. Whatever Jake and Angela had done, it must be over because his arms were wrapped around her now.

"Oh, all right. As long as it ended before we began this marriage again, I'm not going to allow it to come between us."

Jake's face lit up with a smile. Just as his lips moved to connect with hers, Anna noticed his eyes enlarge as though something strange had caught his attention. On the window sill behind them, she watched the orange glow on the back of the Old Widow turn from bright orange to blood red in a second, causing her to turn back around just in time to hear Jake say, "That motherfucker looks like Nathan's twin. Look at the two of them standing there together baby. They're too much alike for it not to be his . . ."

"Oh, my God, please tell me this is not happening!" Anna whispered under her breath as she saw them embrace with smiles and then walk together over to the table. She sat mortified. Raymond Forlorn lifted his tinted lenses and stared down at her with his mouth open. Listening to Nathan introduce Raymond, Carolyn, and their son Jason, a kick from under the table caused Anna to look over at Dee, who was staring from her to the people standing at their table. Anna returned her gaze back into Raymond's piercing gray eyes, and then she looked quickly away. She could not speak when she was spoken to; she just sat there speechless. At that moment Anna felt engulfed by the strange power of that moment. She thought her heart would explode at any minute it was hammering so hard. His familiar cologne caressed her nostrils, adding dizziness to her already dazed senses. She wondered if they could hear how her knees were knocking together or how her heart pounded under her breast as she felt his body all over and inside of hers. What was it she and Jake had been discussing? Oh God, she thought, this couldn't be happening!

The tan casual attire he wore had been skillfully tailored to fit him. There were lips under that mustache she could taste even though they were a few feet away. Electricity charged the air as Anna felt herself being jolted by the energy moving between the two of them. In his eyes, she saw what they both felt. Hers somehow found Dee's, and Anna saw in them that Dee, too, knew the catastrophe that had suddenly come crashing down on her friend.

Nathan guided his brother and his family to the other end of the extended table. Anna turned to Jake.

"Take me home. I don't feel well at all; please let's go now, Jake!" Anna pleaded, almost in tears.

"Now Anna, I thought you told me you could meet any white person without a problem. You're not going back to being afraid of whites again, are you? I can feel your entire body trembling," Jake whispered, placing his arm around her shoulder again. The burning in her throat prevented her from uttering a sound. Tears struggled to make their escape.

"Why are you so uptight? You've already proven you can meet with whites, even strangers, without a problem."

"I don't want to be near these people. Just take me home, please!" she whispered in anguish.

"I know what you are feeling, baby. They are big-time rich and a little high-falutin, but they're Nathan's family. We don't want to insult him by walking out on him just because they have come. Look, they don't die any different than the rest of us. Now hang tuff—I'm here by your side."

"Oh my God, Jake! I don't want to be here!"

"Anna, I keep telling you it is going to be all right. Now calm down. We don't want these rich white people to think we are country and cannot handle being around their so-called blue blood asses, baby."

Anna prayed that she would not be recognized as she listened to Carolyn Forlorn's British accent. She hugged Nathan, telling him she had suggested to his brother that they surprise him by coming for New Years since his secretary had recently informed her it was his birthday. Anna looked at their son, thinking that even though his head was still shaved, he looked to be in perfect health. She wondered what had happened with the illness that had threatened his life.

"Anna, you mind going to the ladies' room with me?" Dee asked staring at Anna, who had turned sideways for the last half hour to avoid giving the new arrivals direct access to look at her. Moving by sheer force, Anna walked with Dee to the ladies' room.

"Sister Girl, you look as though you've just seen a ghost—and I mean one from another planet. We gotta work this. Can't let on nothing is out of order, Anna. Damn that wife of his—she's trippin' like she some kinda queen or something. What language is that she's speaking? Egyptian!"

"Dee, she is from England. She is speaking English."

"What? I speak English—and it sure as hell does not sound like that shit coming out of her mouth. Snooty is what she is. You know how I dislike snooty women. Faking is what they love doing—trying to be something they ain't. I can spot their asses a mile away. She thinks she is too good to include me in her conversation with Nathan's secretary, but it gave me a chance to whisper a few words to that husband of hers unnoticed."

"Dee!"

"I just asked him if he wasn't sure they were twins and not just brothers. Of course he said he was the older brother. Told me he liked the hat I was wearing—it looked becoming of a lady. I told him my girlfriend down on the other end of the table got me to wearing them with my outfits. He smiled, of course, and looked down at you. I told him our husbands had dragged us out to the track thinking we could pick winners, only to discover thoroughbred racing had ended for the season. He asked me if I am a thoroughbred handicapper. Of course, I told him it was you who taught me how to handicap—didn't want to give away my knowledge. I even coughed up enough grit to say you were the best player, winning me and my other friend lots of money, and that's why our husbands had us out here, thinking we could win like that on these trotters or whatever the hell they are called. You think he was happy to hear that?"

Anna sat crying so hard she couldn't answer. Dee continued, "That wife of his wouldn't even speak to me with her snooty-ass self. Him and her don't even look like they belong together. She don't even speak his language—my goodness, he is indeed a Southern-speaking man, Anna." Dee paused as though a thought had just entered her mind. "You know, Anna, I'm thinking Fred has his facts mixed up because looking at that white man's biceps, it seems to me he could handle any woman under his belly. Am I right, sister girl?"

"Dee, this is not the time or place to be discussing sex."

"Sister Girl anytime is the right time to discuss whether or not a man can make good love. And anyway, Fred told me that cat has money to burn. Is that true? And if it is, why would you leave money to come back to this poor sorry-ass city?"

"Dee, money isn't everything."

"When you ain't got none, it is everything, sister girl. Believe me—I know."

"I just hope no one gets wind of anything before it's time to go."

"If Jake wasn't so busy getting looked over himself, he would know who that man is by the way he looks at you. Even Fred picked up on the shocked look on his face when his eyes fell on you. I thought you both were going to pass out. Of course, since I knew why, I assured him the white man couldn't help looking at you that way because you are a beautiful black woman. I asked him, of course, if he saw how you turned away, hating the sight of the white people taking a seat at our table. Like Jake, he probably thinks you still haven't gotten over your hatred of them."

"Dee, what am I going to do? Jake will not take me home as I asked him to do."

"Jake has other things on his mind, honey. Our only cover is your lover's race and his money. He is the last man on earth Jake would give a thought to."

"Ex-lover, Dee. It's the same with Jake—Angela is in the past. We already got that straight right before they walked in," Anna said, almost joining her in laughter as her hand covered her lips. Dee looked at Anna, unable to contain her laughter.

"Oh my God, who is the joke on now? If that slick ass fool only knew how much trouble he has brought on his self by bringing you out here." Dee took a seat next to Anna shaking her head.

"If by some chance Jake discovers who that white man is, we all might die up in here. So come on, sister girl, you've got to pull out of it."

"Dee, we should never have allowed Fred and Jake to find out about the money we were winning, let alone see it. I don't know what I was thinking when I came home that night, leaving my winnings lying all over the bed," Anna whispered, still trembling at what might happen if Jake discovered Raymond's relationship to her.

"I know Anna. We messed ourselves up. This is the last place either of us need to be, least of all you. I must say, though, that picture in that attaché case does him no justice. He is a fine ass white dude, I'm telling you. Look at those arms of his—built like a prizefighter. And it looks like he has been bathed in money. The way he looked at you, I thought that white man was going to jump over that table and grab you. His clear-looking eyes were on you so hard I could feel his thoughts. With him and that wife of his seated next to Fred and me, I got a good sniff of that cologne he is wearing. It dazed my senses—he smells good enough for a woman to want to melt into!" Anna closed her eyes after seeing Dee run her tongue over her lips and then press them together. He is all that and then some, Anna thought.

"Jake would have a heart attack and a stroke at the same time if he knew that white man was the lover you were in bed with for four years, honey. I'm telling you what God loves. He's competition big time. Lord have mercy," Dee said, patting Anna's face with her powder sponge while shaking her head with a big grin on her face.

"Dee, don't you think I know that? I'm going to have a heart attack if you don't get us out of here."

"Anna, he speaks worse than his brother's. I thought I had jumped across the Mason Dixon line listening to that deep southern drawl coming from his lips," said Dee, placing her powder puff back in its container. "And I thought Mrs. Annabelle had a Southern drawl, but his puts hers to shame. This honey of yours must have been born under a huckleberry tree." Down to the tip of her toes, sensations moved through Anna as she thought of that Southern drawl Dee spoke of. No other man sounded out his words as tight. Magnolias echoed in his every word.

"Damn it, Anna! Please don't start crying again. Honey, your mother will never find out, and you ain't gonna have no heart attack. Now stop crying so hard or I'll never get this make up on you right," Dee insisted, taking her powder puff back out.

"My God, I thought after all this time he would seem like a stranger to me. Seeing him again, it's like time stood still. What will I do to make it through the evening?" Anna asked, thinking nothing of the beating her face was taking from Dee's powder sponge.

"Just act natural. He is nothing but an old boyfriend you are seeing for the last time, Anna," Dee said, lifting Anna's chin up to look in her face.

"Dee, you just don't understand," Anna cried, then, stopped talking as three white women entered the ladies' room and looked their way. Anna thought that probably few black women visited this area but before she could cement those thoughts in her mind two black women entered and smiled at she and Dee spoke as they stood at the large mirror powdering their faces. Anna thought about Raymond's baby down in Louisiana she had given birth to. That baby would be three years old in five months. She hadn't seen her mother but for three months to know who she was, while her grandmother did what she should have been doing for her own baby. None of this could she tell Dee.

"I wonder if that brother of his arranged this as some cruel joke . . . the white bastard knew we would be here!"

"Dee, if you put any more powder on my face, I'll look like I'm dead. And no, I don't think so. His look of surprise equaled mine," Anna replied in Nathan's defense.

"Yeah, I guess you are right. He turned so red I thought he was going to keel over. Look, you are not the only one who has to make it through this. When he looked at you, it was as though he saw a ghost who had come back to life. Man, I can imagine how he feels, seeing a woman who was his for four years with another man—and there is not a damn thing he can do but look and wish. That's some hard shit to take. As for you, Anna, you'll make it if things continue the way they are going. Just keep telling yourself it's over. And Anna, it **is** over! It has to be if you value living at all. Not to mention that you have your hands full keeping track of Jake with that Angela woman all over him. Haven't you noticed how she manages to call him away for stupid shit? I just rolled my eyes when she said, 'Jake, I'd like you to see the rest of the rooms that are available for the conferences you and Nathan plan to have.' And you just sat there saying nothing. She knows I am on to her game. I started to get her straight for you, but I didn't want to start something when you are already in a crisis."

"Dee, Jake is going home with me tonight. I'm not worried about some woman wanting or liking him. That is her problem, not mine." It better be over between them.

"I heard that. I know Jake don't want his ass cut up. He's already limping. If the phone rings after the two of you get home and he says he has to take care of something, you jump your ass up out of that bed with him, put on your clothes, and follow him right out the door. There is no emergency you can't help him take care of that is legit," Dee insisted, placing more lip-gloss on Anna's lips.

****

Anna sat in a daze. Her hands trembled as Raymond's son, after not being able to gain his father's attention, mentioned to his mother that he thought the lady seated down from them was the servant they had met in his father's apartment when they were in Las Vegas.

"Of course not, darling," Anna heard Carolyn say to him. "That person is still there, no doubt working for someone else, unfortunately for them—a servant dressed in pink hot pants and a tank top that her breasts bubbled out of! Had it not been for that towel covering them you would have seen all of them. Of course, in that awful city, what can one expect?"

Anna listened to Angela, Carolyn said, "All blacks look the same to Jason. I have explained so many times that there is a difference." Neither Dee who sat next her nor Angela made a comment. Jake had disappeared somewhere. Anna was glad Fred had gone out to see the horses run and had not overheard that comment or the night would have ended right then and there.

"Your son is so adorable," Angela said, gazing at Jason who smiled back at her. "What interest you, young man?" Anna heard Angela asked him.

"Rugby. I've been preparing to become a player. See my muscles are growing so strong," he said, smiling as he displayed his upper arms.

"Yes," Carolyn whispered, "unknown to his father, he is becoming a great rugby player." Anna almost dropped the glass she had just lifted to drink from, hearing Carolyn's admission of what her son was involved in. Even though his head was still bald, at close examination he looked as rugged as any healthy ten-year-old boy. "He wants to wait until he is accepted by a ruby youth team before telling his father," she whispered, smiling at Angela, to whom she directed her attention as she dismissed Dee and Anna from the conversation.

The game she spoke of would not be something a child as ill as he had been would be able to participate in by any means from what Anna had seen of it. When Fred and Jake returned, Dee's hand raising her drink became the tool that brought Anna around when she began to drift or she and her former lover stared a little too long at each other.

"We are going to make it, Anna," Dee said, after getting her to go to the betting window with her. "We only have two more races and we are out of here." When they turned to leave, they ran right into Nathan and Raymond walking their way. It was as if Anna's legs suddenly turned to rubber. Desire for him overwhelmed her. She stood there unable to move as their eyes locked on each other. He reached down, touching the horse on the gold chain around her neck

"Ms. Anna, I love you still! You are and will forever be my beautiful lady," he whispered as she looked into his consuming grey eyes and listened to the gentleness of his Southern drawl sweep her into the past. It took all of her efforts not to fall into his arms as her vagina ached to have him touch it. She felt it become wet between her legs. If only her clitoris would stop vibrating.

"Ray, I . . ." Nothing else was said as Nathan turned him in different direction while Dee propelled Anna back toward the betting windows.

"Damn it, Anna! Are you trying to commit intentional suicide?" Dee asked, pushing Anna ahead of her.

After winning the eighth race, Fred, Jake, and Dee went up to cash in their winnings. Nathan took a call. Anna could not recall what had caused Jason or his mother to leave the table. Raymond sat alone. His eyes followed her every move. When their eyes finally locked, Anna heard the voice of Linda Klein speaking as clearly as if she sat next to her.

"'Are you not listening to me, Kid? Its death row for the both of you and neither of you knows it.' She remembered looking at Linda at a loss for words. "There ain't no sense staring at me like I'm crazy. When you walk through the door of that apartment and he's standing there waiting for you, everything in your body wants to be touched by him and his. You know what I'm talking about and that I'm telling you the truth. He is more your husband than the one you left behind, ain't he?'

As the voice in her mind quieted, Anna felt her body heat up as desire for him intensified inside of her. Rubbing her left palm, she allowed her mind to expand to know his thoughts. She stared at the scene he was remembering, the memory still so fresh in her mind. He stood at the window, waiting for her to return from visiting with her lady friends. It was shortly after he had received the letter from his wife telling him she wanted him home. Everything had been placed just as he knew she would like it. Aretha's *You Make Me Feel Like a Natural Woman* sounded on the stereo. The candlelight dinner made for two waited. Her favorite white and lavender orchids stood as a centerpiece, completing a breathtaking surprise. Anna watched him watching the corvette and knew he wondered why it was taking so long for her to get out of the car. She watched him breathe easier as she slammed the car door and came up the stairs. Hearing her unlock the door, he lit the candles. When she walked into the apartment, her purse dropped from her hand as it had done when she was surprised in New York with the visit he had arranged with her father. Into his arms she fell, all her fears forgotten. The beauty of the room caused tears to slip down her cheeks, thinking his thoughts. Soon they were in the bedroom.

"'I can't lose you again,' she listened to him whisper, holding on to her as their bodies wrestled to grasp each orgasm. "'I'm yours forever! Now make those violins ring in my ears, baby—plllleeeaasseee!' Her moans sounded as whispers. Anna struggled desperately to stop her thoughts.

"Oh my God, Anna! Can't you hear those violins playing for us?" She felt his hands as they reached and locked with hers to bring her back to the present. Moving her hand quickly away from his, she realized he had taken Jake's seat. Anna shook her head, whispering to him.

"Please, don't sit here—not now!" Listening to Ray Charles singing *"I Can't Stop Loving You"* through the music system, Anna again heard Linda's words.

"I can do nothing to stop my thoughts, my dear. How have you been?" he asked as Anna felt her heart still racing from her memory of that special moment. She bit her bottom lip to calm herself and tried to act as though this was just a casual conversation she might be having with anyone.

"I've been fine, Ray, just fine. How else would you expect me to be?" she asked as they continued to gaze at each other.

"Ms. Anna . . . I miss you. My God, I still love you so much," he said shaking his head as though trying to make sense out of his feelings, something she knew he did when showing concern about matters that troubled him.

"We cannot be this close to each other," Anna whispered, looking away from him as she dotted her eyes so her tears would not show.

"You have no idea how I have wanted you in my arms . . . to feel your body under mine!"

"Don't say those things, Ray. I am telling you it's too dangerous!" Anna whispered again.

"I don't suppose you will believe how much I have wanted to see you, but not like this. I had no idea you would be here. As far as danger, I embrace it, as you must know," he said, his eyes never leaving hers.

"Ray, this is madness," Anna replied, seeing the Old Widow crawl down the windowsill just as he reached across the table and again took her hands into his.

"Forgive me, I must touch you," he said as Anna felt his touch start the tug in her heart. A charge moved through her so strong it was as if she had been shocked. She snatched her hand away in fear of what might happen next. "Leave with me," he whispered.

"I can't," she said. "It has to be over whether we want it to be or not," she whispered as they both looked up to see Nathan and Carolyn Forlorn staring down at them.

"Raymond, I forgot to mention," Nathan said, "Arnold sent papers here for you to sign. Come, I will show them to you." Reluctantly Raymond rose and followed him out of the room. Giving Carolyn Forlorn no eye contact, Anna rose from her seat and walked to the ladies' room closing the door behind her. "Oh my God, Old Head! Why can't you take my heart from him? I don't want to love him anymore. I don't want these feelings. I thought I was over him. The way you've connected our lives will destroy us both." She stood with her back to the door, crying so hard that she didn't hear it open.

"My son was right—you are her. A servant, I thought." Anna turned to see Carolyn Forlorn standing there. She closed the door behind her saying with much bitterness. "His irresistible Ms. Anna!" Her voice assaulted Anna's space as she watched his wife's eyes turned to slits as she spit out her name. "I've had to listen to him calling out to you night after night until I removed him from my bed. So it was you—the genius who gave him back his life after somehow returning his face to its handsome appearance again. I must thank you for the miracle you performed."

"You are quite welcome, seeing as how you were ready to demand he kill himself when his looks didn't suit you." Carolyn Forlorn walked closer to Anna as if to examine her in much the same way as her downstairs neighbor in Las Vegas had done when she knocking on her door claiming to want to see her competition.

"Ms. Anna—his perfect woman. I could never fill her shoes. Before I tagged him for myself, it was always you he spoke of. His lady—a genius he missed with all his heart. Damn you, his unforgettable Ms. Anna!"

"And damn you, his wife who buried him as though he had died."

Carolyn tossed her head, refusing to reply to Anna's accusation. "You are his little black filly—the woman who showed him how a real woman makes love. He has apparently never wanted to forget what you did for him. He wakes up in the middle of the night calling for you. I, of course, thought you were a figment of his imagination, especially after his miraculous recovery from that hideous disfigurement he should have died from." Anna gave no reply. "Yet I've waited, knowing someday, someway, somehow if you were flesh and blood, you would materialize." Carolyn hissed her words as she continued glaring hatefully at Anna.

"I don't know what you are talking about," Anna replied, turning from her harsh gaze.

"Are you telling me you are not the irresistible Ms. Anna he speaks of, even in his sleep? I've been waiting for this moment and look at what confronts me, Ms. Anna." Anna listened to Carolyn say her name with so much venom it was as if she were spitting out poison. "I knew it would happen sooner or later—a man as obsessed as my husband has been with this phenomenal woman . . . I knew, somehow he would find a way to return to the source . . . and of all things—his servant." Anna's eyes widened as she turned to give Carolyn Forlorn her full attention.

"I'm afraid you are mistaken. Anna has never been a servant for anyone. Just because my skin is black, don't fool your racist thoughts into thinking that makes me any least a servant than you, white woman."

"And to think he wanted to divorce me to be with a black wench." Listening to her, Anna felt her anger explode as it had when Barb had disrespected her in Dee's apartment. She knew the words Carolyn Forlorn had just spoken would have at any other time gotten her worse than what Barb had gotten. She felt the switchblade lying in wait inside her bra. But Anna knew this was neither the time nor the place for any such action.

"You say your son is playing rugby. How is that possible? With an illness as serious as you and your son indicated in Las Vegas, something is amiss. I would surely like to examine those medical records to see what the real diagnosis was." Anna watched a sudden look of fear appear on Carolyn's face.

"That's none of your damn business, you bitch."

"A bitch is what you are—a damn wicked bitch having your son lie about an illness to fool his father back into your life. How could you do something that disgusting?"

"It worked," Carolyn replied, a smile smoothing out the frown on her face.

"You didn't want him when you thought he was dying. Once you discovered he would live and looked like someone you wanted to hang on your arm, you just happened by to pick him up. I cared for him well; you should be pleased," Anna said, matching her eye level.

"Yes, I must say you did! Walked right in on you and didn't have sense enough to realize it. Should have guessed he'd dig out of the bottom of the barrel. How will I ever be able to stand his touching me again?" she said, tossing her flaming red hair that Anna remembered so well.

"From the bottom of the barrel is where he found your worthless ass. And what you had better do is whatever you were doing before you discovered Ms. Anna. We were finished the day you walked into my apartment. He's yours now; you had better pretend I never existed!"

"The hell I will! You stand there wearing that damn precious chain of his around your neck—the one I begged him for. All I got was an expensive imitation." Anna reached up and touched the chain. "A living testimony of his infidelity—I'll forget it all right—when we are in the divorce court and I'm taking him for every penny he's worth. His name will be mud when I'm finished with him!" she hissed, again tossing her red hair as though in disgust. Anna frowned, remembering how Julia had shared with her that scandal had never touched the Vanderlin or Forlorn names. She knew it would crush him to have that happen.

"Damn you! You try it and Ms. Anna will go have a little talk with those British tabloid papers in London. I'll give them the story of the century. Imagine what those lovely British blueblood lady friends of yours will think when they learn how you left the grandson of John Vanderlin to die during the worst of his illness, not to mention how you manipulated getting him back by using your son as bait—pretending he had a deadly illness that was all a lie."

"You wouldn't dare, damn you!"

Anna's, body turned cold, remembering the oblong tube on the back of the Old Widow that she had ridden on through hell before reaching the Land of the Healing Tree to bring back the tears to save the life of the Young Chemist "I went through hell to restore his life and I will slander your name in hell if you take one penny of his money or link his name to a scandal that would destroy it." Anna watched Carolyn's eyes enlarge as she walked up inches from her face.

"Let me repeat myself. If you want to see what I will do to stop you, take one penny of his money or seek to destroy his family's name and when I finish with you, white woman, the world will not only know about the black wench your husband preferred over your white ass, but those lily-white blueblood English ladies who now welcome you into their circle will read about a woman who used her son in the scandalous manner you used yours. Do you think after learning these things that they will allow you to enter their homes, not even to scrub their dirty floors, you lowdown bitch?" Anna turned and walked toward the door, stopping to speak without turning to face her. "You better stop and think about that circle you are so in love with dumping you after that ugly scandal spreads all over the world."

"You have a husband who would find out."

Anna paused giving her words some thought. "You said it yourself—I must still love him to wear his chain even with a husband. Leaking your dirt to the syndicated columns will be only one of many things I would do to protect him. Try me if you dare, and you will find yourself kissing the devil's ass. Think about it a moment—a woman who can bring a dying man back to life. There is nothing I wouldn't do to save him again, nothing!" She turned to see the stunned look in Carolyn's eyes. Anna knew she had her. Standing with her mouth open and holding her throat, tears flooded Carolyn's face. With her hand on the doorknob, it came to Anna that she must leave the racetrack at once and never return.

"Just out of curiosity, tell me, Ms. Anna. How many illegitimate bastard babies of yours is he paying for?" Anna stopped dead in her tracks, turning back to face Carolyn, whose words cut so deep into Anna that she felt her insides tearing apart. Her temples pulsated as though they would burst. And there sat the Old Widow with her orange light pulsating as red as blood giving life to her secret. There was a baby she had hidden away, as ashamed of her existence as she was of the fact that her father was a white man who had no idea of her birth.

"For that goddamn answer, Mrs. Forlorn, you had better ask your damn husband while you are telling him of your own deceit and leave Anna the hell alone!" All her vibes said to kill this white woman for having the nerve to talk to her in such a manner, but what could she say? The child did exist, was she, Anna asked herself as deceiving as his wife?

Her heart racing, Anna walked out of the ladies' room on her way toward the exit sign. She planned to get out of there no matter what Jake insisted they do. He could stay as long as he wanted. He would find her at home. As she turned the corner, she ran into Dee coming her way fast.

Anna stopped, looking down at Dee's feet and wondered why she was carrying her shoes.

"Take your shoes off and come with me, Anna."

"Why?"

"Take your damn shoes off like I told you and come with me! Stop asking questions. You will get answers soon enough," Dee insisted as Anna slipped out of her shoes and hurried behind her. They entered a room where Dee turned and placed her finger up to her lips to indicate that Anna should be quiet. She slid a sliding door open just enough for them to see and hear the voices inside. Anna stood behind Dee in shock, recognizing the people inside.

"Jake, are you going to come over again tonight? I can't get enough of that body of yours. I didn't want you to leave this morning."

"This is too dangerous, baby. You remember when Fred came and told us Anna had cut up Barb. I might have to wait until next week to get out. I'm not getting my ass cut up letting her catch us out at this track."

"She wouldn't dare cut a white woman," Angela assured him as she slipped to her knees, opening the fly to Jake's pants. The shock of what she was about to do so overwhelmed Anna she could feel her blood draining from her face. He had fooled her again. The switchblade Jake had placed in her bra popped open as she snatched it out when her lips closed around his penis, only to feel Dee's grip as she grabbed her hand much the same as her lover had done the night at the club when she was about to cut her downstairs neighbor. Shaking her head, she pushed Anna outside into the hallway.

"I will go back in there and help you show her what a black sister will do to her white ass, sister girl, but only if Jake is the man you are in love with. Otherwise, it makes no sense to go to jail over his ass when your heart belongs to another man. Think about what I'm telling you. Why rot in prison over a man you don't even love?" Dee looked hard at Anna as she waited for an answer.

"That son of a bitch lied to me, Dee. He's been lying all along. I will kill his ass for that reason alone."

"You cut the hell out of Barb, but that didn't stop him from doing what he is doing now and has always done. Let's get the hell out of this place, Anna, before there is a killing up in here."

Once the car was driven up by the valet attendant, Dee pushed Anna into it. "Tell that husband and brother-in-law of mine to catch their asses a cab when they come for my car," Dee shouted out of her Oldsmobile at the parking attendant as they took off leaving the racetrack.

"Sister Girl, I'm so sorry," Dee said after they had driven in silence for a half hour.

"What happened here tonight has fucked your entire life up." Anna sobbed into her hands, understanding the truth of her friend's words.

"He took me home and made love to me. When the phone rang, he said it was Fred wanting him to join a poker game." Anna laughed in the midst of her tears. "Angela probably made the call. The only poker game he had going was in bed with her. He never stopped seeing her, even after we got back together. Oh Dee, you knew there had been no poker game when I spoke about it on the way out to the track, am I right?"

"Jake came over to get Fred out of the house, but I told that bastard if he walked his ass out of that door at three in the morning, he might as well find a home wherever he was going because the locks would be changed when he returned. He got his ass back in bed and left Jake standing in the front room after telling him it was too late for him to be out unless he was going to sleep in another woman's bed."

"Why didn't you tell me so my ass would not have looked like the fool I feel like now?"

"The same reason you didn't tell me when you saw that woman seated on Fred's lap, something he came back and told me because he thought you would tell me." Anna sighed as she shook her head remembering the night she had went to Foral's looking for Jake and discovered a woman seated on Fred's lap keeping quite because she did not want to tell Dee something she knew would hurt her.

"I sensed shit wasn't right tonight, so I ran back up to where we were seated, leaving Fred's ass outside watching those damn horses run. To my shock, you and the white dude were talking. Before I could get over there and pull you away, his wife and brother walked up. Even though he left with his brother, when I saw you get up and leave, I knew shit had hit the fan after seeing her following you, and I planned to follow her when I saw her slip behind you into the bathroom. But just as I was about to head that way, I spied that Angela woman and Jake slide around a corner. Taking off my shoes, I followed them to see where they were going. When I found out I hurried back to get you. Of course, by then you were coming out of that bathroom and walking away fast. I knew you and his wife had somehow tied up in there. I was so glad it was a verbal encounter and not physical like with Barb, Anna," Dee said as her voice softened. Anna sighed, knowing Dee had saved Jake's and Angela's lives, not to mention her own.

"What I didn't know was that there was a relationship going on between those two before tonight. That is what Fred and I discussed down on that field. I cussed his ass out for bringing us here, even knowing that was going on. It was what he and Jake argued about earlier. He didn't know Jake would be stupid enough to get into her with you here."

"I'm divorcing that husband of mine, and I don't want to hear no shit from you about putting family first." Anna said staring ahead, waiting for Dee to give her reasons why she should not, knowing it would do no good.

"Find you a good lawyer, sister girl—one from out of state that your dirty low-down husband will not be able to intimidate. Now where do you want me to take you?"

"To my car. I need to go somewhere and think. This night has been too much—way too much for me!"

"Anna, after tonight, anything you want me to help you do to leave his ass I will." They drove the rest of the way in silence. Once Dee's car stopped in front of Anna's house, she turned to her. "This night has been an eye-opener for me, too—seeing with my own eyes what true love looks like—I saw it tonight between you and him. Yes, I smelled the magnolias tonight for real, sister girl."

"Dee, love is nothing but a lot of pain. You take care, sister girl, and thank you for everything." Dee hugged her before driving off.

Anna hurried to her car, backing it out of her garage. In minutes, the horrible night replayed before her eyes. *I should have walked right out of the door as soon as they arrived. It would have been best for everyone. Jake might have been a little angry, but so what?* Anna thought, still trembling at all that had taken place. *That husband of mine played me. Had I left, I never would have known.*

How does it feel, she asked herself, being the other woman? She had to face that fact. The wronged wife confronting her with the results of Anna's affair with her husband—seeing the kind of hate in her eyes that was once in her's for Barb. The same pain that was in her's tonight after seeing Jake's woman reveal the length of time they had been and was still seeing each other. Looking into eyes that held so much pain she knew if she could have, Carolyn would have killed her right there on the spot. The same kind of pain Anna felt seeing Jake with another woman she had not known he still slept with until Dee took her to the room where they were. Watching Angela move to her knees to give him the kind of sex she knew he loved. She realized he had been seeing Angela all along, while telling her he loved only her and that there was no other woman in his life. The same lies he always told. But what could she say? Anna wondered if her entire life had been a lie. She needed to get away from Jake and his town fast.

Suddenly, the Old Head's voice vibrated throughout the car, causing her to stop. Looking around her she found she was at the riverfront. The arch stood high in the sky. Three half moons neon yellow and green signs lit up the overhead bridges.

"You must go before the storm comes, Daughter. Your life is unfolding, leading you on another path of this journey you must embark upon!" Anna sat watching an orange hue melting inside the blue magnetic ring. She moved out of the car into its circle.

"What journey, Old Head? To where? I'm already in the middle of the storm. Can't you see my life has fallen apart right before my eyes?" Anna cried, her tears sliding down her face as she remembered the pain she felt at knowing even her husband was never hers to claim.

"You must save the Young Chemist from himself or many will die."

"Old Head, I can't even save myself. How can I possibly save him?"

"Look, Daughter, and see your world through my eyes." The eyes whirled around Anna forcing her to engage them. She stared at Jake and Fred flagging down a cab while Fred cussed Jake out.

"Look further, Daughter, as my eyes allows you to see what lies in the heart of the Young Chemist's mate when race is added to life's equation."

Anna did not want to look, but the eyes of the Old Head moved her into its circle of light, causing her to stare into the faces of Raymond and his wife back in their hotel suite.

"'What a horrible joke!' Anna listened to Carolyn's laughter. "'Now I remember that the detective I hired to find you alerted me that a black woman was the only woman ever seen in your company. I of course waved him off, insisting it must be a servant of some sort. I insisted she was a white woman by the name of Ms. Anna when he wrote me that she was with you. He appeared distraught that I could not come to terms with the race of the woman he insisted had to be the woman of interest. What a fool he must have thought me to be.' Anna slowly released her breath as she listened to Carolyn Forlorn's assessment of her identity.

"'I'd like to think that all that little black wench of yours wanted was your money, but oh no, her heart is most surely yours. I found her crying a pail of tears over losing you and would you believe it—even after I took you from her, she still wears your chain, no doubt unknown to that cheating husband of hers. I wonder how she was able to explain the expense of it to that black one following after Angela, my dear. He did introduce himself as her husband, I believe.

"'One has to wonder what you saw in her that he has not.' Anna listened to Carolyn chuckle as she looked Raymond's way, saying, "'Of course, there is nothing about women of her race that indicates beauty of any kind, even to their own men.'

"'Carolyn, real beauty is so rare that few men ever see it, but when it is felt, it becomes an experience never forgotten.'

"'Well, her husband certainly never felt it for the black wench. The way he was tagging after Nathan's secretary, it was apparent he saw beauty, but it surely was not Ms. Anna's black ass. What makes you so different, coming to my bed after sleeping with the black wench?'

"'If I recall correctly, Carolyn, wasn't it you who came to my bed and insisted we become a family for Jason's sake? A part of that was that I perform my husbandly duties. As many times as you have since visited my bed, I'm sure there has been no disappointment in that department.' Anna watched him turn his back to her. "'As for me and Ms. Anna, when you sent the cable looking for me, I informed you she was who I was with.'

"'Yes, after that first night in your arms, I knew something had changed. She must have taught you how to thrill a woman's body. My God, how you've improved!" She smirked as if she were remembering something. "You never told me everything about the bitch, damn you!" Anna was reminded of what she meant as she thought back to her first meeting with Julia.

"'When we were mere friends, you knew she was a part of my life, something I never kept from you. As for as her race, for what purpose would I have mentioned it?' Anna shook her head again, thinking of Julia and her look of shock when she learned she was the Ms. Anna her cousin spoke of with such reverence.

"'Only in your dreams, I was led to believe. And you're damn wrong. It is the first thing you should have mentioned to me, especially after we were to be married—before I became your wife.'

"'At the time, if I recall, you needed a husband. That was all that mattered to you. And yes, my wife, until you decided I was dead meat your thoughts were never on who Ms. Anna might be or her race. Thank God she arrived in the flesh to make sure this life of mine remained intact, even loving me with that monstrous face that caused you to flee.' Anna watched her turn from him and walks over closing their bedroom door.

"'After your return, I had to have our bedrooms separate because of your calling out to her.'

"'You insisted we sleep in different bedrooms because of my calling out to her in my sleep, and I agreed, having no control over what happens to me when I'm not awake.'

"'Damn black whoring wench.' Anna's fists tighten around her arms hearing his wife's assessment of her.

"'Why would you fill your mouth with such dirty words about someone you know nothing about?'

"'She's a damn black nigger bitch—I now know that! You had me thinking she was a white woman, something I could have dealt with since she saved your wretched life,' Carolyn cried, as Anna watched Carolyn walk into the next room where Jason sat on a couch with his hand over his ears.

"'Carolyn I do not want to discuss this matter in front of our son,' Raymond said, leaving the room and again entering their bedroom. Anna watched Carolyn follow him, closing the door as she confronted him.

"'Raymond, I simply want you to tell me the truth, and we need never speak of it again.' Anna listened closely.

"'What truth is that?' he asked. Anna sighed seeing her sink down on the bed.

"'These feelings you have expressed having for her are only because you are so thankful she saved your life. Tell me the black wench has been just a little play toy you kept around to keep you entertained once you were well again. I'm told they are good at that. I know you could not love her.' Anna held her breath waiting for him to reply.

"'Carolyn, we have discussed this subject too many times,' he said. Anna watched him take a seat on the bed. "'As I have told you many times before, Ms. Anna is my lady. She is no wench, nor is she a whore. And since her parents were married before her birth, she is not a bastard. She has been my lady since before you and I first met, and she still is.'

"'What you are saying could not be true! Not her!'

"'As you already know, long before our marriage or my tragedy occurred, Ms. Anna was in my heart. She is the only woman I have ever loved with the exception of my mother and grandmother.' Anna's heart sank with sadness, hearing his Southern drawl as he spoke words that would cause him trouble he did not need.

"'No decent white man would ever admit to loving any black woman.' Seeing Carolyn wiping tears from her eyes, Anna realized the white woman's reality did not permit what he was telling her.

"'Carolyn, any man who would shrink from acknowledging his feelings for the woman he loves because of what others might say or think is a pitiful soul, fearful of taking one footstep before the other unless another man okays it. I am beholden to no one as to my feelings or anything else for that matter. I have loved Ms. Anna since I was seventeen years old, something I shared with you when we met just as you shared your true feelings for the Duke after discovering too late he never planned to marry outside of his class. I never fooled myself into thinking I was your first love. We made a pact as friends. I believe I have fulfilled my part.'"

"Oh my god, Old Head! He'll never save his marriage by telling her that he still loves me. She is going to hate him for even suggesting he could love a black woman."

"When the Young Chemist came to teach you and the others, the fear of race claimed him as well, Daughter. My eye, during the nine years it lay encased in his head, unraveled his brain, freeing it of illusions that lay claim to human fears. Race, as I assured you, is one of those illusions of the mind that controls human feelings, feeding the

mind with thoughts of race fear in terms of superiority and inferiority. The illusion that race matters in this world of humans was the first to be unraveled. It no longer holds him hostage. He has been freed of the illusions that cause that fear. His mind receives no messages that permit race thoughts to cloud his thinking as it does yours and other earth creatures still burdened with those fearful thoughts."

So that is why he never thought to tell Julia or his wife of my race, Anna thought to herself. "Old Head, the unraveling of his brain that your eye caused has presented him with many problems, and the seed of hate for him will crowd the minds of those who are still living under those timeless illusions caused by the fear of race."

"Yes, Daughter, I'm afraid you are right—as we now see from one controlled by those illusions."

"'Damn you, the Duke is a white man not a black nigger!' Anna continued to listen as Carolyn screamed at Raymond, understanding what it meant for her, a white woman living in a world where the fear of race and class is forever present. "Only a Southern cracker like you would say you love that black-ass nigger wench. Your mother, damn her soul, laid her ass down and slept with a Southern cracker, producing another damn cracker. All are known for that sort of behavior,' she hurled the words at him while laughing. Anna watched Raymond turn and walk toward the door.

"'Where the hell are you going?' she screamed, following behind him out of the bedroom.

"'I should leave and allow you to calm down before things are said that will ultimately destroy this marriage.'

"'And go where, husband of mine? To bed that black wench of yours you have found again? Damn you!' Anna saw their son continuing to look up at them with his hand over his ears.

"'Carolyn, can't you see our son is listening to this raw conversation? This should not be discussed in his presence.' Realizing Carolyn would never forgive Raymond's relationship with her, Anna did not want to see any more, but the Old Head held her locked into the scene.

"'Was she with her true husband or another lover she acquired after I came for you?' Anna saw a pained look cover Raymond's face, yet he gave no answer to Carolyn's question.

Anna twisted her hands, wanting him to say what was needed so that he could keep his marriage intact. Didn't he realize his wife would never forgive him if he did not deny loving her?

"'And to think you had your filthy body in mine after lying with that black-ass bitch. Just know, you white dog, you'll never, never put your dirty nigger-loving hands on me ever again!' Anna watched Raymond twist the door knob.

"'I asked you where in the hell you are going!' Anna heard Carolyn scream as clearly as if she were in the room with them. Raymond she saw gave no answer as he walked towards the outer door. "'Going back to that black whore, I suppose!' she continued to scream as tears poured down her face. "Damn you, you think I mind that you insisted on using protection so there would be no future children for us? I'm so glad Jason is not your biological son and that he was conceived with another man of much finer breeding. There were never to be any babies for you by me—never! How was I ever to be sure they wouldn't turn out deformed like you had become because of that illness that made you look like a monster?" Anna could not move. She wanted to run from the scene before her. It terrified her to see him learn how revengeful women can become when deceitful thoughts enter their minds. "Not to mention those dreadful horses you smell of." The words that sprang from Carolyn's lips tore into Anna as she watched Raymond's pain turn to rage by the way his eyes narrowed.

"My son was made aware that you were not his biological father when you turned ill from that deadly tumor in your head you bastard." Anna watched him close the door he had just opened. You think you are the only one with surprises, guess what? He has never been ill a day in his life. Their eyes locked as Raymond turned back to face her. "'We planned it all along so that you would feel you had to return to us. Tell that to that black-ass whore when you meet with her. She seemed to have known it all a long.'

"You are saying this to hurt me, damn you!" Raymond hissed as a hard frown crested his brows.

"I used you to give him an inheritance, you fool. Why the hell do you think I named him Jason instead of Raymond Forlorn III? He has known since before you took ill that you did not father him to be truthful. He sees his father often enough to know him well. That's why I never allowed you the privilege of seeing him after you called to say you were well again. He was never ill. Never! His illness was planned so that we would get what was coming to us. You got your wish—a child who was never yours from the start. I knew you were too busy grieving over the loss of your Ms. Anna when you didn't question the doctors and believed what I told you about the seriousness of his illness."

"What!" he screamed. Anna felt the horror of his discovery as Carolyn's laughter filled the room.

"Mother, you have destroyed my inheritance after insisting I call him father and having me shave all my hair off and spend time in that horrible hospital when nothing was wrong with me. Now it is all for nothing. You might as well tell him I'm playing rugby as well." Anna listened to Jason speak as he ran his hand over his baldhead.

"The two of you planned his illness?" Raymond asked, looking from the boy to his mother.

"Yes, damn you! I only came back to you for legal purposes. It galled me having to allow you to touch me after living with that hideous distorted face I hated. I simply endured it to get my son the inheritance I felt he deserved, you bastard. One day you may get to see him play rugby. He is getting so good at it. There is no way he could have faced that kind of competition if he were as ill as you thought. We planned it after you sent me that telegram, talking about a damn divorce." Tears fell from Anna's eyes as she watched Raymond move toward Carolyn and saw in his face the danger Carolyn was unaware of.

"Old Widow, do something please!" Anna shouted as her hands moved up to her face when Raymond's hands clenched into fists as he started toward Carolyn.

"Father, there is a large black spider with an orange light on its back crawling down your arm." Anna watched Raymond take the Old Widow and place her between his wife's breasts, leaving her screaming as he turned and walked out of the door.

The eyes closed as Anna stood at the river's edge in the middle of a black night looking up at a sky full of stars shining down on the water flowing just beyond her. Her tears were a true indication of the pain she felt for her lover. The things Carolyn Forlorn had admitted to because of her hatred of Anna's race had destroyed the man the Old Head called the Young Chemist. A man she still loved.

She would have to deal with Jake and her own marriage the same way. She felt the orange light in her palm begin to pulsate. Looking down at it, her mind began to expand again. There Raymond stood in the apartment. Looking closer, she saw the file marked CONFIDENTIAL. He had listed chemicals from a formula they had developed. The chemicals needed to kill hundreds of people stared her in the face—she had discovered the combination and shared with him in Kentucky while looking for a cure for the Tack Disease. They completed the formula together only to discover its deadly effect once it was released. According to the combining ions connecting it, everything it touched within a hundred mile radius would evaporate.

They had never tested it. So frightened was Anna of the damage it might cause that she had made him promise never to use it for any reason. He must, she thought, be out of his mind with insane rage to think of such an end. She would have to give him something else to think about. It came to her—his daughter! She must tell him about her, hoping it would stop the rage she knew boiled out of control inside of him. Her thoughts turned back to her horrible confrontation with his wife at the racetrack realizing her anger had spilled over onto him.

I must let him know he has a child. He can take her and make a home for her if he wants her now that he has lost the family he thought he had. Granny said one or the other of us must come for her. I'll go to the apartment and let him know he has someone to live for. He will have his child—one that is biologically his if he wants her. It was her only hope of stopping him.

All the way to the apartment, Anna kept thinking about how she would word telling him of the child. He might not believe her after so much had happened to him. What if he refused to accept Raspy as his? She was two-and-a-half years old now, and he might think . . . the child could be by another man. Too many thoughts crowded her mind. She knew she could not turn around; what might happen would be on her conscience, she thought as she drove through Tora. If Ray planned to do what she was thinking, his end would be a part of the outcome—his and too many other innocent people.

Pulling the tiny remote out of her purse, she hit the green button and watched the garage door open. Her heart began to race. A black Mercedes sat in his parking space. Sudden fear caused her to want to turn around and leave. But she knew he stared down at her. He had long ago informed her that as soon as the garage door opened, a buzzer would go off to alert him that someone had entered. He had had a TV installed in his lab that would immediately identify the visitor. Taking a deep breath, she pushed the elevator button and walked in, thinking all the way up, *what if*. There were so many she became dizzy thinking of them all.

As she entered the apartment, he stood there naked from his waist up, his biceps tight. Gazing at her as she walked in, he allowed no conversation between them as he pulled her into his arms, planting kisses all over her face and down the side of her throat. Anna felt his heart racing as she had felt it when he fell into her arms the day he'd come to her all shot up. His pain became hers as she held him as tightly as he held her.

"Please Ray, I came to…," Her words sounded as a whisper allowing the magic in his body to cause the essence of her passion to rise. He lifted and carried her into the bedroom; his lips never leaving hers. It was as if they had just stepped out of the pool of passion, whirled into a sexual ecstasy as his hands moved over her body to rekindled feelings she thought no longer lived in her. It occurred to her that she had promised never to allow him in her bed again, but there were things only he knew about her body. Now inside of her, he reclaimed the magic only he held the key to.

Once the black box opened, its stringed instruments began to play their melody, sucking the two lovers into a continuous orgasm with all thoughts of the outside world forgotten. Her reason for coming to the apartment faded as passion took its place. Every warning evaporated into oblivion as their lips locked and their bodies became one with the sound of the stringed instruments. Hearing her name called over and over again, she whispered his in response, allowing him to once again awaken the love song her body hurried to sing to his after waiting so long for his return.

****

Lying next to him the next morning after more intense lovemaking, she eased his hands down, looking into his tear-stained eyes.

"Ray, I did not know you would be there. I tried to get my husband to take me home so that our relationship would not be discovered, but because of his own agenda, he refused to do so.

343

"Seeing you seated there it was as if my midnight star had come for me. I was so ready to go with you right then and there."

"Oh Ray, things went bad for you, didn't they?" Anna asked as he pulled her back into his arms.

"She fucked me, baby. My god, she played me like a ten-cent sucker, licking me all the way up my ass. Jason helped in her deceit. Even though I knew someone else fathered him, I loved him as though he were my own son. The reason I had not pushed for the divorce was because I had been trying to get her to let me see him ever since my recovery. I knew there was no love between us but I wanted to make sure my relationship with Jason remained close. Their deceit cost us our relationship, Ms. Anna." Her heart burst seeing tears slip down the side of his face. Believing Jason was ill, I was thankful you understood I had to return to her to be with him. Nothing else mattered at the time. When he seemed to respond so quickly to treatment, I thought you had somehow played a part in his recovery.

"No, I discovered after listening to her conversation with Angela that he was never ill, Ray."

"The only ill person in that family was me," he replied as Anna felt his lips tasted her breasts. "What a sad joke she played on my stupid ass. Jason never thought I was his father. She must have told him years ago, yet he kept up the farce right along with her just for the inheritance. And to think I would have given him everything I owned."

There will never be another child to carry the Forlorn name—ever. Not by me. About that Carolyn was right. She stated she never wanted children by me because of my illness. A child by me could end up carrying the genes for that tumor that nearly killed me and become hideous to look at just as I was. I could not even fathom having that horror happen to a child of mine." His words stunned Anna as she realized he had believed the reason Carolyn had given for not having children by him.

"Ray, don't say that. Sometimes God is blessing you and you don't even know it." Anna heard her grandmother's voice before the words left her lips. Fresh tears found their way down her cheeks as his next words crushed all thoughts of what she was about to tell him.

"How can God bless a deformed child? No, Anna, not by me," he insisted as Anna looked away from him. You were right in your desire to abort my child. As for Carolyn, I'm sure her lawyers will find a way to get her as much as they can squeeze out of me. I've got it all figured out, baby, it's all good' because Old Ray will be sitting there in court smiling. As soon as she brings up our relationship in an attempt to destroy you and me, I'll wait for the judge to order me to hand over everything to her and her son, and there will be one helluva explosion that sends us all straight to hell in bits and pieces."

"No, Ray! You can't do anything that destructive. That sure as hell is not the answer," Anna insisted, laying her head on his chest as she held him. "You don't know everything! And sometimes blessings are unknown to those receiving the blessings" Anna whispered remembering when she thought death was the only solution to her own crisis."

"I have not been blessed with anything to live for but a scandalous divorce. I'll be damned if she lives to laugh about destroying my grandfather's or father's name—that is one thing you can count on. Everything I own has been willed to you and my brother. When I go, there will be nothing you'll ever need that money can't buy." Anna's tears came so fast that she almost choked trying to speak.

"No, Ray! What in the hell are you thinking?" she cried, rising in bed as she pulled the sheet up against her and stared down at him. I don't give a damn about your money," she said between sobs. "Don't you see that her exposing to you her deception has at last completely freed you?"

"What good is that? Because of her deceit, I lost you and everything we had together," he replied, rising up to kiss her tears as they spilled down her face.

"What do you mean lost me? Don't you know I have you here?" Anna moved his hand to touch beneath her left breast. "In here, we breathe together in an endless dream. Even though we are a million miles apart, we are forever together in our hearts—a place no one has ever been able to destroy."

"Anna . . ."

"Your death would destroy me and everything we have. Please, baby, let it go, just let it go. Do that for me," she cried, her naked breasts buried in his chest as she cried in his arms. "You never know, maybe one day that perfect baby will come for us, but not if you kill yourself and lots of innocent people who don't deserve to die because of what Carolyn did to you."

"I've missed you so much! The shock of seeing you seated there so overwhelmed me. I couldn't believe my eyes. When I looked down and saw my chain still around your neck, my first thought was to grab you up into my arms and kiss you right there in front of everyone. That husband of yours had no idea what was on my mind. I, however, knew you would be hurt by being exposed as my lady. That is why I stopped myself from walking out of there with you in my arms!"

"Ray, I came here . . ." The words would not come, not that it mattered because once again he reclaimed her as his own.

****

Anna lay still under Raymond Forlorn, having no idea what day it was. The watch on her arm had gone somewhere. He slept, his head resting between her breasts. She could not bring herself to leave him during his suffering. She now thought of her own life and knew that after all that had happened to him she could not tell him of the child she had borne him—not yet. He needed time to overcome the devastation of the recent events.

During the night when he cried out, Anna comforted him with her arms around him, hating what his life would be like after this crisis he could not seem to live through. Three days later, she kissed his lips, leaving him sleeping realizing as her father had once told Raymond Forlorn, until they both divorced their ways out of their present marriages, they could never belong to each other.

Chapter Twenty-Six

Hearing dishes rattling in the kitchen and the smell of bacon frying, Anna took a deep breath, preparing to face what lay ahead in a doomed marriage. She walked into her home, placing her purse on the hall table. They stood staring at each other as Jake entered the doorway of the living room from the kitchen. She could smell the bacon he was cooking.

"Why did you leave without me, Anna?"

"Did my leaving matter? I'm sure you found a way to get back to Angela's house. You stayed out all night long with her the night before. Wonder what kind of poker game you were enjoying?" Reaching down to pick up the mail that lay on the coffee table, she was startled to feel Jake's hand run through her hair.

"Did you think a goddamn shower would help you, black bitch? You still smell of another other man. Why did you bring your black ass back here?"

"To get my kids and to let you know I will be filing to divorce your ass even if I have to get an out-of-state attorney to get it done."

"Why? So you can go back and lay up under that nigger's ass you just left?"

"No, Jake. I'm going back so I can get down on my knees to please him. After all, you are not the only man who likes it that way." Before Anna knew what had happened, she felt her body sail through the air from the force of his hand against her face. The end table broke under her weight as she fell to the floor, stunned.

"Bitch! You stand in my face telling me about giving some motherfucker a blow job; I'll kill your goddamn black ass!" Groaning, Anna attempted to rise.

"Where is the motherfucker? Take me to his ass, goddamn it, so I can kill him!"

"I thought since you were laid up with your white woman, you wouldn't give a damn where Anna laid her black ass." Anna fell in the opposite direction as he struck her again; her fall broke the lamp that sat on the other end table. Anna began to realize her life might quickly end.

"Why the hell didn't you stay with the motherfucker?" he screamed, kicking her in her ribs as she lay on the floor.

"Because of my kids, Jake Bradley, I plan to take them and leave you if they are willing to come with me. Our marriage is through—finished, damn you! It is only because of them that I am here. If you hit me again, I will kill you. I swear I will!" Anna cried out in pain as he kicked her again and again, causing her to feel a burning sensation between her breasts.

"Not if I kill your ass first, bitch!" Anna screamed from the pain of his next kick.

"Daddy, it takes a coward and fool to speak to a female like that!" Jake Jr. screamed, running downstairs from his bedroom and standing in front of his mother, daring his father to strike her again. Jake's hand went up in the air as Anna crawled toward the kitchen.

"Don't you dare, Daddy! It was you who taught Jake Jr. those very words," Sheri' cried out, jumping in front of her brother. "You can't hit him for saying what you taught him to believe." Sheri' quickly turned to help Anna up as she made her way into the kitchen.

"You goddamn whore!" Jake screamed as he swung and missed.

"It seems to me we both have been doing a lot of whoring." His kick landed her on the kitchen floor. Something in her told Anna she was giving all the wrong answers.

"Daddy, we don't care what she has done. She is still our mother, and we don't want you beating her like that!" Sheri' cried as she covered her mother's body with her own. Hearing the door bell ring, Anna heard her daughter say that it was their Aunt Dee as she watched the Old Widow's young wrap its silky threads around the hot handle of the skillet that was smoking on the stove. Jake tripped and fell when Sheri' ran to answer the door. As he tried to rise, Anna struggled up and, grabbing the covered handle of the smoking cast iron skillet, pouring bacon and the steaming hot oil right onto his chest. Jake screamed, falling back to the floor as he grabbed himself.

Entering the kitchen, Dee screamed, "Run and call the ambulance. Come on, Anna. Let me get you out of here before he comes after you again." Dee helped Anna out to her car. Her daughter's voice blended with her son's saying their father couldn't get up from the floor. Anna heard his screams behind her as Dee pulled out of the driveway.

"How did you know to come, Dee?" Anna whispered, doubled over from the pain in her sides.

"I told Sheri' to call me the moment you came home. I knew he would be in a rage, and I didn't want him hurting you. I guess I got there too late," Dee said, giving a tissue to Anna as blood spilled from her lips.

"You know he blames me for exposing his no-good ass to you." Anna looked over at her friend. "Yes, I told his ass I took you in there to see for yourself what his ass and that white bitch were doing. I also let him know that had it not been for me, the two of them would have had some cut-up asses."

"Dee, I hate that you are involved in this."

"I ain't. After all, it was me who talked you into taking the fool's ass back. I thought he had learned some sense. Apparently not," Dee said, shaking her head as Anna thought about her situation. "The stupid bastard came to my house talking about whipping my ass for fucking up his marriage. Can you believe that?" Anna looked over at Dee, saddened by the turn of events. "Fred told his ass if he didn't get the hell out of his house, he would kill him where he stood for talking about hitting his wife when he fucked up his own damn marriage.

Anna listened to her share her knowledge of that night under the bridge. "Fred told me he had him and James out there trying to kill some man over you when he was still doing the same whoring that broke you two up in the first place. He told him he was a bigger fool than James had been, but at least James learned from his mistake. Said he was a brother who would never get over thinking he was every woman's dream. To even suggest he wanted to hit his wife, he must be crazy." Dee sighed. "Where do you want me to take you this time, Anna? Over to your parents' home?"

"No, Dee. Take me to the bus station in Godfrey. I need to get a ticket to go down South. I have business there that has been waiting for me too damn long." Anna hugged Dee when they finally arrived in Godfrey. She refused to allow her sister in law to take her to the hospital or to help her walk inside the bus station. Anna struggled to make it alone. The ticket agent asked if he might call an ambulance for her. Anna accepted the tissue he gave her to stop the blood that was dripping from her mouth.

"Pl…e…as…e, please, don't. I'll be all right. If anyone comes asking you if you saw a woman of my description, you never saw me."

"I never saw you—yes, of course," the ticket agent said. Anna turned from the look of concern on his face.

When the bus stopped in Memphis, Anna talked awhile to an older woman who was concerned about her condition. She was also going to Oinston and, of course, knew Granny and Jessie Bailey quite well.

Two days later after passing out on the bus Anna woke up in a hospital. Tearful eyed Frankie Lee stared down at Anna telling her how she came to be in the hospital in Oinston and the totality of her condition. It all came back to her.

The doctor she remembered came into the room and smiled down at her. "I remember you! It's Mrs. Anna Bradley I have the pleasure of taking care of."

"Doctor, I can hardly move," Anna whispered, attempting to sit up.

"With three cracked ribs, it's understandable," he said, moving his hand over her abdomen something that caused Anna to wince in pain as she felt her swollen face.

"I don't think my husband intended for me to have any ribs left."

"It's a shame some men have to use their physical strength in such a brutal way. We will take care of you, don't worry," he said in that Southern drawl she remembered.

Frankie Lee came in and kissed her on her forehead. "Who the hell did this to ya, Anna? Not Jake, I hope." Looking over at Frankie Lee, she hated seeing the hurt look on his face. "I was afraid to call anybody 'til ya came to. Didn't know the circumstances dat brung ya hare, and if dat husband of yers was the cause, I didn't wanta 'lert him as to yer whareabouts."

"Who else would Anna take a beating like this from but Jake?" Anna said, turning away from him. "When he knocked me to the floor and started kicking me, I began to realize that if I didn't do something, I'd end up dead. So I threw hot grease and bacon right on his chest. That took the sting out of him long enough for me to get away."

"What? Damn! He musta caught your ass with another man."

"Not quite, but I was away from home for three days, and to him that was admission enough."

"Who ware ya with?" Anna turned away from his stare. "Musta been the Ice Man. Who else would you be fool enuff to give dat much time?" Anna listened to the name Frankie Lee had tagged Raymond with. At least he no longer called him the white man.

"He needed me. I couldn't leave him until I knew he would be all right. After seeing Jake's white woman unzip his pants to give him what she knew would keep him there with her, I didn't think it mattered who I stayed out with," Anna said, telling Frankie Lee the details of what had brought her and Raymond together again.

"What the hell are ya folks tryin' to do up thare, win the award for mixin' the races? When ya was getting yer ass beat, whare the hell was his white ass? Ya should've gone back and showed him the trouble he got ya in."

"You don't understand, Frankie Lee," Anna whispered, holding her stomach to keep from gasping at the pain. "Ray was already in a dangerous state of mind. If I had gone back to the apartment all beat up with my ribs cracked, he would have gone berserk. I could not have kept him from going into Session and destroying the entire city in order to find Jake if he had to. When his rage gets out of control, he might do anything."

"He'd probably gather up them sheet-wearin' clansmen."

"No, Frankie Lee. There would have been no sheets, no mob—nobody but him and dead people everywhere. He believes a man should take care of his own business man-to-man, no hiding in the weeds or behind sheets to kill. Ray doesn't get a thrill from hurting helpless people but when someone does something to him—he goes crazy on his road of destruction. He seeks out death, even his own when his rage is out of control." Anna listened to the whistle blow from Frankie Lee's lips as he sat back in the chair beside her bed.

"Jake insisted I take him to Ray. What he doesn't know is that he doesn't want to meet up with Ray—he just thinks he does," Anna added remembering the deadly chemicals she prevented him from using to kill again.

"Ya don't think Jake could handle himself if he squared up with the Ice Man?"

"Frankie Lee, neither you nor I want that meeting to ever take place, trust me. While Jake doesn't mind killing, he is not willing to give his life to get it done if it comes to that. Ray would not let his own death stop him if it stood in the way of getting whoever he is after. Believe me, he is no ordinary man."

"I guess I wouldn't want to meet up with him, but Anna, you gonna let Jake kill yer ass yet. No white man can protect ya from a black man dese days, especially thare in Session whare nearly every damn body is black. If he finds out the man ya was with is a white man, he's sho nuff gonna kill yer ass and ya know it. A man is never as forgivin' as a woman."

"Why should he care that Ray is white? The woman he is sleeping with is white," Anna replied as Frankie Lee shook his head.

"Anna, black men don't care 'bout how many white women thay bed. Don't ya know we ain't no different than the white man when it comes to our black women? He tole his woman our women were dirty and nasty yet he found his way to hur bed agin and agin all the time lying to his woman about hur being the best. No man leaves a warm bed to wallow in the dirt unless what's in dat dirt is the best. We are gonna to tell ya how low-down and dirty the white man is to ya and his women. We don't care what their white women did to help the white man in his rapin' ya or hangin' us now that we can fall in bed with hur. Ever chance the black man gits, he'll be in dat bed 'tween those legs still telling ya what no-good motherfuckers white men are just like the white man still tells his women about how disgraced she would be sleepin' with a black man while fallin' in bed with our women often enough, as ya can see, to change the color of our black skin."

"Frankie Lee, that's not right when a man can sleep with whomever he wants!"

"Anna, thare ain't no right and wrong when it comes to men and ya'll women gurl, 'pecially in dis country whare men especially white men are in control of what's right and wrong. Anna shook her head indicating her disagreement with his analysis.

"I keep on telling ya. The black man wants what he sees the white man with, be it his women or whatever else the white man has. Same as the white man cain't stand seeing us with somethin' he thanks should only b'long to him. We're now same as the white man when he could have his way. Like dogs, we bury our bones and dig 'em up when we want to take ownership of 'em or keep 'em from another dog. Knowin' ya have cheated on him with another man, even a black man, is death to yer relationship 'cause even if he says he forgives ya, he never does, not reilly. Ya done the right thang comin' hare."

"Where else could I go? I found out Jake has been cheating on me every since I took him back," Anna said, biting on Barb's assessment of her husband's bedside manners after she left him. "He got himself tied up with Ray's brother's secretary. Started while I was away those four years, I guess. You never know with Jake. He may have been bedding both Barb and Angela. Of course, he doesn't know the connection between Ray's brother and me," Anna assured her cousin.

"What a damn mess ya'll got up thare! For Christ sake, Anna, please don't go back to him. Ain't no telling what he'll do if he's all scarred up from dat hot ass grease ya scalded him with—all dat shit leaves one hell of a scar. Ya listen to me—no matter how many women a man is caught with, he is not forgivin' his woman cheatin'. Trust me, I know—especially after she brands his ass!"

****

Three weeks in the hospital had Anna working hard to get her body moving again. Frankie Lee was there questioning her some more about the turn of events that had led to her beating.

"What went down with you and the Ice Man? Now that he and his old lady made the split, you ain't good enuff no more?" Anna looked at her cousin, seeing the hate in his eyes for the white man she had been with; she knew he felt Raymond was responsible for her troubles.

"Frankie Lee, he wanted me to go away with him. Though I was tempted, I couldn't do that. I had children at home I needed to see about first, not to mention a divorce I need to get. He still doesn't know about his baby I have here, the one you insisted I had abandoned. And like I keep telling you, if I had gone back to the apartment all beat up, Ray would have felt the need to avenge my suffering in a way that would have caused problems even you would not have wanted." Frankie Lee looked at her and shook his head. "Why is it that I'm forever in trouble, Frankie Lee? It seems trouble follows me everywhere I go."

353

The only way she was going to stay away from trouble, Frankie Lee advised, was if she got those two men the hell out of her life. "Try somebody new. Somebody hare in Louisiana. The men hare got a soft touch for thay women."

"Is that what you would want someone to tell Kate?" Anna listened to him agree with her stating he hoped that if his wife found someone else he could deal with it and go on with his life But for her situation he felt he knew how the men of his race dealt with the women in their lives. Their pride would not allow them to forgive cheating by their women no matter what whorin' thay've done. He wanted her to listen to him and take his advice. Telling her it would save her a lot of heartaches."

"What do I need to listen to, Frankie Lee?" Anna asked, eyeing him as she eased herself higher in bed.

"Like I just told ya, stay hare with Frankie Lee and git one of these country boys who'll work hard and brang all his money home to a city gurl like ya."

"What about my half-white baby?" Anna asked; her mouth set as she stared at her cousin.

"Ya're in the South, Anna. No black man hare gonna worry 'bout some white man in yer past life. Ya just give his ass a couple of crumb snatchers and he'll be happier'n hell." Anna would have laughed but her abdomen hurt too much.

******

Still taped up, Anna accepted release papers from her three-week stay in the hospital. Granny had visited when she first came in, paid for her stay so none of it would get back to Session, but she had not brought Anna's daughter in leaving her with Frankie Lee in the car on her visits. Now, being wheeled out by Frankie Lee, Anna flinched at the pain still with her. Her heart pounded as she eased into the backseat, seeing Granny up front with Raspy. The wiggling toddler hugged Granny tight as she looked back at Anna, her forefinger stuck in her mouth. Her wide gray eyes stared into Anna's with a look of puzzlement. Anna sat mortified they looked so much like her father's eyes that they caused Anna's heart to thump. The child staring back at her had skin as white as the first time Anna had laid eyes on her. Thick golden locks covered her once-bald head, reminding

Anna of the hair on Ray's head except that his was straight instead of curly. She thought of him, wishing she had had the courage to tell him about his baby. She had believed after all the time they had been apart that he no longer mattered to her. Whatever love she had once felt for him she thought had long since died. Now she knew, having seen him again, it was as though she had left to go shopping that morning and returned to him waiting for her that afternoon.

Seated in the back seat, looking at the toddler in Granny's arms, Anna could not believe she had given birth to her. Granny said she was walking and getting into everything. Anna noticed that she had that hard intense look that Ray was known for. Her child, she thought, stared back at her as if to ask why she was looking at her—didn't she know who the hell she was? Anna wanted to laugh, but she remembered the pain she would experience. There was nothing Anna saw about Raspy that indicated her mother was a black woman. Except for the deep dimples like her own, it was as though she was looking at a white woman's child.

"Granny she looks too much like him now—it's unbelievable! There is nothing of me in her at all except those silly dimples," Anna said, shaking her head, as she looked closer at her daughter by Raymond Forlorn when they got home.

"It's dare, Chile. Just all inside . . . like my own chilens, I reckon," Granny said in her pronounced southern drawl, "Mr. Porter plum glad dat all dem younguns come hare lookin' so much like him. Mabel, she hated all dat white showin' so much. Folks knowd fer sho' what thay is and who thay come from. He just come to lovin' 'em all even more'n me for a long time." In her grandmother's eyes, Anna saw a glow as memories of the past flashed back to her.

Anna wondered why she hadn't told Raymond about her baby by him. Why did she allow that one opportunity to escape her? She knew, however, deep down in her heart that she could not have stood his probable denial of having fathered the child . . . she had told him her test had come back negative . . . now to tell him there was a child she had had for him? He had let her know in no uncertain terms that he would not give another child his name. He didn't want a baby that might one day become deformed as he had become, and she could not have stood his rejecting her baby for that reason. Better for them both that he never know about her. But like her grandmother and Frankie Lee had expressed, she would have at least known the worth of the man.

Before long, she was able to sit and hold her child, learning what it was like to have a toddler to love and care for again. At first, Raspy addressed Anna by her first name as Granny, something Anna encouraged. One day when Raspy walked up to her mother calling her by her first name, Granny rose and walked over to Anna saying, "Anna, no matter who it is she looks to be, ya mothered her and she should be callin' ya Momma. Anna be nobody special to hur." She added with a stern frown on her face as she stared from Anna to Raspy, "Ya still shame of hur, Chile?"

"Granny, I'm not ashamed of her. She just does not look like she belongs to me. It is easier on both of us if she calls me Anna."

"Dat way nobody knows she belong to ya. Is dat what I'm hearing ya sayin'?"

"Oh, Granny! I know she is my child, and it's not that I don't love her . . . but just look at her . . . she's so white looking . . . too much like him. If he were with me, it would be different." Anna shook her head, still looking at her daughter. "Just think what people will say." Anna spread her arms in a hopeless gesture. "The only way I can feel love for that white body of hers is when I'm squeezing her to me and some of him passes from her into me; otherwise, I just can't see her as being a part of me or as my child."

"Hit don't matter how ya feel—ya be hur Momma. And Momma is what she be callin' ya. Ya soon learn what she be to ya, and she will know too. I heard ya tell Frankie Lee ya slept with the white man last time ya done seed him." Anna turned her head, shocked at her grandmother's directness—that was too much like her mother's. Anna did not answer. The look in her grandmother's eyes that said she knew everything.

"How is it my granddaughter done laid up in the white man's bed and be so shame of the baby he done geed hur?"

"Oh, Granny!" Anna replied, turning her back to clean the kitchen table. "No one was there looking."

"I makes 'em see, don't I," Granny said, talking to the child now seated in her lap. "Raspy, dat be yur Momma, no matter she don't look to be." To Anna's dismay, Granny began teaching Raspy to call her Momma. When she took this near-white baby out in public, if Raspy called her Momma it would be the death of her—she just knew it.

However, after a short while, it seemed Granny had been right—Raspy's calling her Mommie tightened the bond between the two of them. Raspy began following Anna around the house, calling after her. Having learned how to say Mommie, she repeated it constantly. Anna would turn, finding Raspy with her arms in the air calling her Mommie and wanting to be held. Anna allowed her to join her as she fed Granny's chickens and played games with her when she asked to sit in her lap, teaching her to say the parts of her body she could see. After awhile, hearing her child call her Mommie seemed natural, and when the child climbed in bed beside her to sleep at night, Anna knew it was not just a child but her child there beside her—a child she was developing a relationship with.

****

"Granny, I've often wondered," Anna asked one afternoon while helping her grandmother clean house. "How was it that Mr. Porter discovered your plans to leave with your husband?" Anna watched her grandmother stop wiping the what-not she held in her hand and turn to her.

"It be Lilly Mary overheard me and Mrs. Josephine talkin'—done gone back and tole Mr. Porter what I'm aiming to do, hopin' he'd take up with hur," Granny said as she began again to wipe the what-not until it held a glow. Anna shook her head. Now that was a cold bloody sister, she thought. Life can be hell, especially when envy and jealousy are involved.

****

"Anna, Granny glad ya hare to take Raspy for her shots. I don feel like sittin' all dat time down in dat clinic." Anna listened to Granny. She had mentioned that the baby needed her shots. Anna hoped it would at least be a private doctor she would be taking Raspy to see. Frankie Lee assured her they would be going to the clinic where all the black babies were seen. It would be the first time Anna would take Raspy out in public as her daughter. Granny called for Frankie Lee to come and pick them up, saying she was glad to get the rest. Six months with Raspy had brought out Anna's mother instinct. She grew to love hearing the baby calling her Mommie while she followed her all over the house until she finally fell asleep in her arms.

"I can jus' see ya back in Session with them big city niggers showing hur off," Frankie Lee said and whistled. "The names they'd have for ya, Cous."

"Shut your damn mouth, Frankie Lee. She's my baby. I can't help what she looks like. Anyway, I don't ever plan for those nosey blacks back in Session to set their eyes on the likes of her. And how many times have I told you about using that dirty word?" Anna asked, holding Raspy closer to her. "I don't want my baby hearing it."

"You can't hide dat baby forever, Anna," Frankie Lee insisted, ignoring her question. "She gotta grow up some day . . . than what?"

"I'll worry about that when the time comes," Anna replied, looking away from him.

"We southern black folks is use to the mixin' of the races. What happens is, thay mix down hare in the South and then move up North, lettin' the big-time city niggers know we at least sleep equal." Anna dismissed Frankie Lee's unwelcomed humor.

"Just keep your mouth shut and hurry and get us the clinic before we miss her appointment. I don't want Granny angry with me, thinking I'm trying to get out of taking her."

To Anna's dismay, the clinic was packed with black people. Granny had told her that Monday was the only day black children went to in the clinic to get their free shots. Frankie Lee let her know that while segregation was no longer the law people there continued to practice separating themselves. Granny had not, Anna discovered, spent one penny of the money she had given her except on her hospital bill. She could have at least used some and taken Raspy to a private physician, saving her the embarrassment of having to parade her daughter in front of all these blacks who looked strangely at Raspy seated on her lap, Anna thought disappointed in having to take her where all those blacks were.

A young girl with a toddler about the same age as Raspy looked from Anna to Raspy and then to Frankie Lee once they took a seat.

"What ya doin' hare, boy?" Anna cringed at the sight of another gold eye tooth.

"I come to brang my cousin, Clara." Anna watched Frankie Lee point at her.

"I thought white folks took thay babies up in Portland on Mondays now dat thay let us come hare?" She replied in the deep southern drawl similar to Frankie Lee's. Frankie Lee laughed as he eyed Anna, who refused to look at either of them.

"Gal, dat ain't no white baby—dat's hur baby." Anna could have choked Frankie Lee as she watched the girl and the other women in the clinic that had heard him look her way with their mouths wide open.

"She had dat baby?" The girl spoke so loud that the others looked closer to see the baby she was speaking of.

"Yes, damn it!" Anna said. "She is my baby! Now that has been established, do you suppose we can drop the subject?" She stared hard at the young girl seated next to her.

"Anna, she just curious," Frankie Lee said, a big grin on his face.

"I'm curious, too, as to whether she was eleven or twelve when she mothered her child, but I'm not curious enough be poking my nose into her business," Anna said loud enough for everyone to hear. The girl closed her mouth, saying not another word to Anna. The other women who had been listening turned to mind their own business. Anna guessed they didn't want her prying into their business, either.

Raspy Bradley was finally called, to Anna's relief. The old white nurse working there looked up at Anna and then at the baby she held.

"We can't wait on dat chile. Hur momma know ya brung her hare?" the nurse asked, peering at Anna over her glasses. Anna's face burned, seeing all the women gazing from Raspy to her. The least the nurse could have done, Anna thought, was to ask whether or not Raspy was hers. Now that Anna had been with her daughter nearly seven months, she felt like her mother.

"What do you mean? She is my baby! I am her mother." From behind a curtain appeared the black doctor who had come to help deliver Raspy and who had been at the hospital taking care of her when she came in with cracked ribs. Frankie Lee had informed Anna that ole' doctor helped out on those once a month clinic visits for colored babies. And that was probably why Granny took Raspy there. The doctor looked from Anna and Raspy to the nurse and verified that Anna was the child's mother. He told the old nurse that Anna was Granny's granddaughter from up North. And to send them into him once the baby was weighed.

Taking Raspy to be weighed, the old white nurse mumbled so that Anna could hear her, "I knowd bout Jessie and Paul, Mabel's colored sons hare, but I sho' ain't knowd bout no granddaughter yer age up North." Anna watched her examine Raspy carefully after she undressed her.

"Dis baby looks like she's got a good sunnin'—sho' don't look to be mothered by no colored dark as ya."

"You know," Anna said, watching the nurse weigh her baby, "I keep telling myself that very same thing, but she was born at home ask the doctor here. I saw her moments after Granny and the doctor pulled her out of my body. She was then as white as you are now, proving that not all white men's genes are as weak as some people have been led to believe they are." That statement put a button on the old white nurse's lips, and she said not another word about Anna or her offspring.

****

After Anna finished with Raspy's clinic appointment, Frankie Lee stopped off to pick up his wife Kate. Anna liked her at once. She introduced herself by hugging Anna and Raspy, stated that they were just more family to love. The four of them sat in the small restaurant Frankie Lee took them to waiting to be served. This was the first time she had met Kate. As tall and as dark as she and Frankie Lee, Anna looked into Kate's large marble dark bright eyes. Her skin was smooth and pretty white teeth appeared when her lips parted in a smile showing her gold eye tooth. Her hair was cut in a short natural with large gold loops hanging from her ears. She wore a wide tail multicolored blouse with blue jeans that hugged her wide hips and butt.

Once they were seated and had ordered from the menus Anna noticed Kate looking so hard at Raspy that she realized all the while she was dealing with her pregnancy Kate and Frankie Lee had been separated so she never really knew about Raspy.

Anna asked, "What is the matter, Kate? Surely you have seen my baby before."

"Oh Anna, Kate never seed Raspy. She just heerd about hur from me," Frankie Lee said.

Anna was not happy with how Kate looked at her daughter. "You are looking at her so strangely like you are trying to figure out how it happened," Anna said, realizing she had read her thoughts by the look Kate was giving her. "I didn't just pick up a stray white man off the street, Kate. I've known Raspy's father since I was fourteen years old."

"Anna, she is a beautiful chile. I jus' didn't know ya were from the South," Kate said, still gazing at Raspy.

Does she really believe only Southern people have mixed relationships? Anna wondered. "Kate, I am not from the South. My baby's daddy is not from the South. Well, he is . . . but that is not where I met him."

"I didn't know white men mixed the races up North." Anna looked at Kate, thinking to herself that Kate must have never been outside of Oinston, Louisiana. Instead of verbalizing that thought, she said instead, "Kate, the South is not the only part of the country where white and black people have relationships. It might have started here, but believe me, it has spread."

"For real?" Anna looked at Frankie Lee's wife, wondering how in the world it was possible that she didn't know that.

Anna said to Raspy, who had begun to whine, "Our food has been ordered, honey. If you'll be a little patient, it'll be coming soon." Anna looked around her, wishing they would hurry and bring the order. She was hungry herself, they had not eaten breakfast before leaving for the clinic early that morning.

"I have to get home before 4:00; Sheri' and Jake Jr. will be calling me," Anna said to Frankie Lee.

"Who are they?" Kate asked.

"They are my children, Kate. I have a set of twins—a boy and a girl."

"You do? Are they white looking, too?" Frankie Lee interrupted before Anna could answer his wife.

"Aunt Annabelle know ya down hare with Granny, Anna?"

"Of course not, fool. My kids know to call me from their Aunt Dee's house. She takes care of all her phone bills so I don't have to worry about her husband looking at the phone number and asking about the calls. And no, Kate, they are black like my husband, their father."

"What are thay sayin' about thay daddy's condition?" Frankie Lee asked, not allowing the conversation between his wife and Anna to continue.

"What condition?" Kate asked, staring at Anna.

"He was in the hospital for three months. I must have burned him pretty bad. He's telling everyone he let his anger get out of control. He is lucky to be alive," Anna said, looking at the orange spot on her hand.

"Damn Anna! Ya're a dangerous woman. I sho' don want to git on yer bad side." Frankie Lee laughed. Anna turned her head, dismissing his assessment of her.

"My kids want to come down here, Frankie Lee. Wouldn't that be something? I sure would like for them to meet Momma's mother, but I can't see that happening soon," Anna said, kissing Raspy's forehead as she pulled her closer.

"Frankie Lee, she do love hur baby. Look how she's cuddlin' hur," Kate said, smiling.

Anna's mouth flew open as her eyes narrowed. "Frankie Lee, what have you been saying about me? That I don't love Raspy because she looks so white?" Anna asked, rolling her eyes his way. "To set the record straight, my dear cousin, I fell in with love with my baby once you took me to Granny's house and I knew I would be having her," Anna said, staring at Frankie Lee's smiling face. "I've got to get away from this hick town; it's too far south and the people in it are too country!" As soon as the words sprang from her lips Anna noticed Frankie's eyes narrow as his face formed a frown. She realized immediately her mistake. Southern blacks did not like being referenced as country, a term they felt, was used by Northern blacks to demean them.

"This is the place to be . . . ain't nothin' wrong with bein' country cous. Ours is the backs ya Northern niggers crawled up on thinking ya so much cause ya learn to speak and act like dat white man." Anna knew she had upset her cousin by the tone of his voice.

"Ya think dat makes ya better, well ya better be askin' the Cherokee Indians how much dat white man preciates them trying to be like him. Run 'em off 'f thay land in Georgia and in the Carolinas in the trail of Tears cous same as he go do ya northern niggers when ya try to get too white or he thanks ya is. Ya watch'n see."

"Oh now Frankie Lee I am not saying being country is bad." Frankie Lee stared back at Anna saying,

"I know damn well ya ain't cous. Ya thank of learning a language ya ain't never heard of. Being beat to death cause ya can't understand whats bein' tole to ya but trying to learn it the best ya can to keep from being killed. What ya thank woulda happen if dat white man and his woman and children had been dragged to Africa and had to learn fifty dialects not to mantion made to sleep on the ground with snakes and lizards comin' out to fed at night. Dat fool would not have lasted a yeer ya can bet yer life on dat."

"Not a even a week, with all those lions and elephants roaming around," Anna added rubbing her chin as though giving serious though to Frankie's assessment of was white slave life would have been like in Africa. The mood became warm again as Frankie Lee and Kate laughed at Anna's comment.

"Did you see how that old nurse and the rest of those black women looked at me?" Anna asked as Raspy bounced up and down in her lap. "You would have thought I was the one who should have felt privileged having Raspy as my daughter just because she is so light—can you believe that? The white and black people here are something else, I'll tell you. It was as though I was the freak, and Raspy accidentally had me for a mother." Anna listened to both Kate and Frankie Lee burst out laughing at her comment.

"The niggers up thare in Session say whitey, whitey git back 'cause black is whare it's at. That's why ya can't take hur back home, Anna."

"Frankie Lee, you are getting crazier and crazier by the day. And that's another thing—taking on the slave master's labels to refer to yourself. You need to bury that word nigger. It should have died with those old slave masters who coined it."

"Who saved it? You people in the North?" His laughter broke out again. He and Anna both looked up as Kate rose from her seat.

"Thank ya, gurl. I've been tellin' dis fool he needs to git some black sense in his head. He knows how we hated white folks callin' us niggers. Every day dat word come out of some white bastard's mouth 'bout us. I don't want my children growin' up thankin' the meaning done changed cause it ain't. So give it up, Frankie Lee. Yer cousin's right." Anna clapped. Raspy squirmed out of her arms onto the floor, standing there looking up at her with a big grin on her face. Suddenly, she ran across the floor to the other side of the room. Anna called to her.

"Let the kid play, Anna. She's dog-tired of sittin' . . . should be glad she ain't cryin' after those shots she got," Frankie Lee insisted, looking up at his wife. Take a seat, woman . . . standin' over me like ya the law or somethin'. I know my history as well as ya two. It just don bother me none, but trust me, I know what ya're talkin' 'bout. Got to cut it to the quick like," he said, pulling Kate down in her seat.

Kate looked at Frankie Lee and Anna, shaking her head. "This man is somethin' else, Anna. I tell him all the time about dat word." Anna shook her head looking at Frankie Lee then noticed Raspy was nowhere in sight.

"Frankie Lee! Raspy is gone! Where could she be?"

"Ya better go git hur. She probably gone through them swingin' doors to whare the white folk sit." Anna hurried though the doors. Sure enough, there Raspy sat at a table with two white women and a child whose glass Raspy was drinking chocolate milk from. Anna's eyes grew wide in alarm as she hurried over to the table, noticing there were only whites seated in the room.

"Raspy, don't let me have to spank your butt—coming in here like that drinking out of her glass. You know better than to leave me."

"Mommie," Raspy said as Anna snatched her up from the table and walked hurriedly away but not before hearing one of the women remark, "Wish I knew who that child's parents were; I'd tell them what kind of nigger they've got tending their kid. Got that white baby calling her Mommie" Anna carried her daughter back through the swinging doors without even looking back.

"Just wait until I get you home, little girl. You and I are going to have a talk about your behavior. Frankie Lee, what kind of place is this anyway?" Anna asked, looking back at the swinging doors.

"What ya mean, what kinda place is this?" he asked.

"You know damn well what I mean. Blacks seated in here and whites in there. That's segregation," Anna said, remembering the cafe in Kentucky out on the ranch.

"So?"

Anna looked at Frankie Lee, wondering what planet he was living on. "So? Are you crazy or am I? This is 1982, Frankie Lee. I have been under the impression that segregation was over—if not for you two, it sure as hell is for me!"

"Yeah, we see," Frankie Lee, said, looking from her to Raspy.

"Don't be funny," Anna said, placing Raspy back on her lap.

"Look, Anna, it ain't as though thay can tell us we can't go in thare. We just don't choose to. We know thay don want us to be with 'em no how, and we don want to be with 'em. Like I said, it's just ya Northern black folks thank everythin' the white man says is gospel. And if you ain't with them you ain't shit. We already know better. Ask yur Momma—she sho' nuff know better."

"Say what you want to, Frankie Lee. It looks like segregation to me."

"Anna, thangs hare ain't like thay is in the North. Thare is still certain thangs we can't do hare. Ain't no sense in sayin' it is, Frankie Lee," Kate insisted, turning to her husband.

"I know, Kate. But we don look at it the same way Anna do. We don't like 'em so we don want to eat round 'em no how." Anna looked at him, shaking her head like she didn't understand what he was telling her. "We 'bout them same as thay is 'bout us—it's simple as dat. Thay thank thay segregatin' thayself from us . . . we just laugh cause what they don't know is we segregated ourselves from them a long time ago. As long as we know we can go through those swingin' doors without getting hung, we choose what white folks we want in our company. Ya git whare I'm comin' from?" he asked, gesturing with outstretched hands.

Anna felt like she was on another planet as she listened to her cousin. "Frankie Lee, I don't like your logic at all." Anna replied.

"Listen to this city gal talk. Logic . . . what damn logic? All ya Northern city niggers b'lieve ever thang dat white man says is how life spose to be. Not realizing he don know no more'n nobody else. Dat's why his laws change all the time. Dis month he might try somethin' and tell ya it's the way it must be done, den come to find out he done messed up. Ya thank dat white man gonna 'mit it? Hell nah, 'cause he knows he can't be found wrong. If he says the moon is purple, ya Northern niggers say yah, it sho' is purple 'cause the white man said so.' Anna and Kate looked at each other both laughing.

"I heard a white man ask a black brother why he was so lovin' to his wife and kids. The white cracker was mad 'cause his wife had probably compared his ass with dat brother. Ya know what dat fool said? 'Nah sir, I's just like y'all—ain't no difference in us.' Do ya know dat fool went home and kicked his wife's ass and his kids just so he could be more like that white-ass cracker who was kickin' his wife and kids' asses?"

Anna stared at Frankie Lee, not believing her ears. "Frankie Lee, you are lying, but you have made your point. I understand where you are coming from."

"White man say ya niggers like to cut and kill. B'fore daylight in the mornin', some fool done killed him another black man thankin' he gotta prove dat white man right. I ain't in to dat. What dat white man do is his business. What Frankie Lee do is mine. I don need him to tell me how long I can live and what I must do to be more like him 'cause I don choose to do my thang the way he does his or like his taste in women unless, of course . . ." Frankie Lee smiled at Raspy, "unless he step up to the plate and start hittin' on my women the right way. Telling me I gotta take care'f mine and he ain't cared for none he had. Ya don't see me with no white-lookin' babies floatin' around nowhares I ain't here with. All my babies got nappy hair like mine, and that's the way I like it." They all looked at Raspy, who grinned up at Anna and then rested her blonde head on her mother's chest.

"Let me get my baby out of here before I have to knock you on your butt . . . talking about her that way."

"Hey Anna, ya thank that's somethin'? See that door back thare?" Anna looked around to see a door with a sign that read STORAGE.

"What about it, Frankie Lee?"

"That's whare Mr. Porter use to take our grandmother to git a little piece."

Anna's mouth flew open as she placed her hands over Raspy's ears. "I don't believe it . . . anyway, it's a disgusting thing to even mention, Frankie Lee. You should be ashamed for dishonoring Granny that way."

"Now ya see why this husband and me can't git along. He's too much," Kate said as they all looked up to see the hot steaming plates of food arrive for their table.

"I'm no longer hungry, and even if I were starving, I wouldn't eat in here." Frankie Lee laughed, moving Anna's rejected plate over next to his and taking Raspy into his lap then placing a spoon of food in her mouth.

"Cous, you don understand the South and how we coloreds see white folks hare. I lived through them days when black folks had to say 'yes sir' and 'nah sir' to little white kids. Ya see, thare was a time when one white man could come among fifty black men, pick one out, no matter how big or strong and beat the hell out of him—and thare was nothing he or the

366

others could do but stand thare and watch less thay wanted to die. The white man could take the poor man's woman, makin' as many babies as he liked, and the black man had to take care of hur and them, back child support this government has yet to pay for." Frankie Lee shook his head his eyes looking beyond them. "Long as dem days is gone and I am free to go in and out of where ever I want, I don care if I never sit or eat side of a damn cracker another day of my life. Integration is all right on one hand, but on the other hand, coloreds in the South lost a lot of thangs we valued because of it."

"Like what?" Anna asked, wondering to herself what could be more important than freedom.

"For one thang, when integrated came to Ointon we had just had a new school built, The white folks tore it down brick by brick cause thay didn't want thay white kids going thare. The black kids going to white schools lost a lot of the programs thay were traditionally accustomed to in thay own schools, thangs white schools didn't know nothin' about and sho' didn't intend to implement in thay school programs."

"I see you can sound educated when you want to, Frankie Lee. I didn't think you knew a thing about education, but here you are talking in the King's English about implementing programs.

"Anna, ain't no fun for our kids doin' thangs the way white kids do them all the time."

"Anna, he's right. Now dat our schools are integrated, white folks feel we wanted so bad to be with 'em dat we were willin' to give up all our traditions and take on theirs . . . which I guess is what's happenin' all over. Seems to me like the black man don't want nothin' of his own if the white man didn't come up with it first."

Anna listened to what they were telling her. It reminded her of what Jake had called the White Man's Syndrome. "We can't tell 'em what's best for us cause we chose to go thay way and thay sho' nuff didn't want us . . . so we must do it thay way or go back to a one room school . . . it's as simple as dat. What meant somethin' to us don't mean a damn thang to them . . . course most of ya Northern black folks thank the white way is logical and the only way thangs should be done; otherwise it's country," Frankie Lee said, placing another spoon of food in Raspy's mouth.

Anna began to realize that there was a big difference in the thinking of Southern blacks and blacks not only in the North but, even in the Midwest. "You could always set up groups to object to the things you feel are unfair." Anna quickly realized she must have made a stupid statement by the way Kate and Frankie Lee looked at each other and laughed.

"Ya sho' nuff been in the city too long to live down hare, Cous. These snitchin' white-lovin' black-ass niggers—oh, let me get rid of that slave word, but niggers is what thay is—would run to the white boss b'fore the sun rose the next mornin', tellin' what we planned to do like dat Lilly Mary done to Granny. I guess by now she done tole ya," Frankie Lee said as Anna nodded her head.

"All of us owe that white man something," Kate said. "B'fore daylight, his nigger boy say, 'Look boss, thay tryin' to start up somethin' down dar go hurt ya.' Boss man smile and say 'thank ya Henry, two payments off that debt ya owe.' I know I hate dat word, but for them kind of folks it fits, Anna."

"The nigger knows he done helped hisself, but whare's dat gonna to leave the rest of us with Johnny-white law then? Hare is my poor little cousin caught right in the middle," Frankie Lee said, lifting Raspy up and kissing her on her cheek, causing her to laugh out loud. Anna looked over at her child, hating the predicament she was in.

****

Anna attempted to give her sleeping baby to Granny after they arrived home, but when she woke up Raspy began to cry and refused to go to Granny. "Why I b'lieve that gal done got 'tached to her momma," Granny said. Anna took Raspy back as Frankie Lee laughed along with Granny.

"Raspy honey, you need to finish your nap."

"I want you to nap with me, Mommie," Raspy begged, clinging to her. Granny's smile told Anna her grandmother was not sad that her daughter preferred her. In the months ahead, Anna couldn't move for Raspy tagging along, holding on to her skirt tail whenever possible. Taking country walks, she talked to Raspy about the trees and plants, asking what they were and discussing their importance, even though she knew the child did not understand much of what she was telling her.

Some days, Frankie Lee came to take Anna to town to visit Kate. Raspy cried to come along. When Kate had guests, Anna noticed the stares and assured them her baby had taken her looks from her father. Nothing more was said on the subject. The closeness between Anna and Raspy soon became a bond that Anna did not want to lose.

Holding Raspy in her arms, she looked over at Granny and smiled. "I would die for her, Granny. I love her so much. Can you believe I wanted to give her away? Now I can't see that happening no matter what. She is mine and I love her."

"Ya just like me back then. I know'd ya had feelin' for yur chile. I had love for Mr. Porter's chiles. I tole myself a thousand times I didn't, but I know'd I did. Seen the same thang in ya as was in me. Love for hur is in ya, and I knew I couldn't let ya be like Granny was back then." Admitting she loved Raspy caused thoughts of giving her away to slip from Anna's mind.

Finally learning how to get through the maze of driving to town from the country where her grandmother lived, Anna drove Raspy back home in Frankie Lee's car when he claimed he was not feeling well enough to bring them back one evening. She was now on her way into Oinston to her uncle's house to return Frankie Lee's car because he would need it to go to work the next day. Anna first dropped off Granny at Paul's clinic to see him and then drove over to see Frankie Lee at her uncle's house where he waited for her. Raspy sat next to her with a teddy bear snug under her arms. She watched as Raspy clapped her hands in an effort to get Anna to sing along with her. The few words Raspy knew included "Mommie," something she repeated while Anna began singing the "Three Little Kittens," feeling so happy she had come back and finally claimed her child as her own. Love for Raspy filled her heart as she looked down at her, thinking no matter how white she looked, she was her daughter. "Mommie loves her baby," she said to Raspy,

"Raspppy loves Mommie," Raspy said. Anna saw the look of love Raspy gave in return as she smiled up at her, calling her Mommie again and again. Glancing up, she spied the Old Widow its back glowing bright as it crawled right across Frankie Lee's car window. That morning, she had seen the spider crawling down its web. Thinking it was just a country spider, she had ignored it, but after seeing the Old Widow slide across

Frankie's window with its back pulsating like crazy, she knew something was amiss.

"Oh shit," she said aloud.

"Oh shit," Raspy echoed her.

"Raspy, Granny would be on us both for using that word. Shush, don't say it," Anna whispered to her, placing her finger against her lips and watching Raspy place her finger against hers. Looking up at her, her blonde curls moved back and forth as she shook her head no. Anna watched the Old Widow disappear.

Driving up the short road to Frankie Lee's father's home, Anna's heart began to pound when she spied Jake's red Seville Cadillac parked in front of her uncle's house. Her eyes grew in terror seeing Frankie Lee talking to Jake in front of the house. At last she understood the spider's warning. Jake turned staring her way, Anna panicked and applied the brakes so fast that Raspy fell under the dashboard, hitting her head on Frankie Lee's CB radio. Both Anna and Raspy were screaming when Frankie Lee and Jake came running.

Blood poured from Raspy's forehead as she screamed. Moving Anna over, Frankie Lee jumped into the front seat while Jake jumped into the back. No one said anything. They hurried to the hospital as Raspy continued to scream. The nurse came out, took one look at the child, and asked for her parents. Anna didn't know what to say to the black nurse staring hard at her.

"I'm sorry, but we have to have her parents here before she can be treated.

"Oh my God, Frankie Lee, what am I going to do?" Anna asked desperately as Jake stared at them.

"Anna, call the kid's parents like the nurse told you to do," Jake insisted.

"Can't the parents give consent over the phone? The damn baby will bleed to death before thay git hare, woman!" Frankie Lee shouted at the nurse.

"This is a white baby she is caring for and her parents may want it treated up in Portland since we treat mostly blacks here," the nurse replied, giving Anna a towel to press against Raspy's head.

Anna's eyes fell on the black doctor she knew so well coming out of one of the emergency rooms. Terrified that she might be exposed, Anna ran up to him, pulling him away from the others. "Doctor," she whispered, "my husband is here from Illinois. He came unannounced. He knows nothing about Raspy. Remember, we discussed it. I was driving too fast and she fell and hit her head on the CB in the car. The nurse says you can't treat her without parental consent. Please think of something," Anna whispered tears pouring from her eyes.

"Take the child into the room there, nurse. You gentlemen wait out in the waiting room. Still protesting, the nurse followed Anna and Raspy into a room. Anna fell into a chair and broke down crying out of control. The doctor lifted the still-screaming Raspy from her arms.

"Oh doctor, I know I should be ashamed of myself, but he knows nothing about her. If he found out she is my child it would mean . . ."

"I understand your situation. It would do no one any good; least of all the child if you were dead, now would it? Get control of yourself. I'll call Paul, explain everything to him, and have him bring Granny down here. Once your husband sees Paul, he'll believe the child is his." The nurse said not another word as she stared from Anna to Raspy.

"You are ashamed of me, aren't you doctor?" Anna cried, hating what she had to do.

"The only way I would have been ashamed of you was if you had destroyed a child as precious as this one. Go get the papers for her to sign Nurse I will be back in a minute," the doctor said, smiling at Anna. Once they were out of the room, Anna turned her palm up.

"Old Head, this is my baby. I love her too much to see something bad happen to her. I don't know how things will turn out. Please take the spider from my palm and place it into hers so that if things go bad the Old Widow's young will protect her. Anna placed her daughter's hand against her own and pressed hard. When she looked again, a tiny orange spot glowed in the child's palm. Hers showed nothing. Anna felt that if it came to a choice between her life and that of her child, she would rather die than see Raspy hurt. Raspy laid her head on her chest as the sound of her crying ceased.

"Remember, Mrs. Bradley," the doctor said when he stepped back into the room, "all God requires of you is that you love and protect the gift he has given you as best as you can." The nurse assisting the doctor stood staring with her mouth open.

"I know, Doctor. I love her too much to see her hurt," Anna said, signing the papers as he and the nurse treated Raspy. Anna walked back into the lobby and overheard Frankie Lee saying to Jake, "First I seed of my cousin; someone was calling my ass from Arkansas 'bout eight months back." Anna slowed her pace as she listened to their conversation. "Yeah, I thank dat was when the call came. When I got thare, I found my cousin all beat up with three broken ribs . . . unconscious near bout. Dirty shame it was."

"Yeah," she heard Jake say, "Guess I let my temper get the best of me. Anyway she paid me back with that hot-ass grease she threw on me. Came to make it up to Anna—straighten things out if I can," Jake said.

"Yeah, I know bout that straightenin' thangs out shit . . . my guess is that ya come to take her back and make hur life a livin' hell," she heard Frankie Lee telling him.

"What makes you say some shit like that, Frankie Lee? You got a wife. Would you want some son of a bitch telling you some shit like that when all you wanted to do was to make things right?" Anna listened to Frankie Lee's laughter.

"Come on Jake, man, we cut from the same black cloth. Ya know well as I do we black men ain't forgivin' no foot slippin' from our women. It looks like she burned yer ass good, so she gonna have to pay for dat, too." Anna saw Frankie Lee pull Jake's shirt open and knew he was looking at Jake's scarred chest.

"Don't know what you are talking about, man. All I want is my wife back home," he insisted, moving away from the hands on his shirt. Listening to Jake, Anna knew better. Sheri' and Jake Jr. had already told her how Jake had had to have skin grafts from his back to replace that burned skin on his chest. They had overheard their grandmother say that his long stay in the hospital had made him an unhappy man.

When Granny and Paul Porter arrived, Anna stood by the window, crying so hard she was unable to look their way, her screaming child within hearing distance. Frankie Lee told Paul and Granny what had happened. Jake stood at Anna's side. Paul walked up to Anna, placed his hand on her shoulder, and told her he did not fault her for what had happened to his daughter.

Raspy was given to Paul, and Anna knew Raspy was unfamiliar with him because his infrequent visits. Not even Granny's outstretched arms kept Raspy from screaming for Anna, calling "I want my Mommie! I want my Mommie!" Anna listened to her scream over and over but made no move toward her as Granny and Paul after signing for the doctor's orders taking her out of the hospital still screaming for Anna. Her shoulders shook as tears flowed from her eyes as she turned her back on her screaming baby.

After leaving the hospital, Jake went to have the oil changed in his car. Anna stood with Frankie Lee on his father's porch. "You were right about me, Frankie Lee. I'm a no-good mother," Anna cried, wiping tears from her eyes.

"I never said dat. What ya did today proved dat's a lie. Ya loved her enough to turn away from hur, knowing what might happen otherwise," Frankie Lee said, taking her in his arms.

"I guess I never tole ya, Anna, but other than Granny and the old man, ya the closest relative in my life. Ya and I was only children when ya came up and stayed with Granny dat yeer. I've loved ya ever since. Ya are the sibling I never had. I'm my father's only child, and ya are Aunt Annabelle's only child. Ya know I love ya, gal, no matter how I tease ya. Anna felt Frankie Lee's arms tighten around her.

"I guess I see Raspy like I see myself living without my own mother. Cous don't go back with him. Stay hare. We will work somethin' out fer ya and Raspy." Anna listened to Frankie Lee, wishing it were that simple.

"Frankie Lee, Jake is not going to leave here without me. As long as I am here, he is going to hang around. There are too many people in this town who now knows I am the mother of a half-white child. There is no way he won't hear of it sooner or later from someone somehow and that is, you know as well as I do, when the killing will start." Anna allowed her tears to fall. "I cannot risk having my baby harmed because of my foolishness. I can only harm us both by staying here. His name had to be given on Raspy's birth certificate as her father. He is, after all, still my husband, so I couldn't use Ray's last name. Once Jake finds out about Raspy and that her last name is Bradley, he will claim her as his daughter just to get her back into Session."

"To tell Aunt Annabelle and the rest of those Session blacks . . . I know," Frankie Lee sighed, blowing out smoke from his cigarette.

"Anna, seeing Raspy crying like dat for ya, I had to thank of dat daddy of hurs. He has a right to know 'bout hur. She has a right to know her own daddy, Anna, and see if he would 'cept hur as his chile besides hur lookin' at some damn pictures ya got hung upside the wall."

"But Frankie Lee, he is . . ."

"White? Ya think I can't see dat? What I'm wonderin' is what kinda white man is he reilly? Ya said he would die for somethin'. Let's see if he is willing to put up some skin for his own daughter or if he is just another redneck dirty white cracker, Anna. If ya don't know what dat is, it's a white man who lays his ass in bed with black women and then gets up, leaving his seed for other men to care for. And b'lieve me, I've known plenty of white good for nothing crackers just like dat," Frankie Lee threw the butt of his cigarette across the yard, shaking his head as he lit another. "If he is, then he ain't worth the time it took to meet his ass in that apartment for three damn days and nights, was he? Worse than dat is Jake finding out his ass is white."

"Frankie Lee worse than that is if Jake finds out my baby is half-white and insists on bringing her back with us. By the time we reached Session, he would know everything there is to know about the father of this half-white child I have without lifting one finger to harm me."

"Yeah, I know. It'll be Raspy who'd take all the punishment. All ya could do is watch, unable to do anythang to help hur." Frankie Lee blew smoke from his lips as he sighed and spat across the yard. "I hate with all my heart yer havin' to go back with him knowin' how it's gonna be. I also know ya're right. It's a must for Raspy's protection. He won't rest til ya on yer way back to Session with him. Raspy don't deserve him or Aunt Annabelle taking thay hatred out on hur, poor kid." Anna listened to his concern for her daughter and knew he loved her, too.

"All these Oinston women are already fascinated by his fancy car and clothes, not to mention his good looks, Frankie Lee. He would find one of them who knows I'm Raspy's mother . . . someone who would tell him about her. Jake never even connected her to me . . . not once did it dawn on him. I was terrified he would somehow figure it out," Anna shared, crying uncontrollably in Frankie Lee's arms. "But we both know after being told often enough, he would make it his business to find out the truth."

If ya have to go back, Cous, play it cool til ya can git away agin. Call me and I'll come help ya git away so he can't ever find ya—like I did when ya was carryin' hur." Frankie Lee kissed Anna's forehead, hugging her to him as she cried out loud, still hearing her baby screaming for her.

Chapter Twenty-Seven

— ∾ —

After Jake returned with a full tank of gas and having the oil change he had stated he needed, he blew the horn for Anna, saying nothing else to Frankie Lee. Anna swung her purse over her shoulder and got into the car. When he reached over to kiss her, all Anna could envision was Angela kneeing down before him to take his penis inside her mouth. She shook her head and turned away.

"What the hell's wrong with you?"

"I can't taste any woman's body fluids but my own, not and know it," Anna confessed.

"What kinda shit is this you're talking now?

"If Angela is down on her knees for you, you must be sucking in her body, too. No, I just can't do it—I will vomit in your mouth," Anna insisted.

"What the hell are you talking about? I was in the hospital three long months on account of that grease you threw on my chest. The only shit I have in my mouth is the bitter taste of them damn pain pills you caused me to have to take." Anna shook her head now moving farther away from him.

When he tried kissing her again Anna gagged as though about to vomit. His face suddenly held a look of anger that scared Anna even more as he pushed her away. She knew she would have to get away from him as soon as they arrived in Session. With Al Green playing on his stereo, Jake sped away, not looking back at Frankie Lee who stood staring at the car. Anna's heart was pounding with worry about the seriousness of Raspy's head injury. Frankie Lee, fearful that Jake would take revenge on Anna for burning him, had given her a gun larger than the derringer Madria had sent to the ranch for her but small enough for her to carry in her purse.

Frankie Lee had said, "If he starts actin' like he wants to hit on ya, ya reach inside yer purse but don't take it out—he might take it from ya. Just start shootin' until the gun is empty."

She had assured Frankie Lee she would do as he told her if matters came to that, while also assuring him she would be getting away from Jake as soon as possible.

He had told her, "Call me so I know ya alright, Cous."

Now on the highway after having refused Jake's advances, Anna felt her body shaking so badly that she doubted she could use the gun Frankie Lee had given her even if she needed to. As if on command, everything turned bright orange. The Old Widow crawled along the edge of the passenger car windowsill, its orange back glowing as red as fire. All at once Anna was no longer in the car with Jake but in the rainforest. The blue magnetic field of thirteen eyes stared down at her. Looking up, she stared up at the pulsating brain moving around inside. Settling on a giant lily pad Anna felt light rain warm her body as she inhaled the intoxicating fragrances of different flowers.

"Daughter, you must drink from yonder pond."

Anna looked to see water so clear it reflected her image and the lily pad on which she sat. She reached into the pond, her hands cupping the water.

"Its water shall calm your fears on this journey you must embark upon with your earth mate. Listen carefully to his words for he will teach you how collective thinking rules your world. His human mind, like all human minds of this earth world, has been taught collective thinking—thus missing the true realities of life that moves them through it. While under the conjuration of the Healing Tree, you pulled from it the leaf of endurance, drinking in its powers from the cauldron left for you during the Young Chemist's healing. It has enabled you to endure many of life's lessons you must learn. Soon your journey shall call you away again. It is the path you must follow. Your young's wound has healed. Fear not for her safety—she now has the Old Widow's young to protect her life."

Anna felt the fear inside her subside as she continued to drink from the pure waters flowing before her.

In a blink, she found herself back in the car with Jake again, noticing him driving down the highway at eighty miles an hour. She no longer felt fearful—in fact, her worries about having to get away from him had calmed. It came to her that it would be best for her and her husband to come to an understanding before they arrived in Session. There was no way at this point in their marriage that he couldn't realize it was over for them. She was not angry about his infidelity. It was bad enough thinking about her unfaithfulness. She would not have to run from him if she could get him to agree to a civil divorce and shared custody of their children. She could then go on with her life and not worry about him continuously hunting her down like he owned her.

"Jake, we cannot go on with our marriage," she said, staring out the front window, hopeful he would be in agreement with her. "I know you have been unfaithful to me. And I will not deny my own transgressions. I just want us to agree to a civil divorce so that we both can go on with our lives. I'm sure Angela will be happy to have you all to herself."

"Angela who? I don't know who or what the hell you are talking about. You have never laid eyes on me and any other woman since you caught me dirty with Barb and her friends. We had a goddamn perfect marriage until you fucked it up by listening to that shit Dee's ass brought to you. I'm not copping out to anything you haven't caught me doing. What some fool told you trying to destroy our marriage doesn't mean shit to me. I came to get my wife back so that we can go on with our lives together."

"Jake!"

"And about you and that nigger you stayed with three days because you believed some lies Dee told you . . . I'll just wait on his ass to come again—and he will. When he does, a good killing is what he's got coming. You are still my wife, and no man can have you but me until they carry you away in a box. I thought I told you that. He will find that out as soon as I get my hands on his ass. You can bet your life on that shit."

Anna sighed, saying nothing else. Looking straight ahead, she began to wonder which one of them was crazy—him or her? She thought of how his mind worked. Dee had stopped her from going into the room where Angela knelt, giving him oral sex. If she did not walk in on him in the act, he would deny what he knew they both knew until his dying day. If she had gone in and killed them both, she would be in prison right now. She wondered which was worse.

She also knew her husband was obsessed with not allowing anyone to take what he believed belonged to him. He had once told her, "If I own a broke-down dog and someone takes it, I will be getting it back. Nobody takes from Jake Bradley. If that gentleman you say you got comes to my town after we are married, talking about you're his, I will kill his ass Anna. You can bet your life on that shit." At the time, Raymond had simply been a boy in her dreams, as unreal to her as were the dreams. There was no one to kill. Now that she knew he was real, she also realized her father was right in his assessment of their affair. Jake would kill him and her if he knew who he was. His pride at having his wife taken by any man had him spitting blood. Her affair with a white man would be his undoing. He would go berserk. Before that happened, she needed to talk him into giving her a divorce without any casualties.

Anna remembered Raymond pleading with her to leave with him and go abroad. They could marry and buy a home there. Once they were settled, she could send for her children. No more problems with race once they left the United States, he had assured her. No, their divorces needed to happen first, she had insisted. She did not want a scandal smearing his family's name. They should not give Carolyn that satisfaction. After her discovery of Jake and Angela's affair, Anna had thought she would have no problem getting a quick divorce. Then, once Raymond's divorce was final, they could once again think of their life together. She had never dreamed that Jake would still want their marriage to continue.

Thinking back to Carolyn's deception, she could not believe a child as young as ten would have come up with those deceitful thoughts on his own. It's funny how anger will make you reveal things you would otherwise never tell, Anna thought to herself, wondering if Carolyn Forlorn regretted her outburst. She would never realized the price that outburst almost cost her. Ray had planned to kill her, not caring that he would die himself. The way he had planned to carry it out would have cost many innocent people their lives. Anna knew that because of his anger at the time, he did not care who died as long as her life ended. He was The Chemist, and when The Chemist set out to do a job, he did not get paid to think about the outcome or what victims might fall in the aftermath of his destruction. As long as he got the job done, nothing else mattered. She knew, as did the Old Head, he had to be stopped.

He had found her the next morning in the apartment's small lab, deactivating all his explosives. She had already boxed up many of the test tubes and chemicals. Little was said as he began helping her dismantle his plan of destruction. After several hours, she had rested her head on his shoulder and let him wipe sweat from her brows.

"The man I fell in love with is better than this," she had assured him. "You and I found a way to put these chemicals to good use when your thoroughbreds' lives were threatened. In fact, it was you who insisted I use this brain of mine to help save their lives even though I didn't want to go to Kentucky to help you, remember Ray?" Anna had asked him as he stood next to her, helping to stabilize the explosives so that they could be disposed of without danger of contamination.

"I do remember, baby," he had answered, kissing her cheek as he anticipated her moves while they studied the combinations he had put together. It had taken them two days before they came up with a stabilizer that matched the type of chemicals needing to be neutralized. "Mix needed to find another way to make money. Remember me telling you that?" she had asked when they finally found the match they needed. "How I didn't want you somewhere blown to hell killing for him or anyone else? Like I said, you are better than that. I knew it when I was fourteen and I know it now. You are the man of my dreams. Life without you in it would be impossible." He had kissed her lips and smiled as they continued their work.

"Who knows, I might need you someday," she had said, smiling up at him. "If you are blown to hell with your wife and a hundred other people, what would I do then?" She had almost said "Raspy and I" but stopped herself in midsentence. Thoughts of the baby brought tears to her eyes as she became too weak to stand. What could she say about Carolyn when she was also deceiving him by not telling him of his child she had given birth to? It was at that moment she had been tempted to tell him. Instead, she had allowed him to take her into the bedroom and make love to her again, not really wanting to challenge his feelings about the baby he might not accept and missing the last opportunity to tell him about his child. After everything had been deactivated they placed the chemicals in his safe and locked it.

As her mind returned to the present, Anna wanted to assure Jake that she and Dee had seen him and Angela in her office out at Looper's racetrack, but she remembered the beating she had taken after mouthing off to him when she returned home from being with Ray. She decided to try another tactic. Looking over at him, Anna wrestled with how she would word what she needed to tell him without starting a fight. He had already proven that he didn't do well with facts he did not want to hear.

Why did he insist on keeping her as his wife, she wondered, when so many women wanted him? He was a handsome man even with his limp; she believed it actually had the women more interested in him than ever. His curly hair matched those long eyelashes she had listened to the white wives admire when they went to Tora's gala banquet. His hair had been cut so that his black curls lay thick on his head and long enough to wrap around the edge of his earlobes. His thin mustache lay over a full set of lips that looked as though they needed to be kissed. Wearing a gray double-breasted suit over a white silk shirt, her husband would have looked enticing had she not been made aware of his adulterous ways that had continued though out her return to him, something he had vowed would never happen again.

She believed Jake only wanted a wife to go with his need for having women run after him—women he could refuse to have a permanent relationship with because of a wife he would tell them he could not get rid of. This time she would help him realize he no longer needed to lie. There was no love lost for her. She wanted him out of her life once and for all. And as soon as she got back to Session, he would find that out. Taking a deep breath, Anna turned down the stereo and spoke in as friendly a tone as she could manage.

"Jake, I can't blame you for wanting Angela—she is a beautiful white woman." The look Jake gave her caused Anna to turn and look out of the window, not wanting to hear his response.

"You must have forgotten about all those black people at that meeting the night I took you to the city council with me, woman.

"What black people? What meeting are you talking about?"

What meeting am I talking about? You sat with your parents on the front row. That crowd lifted me, Jake Bradley, up on their shoulders, screaming my name because they love me so much. I am their man. With as much power as I have with the blacks living in my city, can you imagine me sporting some white woman on my arm, telling every black citizen in

Session how beautiful she is? As hate-filled as your mother is, she and the rest of those old biddies who caught hell from white women back in the day would run my ass out of town on a rail."

"They haven't run James or the other black men with white women out of town."

"Those brothers aren't striving to be anything but workers. I run that city. It belongs to me. There is nothing I can't get done. The people old and young love Jake Bradley's black ass. Whatever goes down there, I am the man they call on. No, Anna, there can be no white woman I'm marching into Session talking about being my woman. I have too much at stake to give it up for some shit you call beauty. The motherfucker who is sporting a woman he thinks looks better than his ass is a fool other men look for. Sooner or later, her real beauty is going to be auctioned off to the highest bidder. I'll stake my life on that shit." Looking over at her, he shook his head. Anna realized the truth in what her husband said about what the people in Session thought of him, she knew he would never give it up for a woman he could have on his own terms.

"Anna, I thought you knew American history."

"American history? What does beauty have to do with American history?" she asked, startled by his statement. He slowed the car to the posted 65 miles per hour instead of the 80 miles per hour he had been driving.

"As many times as you have been to the South, you don't know a thing about American history in this country, do you?"

She gave him a strange look as he continued. "The white man changed who looks beautiful in this country, Anna, after he got his marching orders from his white woman telling him that he better see no woman's beauty but hers and while he could bed the female slaves all he wanted, they were still animals up for sale—animals he better not make equal to her. He could make as many babies as he wanted with you black sisters, but your babies would be born animals too—animals he could never claim as his children."

"What!" Anna thought he had lost his mind as she listened to his assessment of the black woman's place in American history while thinking of her own half-white baby.

"You didn't know that! Where the hell have you been? The white man may have had all the power and the property and thought he was in control in this country, but when that white woman gave him his marching orders, he had to go along to get along."

"Marching orders?"

"What he could and couldn't do when it came to you black sisters, those marching orders. Naturally he didn't want it known that he had had to concede to those orders so he made up his own lie," Jake continued as he leaned back in his seat driving even slower, "Her orders told him what he could and could not do with the black sisters he was bedding. His orders told everyone that it was the white woman's beauty he didn't want the black man to have, making the black sister appear less beautiful, even to her own men. When in reality, that white motherfucker knew if he tried to put that black sister over her, his white woman would blow up every goddamn slave ship he tried to bring in to port, something that would have destroyed the wealth he had established and that promoted his leisurely lifestyle." Anna stared over at Jake. "He also knew," Jake continued as he rested an arm on the back of her seat, "that in the dark, all women's beauty is the same.

After sleeping with his slave and loving the way her body felt to him, he had no plans of giving her up but he was terrified that if the white woman found the black man's body as sexual enjoyable as he found the black sister's, she might just dump his ass for good. Then where the hell would that leave his ass? It would mean the lost of his control over everything he had going for him! The white man couldn't have that shit happening."

"Jake, you are too much."

"Your history books don't tell you he was out there making out with his pigs and horses, do they, huh? You're talking about sick—think 'f that. So you know he knew better and wasn't about to get in the sack with no real animal when what he really wanted was some sweet black-loving—something he could have as long as he followed the white woman's marching orders." Anna shook her head but became curious as to his logic.

"Think about it. Can you see yourself in some white motherfucker's arms after lying in these?" he asked, looking down at himself with one arm stretched out. Anna stared over at him as the image of Raymond's naked body covering hers flashed in her mind.

"That smart-ass motherfucker was not going to take a chance on her unleashing her fury after coming up with a way to have the best of both worlds. What the hell did he care what she called you black females when he gain pleasure out of bedding you both. He definitely knew you both functioned the same?"

"How do we function the same?"

"In bed, Anna. The cat wasn't stupid enough not to know no matter what his woman believed; all women function the same in bed. He had no problem with her referring to the black woman as an animal or selling her kids as long as she could deal with what he felt was his right." Jake's laugher filled the car. "After all, selling the babies the black woman had meant more money for him, further enhancing his and her already elaborate lifestyle. And get this. Not one of those babies he sold left the country, which meant they would be available for other white men either to work or bed. You think about all the street marching you black women were doing for equal rights? It was for equal rights all right—so those white women could have the same sleeping rights as well as working rights as their men."

"What the hell are you getting at Jake Bradley?"

"Dear wife, they wanted equal rights—the equal rights to sleep black like their men slept black and everything else he took privilege in doing for so long. That was something they could never do until you black women helped make it possible for them."

"What? I'll have you know we were dealing with oppression from our own black men! That is the only reason we wanted women's rights.

"That white man still has his marching orders, my dear wife, and he knows his place. As for you black-ass sisters being oppressed, as long as you had that white man wanting your asses, we were the only ones oppressed— the black man and the white woman."

Anna's mind went back to Linda and her assessment of the women's movement and what it meant for white women versus black women. Oh my God, she thought, she had the same take as Jake on the white woman's feelings about the women's movement.

"Jake, you are crazy coming up with something that outlandish, knowing good and well it was you black men helping white women get into your beds."

"Outlandish, my ass! You see how Nathan's brother looked at you, baby?" Anna suddenly felt her palms begin to sweat. She hoped Jake would not notice that she had begun to tremble.

"I am not interested in how I am looked at by any white man, Jake Bradley—you know that," Anna replied, turning her head to look out her side window.

"Baby, he looked at you like he had never seen a lovely dark-skinned black woman in his life. I thought he was going to jump over the table and eat your ass."

"Jake, there's black women darker than I am all over this world," Anna insisted, rolling her eyes his way but feeling a newly born fear in her heart that one day he might find out the truth. Her life would be done.

"Not in his rich white world there ain't. All the women in it are lily white, believe me, I know."

"Oh my God Jake!"

"And you know what else I know? That southern-speaking brother of Nathan that stood staring at you, who, by the way, I'm told has got money he ain't never seen, money enough to buy a country but you know what, he can want all his ass wants to but he has his marching orders and could never be seen swinging a black sister the likes of you on his arm in public." Anna stared straight ahead, feeling a cold sweat sweep over her body, thinking if he only knew . . . "That wife of his is so white she doesn't even speak our language. Anna, the motherfucker has so much money that he bought her white ass in another country. Can you imagine me taking my black ass over to some African country and buying me a black sister?" They looked at each other as Anna shook her head, trying not to laugh.

"Even with that southern shit coming out of his mouth, he got himself a pure white woman because he knows he can't be seen with no black-ass sister acting like she's beautiful." Anna moved over next to the door, remembering the Old Head's warning about collective thinking. She realized her husband had no way of knowing his thoughts of black women had been placed in his head long before he became a man, and they reflected how he saw himself. After all, she thought, the black male's sperm produced every woman of his race—women he thought as little of as he did of himself. Anna watched a smile form on Jake's face as he cast his eyes over to her Anna thought, No you don't know, Jake Bradley. You only think you know what's in a white man's world. Instead, she said, "Jake, I am sure the white man no longer publicly limits himself only to women of his race. You have been confined to Session far too long if you believe that is still true." Anna remembered the many times Raymond had publicly embraced her with no thoughts of who might see them.

"You need to watch television more, Anna, instead of keeping your head stuck in those silly science books."

"Television? What's on television that I have missed?" Anna asked, realizing that television watching promoted the worst kind of collective thinking. It distorted reality, causing people to more readily accept group thinking without the benefit of personal assessment and fact-finding as is conducted in science.

"I don't have to leave my living room to know what I'm telling you is true. You see it every day on television!" Anna threw her hand his way as if to dismiss him.

With one hand on the steering Jake pointed her way. "If you watch television, you'll see a brother swing a white girl on his arm, talking about how she is his woman or his wife, but that white man still has his marching orders baby, and the only way he is going to embrace a sister talking about how she belongs to him is in a dark room so no one sees his ass. I hate to tell you, wife of mine, but that white motherfucker looking at you at the racetrack has not forgotten his marching orders, even in this century. You would have to fill out an application to get hired as a maid in his world, and once race popped up, you would receive it back stamped 'hell no.' You know why?" Anna refused to make eye contact with him. "He has his marching orders, and he would never be caught with a wench cleaning his house."

Anna's mind flashed back to a time in the past. Having spilled food in the oven, she had gotten on her knees to clean it. Raymond had said, "Ms. Anna, why do you insist on cleaning? Allow me to have someone come in." Anna remembered smelling his Wild Passion cologne that filled her with desire as he walked into the kitchen. She had smiled, moving into his arms as he knelt beside her. With their lips locked together, they had arisen from the floor.

Anna had to admit that in some ways her husband spoke the truth in his assessment of collective thinking. When Julia Mike had walked out on her porch and looked down at her, she had immediately called for her maid. If nothing else, the white woman had thought she already knew the race of the woman her cousin would be bringing to meet her. She could hear the whispering voice of the Old Head embrace her mind

"His human mind, like all human minds of your world, has been taught collective thinking—thus missing the reality of life that moves them through this earth world."

Yes, Anna thought, the Old Head had been correct in its assessment of her world and collective thinking. Even at the ranch, she had seen the shocked look in Julia Mike's eyes as well as the others' when Raymond Forlorn wrapped his arms around her and had announced that she was his Ms. Anna. The Old Head wanted her to learn from Jake's collective thinking about white women versus black women, but how many times had she not learned from many others how the minds of humans of her earth world moved them through life?

Carolyn Forlorn's first thoughts were that Anna must have been a servant to her husband. She could not have fathomed him with a black woman in any capacity but as a servant. Taught collective thinking, as the Old Head called it, Carolyn had never given a thought to Anna being a serious threat to her marriage. Having accepted what others believed to be collectively true as to where the black woman stood in the scheme of things, Carolyn had missed the one woman who had happened to be the most important person in her husband's life. What a shame, Anna thought. As early as ten years old, Carolyn's son was learning to become the same collective thinker, having called her a house servant when he saw her at the racetrack.

Maybe most American white men were as her husband stated, Anna thought as she listened to Jake's assessment of the black woman's place in the white man's world. But about the white man she had been with, she knew Jake was mistaken. Still feeling the warmth of Raymond's embrace, she was reminded that the Old Head's eye had indeed unraveled his brain, leaving no marching orders he was forced to adhere to. Had her husband, she thought to herself not been so involved with his own behavior with Angela he would have discovered that not all white men lived under marching orders.

"So what does that have to do with a woman's beauty?" Anna asked glad as hell her husband's collective thinking had caused him to overlook the most important man in her life.

"The only way that white man could take the sting out of his woman's orders," Jake went on to say; "was to tell her and everyone else she was the only beautiful woman in the world because she was white, and no nonwhite woman could ever be as beautiful as she was. Being a woman, she fell for that shit, of course and because the white man proclaimed it to be so every other man in this country sucked it up. That's how we got our ideas of what beauty should look like baby. Let no one tell you any different." His laughter filled the car as Anna shook her head, having no understanding of his logic.

"Why do you think she liked calling the Indian woman a squaw and you black women wenches? It made you less than her, something she still believes, and, of course, everyone fell for the lie. Only her men knew better. It worked that's all they cared. She watched him smile and she knew he knew she did not like what he was telling her. "Don't feel bad. Wasn't no black brothers allowed to have white women so they believed it to be true to. No Anna, you could never be a wife to any white man. His wench maybe, but never his wife." Ain't no white man with money, especially a southerner going to be seen with no squaw or a wench, much less marry one—not with those marching orders still in his head." Again his laughter filled the car as they looked at each other.

"So where does beauty play in the scheme of things, Jake Bradley?"

Still smiling, Jake looked over at Anna and said, "The only beautiful woman in this world baby is one who listens to what her man tells her and keeps her damn mouth shut, not trying to tell him how to run his business. The Bible tells you women that the man is the king of his castle. He is the rooster of his hen house," Jake insisted, throwing back his head. "Ain't no hen chickens running shit in a rooster's house, Anna Bradley."

"That tells me nothing about how you see beauty playing its part in a woman's life," Anna said, wishing her last name was still Drake and thinking about how quickly she planned to change it back to Drake.

"Every woman in a man's life is beautiful if she is doing what he wants her to do. You see, that white woman became the most beautiful woman in the world when she allowed her man his pleasures and kept her damn mouth shut about it."

"You are out of your mind, Jake Bradley." He looked over at her, still smiling.

"My mind is tight, baby, and no man knows women better than Jake Bradley. When the right man comes to her—and that, my dear wife, is a man who studies women and knows how to tell that certain woman about that beauty she believes she has—that woman, if she likes how he tells her she is beautiful, will then be willing to give up what is most beautiful to him. And that beauty no one can see." Anna turned from his gaze, realizing where he was going with this conversation.

"Once she gives it up, he is locked into it until she turns cold. He will then go looking for other unseen beauty that will warm him. You remember what I'm telling you—that beauty everyone exclaims over in awe is only advertisement that a woman displays to a man who hopes it is an indication of that real beauty he is seeking."

For some reason, the Madame's face came to Anna's mind as she remembered her thoughts of the Western woman and beauty. What her husband spoke of surely was not that eternal beauty the Madame had had in mind. Was the Western thought of beauty so superficial? Anna hoped not as she sat listening to her husband's assessment of the meaning of beauty.

"The ugliest woman in the world Anna is the woman everyone says is beautiful but who has no idea what real beauty is to a man." Anna stared over at her husband's smiling face.

"Once he seeks that unseen beauty and finds himself in a freezer, she becomes the ugliest woman in the world to him. There is no doubt about it." His laughter once again rang out in the car. "So that you know, wife of mine, the beautiful woman knows the beauty a man seeks but is unwilling to give it to him except on her own terms."

"That's bullshit, Jake! It will be the woman who dumps him when she discovers he has no idea how to arouse a cat, let alone a full-grown woman. You know there are some men who think it's all about satisfying their asses—thinking their hands are for holding onto instead of caressing that which will get them the fire they want instead of the freezer they turn the woman into by humping like a dog. Meanwhile, the woman looks at the man, thinking he is an animal, all right, and sorry animal at that."

"See what I mean? You are cold—downing a man because he is lacking in his abilities."

"I don't know why you married me, Jake Bradley, when there were so many other women out there willing to accept you on your terms."

"I gave you my name, Anna Bradley, because you refused to see me as every other woman in my life had seen me. You insisted the only way I could have you was on your terms." Anna watched Jake shake his head as he continued to drive. "You always thought you were smarter than me—you and that damn tough-ass, white-looking mother of yours who thought you were too good for me. She talked about how she wanted her daughter to have a virgin man. That made me know I had to have you."

"Is that the reason you married me?" Jake pulled his shirt open to expose his burned chest.

"There has always been something mysteriously evil about you when you were mad that sent thrills through me, woman. I knew it when I first pissed you off at the job after I took over from my old man. You would have killed Angela's and my ass had it not been for Dee—that is the lie Dee told me. But I knew it was her ass that told you that shit about me and Angela. After seeing Barb's marred face and being branded with that grease, I knew if you had seen what Dee had told me you had seen, both Angela's and my ass would be dead right now from more than some hot-ass grease. You can do some crazy shit when you get mad enough, Anna Bradley. We would never have lived through the night with you having that switchblade I gave you that night. Nothing could have stopped you from killing us."

Jake suddenly stopped the car, pulling over along the side of the highway. Turning her to face him, he again attempted to press his lips against hers trying to force the kiss he wanted.

"I will throw up in your mouth if you kiss me Anna screamed turning away from him. "Dee wouldn't lie to me or to you, damn it!" Anna could still see Angela's mouth closing around his penis. I saw the two of you, Jake Bradley, in that conference room with her kneeling in front of your ass. And you telling her about the night I cut Barb."

"Stop lying! You ain't seen shit. Like I said, you are an evil bitch when you think shit is happening you don't like. When Dee told you that shit you went insane, and there is one thing you are to a fault, Anna Bradley."

"What the hell is that?" Anna asked, moving farther away from him.

"Like that mother of yours, you are a revengeful bitch. That is the only reason you returned to Session in the first place. To get revenge for what you felt I had done to you with Barb. You could have taken our kids and run off. But not you—you needed to see the look on my face when I saw what everyone else was seeing."

"And what the hell was that?" Anna asked, watching a grin spread across his lips as he stared her way.

"That goddamn beauty you were advertising. Beauty that only I knew of before you left me. Yes, dear wife, you needed to see me want you the way you felt I had made you want me. Threw that leg of yours in the air so I could see that beauty you would no longer allow me to have on any terms, damn you!" Anna turned her head staring out the side window "Beauty that was mine alone at one time.

"You think I cared about some Joe you met up with after leaving me? Hell no! But that night down by the river when you spoke up about the abilities of your lover, something told me he was the same one you had told me about when I first made my play for you. He has been lingering in the background waiting to take you from me from day one, and he plans to do it in my town. When you told me this motherfucker had already killed for you, my sweet wife, you meant it on your life and the life of that nigger I was about to kill. No man kills for a woman his heart does not throb for. That the motherfucker has killed for you was no lie! He must love your ass if he is willing to take a life for you."

Anna's eyes widened as she sucked in her breath. "I told you I was lying about that," she insisted, turning away from the eyes on her.

"No, wife of mine! You are lying now! That night under the bridge, you were in rare form. Everything you screamed in my face at that moment came out before you had time to think. You were so terrified I was about to burn that nigger's ass who was trying to get into that beauty that still belongs to me that you told the truth. Your goddamn lover had already killed for you, and I knew you believed he would kill for you again. What I wondered is why he didn't come for me after I beat your ass. Of course, you both probably felt that hot grease you cooked my ass with was payment enough, huh?" Anna said nothing.

"A man loving my wife enough to kill for her is a man I must meet. There is something to say about a woman men are willing to kill for, Anna." Anna breathed in, still looking out the side window and saying nothing. "You know countries have been blown to hell because of a man's love for a woman." Anna shivered, not wanting to think about him and Ray meeting up and what might be blown to hell if they did.

"And you want to know why I married you? One reason is because I needed to have that beauty you so thoroughly guarded. The second reason is that you told me you belonged to another man I could never catch you with but always knew was somewhere lurking in the wings waiting to take your ass from me. I had to have you belong to me and not him." Anna turned from him to stare out the window.

"Whoever the motherfucker is, he sure as hell was not marrying you before I did. And now that your ass is mine, he will learn what I do to niggers trying to take from me." His smile let Anna know he had no intention of giving her a divorce anytime soon. She stared back at him, thinking how conceited he was in placing his own race of women at the bottom of the barrel when it came to white men and then claiming that no man could have her but him. Well she could tell his dumb ass a thing or two that would knock the socks off his feet regarding the man he called a nigger and his black woman. Fear lodged in her heart thinking about that deadly meeting between the two men, sending a cold chill through her so strong she felt the sting of a winter's storm.

"Jake, you need to travel out of the country. Session gives no one a full understanding of race and white men." She noticed a frown crest his face.

"What the hell are you talking about? I was a marine in Vietnam. What is there about white men you know that I don't?"

"You knew my take on white men when I insisted you take me home from that racetrack after that white man looked at me the way he did. But for some reason, you insisted on staying there. The question I have is why you insisted on staying there?" The menacing look she gave him caused Jake to reach over and turn up the stereo, allowing Al Green to entertain them the rest of the way home. Anna stared at him with a frown on her face, realizing that was one question Jake Bradley did not plan to answer.

Chapter Twenty-Eight

—∽∽—

As soon as they arrived in Session, Jake immediately took Anna to her parents' home. This would be the perfect place to let him know she would not be going home with him, Anna thought to herself, as they drove up into their driveway. She watched Jake smile as he hurried in and kissed her mother on the cheek, then shared with her that he had found Anna down south wet nursing a white baby. Anna stood stunned listening to him divulging information he knew would enrage her mother. Their eyes locked. He had been plotting right along with her she realized too late. He knew she had no plans to take him back. It also occurred to her that he knew he would need an ally. What was she thinking trying to outwit Jake Bradley? He had rubbed shoulders with the preachers and politicians he called pimping hustlers. He knew how the game was played as well as they did. She had been no match in her scheme to get away from him. She watched his smile grow seeing the scornful look her mother gave her.

"Ask her yourself if you don't believe me, Momma. Had the white baby calling her Mommie," Anna noticed that even her father raised and eye brow hearing that information.

"Anna, what's dis he tellin' me? Ya been down South wet-nursin white devils' babies actin' like thay yers?"

"Momma, I had to live. I couldn't depend on Frankie Lee and Uncle Jessie to feed me, could I?" Anna said, reaching for the first answer she could think of.

"Ya coulda come home to me and yer daddy if ya didn't want dat husband of yers no more. I'd ruther feed ya myself than to have ya runnin' off down South taking care of 'em white devils' little demons. I don't want dat happenin' no more. If ya and Jake can't git long, ya come hare and stay. Down thare in Lousanna' carin' for some devil whose granddaddy no doubt help string up my Papa. Hare I am bustin' my back to help ya take care of yers and ya off tendin' dem white devils' little demons—hell no!"

"I'd take care of my children myself if you didn't keep insisting on helping me with them." Anna knew by the sudden change in her mother's expression that she should not have said anything about her caring for her children.

"Jake Jr., Sheri', git yer clothes up! Anna watched Jake's hand move through his hair. Even her father, Anna saw looked surprised. "Ya goin' home with ya Momma and Daddy. It'll be thay job to care fer ya from hare on out." Anna knew this had been more than even Jake hoped for by the wide smile spreading across his face. Everyone knew how much her mother and father loved caring for their grandchildren. Anna and Jake had not had the heart to take the children from them for good. Before she had left, the children had stayed at home on occasion, but as soon as they could talk their grandparents into it, they went back with them again.

Other than disapproving of Jake's adulterous ways, Anna's mother thought of him more as a son than as a son-in-law. She was shocked that her mother's hatred for whites would cause her to go as far as to relinquish care of her grandchildren. Anna's plans to leave Session flew right out the door.

******

Though Anna loved having her children home with her, it changed her plans to leave Session as soon as she got a chance. They were still in school. Jake Jr. bragged about attending the private school in Godfrey. They needed caring for, and since her mother had insisted she take them home, there was no way out of it. It would have been shortsighted for her to rush and take them anyway. Jake would come looking for her and them. Not only that, they were not close enough to her to want to stay wherever she took them, especially not another country. She would simply have to build that trust, and given a little time, she would accomplish that. Anna wondered why the Old Head had not alerted her to her husband's plot. Something was in the air she thought remembering how Granny had entered her life.

For Anna things did not seem the same without Raspy pulling on the hem of her dress when she wanted her or hearing her call her Mommie over and over as though repeating the word to learn its meaning. Anna, of course, had given her sweet kisses every time she had called her, and that had brought on more Mommies. Outside, they had fed the chickens together with Raspy running around the yard and Anna insisting that she had just dressed her and didn't want her getting all dirty. At night after Anna had given her a nice warm bath, Raspy switched from Granny's bed to hers, crawling around in it until she fell asleep with her head on some part of Anna's body.

Until she had asked Frankie Lee to buy a rubber sheet, she would wake up soaking wet in the middle of the night. Granny did not believe in disposable diapers—said they did not allow the baby's body to breathe and caused sores. Anna had issues with Granny's opinion but knew it was useless to argue with her when she had her mind made up about something. She was, in a way, like living with her mother—just a lot sweeter.

Standing at the kitchen sink back in Session, Anna's thoughts turned to Raspy. It felt as though she were right there behind her. Her soft body would be standing next to hers as she pulled on the hem of her skirt, begging for her to take her in her bedroom so that they could look at the pictures of Anna and the man posted on the wall. Raspy had learned to call the man "Daddy" soon after celebrating her third birthday. Although Frankie Lee and Granny enjoyed hearing it, Anna assured them that Raspy would never be saying it to her father, so what difference did it make whether or not she learned the word?

Now back in Session, all that was gone from her. It would be a long time coming before she would be able to get away again—Jake called like clockwork every morning, afternoon, and evening to make sure she was home and not gone before he returned home from work. Nothing about their marriage after New Year's was the same. The love for Jake that had started to rekindle died in that room as she and Dee listened to him inform Angela that they could have been victims the night she cut Barb. Yet it was nice being home with her children. Anna knew that, as she had done with Raspy, she would have to let them acquaint themselves with her in a way that allowed for trust, so that when she did leave with them, she would not have to worry about them running back to Session.

As soon as Anna escaped Jake's watchful eyes and the children were in school, she went to visit Dee. After they hugged each other, Dee reprimanded her for returning home with Jake, telling her he was no good for her and she should never have come back with him. Anna explained that her plan was to leave at the first opportunity and go abroad instead of staying in the country where Jake could find her—but that all that had changed after what happened when Jake had taken her to her parents' home as soon as they arrived there. Maybe she would get one or both of her children to move abroad with her. How she would tell them about Raspy was something else she would also have to figure out. This she told herself.

"You know that husband of yours no longer speaks to me."

"Oh my God, Dee—I hate that! You always cared a lot for Jake."

"Not after I saw him out there at that track showing no respect for his marriage. Seeing how he kicked you for telling him the truth. The bastard stayed in that hospital over three months from that grease. I thought his ass was a gonna for sure. Jake thinks he is one slick brother. See, I have not forgotten your thing about that N word," Dee said. "But he can't get it out of his head that the women he thinks he is playing are really playing his ass. When he loses everything, he will find out that that little head between his legs ain't got the brain God gave a goose."

There was no romance in their lovemaking any longer, laying unmoved under him. He hissed that she had become a freezer in bed. She knew he remembered how it was before, something that caused him to become outraged with bitterness.

After she and Dee talked, she asked to use her phone. She needed to call Frankie Lee and let him know she was all right. A public phone booth would not be a good idea. Suppose Jake walked up on her and accused her of calling a man. The fight would be on after he insisted she let him talk to "the man," which would be Frankie Lee or her grandmother—and she was not about to let Jake get on the phone talking nonsense to her.

Talking to Granny proved to be the hardest for her. While Raspy had no serious head injuries, she constantly asked for her. It brought tears to her eyes when Granny further informed her that Raspy ran around the house looking for her most of the day as if she were still there.

"Granny, my baby is going to hate me one day. I just know it. Leaving her like that was the hardest thing I have ever done in my life. I can still hear her screaming for me," she said, sobbing over the phone to her grandmother.

"God will work it out," Granny assured her.

Three broken ribs had brought her down there to see her baby. What horrible tragedy could God possibly bestow on her to take her back again? She did not like how God worked out problems, she thought, but Anna did not tell this to her grandmother because it would not be something she would be happy to hear. God fixed everything in Granny's life, and no matter how it was fixed; she accepted that that was how it should be fixed.

"Granny, you could not have told me that generations later I would be living your life all over again."

"I know how it feels hearin' yer baby screamin' for ya, Chile. Granny knows,"

"There I was down there telling you how you should have solved your problems fifty years ago, and now I'm having the same problem and don't have the slightest idea how to solve my own. My God, what a fix I'm in! I tell you, Granny, Raspy is going to hate me. It's no different from Momma hating you. I am living your life all over again, Granny—can you believe it?" By the time Dee came to the phone, Anna was crying so hard she had to hang up for her. Nothing was said about the conversation. She had not told Dee anything about Granny. Anna knew it was Frankie Lee Dee thought she was talking to. To tell her about Granny would mean she would have to tell her about Raspy, and she was not about to do that.

****

With two children underfoot all the time, Anna had a busy schedule all day, every day. After school there were lessons to help with and arguments to settle. Worst of all, the children had become lazy. Their grandmother had gone behind them cleaning their rooms and picking up after them. Unlike at her mother's home, their rooms at their parents home were upstairs, which meant Anna was up and down the stairs all day, picking up, washing, and cleaning with not relief since they could not return to their grandparent's home.

The living room and kitchen that had once been spotless was now left dirty after dinner every evening. After watching television or playing their games, Jake Jr. and Sheri' got up, leaving their books, games, and other debris for her to clean up.

"You kids are going to start doing some work around this house . . . cleaning your rooms first of all . . . and picking up in here after yourselves." Turning off the television, Anna listened to their groans.

"That's your job. Grandma does it and she is older than you. Anyways, she didn't send us over here to be worked to death," Sheri' said, pouting about the work she was asked to do.

"Yeah, you got us here to work us to death," Jake Jr. complained, his lips also stuck out.

"I'm calling Grandma to ask her to let us come back to live with her and Grandpa," Sheri' grumbled.

"Grandma and Grandpa have been taking care of us all the while you were gone. How can you tell us what to do . . . you don't seem like my Momma anyway," her son said, sounding angry and rebellious. Hearing her children's comments, Anna turned and picked up their dropped articles from the floor, saying not another word about their conduct.

It was not the children, but Anna, who went to ask her mother's advice, feeling her children, had defeated her.

"Anna, Chile . . . when will ya ever larn?" Annabelle said to her, as they took seats at the kitchen table with cups of tea in their hands. "I know ya said ya ain't go take no switch to yer chilens. One thang for sho', ya ain't never give me no back talk. Ya respected what I done tole ya and did what I tole ya to do like it or not."

"It's hard raisin' chilens in dese days and times," her mother complained gazing beyond Anna as though recalling some forgotten memory. "I know them babies lazy, but I'm so use to doin' for em it's hard to be bothered tellin' em what to do. But gal, ya can bet what I do tell em to do, thay do it and thay don't give me no back talk. Thay knows them switches I got in the shed and I won't hesitate to go git 'em. Them's my rods of correction. Ya been listening to them white devils tell ya whippin' is bad. When I was comin up, colored chilens didn't go to the white devil's jails. When thay got sassy and smellin' thayselves as my ole grandma use to say, thay was taken behind the shed and when thay come out, b'lieve me thay was corrected." Anna thought about all she was hearing. Her mother's sermon was interrupted when she got up to see about her food in the oven.

"I ain't taking em back, not less ya sick and can't care for em. Go in that shed and git some switches and beat thay asses 'fore they be beatin' yers like I guess Jake done started doing' causin' ya to run off the way ya done adder ya threw that hot grease on him. Ain't been long got outta the hospital fore he come adder ya. Ya two gonna kill the other yet."

****

Though Anna did as her mother suggested and took some switches home, she was determined she would find a better way of getting her children to do what she wanted them to do. Gifts and bribes worked only when she had something they wanted—but not all the time even then.

One Saturday afternoon after arriving home from grocery shopping, Anna asked her son to help get the groceries out of the car.

He insisted that he was tired and that she should get them herself. Anna looked at her son who sat slumped in a chair where he had been watching TV with Sheri' most of the day. She knew he would not have hesitated if it had been her parents or his father who had asked him to do what she had just asked him to do. Anna had to admit her children had no respect for her. As much as she hated to, Anna went outside, opened the trunk of her car, and pushed the cloth from the hidden switches. It occurred to her that it was not the switches that had marred her back but the cougar's claws. Coming back into the house, she found her son unmoved. Anna passed Sheri' coming into the house with her hands filled with switches, Sheri' jumped up and hurried out to the car. Before he could move, Anna grabbed the thin T shirt Jake Jr. was wearing and beat him anywhere the switches landed. She then took him outside by the ear and had to run to keep up with him. After the groceries had been brought in, she led Jake Jr. up to his dirty room.

"Boy," Anna said, staring hard at him, "if you don't have this room cleaned spotless in an hour, I'll be coming back up here and throw your little ass out of this window. Do you understand me?" she asked loud and with anger in her voice.

"Yes," he whispered between sobs. Turning to go find her daughter, Anna saw her already in her room cleaning it as fast as she possibly could.

"Please Momma, don't whip me!" she cried. "I'll do what you say. Jake Jr. is the one who said I didn't have to."

Anna picked up the phone later to call and tell her mother that her way worked only to find her children on the extension complaining to their grandmother about her. She listened to her mother say, "Ya chilen tell yer Momma she better use them rods of corrections on yer behinds ever day. When she run out, Grandma is go brang her some more. So maybe when ya git back hare, ya'll be able to help yer po old grandma and grandpa instead of workin' us to death."

Anna smiled as she eased the receiver back into its cradle. Now she knew her children truly belonged to her.

****

Several months after Anna's return, Dee called and asked if she would like to accompany her and Shirley to a movie. Anna agreed, thinking it would give her a freedom break from her daily housework. It occurred to her she needed a job. Next week she'd go looking.

Anna called Jake to tell him of her plans. He agreed to come home early to be with the children. When it came time for her to leave, he had not arrived. Anna instructed the children to lock the door and expect their father soon.

It turned out to be a nice movie without all the gore of killings and violence Anna had grown to hate. She returned home and was surprised to find the children still up. Jake had never made it home. The phone rang just as she got them off to bed. Anna looked at the clock. It was past eleven.

"Oh no!" Anna cried, listening to her mother over the phone. She had had to take Anna's father to the hospital. She was there waiting to hear what the doctors had to say. Anna hurried upstairs to tell the kids their grandfather was in the hospital and she was going to be with her mother. She wrote Jake a short note and left.

****

"What I'm gonna do if yur daddy passes? He's all I got cept ya and them chilen," Her mother cried as she grabbed and hugged Anna when she hurried into the waiting room. "I'm so glad Jake brung ya back"

"Momma, he's not going to pass."

"It's cancer eatin' away at him. Got him right adder ya left when ya and Barb got into dat fight a while back."

Anna's heart grew heavy. She found her father in so much pain that it frightened her. When he began to cough up blood, she knew it was serious. The doctors wore grave expressions on their faces as they took him up to surgery. Anna held her mother as they watched them wheel him away.

"Thay don't thank he'll come out alive," her mother cried.

"Why didn't you tell me Daddy was so sick Momma?" Anna asked, feeling her own tears escape.

"He didn't want ya to know . . . begged me not to tell ya."

Anna cursed herself. How many times had she reminded herself to ask her mother about her father's health? Every time she had looked at him, she had known something was wrong.

"You stay here in Daddy's room. I need to walk to the chapel Momma," Anna said to her mother. She left her in the room as she walked around the corner to the chapel and took a seat. Praying, she wept out of control, asking for the life of her father to be spared. In the midst of her prayer, the room turned orange then blue as everything around her began to spin. Anna opened her eyes to find herself in the rain forest where peace and harmony had always revived her. There they were—the thirteen eyes surrounding the Old Head in the blue magnetic field looking down at her.

"My Daughter, what burdens your heart?"

Anna's heart filled with joy at seeing the Old Head. She cried out in a hopeless plea, "Old Head now I realize why you didn't allow me to escape my husband. I would have discovered my father's illness too late, please help me help him!"

"How shall I help you, Daughter?" the Old Head asked as its eyes revolved around it hovering above Anna.

Anna closed her eyes and allowed her mind to take her to a time in her past. She was a little girl, standing with her father over his barbecue pit.

"Baby Girl, I can't understand no French. Who taught you to talk like that?" he asked, smiling over at her with his Lucky Strike hanging from his lips. Anna saw herself hunch her shoulders. She had just returned with her mother from Louisiana.

"Your Daddy needs you to talk like him so he can understand you." Anna saw herself looking up at her father. She wanted to speak as he asked, but only French words came out. Smelling the barbecue cooking she tried to tell him how good it smelled.

"Your Daddy can't teach you how to work this big old pit if you don't talk to him so's he can understand what you say." Anna looked up to see his big smile as he bent and kissed her dimpled cheek. She wanted so much to tell him how much she loved him but she knew he did not understand the words she spoke.

Late at night he was in her bedroom when the nightmares came, whispering that he was there to keep those bad dreams from bothering her. After taking her into his arms, he had told her nobody was going to hurt his Baby Girl. He said it so often, Anna began to repeat it. One night she answered, "Never, Daddy?" To his surprise, she spoke in the language she knew he understood.

"Never, Baby Girl—not ever again as long as your daddy lives." She smiled and began to speak to him in the language she knew he understood.

Now he lay on the operating table, possibly dying. "Old Head, you must take me back to the Healing Tree so that I can saturate my body with her tears. It is the only way I can save my father's life. I'll do anything—anything—you ask to make that happen!" Anna cried.

"The only way you can give your father the tears from the Healing Tree is if it enters his body from yours Daughter. What you did to retrieve my eye from the Young Chemist will not work on your earth world with any other human because their raveled minds will not receive it as the Young Chemist received it. As I explained to you the nine years my eye lived in his head it unraveled his brain. He is no longer a collective thinker unlike others of your earth world. You have given the young spider to your child so that she will be safe. The only thing you have left is the Healing Tree's life strength to combat all earth illnesses that you consumed from the cauldron when the Young Chemist became a normal man again. If you give it away, your body will be subject to sicknesses and suffering just as any other human making you helpless before your enemies, especially since the Old Widow's young now live in the palm of your young one down in the land of your ancestors."

"I don't care, Old Head! I want him to have it now. I will still have the power of endurance from the leaf I absorbed from the top of the Healing Tree. That means I can endure the worst and still survive. Anyway, wasn't it you who taught me that I have no enemies—simply lessons in life learned through traveling roads already predestined for this journey we are moving through together? Give him my life's strength and allow me to face life's lessons so that I learn to endure as the Healing Tree has endured for an eternity." Anna looked fearlessly into the eyes staring down at her. "Remember Old Head I must grow strong enough to confront many forces of evils when it is time to keep the promise you made before I was a thought on this earth world.

"Even so, my Daughter, his life won't last forever. All life on your earth world must end."

"Yes, Old Head, I am aware of that—but not now. Give my father all my life strength so that he will live the life he has left as a well man. If I must suffer, so be it. Do what you must, but please heal his body so that for as long as time will allow, he will live without pain or suffering, as you prepare me for that which I must face in order to keep the promise made when you journeyed to my world to find me." Anna beseeched the supernatural force guiding her life. The thirteen eyes moved toward her. Feeling light inside, Anna closed her eyes and felt an electrical shock move through her body. When she reopened her eyes she was back in the chapel. Leaving she hurried back to be by her mother's side.

When her father returned to his room, he exclaimed feeling no pain. The doctors looked mystified, stating that all his tumors were gone. What they had found formed the appearance of cobwebs. Her father, looked around the room at the doctors and Anna and her mother, wanting to know when he could go home.

Anna's mother grabbed her husband kissing him all over his face. Turning back to Anna, sobbing she kissed her while telling her God in his mercy had spared her father. Anna smiled, thinking about Granny and how she equated all blessings with God. Kissing her father, Anna left the hospital, grateful that he would live in good health for a time.

A puzzled expression appeared on Anna's face as she walked into her home at three in the morning after leaving the hospital. Jake stood there in the dark with his hand in his pocket.

"Well, at least the nigger let your ass come home before three days. I asked myself how long will the bitch be gone this time?"

"What are you talking about?"

"You think I believe that shit about you and Dee going to some movie? You used Dee's ass because she will lie for anything you pull, bitch!"

"You must be out of your mind to have come up with something that dirty! Didn't you read . . ." Anna never finished her sentence, finding herself falling between the coffee table and the sofa. The lick had come without warning.

"Goddamn you, bitch! I'll kill your ass! Do you understand me?" he screamed, grabbing her up by her hair and smacking her senseless. "And this time there won't be no grease you'll be throwing to fuck up my ass. I was in that hospital three damn long months in pain because of what you did to me, bitch. Your ass will pay—and I do mean pay—for that shit! Do you hear me?"

"Daddy, why are you hurting Momma?" Sheri' screamed from the top of the stairs. Both she and Jake Jr. stood there crying.

"Shut your damn mouths and get the hell back into your rooms before you get some of the same!"

"But Daddy!" Sheri' screamed.

"I said get back into those damn rooms before I come up there!" Anna heard the slam of doors. Looking up, she stared into eyes that had become wild. Jake pulled her up from the floor.

"You lousy whore you're cold as a freezer when I'm in you. I know you've been with the motherfucker. Think you are going to start your shit again, huh? You don't go no damn where until I take you or you are with my kids! If you do, I'll kill your goddamn ass! Do you understand that shit, you black-ass bitch?" Anna could not help but scream "yes" as she felt a handful of her hair being pulled from her head.

"You are just one step from the grave as it is, goddamn you! Do you understand me?" he shouted in a terrifying voice that filled the entire house.

"Yes!" she screamed again.

"If you decide to run again from here, you had better sure find the road to hell because I'm coming—and wherever I find you, it will be a dead ass you will have, whore!" Anna fell to the floor as he pushed her away from him. When he left the room, Anna felt the presence of her son and daughter approaching her.

"I hate him, I hate him!" Jake Jr. cried.

"So do I!" Sheri' cried as they sat on the floor in their mother's arms, sobbing.

****

"Sorry about last night. Your mother called and told me what happened, okay? This morning I found that note you left last night. Listen honey, I want you to take my beige suit in and have it cleaned." Anna said nothing.

"Did you hear me, Anna?" Jake pulled her swollen face around to face him. "I said I was sorry. What do you want me to do—kiss your ass?"

"Yes, Jake, I heard you," Anna answered, turning her back to him. He left early without his usual coffee.

"Momma, we would have cleaned up, but Daddy hollered and screamed at us and made us go upstairs," Sheri said as she touched the bruises on Anna's swollen face. "Daddy hurt you like this, Momma. He didn't let us tell him what happened to Grandpa. We saw the note you left."

"Don't worry, baby. You go get ready so that I can take you and your brother to the bus stop."

Anna sat in her car as she watched her children catch the bus to two different schools. Dark glasses covered the bruises on her face. In the quiet of the car, she felt the energy of the Old Head moving, and soon she was no longer in the car but seated on a cloud. The thirteen eyes hovered above. Seeing blue tears fall from their eyes into empty space, she felt her own tears fall as well.

"Let us take you away Daughter. The dangers that confront you are many. Your husband lives without reason as a man possessed. We will take you away from this earth world forever if you wish it to be."

"Where will I go, Old Head? Isn't this the journey you said I must embark upon so that the promise you made will be fulfilled? I cannot let you down now just because I must suffer to get us there. That is what I tried to do when I discovered I was pregnant and did not want my child I now love. The dawn awaits me. I want to run again, but you have allowed me to get to know my children as I have never before known them. It might be my last and only opportunity to spend time with my father and my mother, who both need me now more than ever. I must thank you for my father's recovery. When I leave again, it must be because my journey leads me away from here. Until then, I will endure for the sake of all that

405

must come to past to live through as much of this as I can, just as my ancestors endured, and, Old Head, just as the Healing Tree has suffered. Blue tears from the thirteen eyes poured down like rain. "Yes, I know her tears indicate her suffering. Why I don't know, but I am a part of this journey to end that suffering that is leading you and me somewhere. We must finish this journey so that one day her tears will no longer be tears of sorrow but tears of joy."

"Yes, it is as it is destined to be, Daughter. We will continue our journey to its end."

Anna opened her eyes to find herself back inside her car, her children already in school.

****

Like most children, Anna's children forgot what their father had done. When his birthday came around, they wanted to give him a party, something they had been unable to do at their grandparents' home. Their happiness in planning the celebration motivated Anna into making it something they would be proud of. Allowing them to buy a separate gift, she chose something of her own, hoping to salvage as much of the marriage as possible.

Invitations were sent out to all his brothers and their families. She begged him to come home early that evening so they could spend time together. He promised, stating that he would take her to a movie they both wanted to see. Everyone arrived, but Jake. The children looked at her with tears in their eyes. Anna decided to go find him. Passing his construction office, she saw that his car was still there. His phone service recorded him gone for the day. A smaller gray sports car also sat in front of his office. She figured he might still be in there, but business or no business she would have to try and get him home somehow.

Knocking on the door and getting no answer, Anna tried her keys until she found one that fit. The door opened. She called out to him. Jake rushed out of the back room. Anna noticed he was bare feet. Hurrying toward her, he buttoned up his shirt and said, "What the hell are you doing here?"

"You promised to be home early. Hearing noise coming from the other room, Anna gave Jake a strange look and started to walk past him. He caught her by the arm, pushing her against his desk.

"Are you here spying on me?" he asked, refusing to allow her to pass him. "Did Dee's ass tell you to come here? That damn bitch still telling lies on me to give you a reason to go see your nigger's ass again, huh!"

"I've caught you again, haven't I?" Anna fell against the door as his hand whipped across her mouth.

"Goddamn whore! What the hell are you trying to say—that we are both out here whoring?" Anna tasted blood and placed her hand over her swollen lip.

"I came here to find you because your kids are home with guests waiting to surprise you when you walk through the door . . . a birthday party for their daddy."

"Well, why the hell didn't you just say that?"

"I figured it might spoil the surprise, but I can see you are full of them as usual." Anna turned and walked out of the door, leaving him still straightening up his clothes. In her preoccupation with trying to gather her thoughts, Anna walked into a white woman hurrying to pass her. She was about to apologize for bumping into her when the woman backed away saying, "Please don't cut me as you did the other woman. I promise I won't see him again. I promise." Anna saw fear in her eyes as she continued to back away from her.

"Why would you think I would cut you . . ." Anna's mouth asked as she recognized Angela, Nathan's secretary.

"I was with Jake the night his brother came and told him you had cut some woman and they didn't know whether she was dead or alive. I promise I won't see him again. I don't want to be harmed like that." Anna looked to see the tight grip she had on her unbuttoned blouse.

"So it was you struggling to get away moments ago?"

"I . . ." she replied, not getting her words out before Anna interrupted her.

"It was you who arranged our seating on New Year's Day?"

"Yes, of course. I wanted to be . . ." Again, Anna interrupted her.

"You wanted to be near him. I saw you kneeling before him giving him oral sex."

"That night, yes . . . you must know, I love him," Angela answered, turning as she hurried to her car. Anna almost laughed at the irony of it.

Entering her home the back way, Anna took out the new seven-hundred-dollar watch she had bought for Jake's birthday, laid it on the floor, and stomped on the watch until it was in a million pieces. Wrapping it in a towel, she threw it in the trash, cursing the name of Jake Bradley before God in heaven.

Still in the bedroom, Anna listened to everyone cheering for Jake when he made his appearance. The entire yard was filled with friends, most of whom had invited themselves and brought food, drinks, and gifts. Anna had sent out twenty invitations. A hundred or more people stood inside the house and around the yard. All the laughter and happiness caused Anna to feel sick; she no longer felt like participating. She was no longer in a partying mood.

Finding her in their bedroom, Jake took a seat next to Anna on the bed. Using a handkerchief he took from his pocket, he wiped the blood from her mouth.

"I'm going to make this up to you . . . I don't know what's wrong with me these days. Come on out to the party; everyone is asking for you," Jake insisted, trying to coax Anna into a better mood.

"That's funny . . . with you here, I'm surprised they missed me at all," Anna said, not wanting to go out to join the party.

Pulling her up by her arm, Jake said, "Come on now—the kids will be in here looking for you."

Before the words were out of his mouth good, Sheri' rushed in all excited. Stopping, she looked from her mother to her father and asked, "What the matter, Momma?"

Jake's arms went around Anna, and he kissed her lips, saying to his daughter, "Nothing, princess. Your mother and I were playing a game."

"But her lip is swollen. How did that happen?" Sheri' asked, touching where Jake had struck her mother.

"I bit her, but it was all in fun—wasn't it, baby?"

"I'm fine. Let's go out to the party before everyone thinks we have deserted it." A smile spread across Anna's face as she looked at her daughter. Sheri' then smiled and caught her mother's hand, pulling her out of the room with her.

Anna waved to Dee and Fred who were out on the floor dancing. She knew if Jake had had his way, Dee would never have been invited, but he would never she knew embarrass his children at a party they had given for him. Anna then spotted her father tending the barbecue; her heart lifted somewhat as she walked over to him. Her mother had not come. Anna had been forced to admit to her mother that James would be there with Tammy and that there would be other whites at the party. Her mother tore up the invitation refused to come, saying it was a disgrace the way the black men had fallen to the evils of those white female devils.

"Daddy, you look the picture of good health. How do you feel?" Anna asked, beaming at how well he looked.

"I feel like I'm seventeen again," he responded with a big smile on his face. "What's the matter, Baby Girl? My little girl don't look like she has stepped out of Ebony Magazine any longer." Anna forced a smile for her father's sake.

Touching the hand that touched her swollen lip, she said, "Daddy, I'm fine. A housewife can't look like a movie star, not with all the housework she has to do." His hand tightened around hers. Her eyes on her father, Anna's heart filled with compassion. Happy that he was well again, she now understood the meaning of true love. At that moment, she wanted to fall into his arms and cry a river of tears, but she knew it would hurt his heart if he knew of her situation, and she couldn't cause him to have to return to prison because of her life with Jake. Her father had gone through too much already. No, she could ill afford the risk of his spending the rest of his life in prison for killing her husband. Jake was not worth it. Her father looked so good that she didn't care what she had to give up."

"Daddy, are you taking care of yourself? Both Momma and I have asked you to give up those awful cigarettes," Anna said, looking up at her father as he turned a piece of meat over on the pit.

"Sho', Baby Girl, just getting old that's all. After experiencing all that pain, I feel better than I have felt in years somehow," he said, smiling down at her.

Anna thought about how Jake had accused her father of allowing her mother to rule his life. Said it showed a sign of weakness and lack of masculine strength. She knew her father was a husband like she wished Jake had been. He always showed love for her mother but never the possessive, threatening kind. Her mother was more like Jake, Anna thought, in that she had always demanded strict obedience with little compassion for human weaknesses except her own. Jake had insisted there was a weakness about her father that allowed her mother to boss him as if he weren't there until she called for him.

"You think your Daddy's old and foolish, huh?" he asked. "Just looking at Sheri' makes me think back to when you were nothing but legs and mouth. Asked more questions than a body could answer," her father said as they both stood staring at Sheri' talking to friends she had invited.

"Oh Daddy, you and I are a lot alike. Momma always said we were."

Her father's hand again moved up to touch the swollen place on Anna's lip. "Your Momma—I never laid a hand on her. We never slept apart one night in the thirty-eight years we been married, except the time I had to . . ." His voice trailed off. "I plan to have a talk with Jake about you, Baby Girl. I might have to kill him yet for hurting you. Never thought I'd see the day I'd rather see you with Mr. Forlorn than with Jake, but I believe it has come to that."

"Oh Daddy, you don't know what you are saying. Jake and I are doing great, really. I don't want you thinking about killing anyone. There is no reason for you to have a talk with Jake about me. Whatever people are saying is just not true. You keep on taking care of your health and showing our dimples if you want to make me happy, Daddy." Anna was shocked by her father's admission to preference when it came to the white man she had been with over Jake who he had once adored.

"From the looks of your mouth, not by what you say, I know how great you are doing. Baby Girl, I see a lot of things you don't think I see. Too many people come into the restaurant for me not to know something ain't right. I also know what people think about your mother and me." His eyes wandered off. "She's a good woman deep down within. Seeing the daddy she loved hung like he was by white men and her mother carried off—and the things she has done because of that tragedy ate away in her so long she can't help the way she is."

Anna envisioned her mother's mother a woman who at that very moment was caring for the half-white child her own mother would have spit on. A lump settled in her throat as her body trembled. "Yes, Daddy," she said, "I understand."

"Baby Girl, I'm taking your mother on a trip to New York City. Since I made that trip there to see about you, I've wanted to go again. I got the hotel stay taken care of and the time I need off is no problem."

"Momma agreed to go with you? I'm shocked."

"Since I almost died, she realizes we need to spend more time together. Who knows, we might even leave there and go see my people in Ohio," he said, smiling.

"Good, Daddy! Never put off what you want to do but feel you'll have another time to do it. I have the kids now, so there is no reason you can't make that happen."

Jake Jr. and a young girl danced as the crowd cheered them on. Anna looked around to see all the children and young adults surrounding the couple. She noticed some trying to get Jake on the floor. Laughing, he politely refused.

"Anna, I got money . . ." Anna turned back to face her father. "I've been saving it for your Momma to take a trip back home if she's a mind to go. She told me she ain't got nothing there but her brother and his boy, and she just don't want to go back down there with so many bad memories."

"Daddy . . ."

"Don't "Daddy" your old man—just take the money. It's always been for you and the kids anyway since your momma said she ain't never going south again. I want to see you looking like you did when you ran into my arms that day in New York City. When my eyes landed on you, it was one of the happiest days of my life, all thanks to Mr. Forlorn, of course. Daddy don't want to see no more killing like I been seeing happening since the shelter closed. There are too many of our women killed by our men. And you scalding Jake with that grease—it ain't good, Baby Girl."

"Daddy, nothing like that will happen to me. I don't want you worrying now."

"When I look in your face and see it all puffed up and swollen, I can't be happy. In God's eyes, you belong to your husband, and it would be a sin to cause trouble in a home God put together. But you just tell your Daddy when you've had enough of being hurt, and I'll take care of the rest. That Negro will find himself six feet under." Feeling her tears about to slip from her eyes, Anna turned her head, hoping no one would see them. Soon, she felt her father's handkerchief being placed in her hand.

"Daddy, I will leave for sure before it comes to that. I promise. Anyway wasn't it you who told me a thinking man will outsmart an angry man any day of the week?" For the first time, she saw a smile light on her father's face as he turned a slab of barbecued ribs over.

With so many guests there, Anna had not gotten a chance to see Tammy or her baby. Somehow they bumped into each other in the crowd. Lifting the toddler from her arms, Anna smiled and kissed his cheek. He looked with suspicion at his new handler. Anna saw his black heritage through his dark color. She thought of Raspy. Her baby daughter's gray eyes seemed to penetrate hers just like her father's. She even switched spoons in the middle of eating like her father, had that little black mole under her butt like him. His DNA was wrapped all over her. Why couldn't she have given her daughter anything to acknowledge her blackness? Anna looked at all the black people laughing and acting happy around her, she shuddered to think what they would say of her if they knew her closet secret.

The child in hiding was a bastard . . . something she knew would never change. No half-white baby would ever infiltrate the Forlorn/Vanderlin dynasty . . . not ever. Tears spilled from her eyes thinking of it.

"What happened to the happiness I saw in the picture so long ago?" Tammy asked. Anna heard the sadness in her voice.

"There is nothing left of her, Tammy . . . not anymore," Anna said, handing the baby back to her.

******

Anna Drake Bradley's life drifted along. The children were happy, it seemed.

With her parents gone on their vacation, Anna and Jake had them all to themselves. Resolving never to regret what her father's life had cost her, she was happy about the return of his good health. Since the party, Jake had been civil, but their relationship remained shaky because as he stated she had become a freezer in bed. It seemed that every day he had a word to say about waiting to kill her nigger's ass. She simply shook her head saying nothing. School was now out, Sheri' and Jake Jr. sat at the dining room table at breakfast, discussing their upcoming camping trip.

"Jake Jr., don't let me forget to pack the medicine for your allergies."

"I won't, Momma. Now I can go hiking and everything."

"We're going to learn how to build a fire without matches . . . whata you think of that?" Sheri' asked, grinning as she took in a spoonful of her cereal.

"What are you going to do while the children are away?" Jake asked Anna, sipping from his coffee.

"I'll find something to do. Probably take a trip for a week or so," Anna said, thinking about how she wanted to go back to Oinston to rekindle her broken relationship with Raspy.

"We'll be gone the whole summer," Jake Jr. said, turning to Anna. "Momma, take a long trip. Go where you can have some fun and be happy!"

"Your mother is not taking a trip no damn where and neither are you two!" Jake screamed, rising from the table. We just got these kids back with us and you want to let them go away for the entire summer? Bullshit!"

"Daddy, we take this trip every year," Sheri' insisted.

"Good. If you've been going every year, it's time you spent one summer at home keeping your mother company. You may be saving her life. As for you, you've had enough damned trips . . . having me following behind your ass like some puppy dog when you fail to return. We don't want your whoring to start again, now do we?" Jake shouted, staring down at her.

"Jake, how can you say something that filthy—especially in front of our children?" Anna asked, rising from the table.

"I'm the rooster running this henhouse, in case you have forgotten, and as long as I'm running it, I'll say whatever the hell I damn well please. I don't intend for your whoring ass to start again . . . from now on, I'll be the only one allowed that privilege," he said, taking a drink of his coffee.

"I can never remember the time you didn't have it."

"You got a goddamn big-ass mouth. The blow numbed her jaw. Sheri' and Jake Jr. jumped up from the table and ran in front of their mother.

"Daddy, don't! I don't want to go to camp! I don't want to go anywhere—just leave our mother alone!" Jake Jr. cried, pushing Anna out of Jake's reach.

"Good, that ends that conversation," he said as he grabbed his coat and walked out of the house, slamming the door behind him.

The kids never talked about their camping trip again. Too many nights, Anna heard their screams when arguments between her and Jake became heated enough to turn physical. No longer was she Anna but every bitch, slut, whore, and fool—Jake called her whatever he felt would cause her the most humiliation. Any movement of his hand in Anna's direction caused her to duck, moving quickly out of his reach.

Anna, at last, admitted to herself that her life with Jake had become a living hell. Without her powers from the Old Head and the young spider no longer in her palm, she was now a victim. At last she was walking in the shoes of the battered women in the shelter she had run—women whose lives she had not understood until her feet began to feel the pain of their shoes. Yet no price was too steep to save her father's life, even if only for a little while.

Chapter Twenty-Nine

———ͽͽͽ———

Anna enjoyed the full time job of mothering her children. With all the added responsibility, she still loved having them underfoot asking for this and that, keeping her busy. As soon as they got up in the morning, it was "what are we going to do today Momma?" The park and the zoo had become something they only wanted to do once in a while. Sometimes, she would just sit and listen to them talk about themselves and what they wanted to become.

Sheri' always wanted to learn how her grandpa made his barbecue so delicious. She told Anna he had promised to turn the business over to her as soon as she was old enough to run it. Jake Jr. wanted to be a scientist. His head was always in a book. He loved any topic that had to do with discovery. He sure had a lot of her in him, although Anna had to make sure he did not bring any of his dissected creatures into the house. He and his father had nearly come to blows when Jake Jr. had dissected a snake and Jake had discovered it in the bathroom. They soon found out his fear of snakes as he screamed bloody murder for whoever had it placed it there.

One evening while watching television, Anna and the children saw a show with scenes of white children waterskiing,

"If that sport wasn't just for white people, I bet I could learn to do that," Jake Jr. said as both he and Sheri' laughed when the white children lost their balance and fell into the water.

"I could do it, too! But you never see black people doing anything that dumb. Standing on two boards being pulled through the water—what black person would do a thing that silly?" Sheri' asked as she threw up both her hands.

"It's a great way to have fun," Anna told them, laughing.

Anna knew her children had never learned the sport simply because they didn't live close enough to water to have the opportunity to learn water skiing. Of course, her mother was not going to take them. As for her father, he was always busy at his restaurant. By the time he got home, it was way too late to take them an hour's drive down to the lake so they could learn to ski. Jake she knew thought the same as his kids thought about skiing.

"I guess your mother must be dumb because she has done it lots of times, and believe me, it is fun!"

"You, Momma?" Both children looked at her in surprise.

"Who taught you, Momma?" Jake Jr. asked. "I don't know any black people who know how."

"I bet it was her guardian angel, huh Momma?" Anna looked at Sheri' in a way that made her cover her mouth. "I mean, was it fun to learn, Momma?"

"Well, do you want to learn or not? If so, I'll get someone to teach you, but you can't mention it to your father. I don't want any trouble out of him."

"Yes, we know, Momma . . . we won't breathe a word of it to Daddy." They swore complete secrecy.

Anna decided to take them to the beach the first thing the next morning right after Jake went to work. They could swim and ski for a couple of hours and then return home before he came home from work. Filling her crock pot full of meat and vegetables she reasoned that as long as she had their children, Jake would not mind where she went as long as they all returned at a reasonable time, which meant before he came home and found them not there—and started asking questions.

****

The boat owner she located was a young white man named Gregg. He suggested that since Anna knew how to ski, she should go first to show her children how it was done. Anna fell a couple of times, causing Jake Jr. and Sheri' to fall over laughing in the sand. After awhile, however, she could hear Ray's voice, and she felt their arms locked together going fast through the water. When she hit the water, she remembered how he had helped her up, telling her what she had done wrong. That, of course, had been between kisses because her Ray had been a kissing man, and he had found her lips no matter where they were.

Going out on the water with each child, she taught them how to hold the rope and to keep their legs straight. They had the time of their lives falling and getting back up, but after awhile they got the hang of it and realized it was a sport for anyone willing to learn it. The boat owner agreed to meet them there the next day if she would bring them back and allow him to ski with the children. Skiing was something he enjoyed also he shared.

"Who will drive the boat?" she asked.

"If you can drive a car, it may take some time to adjust yourself to steering a boat, but it's no different. The important thing to remember," he told her "is to stay clear of other boats in heavy traffic going fast through the water."

"Please, Momma!" both children begged. "Let us come back; otherwise, we'll have to sit at home all summer long watching television."

"Oh, all right! But you better be good and get all your chores done tonight," Anna told them, glad they had enjoyed themselves so much.

For the next two weeks, Anna watched her children learn to enjoy the sport they once thought could only be enjoyed by white children.

After a few weeks of skiing, Gregg asked Jake Jr. if he wanted to drive the boat. Jake Jr. looked at his mother. Anna saw the big smile on his face at having been asked something she knew he wanted to do.

"I guess it'll be all right, but don't you kill us, boy," Anna said, seeing him glow with expectation. Sheri' looked at her brother and smiled.

"Jake Jr., Momma is right. You better not kill us. We don't want Daddy to find us out here in this water drowned—you hear me?" Jake Jr. did not answer as he took over the boat. Anna knew her son's excitement over learning how to drive the boat exceeded that of learning to waterski.

On the way home that evening, Sheri' fell asleep in the back seat almost as soon as Anna drove off. Jake Jr. sat in the front seat. It was his turn because Sheri' had ridden in the front coming up. Anna felt him move closer to her and thought he might soon fall asleep, too.

"Momma," he said, looking up at Anna.

"What, Jake Jr.?" she answered, smoothing his curls back on his head.

"Is it all right to like them?"

"I don't know who the "them" Who are you are speaking of, honey. You must be specific if you want correct answers to your questions."

"You know—white people. Grandma says they are all devils. Gregg doesn't look like a devil, but . . ." His voice trailed off.

"Jake Jr., you can't live your life hating people because they don't look or do things like you. Do you like Gregg?" Anna asked her son.

"I want to like him, but I get to thinking about what Grandma has taught us and the things she tells me and Sheri' about them, and then I don't want to like him. Who wants to be near people with devils and demons in them?"

"Did there seem to be any devils or demons in Gregg when he was teaching you how to drive his boat? He taught you something you wanted to learn. Am I right?"

"No, not at all. You are right. I had so much fun," Jake Jr. answered, smiling up at his mother.

"Has he said or done anything to make you want to hate him?"

"No, but . . ."

Anna interrupted him. "Your father and grandfather talk to and entertain white people all the time. They know that whites are people just like us. Their color is different, but believe me, just like some of us treat you good and love you, some of them act the same way. And just like some of us act like devils and demons and are not so nice, some of them act that way."

"Grandma wouldn't come to Daddy's birthday party because she said that too many devils would be there. Why is it devils and demons live only in white people, Momma?"

"Jake Jr., didn't you just hear me say devils and demons can live in anyone? As a child, your grandmother had a horrible experience involving white people that caused the death of her father and grandfather and the loss of her mother. She has never been able to get over the pain of that hurt. What they did was horrible! You recall her telling you and Sheri' about those deaths and how her mother was taken away?"

"Yes, Momma. She told us that every day before sending us off to school." Anna remembered her school days and how her mother had taught her in the same way. "How did you get over hating white people like Daddy said you once did?"

"Oh, I met a very nice person somewhat like Gregg. I was helped by that person when I desperately needed help. After that, I learned to look beneath the skin color to see the character of the person." Anna leaned over to kiss the top of Jake Jr.'s head.

"Momma, I do like Gregg. He is a nice man. I guess I wanted to make sure it was all right for me to like him," Jake Jr. clarified.

"Jake Jr., you do understand you cannot tell your grandmother about Gregg or any other white person you might meet and like. She will not be happy at all."

"I know, Momma." Soon Anna heard the deep breathing of her son and realized that he had fallen asleep.

Every other day, her kids begged Anna to take them to the beach to either ski or swim and pack a lunch to picnic. Although they were too young to help with the driving, Anna did not mind. As soon as they saw Gregg, they raced toward his boat. When Anna entered the boat, Sheri' threw a towel over Anna's bruised legs.

After awhile, the sun got so hot it caused her to perspire. Anna took off her glasses to wipe her face. The black and blue bruise under her eye still hurt when she touched it. Quickly, she replaced the glasses. The children skied awhile, and then Gregg stopped at a quiet place so that they could swim and play in the water. Anna sat watching her children, thinking that at least she was forming a closer relationship with them by shared this time with them letting them get to know her. She looked happily out at them swimming in the water.

"Anna, you've got big problems at home, haven't you?" Gregg asked, looking over at her.

"I don't know what you are talking about," Anna answered, pushing her glasses securely over her eyes.

"This isn't the first time I've seen you come down here all bruised up. You're a nice-looking woman, but when whoever is physically abusing you finishes with you, you won't look like a hill of beans." Tears fell from behind the glasses Anna wore. She felt the towel being pulled away from her legs, exposing the large ugly bruises on her thighs.

Anna could not help but think back to how they had gotten there. It had rained a few days before and she had been standing out in it after going shopping, angry with herself for having locked her keys in her car. A friend of Jake's that they both knew well had given her a lift home to get her extra set. She hadn't thought to mention their friend's helping her to Jake.

The next day, Jake had come home and played with the kids awhile, asking them where they had been the day before. They had innocently informed him that they had stayed home while their mother went shopping. Anna hadn't given his question much thought at the time and told him how she had locked her keys in her car and the help she had received.

"Hey baby," Jake had said, a smile on his face. "Let's go for a ride."

"I promised to cook pizza for the kids, Jake."

"I'll buy the pizza; that way you won't have to slave over that hot-ass stove."

The kids had been excited to go to the pizza house where huge pizzas were cooked. They got two large pizzas and the two children began to eat theirs as soon as they got into the car. Anna wondered why Jake had stopped in front of someone's house she did not know. She had wanted to get home so she could eat her pizza before it got cold.

"Get out a minute, baby. I have someone I want you to meet," Jake had said after coming around to open the door for her. She hadn't wanted to meet anyone, but she knew he would insist.

Jake knock on the door they walked up to. Anna recognized the woman who greeted them as the wife of the man who had given her a lift home to get her spare keys the day it was raining. She spoke cordially to her. Jake asked if her husband was home. The woman indicated that he was and went to get him. The man appeared at the door with no shirt on and his midriff hanging below his belt. He was not quite as old as her father but she knew he was close to that age. Running his hand over his thinning hair, he then scratched at the beginnings of a beard growing on his face. Anna could tell he had been eating because he was still chewing.

"Hey man, what's up? Come on in—you know you are always welcome here," the man had said, extending his hand outward.

"Nah, Al. I've just come to straighten out a little matter about you and my wife here." The man looked at him as he slowly stopped chewing, a puzzled expression on his face. Anna stood there in shock, not knowing what to think or say. The man had looked from Anna to his wife a big brown skinned woman who stood in the doorway beside her husband with her head wrapped. A look of concern suddenly covered her face.

"Have I ever picked you up and taken you anywhere?" Jake had asked the man's heavy-hipped wife who had a puzzled look on her face.

"Nah, you ain't never took me nowhere, Jake."

"I don't allow no man to take my wife no damn where! If I catch her in a car with any other man besides me or her father, I'm killing his ass and hers," Jake had said, staring at the man.

"Man, I was just helping her out 'cause she was standing out in the rain soaking wet. I call myself doing you a favor. I swear I never laid a hand on her. She can tell you Jake."

"Look, man, I'm not going to take your woman no damn where and I'd appreciate it—even if you see mine standing out in the middle of a tornado—if I'm not around to help her, you just let the son of a bitch take her ass away. You got that shit?" Anna watched a frown solidify on Jake's face.

"I sho' nuff do. If a herd of stampeding bulls come straight for her and it takes these hands to pull her out the way," Al had said, holding out his hands after scratching his naked belly, "she sho' nuff will be a goner for sho'. You can count on that Jake man."

"I'll thank you for that." Anna then remember to farther her humiliation, Jake had grabbed her by her arm, pulling her away from the house and back to the car.

She had been sobbing so hard by the time she got back into the car that she didn't even remember that her children were inside.

"You're out whoring with my goddamn friends now that you can't get that nigger's ass you really want. Must be some kinda fool thinking I'm not wise to your shit, whoring bitch." The back of his hand had sounded against Anna's face, causing her head to hit the headrest as blood poured from her mouth and nose.

"I can't even get a kiss and your ass is as cold as a goddamned ice box when I got you home in bed, but you're good for every other motherfucker in the streets." Anna listened to his abusive language, realizing he did not care that their children were listening.

She had reached for the door to try and make an escape. He quickly grabbed a fist full of her thigh, pulling her back into the car and repeatedly slapping her until Jake Jr. and Sheri' had screamed for him to let their mother alone, throwing their uneaten pizzas out the window as they grabbed his hands.

"You two had better sit back in that seat or I'll be on your asses, too!"

Anna had then realized the danger her children were in and begged Jake not to hurt them. Her fear had increased as she saw his body tremble as he took tighter hold of her already badly bruised thigh.

"If you have to go to the shit house, Sheri' better be in there with you. And you better not leave home without both kids. Woman . . . you keep this shit up, you're going to find yourself an early grave! Do you understand me?"

"Yes!" Anna had screamed back at him.

Now crying shamelessly in front of Gregg, Anna knew she hated and feared Jake Bradley more than anyone else on this earth. No longer having the strength to fight him, she would have to think of some other way of getting him out of her life.

She could have run again, knowing he would not be able to find his way to Granny's house, but Jake had promised to kill Dee for telling on him if Anna ruined their marriage by leaving him. And just as with Raspy, learning to be a parent to her twins instilled her with a feeling she could not explain. When they embraced her, telling her how much they loved her and never wanted her to leave them, Anna hoped for better days so she would not have to leave them ever again. They wanted her to go back to her parents' home, but Anna knew it would do no good. Jake would give her no peace as long as she lived in Session. Now she realized there was nothing left for her to do but figure out a plan of escape, with or without her children. Anna knew she would soon have to run again from the man who had become this horrible stranger she did not know at all. She knew all his threats were meant to scare her but she feared his henchman Jay Man knowing he would kill with pleasure.

The next evening when Jake came home, nothing pleased him. Jumping up from the table, he screamed, "Why don't you go buy a cook book? Everything you cook tastes like shit. You're the damndest fool . . . always have been. It makes me sick looking at you." He moved toward Anna, causing her and the children to jump. "I ain't on your ass yet, bitch . . . when I am; jumping won't help you now sit the hell down!" He returned to his seat at the table as they eased into theirs.

"Daddy, you are always bragging about Momma's cooking" Jake Jr. said, interrupting the argument his father had started.

"She can't cook shit." Jake said staring at his son.

"Jake Jr. as long as you and Sheri' like my cooking that is all that matters to me." Anna realized from the frozen look on Jake's face that she should not have said anything

"What the hell do you mean as long as they like the shit?" he asked, placing his fork down pushing his plate filled with food on the floor.

"I'm sorry. I didn't mean to contradict you," Anna answered, turning away.

"Nah, you ain't sorry. You think you're a damn smart-ass bitch. If you don't shut your damn mouth, I'll be on your ass with both feet! Now get that goddamn shit up off the floor." Anna watched her children hurry to pick up the spilled food.

****

The doorbell rang just after Anna closed the door behind her to Sheri's bedroom where she had been staying for over a week refusing to sleep with Jake. She held her breath, hoping he would answer it so she would not have to go downstairs and face him.

"Woman, get your ass down these stairs and answer the damn doorbell," Jake screamed. Jake Jr. and Sheri' had been allowed to spend the weekend with their grandparents who had returned from their trip, but they had been threatened a severe beating if they breathed a word of what went on inside of their home.

Anna made her way down the steps. Opening the door, she found James standing in the doorway a look of shock suddenly appeared on his face.

"How are you, Anna?" he asked, taking her in his arms and hugging her.

"Jake, James is here to see you." Looking away from James with her head lowered, Anna walked back up the stairs without answering his question. Halfway up the stairs, Anna stopped and took a seat on one of the steps.

"Hey, man—what's to it?" she heard her brother-in-law say.

"It's been heavy on my ass man . . . HEAVY!" Jake said in a loud voice. "How's Tammy and the baby?"

"Fine man—I couldn't have a better woman. No shit, she reminds me of Anna when you guys first married . . . that eighty-percent woman Dad used to tell us about. You know how I always said Anna was a lot like our mother was." There was silence for about three minutes. Anna became worried, and then finally heard James's voice again. "Al, the dude you cursed out about giving Anna a lift home—he and I had a little talk, man. You know damn well you ain't jealous of that old dude. What the hell were you trying to prove going up to his house—embarrassing the man in front of his wife? It made no sense at all."

"Nigger please! He better hope I don't have to front his ass again."

"Anna looks like hell, Jake. You should be ashamed of yourself. Fred told us how you have been beating up on her. And worse—our brother told my ass that you have been having that ugly-ass Jay Man follow Anna around no wonder she tried to leave your ass.

"Had it not been for Jay Man watching the house at night and alerting me her ass was trying to leave, she would have been gone. He helped me drag her ass back inside suitcase and all."

Fred said if that nigger looks like he wants to come anywhere near Dee, he would kill his ass without a thought. The nigger is crazy, and I sho' nuff wouldn't have the motherfucker near my wife, especially and she don't even know he is following her."

"Fuck Fred and that lying wife of his, man. He don't know shit. Jay Man is my nigger. I can always depend on him to take care of my shit. Now that Anna knows that he is watching her I won't have to worry about her trying to leave my ass again." Anna listened to him say. "Jay Man don't be trying to second guess my ass like you and Fred's asses do. I can get him to do anything for me, man. Blew that house Anna wouldn't go back to sky high—didn't leave a trace back to him or me. The insurance company paid off right on schedule. You and Fred are just jealous because you ain't got it like that. He's my nigger. So what if he is a little off? Don't come in here sweatin' me about Jay Man 'cause he ain't going nowhere unless I catch him dirty. I got him following my woman, not yours or Fred's."

"One day," Anna listened James say, "that crazy motherfucker is going to meet up with a motherfucker crazier than he is. It's gonna be his undoing. I remember that night down at the river. I think he was thoroughly disappointed he couldn't kill that nigger's ass who was begging for his life. If it wasn't for Anna telling you the only way she would take your ass back was if you didn't kill him, that fool would have taken the gun from you and shot him himself." Anna knew he spoke the truth.

"Anyway," she listened to James say. "I didn't come over here to discuss your henchman. It's your marriage I'm worried about. I lost my first wife and kids 'cause I thought nobody mattered but me and what I wanted. When she left my ass, I felt like shit. You don't want that—I'm telling you. I am your brother, and I wouldn't lie to you. It makes no sense, Jake. Isn't that the same advice you gave me? I cannot believe you're that jealous of some old-ass man. Come on now . . . as many women as you have been into . . . you're gonna lose your wife. I know you love her as much shit as you put us through trying to help you get her back when she didn't even want your ass. If you don't stop this madness, man, she's gonna be gone again and you gonna be feeling just like you were when she left you the first time."

"I've already lost her . . . ain't never really had her since she caught me dirty and skipped town with that nigger. She came back changed, man . . . I ain't lying. You know how Anna used to be? Hell, the woman was afraid of her own shadow. I was scared to death when they found her car—knew she had been killed or hurt—figured she was somewhere terrified if she was still alive as scared as she was of white people and strangers.

"It wasn't until I met up with Angela that I thought about letting her go even if she came back. We had been into each other about two years. It's just that I had too much to lose here in Session to let it be known I was with a white woman. Can you imagine how Anna's mother would have dealt with that shit?"

"You know I know, she doesn't even speak to me since Tammy and I have been together." Listening Anna remembered her mother telling her as much.

That's why I kept Angela away from Session and our relationship out of the public eye. I know how dangerous her mother's month can be."

"You should have dropped Anna as soon as you discovered she didn't want your ass no more and got into Angela deep man."

"Anna came back here with furs wrapped around her ass, looking at me like I was shit she wouldn't spit on. Wearing what I first thought was fake jewelry and rabbit fur. Jay Man happened to be in the car one day and saw a bracelet she had left inside. Come telling me it looked like real diamonds. I told him it was nothing but fake shit. He asked if he could take it and have his dealer case it. I laughed at him and said okay. When he came back, he told me how it was worth twenty big ones on the street. I went and got the rest of her shit and had it appraised."

Anna sucked in her breath, listening for his next words.

"The shit was worth a quarter of a million dollars plus. I almost dropped my ass on the floor!"

"Damn! Did you ask her about that shit, Jake? That sounds like white man's money to me man."

"Hey, dig this—when I told her I wanted to give that fake shit away and get her some real jewelry, she looked at me and said 'fine, as long as you don't take this.' Man, she was holding onto that cheap-ass chain her father had given her. I looked at her and shook my head. Nah it can't be white man's money, Anna would lie up under a dead black dog's ass before she'd let a white motherfucker touch her. I figure it must be some black entertainer who got ahold of some bread and wanted to impress her. Anna ain't got her mind on nothing but getting back to that nigger she's been with."

Listening to their conversation, Anna sucked in her breath, not wanting to think about what he would do if he really knew who had impressed her.

"Every time I'm with her now, I get that same feeling I got when I first tried to come on to her and she told me she was already in a relationship. I asked her who the nigger was. She looked at me in a way that made me feel like dirt, telling me if I was the kind of man who thought of his race of men as niggers, I was not the man she wanted to wrap her arms around. Had the nerve to tell me she didn't date niggers, nor did she want to know one and that it was now okay for men of my race to call themselves men instand of niggers. That white men wasn't allowed to hang men like they did niggers. It took about a month before I got up enough courage to ask her out again. That time I asked who the gentleman was she was seeing.

"Anyway . . . somehow, wherever the hell she went, she got hooked up with some strong nigger's ass. The motherfucker completely changed my woman. Got her mind all fucked up—she's got this thang for the motherfucker and all she can think about is him."

"Man, it looked like you two were doing fine after you scared her into taking you back. But then she did tell you her nigger was fearless and would kill for her. That's a strong nigger's ass sounds like to me man."

426

"You right man that motherfucking nigger has always been on her mind," Anna heard a loud bang that caused her to jump and move up a step. She wished she could go down and tell her side of it, but she knew that would be sheer suicide.

"You remember when all that shit went down between her and Barb?"

"How could I forget it?"

"I know in my heart she was with him all that time, even though she swore she wasn't. He has been here since her return . . . I know that. That motherfucker has a serious itch, coming to my town serenading my wife. She left me for three days because of some shit Dee told her ass. He sent her ass back to me in the same dress she had on when I took her to the track on New Year's

"If he's that strong, he has already taken her, man. Whoa, you ain't got a pray and no play—it's just a body you're keeping. Until he is dead, she belongs to him."

The quiet scared Anna. She knew when James left she would have to fight again with the state Jake was in.

"I went out," Jake stated his voice low but even, "and bought this thirty-eight a couple of days ago. 'cause it occurred to me, like you said, until I kill that motherfucker—wherever the hell his ass is—things will never be the same between my woman and me. Even when things were supposed to be good between us in bed, I could feel she wanted something I was not giving her . . . fire she got from him and still wanted. Now, she just lays like a board and won't move." Anna heard James's laughter.

"Man, it's that way in some brothers' culture—that's what they expect their women to do." She heard James tell him.

"You gotta be kidding me, man. Those poor brothers are missing what the good Lord meant for a man to let his woman enjoy. What could be better that hearing your woman's body sings to you? I have walked upon women and the way they looked at me I knew they knew I was the man to make their bodies sing my song. If you put it to them right you can hear that music in the sound of their voice."

"You got that right, man! Sometimes it's a low moan—and for some even a loud cry when you light that fire in them. Lord have mercy," James whispered.

"Or whispering your name over and over while holding you tight. If you can't get that from a woman you might as well cut it off and give it away. I know that's what that nigger is doing for Anna. He's willing to risk his life to hear her body sing."

"That's a heavy motherfucker, willing to risking his life to get into a woman like that. He has got to die, man."

"You're right! That motherfucker has got to die, James. That's all there is to it."

Anna wept as she heard his words. She knew that if there were any way she could prevent that meeting, it would never take place.

"Yeah, I know what you mean, my man . . . if the nigger's dead, he ceases to be a problem. Kill his ass if you must, Jake, but goddamnit; get that song back right between you and Anna. She belongs to you; it's up to you to make her know it."

"She'll know it or die with that motherfucking nigger's ass," Jake replied.

"Yeah, but you better remember this, too—If you don't do better by your woman, you are going to wake up one morning with a hard on nobody wants. I ain't lying, man. When you get down to using them fingers, you done hit rock bottom. Fix it, baby, fix it."

"Yeah, I gotta fix it, man. The shape I'm in, I can't get it up for no other woman but her, and then it's for only two minutes at best. I'm finished. I'm sweating so hard it's like I have been working at it for hours. Ain't that some shit, man! Like an old goddamn man."

"What about that white beauty you've been hitting on up at the track? I know you can get it up for her."

"Angela. Man, that is a hit and a miss, right before . . . wait a minute . . . "Anna," she heard Jake scream her name and refused to answer. "She's probably locked up in one of the kids' rooms hiding so I won't get to kicking her ass," Anna heard him say. "So after Anna left after the incident with Barb I tried to get back with Angela. We hadn't talked since Fred came and told me what Anna had done to Barb. I sweet-talked her receptionist into telling me where Angela had gone. After about eight months of not hearing from her I took me a flight to a little town in Vermont just to talk to her. I wanted to see where we stood and why she had left so suddenly without at least telling me she was going and whether she would or wouldn't be continuing the relationship." There was silence. Anna moved one step down to hear her husband's next words. "I rented a car at the airport. Anna's ear tuned in as he lowered his voice to a whisper. "And went out to the address I was given. Boy did I get the shock of my life!"

What was up with her, man?" James asked.

"Man I saw her coming out the house, she was almost ready to pop. I don't know what it is with these women and babies. You could have bought me for a penny, I was so shocked," Jake whispered.

"What did you do? Confront her?"

"Hell no, I didn't confront her! I turned right around and caught the next thing smoking—got my ass out of there quick and in a hurry!"

"You didn't want to know if it was yours or not?"

"Hell no! I knew it was mine. She was in love with Jake, baby—I know she didn't lay for nobody but me. She still is, but when Anna almost caught us in my office, she has been scared shitless that Anna might cut her up like she did Barb, so she won't let me near her."

"But Jake . . . what about the kid?"

"She knew how it had to be. I didn't play games with her like I did with Barb. I came straight out and told her there could be no babies in our relationship, and if my wife returned, it was over between us. So she already knew. But with women, man, if they get caught in that 'I'm-in-love trap,' first thing they think of doing is having your kid, man."

"She has never told you about the kid?"

"Not one word and I haven't given any indication that I know. Before Anna scared her that day in my office, she'd let me bed her even knowing I can't keep it up very long. Now all she talks about is me divorcing Anna and marrying her before she allows the relationship to continue."

"Then you need to do what I had to do and bring her into your world, man. Let Anna go—since you know there is another man she is into." The sound of Jake's laughter sent chills through Anna, and she held her breath waiting to hear his next words.

"Are you kidding me, man? You got away with marrying Tammy because your name don't mean shit in this town. When they hear the name Jake Bradley people jump, baby. I ain't owning no woman's babies but these black ones I got living under my roof right now. If I come up in here with some white broad talking about how she's had my kid, Anna's old lady and those other old biddies she runs with would have me hauled out of town on the back of a freight train. She almost had me gone when Anna's car burned and they thought I was responsible.

"Right now, all I gotta tell these niggers is, it's the white man who's responsible for their lot in life, and it's on with me in front. I ain't doing shit to mess that up. As for dumping Anna, believe me, I have thought about it. But for some strange reason I cannot explain, I just can't get that black bitch out of my system, even knowing I can get any woman I want just by showing up. Man, it's like I'm hexed. When I am away from her, she is constantly in my thoughts. I can't wait to get back to make sure she hasn't left me again. When I am here looking at her, nothing is on my mind but that nigger waiting to take her from me. Until I kill his ass, she will never be my Anna again."

"That's fucked up, man! You had better hurry and get it taken care of or, like I said, you will be thumbing it alone. Pulling that dumb shit you pulled with Al can't be happening when you're running shit and want everyone to love your black ass. And you better make it right with Fred and Dee again. We're family, man . . . we can't have brothers at each other."

Anna heard the front door open and close. Easing back up the stairs, she stopped cold hearing Jake calling for her.

"Anna! Where the hell is your black ass?" She froze at the top of the stairs, staring down at him when he started up. "What the hell are you doing? Hiding in the kids' rooms again?" Anna gave no answer. "I don't hear Sister Franklin drowning out my ears these days. She always had a message for a brother." Anna looked down at her husband with contempt in her eyes.

"When the thrill is gone, Aretha is no longer the messenger." Folding her arms across her chest she stared down at her husband—seeing him as if for the first time since her return. A feeling of rage stirred in every cell in her body as a voice vibrated throughout her brain. *Is death so bad?* It asked. *Surely it is better than this life of brutal oppression.*

Death had to be better, she thought, as Jake hurried up the stairs and grabbed her around the throat.

Anna jerk away from his hold and began beating him in the face with her fists. Because he was down lower than she, he fell backwards with her falling on him as she continued to beat him in the face much the same as she had done Barb when her rage took over and there was no one there to stop her.

"You busted my lip bitch I should kill your black ass." Jake hissed licking his bloody lip when he finally gained control of Anna.

Kill me! You son of a bitch. Lying to my mother about how you never touched another woman all the while I was gone. You bastard! Angela was in your bed two years before I returned. And has been in there ever since."

"I guess I better be glad you didn't have that switchblade in your hand," Jake said laughing as he licked the blood from the cut on his lip as they both sat at the bottom of the stairs with him clutched her hands in his.

"You're damn right, you better be! I know you think every woman loves your black ass, but know this—Anna is not one of them, so do what you have to do because the thrill is gone. You can kill my ass right now! I'm ready to die!" Anna never blinked as she stared into eyes she hated.

"Not before I kill that nigger's ass who's fucking you," he said smiling as his hands moved up and down her throat. "When that's done, then I will think about killing your black ass, bitch." The slap across her cheek caused Anna to close her eyes. Not only did she feel hate, she tasted it.

Chapter Thirty

—〰—

When Anna was forced to sleep with Jake she never refused him sex; she just lay like stone. One night after finishing with her body, he laughed and said to her, "Now baby, you can go and come as you please . . . give that motherfucker you love as much loving as he can stand and see how he likes that gift I'm sending his ass." Anna listened to him but paid little attention to his threat. She knew he was dirty, but she believed he had said this only because she never responded to his lovemaking.

A few weeks later, feeling some discomfort, she went for a checkup and was told she had gonorrhea. She walked out of the doctor's office in total shock after she took the shot the doctor gave her to clear her body of the disease.

Jake will die this night, she vowed, tears streaming down her face.

Anna waited until he was in bed asleep. She made sure the gun Frankie Lee had given her was still loaded. It would be the end of her freedom, but she didn't care. Pointing the gun at his head, she said a prayer and prepared to pull the trigger.

Screams rang out from upstairs where the children slept. Jake jumped up; Anna put the gun behind her.

"What the hell is going on?" he demanded, unable to see the gun in Anna's hand in their dark bedroom. Bending down, she pushed the gun under the bed and told him Sheri' was having another nightmare. Rushing upstairs, she took the screaming child in her arms.

"Momma, I dreamed you and Daddy were fighting again and he killed you!" Sheri' cried and held on to Anna so tightly that she slept with her the rest of the night, even though Jake kept threatening that she had better come back to their bed.

****

While on the phone with her mother later the next morning, Anna watched Jake walk into the living room. She wondered why he was not at work. He asked if Sheri' was okay from the nightmare she had experienced. Not wanting to interrupt what her mother was telling her, she continued listening without answering him.

"Don't you hear me talking to you?" he screamed.

"Jake, can't you see I'm on the phone? I'll talk to you when I'm finished."

"Hang that motherfucker up, bitch! That's all you and those biddies do is stay on the goddamn phone talking about every motherfucker's business. Keep your ass concerned with what is going on in this house for a change, bitch!" He shouted. Then Sheri' wouldn't be screaming her head off all night long," he screamed when she gave no answer. "And I need you in bed with me, damn it!" Jake ranted as Anna placed the phone back into its cradle, bitterness in her voice she turned to address him.

"Why did you have to do that? Can't you even pretend you have some decency to outsiders so they won't know what a dog you really are?" Jake reached for Anna, but both children jumped in front of her.

"Please don't!" Sheri' screamed. "I can't take it anymore!" She grabbed Anna, crying in her arms. Sheri' had not felt like going to school that morning, and Jake Jr. refused to go. Anna felt tears slide down her own cheeks when she saw tears coming from her son's eyes as well. She realized the time had come for her to leave. Not even for the sake of her children could she stay with Jake any longer. She hoped they would join her and not want to run back to Session. If only she could think of a way to outsmart that Jay Man. He watched her every move seated across from their home. She had wanted to prove to the Old Head she could handle her life herself but she knew she needed help.

When the doorbell rang, Jake Jr. ran to answer it.

"Is Jake in hare?" Anna looked up to see her mother standing in the doorway.

"What the hell got into ya, boy, callin' me a biddy? Is this the way ya disgrace yer wife when she's on the phone? Jake eyes grew wide in alarm. "Ain't no dogs been under my dress, so dat daughter of mine ain't no bitch, ya understand me?" The look in her eyes showed danger they both understood, knowing how dangerous Annabelle could be if she got to talking about him around town. People would soon see him in a different light Anna knew he knew it.

"Yes, I understand," Jake, answered. Anna knew he feared what her mother's actions could mean to his standing among the people he felt loved him. They loved her as well and the older ones would hear her words and believe them even about him.

"We were just having a family disagreement, Momma. I had no idea it was you on the phone with Anna."

"It makes no never mind who she's talkin' to—ya should have sense enuf not to embarrass yer wife like dat. How would ya like it if she was screamin' and cussin ya out when ya was talkin' to some of them bigshot white devils ya thank so much of? Ya'd be puttin' yer foot up hur behind right 'bout now," Annabelle said as she turned to face Anna.

"Anna knows I wouldn't hurt her," Jake said staring at her mother.

"Hummm," Annabelle said as Anna saw her look from Jake to her and then the children, who were staring straight ahead with looks of fear. "Gal, ya look like death walkin. Dis man of yers is draggin' ya down to the gutter. Now yer mine and I could kill his ass myself for doing ya dis a way, but yer momma can't fight yer battles for ya. Ya gotta learn to stand and fight for yer own life even if it means dyin', gal . . . 'cause far as I can tell, ya sho ain't got much of one right now. Put dat razor on his ass. He may still go out thare and whore like he been doin' all along, but he'll sho' leave ya the hell alone."

Annabelle fearlessly turned to Jake. Anna knew her mother was angry because she never pointed her finger unless she was ready to fight. "Boy, I never thought ya would turn out to be plum no good. But if my daughter wants ya so bad as to take ya doggin' hur, dat's hur doing. But my babies hare can't fend for thayselves. Ya lay one finger on one of 'em; ya'll have me to kill. If ya don't want this gal of mine, send hur home to me and hur daddy whare ya got hur from in the first place. She sho' welcome thare." Jake stood with his hands in his pockets, staring at her mother. "I told that gal when ya asked hur daddy fer her dat she needed a clean minded virgin man. Course she wouldn't listen."

"Gal," she said, turning back to face Anna, "Ya mind what yer momma done tole ya. As long as he can coward ya down, he sho' gonna do it. Ya better wake up and let his ass know ya Annabelle's daughter and be willin' to cut his ass to death if it's the only way for him to know it." Anna thought of Madria as she listened to her mother's answer to her problems. She felt shame as her mother turned the knob to leave her home. There in her eyes she saw pity for her that she had never before seen but she knew her mother's way always led to a violent end.

"Momma," Sheri' said to Anna after Jake left for work, "why don't we go live with Grandma and Grandpa? They wouldn't let Daddy come there fussing and beating on you." Anna listened to her daughter as she looked over at her son who was sitting with his hand under his chin, looking at a blank television screen.

"It's not that easy, honey. Your grandparents don't need me running back to them every time I have a problem. I have to work this thing out myself."

"Momma, work it out by doing like Aunt Dee does." Anna listened to her daughter tried to coach her on how to protect herself from her father.

"She talks back to Uncle Fred no matter what he says. That's how I want to be. I'll never let a man hurt me like Daddy hurts you—never!" Sheri' insisted.

"I hope you won't, Sheri'," Anna said with tears streaming down her cheeks. Yes, what she had told Tammy was true. The Anna that had once smiled with love in her eyes was now dead and gone to hell. There was nothing left of her—nothing at all.

****

Anna looked with surprise to see Dee standing at her door. They talked only by telephone since Jake had forbidden her to visit his brother's house.

"What brings you over to the haunted house?" Anna asked, welcoming her inside.

"I knew that damn husband of yours was out of town," Dee said, placing both hands on her hips as she walked inside.

"Your mother was telling me the gospel truth. You look as though you are at death's door, sister girl." She took a seat. "I overheard James telling Fred the same thing.

"I'm fine, really," Anna answered, turning away from Dee.

"Jake Bradley has walked your ass nearly to death, woman, and if you don't take a fast look in the mirror, there won't be no need for one."

Going into the bathroom, Dee returned with a large hand mirror and said to Anna, "Take the sucker and look into it . . . see what your kids are seeing—what your father and Mrs. Annabelle see—what I'm looking at right now." Dee held the mirror to Anna's face. You look worse than some of those women that used to come into the shelter.

Anna looked in the mirror, seeing a scarf tied around her head that she remembered putting on the week before. Dried tears marred her face. She looked like hell; she had to admit.

"You sit your ass down on this couch and let me get you back on track, like you were when you first came back from being with that white man you fell in love with," Dee said, pulling her down on the couch beside her. "I don't poke my nose into no woman's business when it comes to her and her man, but you are like a sister to me, and sisters count different." Anna saw the same look in Dee's eyes that she had seen in her mother's.

"Do you think Jake Bradley has ever stopped having himself as many women as would have his ass from the day he told that preacher until death do we part? Something Fred told me after hearing what he did to Al. He also told me that night you left here after cutting Barb he found his ass with that white bitch working out at the track." Anna heard a sigh escape Dee's lips. "Anna, all some men wants a wife for is so they can use her to protect their ass from having to marry another woman. The rest they just uses, coming home telling the wife what she better not do. Wake up, little sister. The only reason Fred can't get away with that shit is because I'm on his ass all the time."

Anna hated hearing Dee's truths coming at her so hard.

Dee continued, "I told him if he starts Jake's shit, he will be out on his ass quick and in a hurry because I am not the one. You need to start that shelter up again and make yourself its first client 'cause sister girl, you sho' need help. If this is what you've got to take, you just as soon be out there doing what he's beating your ass for. The motherfucker can't do you no worse."

"Dee . . ." Anna couldn't talk without choking on her tears.

"Dee nothing, Anna. Look honey, I know back then I put that guilt trip on you about family and doing what it takes to keep it together, but that's only if the man is trying to keep it together as well. Jake is a street-whoring motherfucker whose beating you to hide his own wrongs.

Nothing you have done is worth this kind of treatment—not your kids, your home, nothing—least of all a no-good whoring husband like you have. If it is the house, all of it will be here after you're dead and gone. If it is something I said when you came home that first time, erase it from your heart. I was wrong—dead wrong—about everything. You are not living in a home where the family comes first—you are living in hell, and Jake Bradley is the devil. "How could you love him after all the shit he's putting you though?"

Anna listened to her friend, her tears flowing down her face. "My God, Dee, I'm at the breaking point!" Anna cried so hard that Dee began to cry.

"Anna, don't take this shit no matter what you have done. Nothing is worth it—for sure, not a damn no-good wife beating husband who has no respect even for his kids."

"Dee there are things about me you don't even know. If they were known, a lot of people would be hurt. You think Jake is crazy now; if he had any idea what I have done, I would have been dead a long time ago," Anna said, staring off into space.

"Anna, nothing could be worse to him than your living with a white man—someone he thinks is black. If it wasn't so serious, I would laugh myself to death. I am telling you his woman is white. It's no more for you than it is for him. Now you tell me what could be worse than that? Anna pulled out the small picture she had hidden of Raspy.

"Anna, is that the baby Jake told James you were down south wet nursing?"

"The time I went away after my fight with Barb, I gave birth to her Dee. Anna watched her friend's mouth stretch open. "While I was there, I discovered I was carrying her. That's why I was away so long. Nothing I did to get rid of her worked. Raspy is almost four years old now . . . she lives with Momma's mother."

"Mrs. Annabelle's mother? I always thought her mother was dead. Gee would I like to meet her" Dee said, her eyes growing larger by the second.

"You would love her. She has none of the harshness Momma has in her heart.

"Really?"

Yes, that's who I lived with down in Louisiana. Dee like I said she has been caring for my baby." Anna related seeing Jake in her cousin's yard and then the hospital scene. "She kept screaming for me to take her Dee. I had to turn my back and act like she wasn't mine to keep him from finding out she was mine."

"My God, Anna! If he had, there would have been a double murder."

"Had it not been for my grandmother, it would have been. She came and got Raspy from the hospital—she and my uncle, who looks like any white man.

"Damn! If it wasn't for them, your ass would have been exposed big time. Mrs. Annabelle would kill you herself if she knew."

"Yes, Dee. Momma doesn't know, but if it were not for her mother, I guess I would already be dead, if not in an insane asylum." Anna sobbed as she unfastened the straps of the watches she always wore to let Dee see the cuts across her wrists.

"Every day of my life I sit here jumping at the ring of the phone, thinking it's someone calling to tell me my grandmother has died or is seriously ill and can no longer care for my child. My worst fear is that something awful might happen at any time—something that would expose me to everyone. The hell of it is that it makes it impossible for me to feel Jake's beatings. Dee, I can't feel anything but the heat of the hell I'm living in right now."

"Even that, Anna, ain't worth what you are going through with Jake. Let it go and live again."

"I don't know how to live again, Dee. I just don't know how," Anna replied as they sat crying in each other's arms.

****

Anna and Sheri' stood in the backyard watching Jake Jr. uncovered the dome he and Anna had spent the last month constructing for his science project the next day. Anna watched Sheri' admire the dome. It had taken weeks to get the dome built just right so it would collapse under the pressure of the chemical explosives that would suck everything inward, making the dome collapse the way they wanted it to. Anna had been teaching Jake Jr. about the earth and its elements. She discovered he was intrigued by the science he learned at the private school he attended.

"Momma why do you think God gave Jake Jr. a smart brain and me just an ordinary one?" Anna took Sheri' into her arms telling her God had given her a compassionate heart like her grandfather one she should be proud to have. The smile that spread across her daughter's face caused all three to hug each other.

"Why the hell do you have my kids up this late at night?" Anna and the kids jumped away from each other hearing the sound of Jake's voice. Anna had hoped he would not return from his trip to Chicago until the next day by then they would have taken the project to school. But here he was—and in his usual disgruntled mood.

"You hear my ass talking to you, bitch? Can't you hear?" Anna refused to answer him. "Do you want me on your ass again?" There were tears in her eyes as she looked over at him seeing that he was not only disgruntled but drunk.

"Daddy, Momma and Jake Jr. have been building this incredible dome. Isn't it awesome? Who would have thought Momma was that smart?" Sheri' asked her father, excitement in her voice.

"Yes, Daddy, I've got the smartest mom around. She is teaching me so many things about the earth and its elements. So many things I didn't know before." Anna saw the admiration in her son's eyes as he informed his father about the dome they had built and that it was a project for school the next day.

"What?" Jake screamed, staggering closer to the dome.

"Daddy, Momma came up with the idea for Jake Jr. Momma is a genius, don't you think?" The sudden movement happened so fast that Anna, Sheri' and Jake Jr. could do nothing but stand there staring with their mouths open. The dome fell as Jake kicked the table that held it. Once it fell to the ground, he stomped the pieces under his feet screaming that their mother wasn't shit. Anna had a flashback of too many years ago and a pair of glasses that had changed the course of her life forever.

"Get my kids upstairs and into bed or I will stomp your ass, too." Anna and the children turned and rushed into the house, not stopping until they were inside Jake Jr., room with the door locked. Anna tried to console Jake Jr. by telling him they would build again.

"It's too late, Momma. It's going to always be too late as long as he is around."

****

Anna stood looking at the blue and white Buick across the street from her house, when she heard the phone ringing. Jake's voice came booming through the receiver, telling her to get down to Jake Jr.'s school immediately. Hoping nothing terrible had happened to her son, she rushed out of the house. The blue and white Buick started up, but Anna didn't care that she was being followed.

Finding parking at the school wasn't hard but Anna found herself slowly walking into the school with a heavy heart. After being directed to the principal's office Anna walked in looking from her son to his father seated inside, her mind went back to when she had sat with her mother years ago in the principal's office at Camelot Academy and the terrible results of that day.

"Mrs. Bradley, your husband suggested he call you to come to school so that we can get a clear understanding of what your son wants to happen here today. Because he is one one of our most brilliant students, we have taken his request seriously." Anna's face formed a frown as she tried to understand what was going on. The principal a short white slender middle aged gray haired man took a seat on the edge of his desk gazing at all three.

"Mrs. Bradley your son has asked that his name be changed to Jeff Jr. Drake. He says he is no longer Jake Jr. Bradley and chooses never to be called that name again."

Anna felt her heart began to pound so fast that she thought she would lose consciousness. She took a seat while holding her chest. Closing her eyes, she immediately reopened them when Jake suggested that she, their son, and he discuss the matter privately first. The principal agreed it was a good idea and left the office.

"Son," she listened to Jake tell their son when the door closed behind the principal, "as soon as that white motherfucker steps his ass back into this office and you tell him you want to disown me as your father, I will blow your mother's brains out. You'll never see her alive again. Is that clear enough for that *brilliant* brain of yours?" Anna sat stunned when a small gun appeared next to her head as Jake drew her close to him.

"What difference does it make? You are going to kill her once she leaves with you anyway."

"No son, not as long as she does what I tell her ass to do. When you get a wife, you'll understand how it is with a man and his woman. Now you're just a kid trying to protect this mother of yours from the man who owns *you and her.* So make up your mind what it's going to be."

"You are going to hurt her—I know it."

"I told you I'm not going to touch her ass if she continues to do what I tell her to do. Now what's it gonna be? I haven't got all day for you to make up your mind whether she lives or dies *right now!*" Jake pulled Anna even closer placing the gun at her temple.

Jake Jr. looked at Anna with tears in his eyes. "Call him back in I'll tell him I've changed my mind."

******

She drove home alone but both Jay Man and Jake trailed her. Anna walked into the kitchen and started dinner seeing the Old Widow parked on the window's edge she knew she must call her father to come for her the next morning because the end was coming fast. That evening, Anna saw Jake staring at his son from the dinner table. "Boy, one day you are going to have a wife, and then you will understand how it is with a man and what belongs to him. A man cannot allow what's his to be taken from him by no other man. When that happens, it's his responsibility to see that the motherfucker dies so that his woman can be put in check. That's exactly what you will be doing to yours when you get one. Ain't that right, Anna?"

"Jake, go on somewhere and leave me the hell alone. I hope my son will learn how not to treat his woman by looking at his good-for-nothing father. It hurts our children to hear you talking to me that disrespectfully even if it gives you pleasure. They have never seen me do anything wrong. I'm a prisoner in this house because you know I don't want you anymore and would leave if I could." The slap came quickly, causing Anna to scream out in pain. Everything else happened instantaneously.

"I promised myself I would kill your ass if you ever hit my mother again, you black bastard!" Jake Jr. shouted, rising from the table with a gun pointed at his father. Anna looked in shock realized the gun he held was the gun Frankie Lee had given her. She had searched everywhere for it. Jake Jr. must have taken it from under her bed where she tossed it and hid it in his room because he knew she never went in there except to make sure it was clean. "I'm tired of hearing you curse and beat my mother for no reason. Sheri' and I can't sleep because we hear Momma screaming out when you are beating her . . . all night sometimes. Jake Jr. wiped his eyes, turning his head to his shoulder.

Jake rose slowly from the dining room table as Anna and Sheri' stared at the gun in Jake Jr.'s hand. "Give me that gun, boy! Your mother is nothing but a goddamn whore. She deserves those beatings I give her!" The look in his eyes told Anna her husband knew the danger he was in.

"I have never seen her do anything but take care of us and cry when you hurt her. Momma was right . . . there are black devils . . . and you are one of them, you black ass good for nothing bastard! Those beatings she has been getting are going to stop right now!" Jake Jr. placed his finger on the trigger as his eyes narrowed and his lips grew tight. Anna's heart pumped blood so fast to her head she almost fainted. If the gun accidentally went off, Jake might be a dead man.

Sheri' ran to the phone and dialed, screaming into it that Jake Jr. had a gun and for her grandmother to come over at once.

"You little bastard!" Jake screamed, grabbing for the gun.

"Jake Jr.! No!" Anna screamed. A loud shot sounded as the gun went off and Jake fell back onto the floor. Jake Jr. walked over cocking the gun again. Anna snatched the gun from him causing the next bullet to penetrate the wall behind her.

"No boy! Go upstairs and stay there, Jake Jr.—you too, Sheri'!" Anna screamed. "I mean it—stay there! And no matter what questions the police ask you, say you don't know what happened. You were in your rooms, you understand me?" They ran up the stairs as Anna began wiping all the fingerprints but her own from the gun, and when Annabelle arrived, she found Anna staring down at her husband lying in a puddle of blood.

****

Anna walked out of the city jail three days later with her father as he told her why the police had not charged her. "When Jake came to after surgery, he insisted it was all an accident. I'm not telling you what to do, but he's been asking to see you. Your mother and I have the kids. Are you going back to Mr. Forlorn?" Anna heard the seriousness in her father's voice.

"No, Daddy. Even though I know he is divorced now, I am not going back to him. I have someone I need to go take care of, someone I have neglected far too long as I have been thinking only of myself." Anna reached into her wallet, pulling out the snapshot Frankie Lee had taken of her and Raspy and handing it to her father. His mouth opened much the same as it had when he saw her kiss Raymond in New York.

"Yes, Daddy. She is mine. Her name is Raspy. I didn't know I was pregnant with her until after my encounter with Barb when I took off down south. That is where she was born. Momma's mother has been taking care of her for me ever since." Anna saw a startled look suddenly appear on her father's face as he held the picture and stared from it back to her.

"What do you mean—your mother's mother? Are you seriously telling me she is still alive?"

"Yes, but Momma never wanted you or me to know about her. She despises her as much as she does whites. But without her, I would not be sitting here now. I love her, Daddy. She is everything I wish Momma could be for me. I am going to her and Raspy. Granny is getting up in age, and she is not going to be able to care for Raspy much longer." Anna stood crying while her father gazed at the picture.

"She is the baby Jake saw me with—the one he told Momma I was down in Louisiana wet nursing. He never guessed she was mine, Daddy. Sooner or later you have to come face-to-face with what you have done and own it. I must own my own sins—they have slapped me so hard in the face I have to."

"Does Mr. Forlorn know about my granddaughter?" Her father asked, looking hard at Anna.

"No, he doesn't know about her. I never told him, even when I had the chance to. I just thought he might be like most men who have babies by outside women. She's my love-child, so that makes her my responsibility, not his."

"My God, Anna! We will have to agree to disagree about that," her father said, shaking his head. "All this you have been going through. I would like to see her someday," he said, looking closely at the picture.

"Daddy, you know I can never bring her here and let Momma find out about her, not to mention Jake! As it is, I must find a place he cannot find me or her. She has his last name, and all I need is for him to try claiming her just to hurt me."

"Can I have this photo? You won't need it since you are going to her anyway, and then I can at least look at my grandchild I might not ever get to know," he asked.

"Daddy, if Momma got ahold of that picture . . ."

"I'm not your mother's son, Baby Girl. I am her husband and your father," he said as Anna felt his lips touch her head.

"When I get there, I will send you a better picture than this, I promise—one with me holding her in my arms as a mother is supposed to. I will send it to the restaurant, so look for it, Daddy. I don't want Momma getting her hands on it. Now would you please take me to see Jake? I own him that much for not telling the authorities that it was Jake Jr. who shot him."

"Send it, please. I am not worried about anyone getting their hands on it unless I want them to. Let me get you on over to that hospital before Jake calls out the National Guard."

****

Anna watched a smile light up Jake's face as she walked into his hospital room. His shoulder was all bandaged up and looked a lot like her abdomen had looked when she first woke up in Oinston's hospital.

"Anna, our son tried to kill me. That's messed up. That boy doesn't realize how much I love him and his sister." Anna looked down at her husband, remembering that she had just seen her children before coming to the hospital to see him. She had wanted to let them know she would be taking them away with her—far away so Jake could not hurt her or them ever again. It was her son who had informed Anna of the best way to leave his father.

"Momma, if you take us with you, he will enlist the help of every law enforcement person in the country. We couldn't get into school without him finding out where we were living. There would be no end to what he might do to try to get control of our lives again. You must leave us here with Grandpa and Grandma and go alone. That way it's just his wife and no one else leaving him. He won't hurt us, but since I didn't suceeed in killing him," Anna heard the disappointment in her son's voice, "if he gets his hands on you again, I'm afraid we won't have a mother any longer."

Anna had swallowed hard, knowing what he told her was true but hating it just the same.

"Jake Jr., I have left you and Sheri' here with Momma and Daddy too many times. It's time I take responsibility for caring for my children. I don't want to leave you here. If something were to happen to you, it would be the death of me. I love you and your sister too much to take a chance on that."

"Momma, Jake Jr.—I mean, Jeff Jr.—is right. Daddy's not going to hurt us, but we don't want to lose our mother. Daddy goes crazy when he is around you, Momma. Go on . . . we know you love us . . . that's all that matters. We don't want you killed. I couldn't live if that happened." Sheri' grabbed Anna, hugging her as her body shook and tears streamed down her face. My brother almost killed our Daddy, Momma. I don't want that happening to you."

"Momma, don't come back here. We will come to you. We will, you'll see. Now go." Her son pushed her toward the door. Anna looked at her mother who stood with her hands folded saying nothing as tears fell from her eyes. Anna began to cry as she hugged her children and her mother before following her father out of her parents' home, hating that she again had to leave her children in their care.

"Daddy," Anna had said, turning to her father as they had gotten back into her Porsche that he was driving. "I have learned so much these past months. I will never judge a woman living in abuse or say what she should or should not take like I once did because now I know how her shoes feel. I also now understand why you went to prison for me. Only a parent who loves their child and sees how life can play out understands what one must do when pushed there." Her father kissed her cheek as he nodded in agreement.

Looking down at Jake's messed-up shoulder, Anna was glad his son had not killed him. Anna knew how much it hurt Jake having his son shoot him, but she also knew he would never let it be known. For that reason, she felt she owed him this visit. His son no longer used his name, and she knew he would soon have it changed—she wondered how Jake would handle that now that he wouldn't have killing her as leverage to stop him.

"Anna, I'm sorry for what I've put you through; things will change when I'm able to get out of here. I'm determined to make our marriage work."

Anna's eyes narrowed as she looked down at the bandages covering her husband's shoulder, still remembering the pain she had felt after he had cracked her ribs. Standing beside his bed, she lifted her left hand, taking off her wedding rings saying to him. "Any black man who admits he fathered a baby and refuses to acknowledge its existence simply because its mother is white is a low-down son-of-a-bitch no better than those no good white son of a bitches you are always preaching about!"

Anna watched a look of shock spread across Jake's face realizing that he realized she had overheard the conversation between him and James.

"The only person's pain you have ever cared about is your own Jake Bradley." Tossing the wedding rings on the bed beside him, she gazed down into his face. "You take these damn rings to the river where you planned to kill that man. Throw them in, because I am never ever coming back to your ass. You have given me enough pain and heartaches to last Anna her lifetime. It is over between you and me forever! You don't deserve to be loved—you don't even deserve to be hated!"

Walking out of his room, she heard him scream, "GO ON BACK TO THE NIGGER, YOU DIRTY BLACK BITCH! BUT I'LL FIND YOU AND KILL THE BOTH OF YOU MOTHERFUCKERS, YOU HEAR ME? I WILL FIND YOU, ANNA BRADLEY—AND A DEAD ASS YOU WILL HAVE! I PROMISE YOU ON MY DEAD MOMMA'S GRAVE—YOU WILL DIE BY THESE HANDS!" Anna walked out of his hospital room without looking back.

****

"Take me by the restaurant. I need to get my car and make a stop at the bank," her father said to Anna as she slid into the driver's seat after walking out of the hospital. "I'm worried about you, Baby Girl," he said with sadness in his eyes.

"Now that Jake is out of my life, I will be fine, Daddy."

"What has puzzled me since your return to him is the conversation we had when you came to see me and you told me you would never take him back. Several nights later, you and Jake appeared at the house as husband and wife again. How did that happen? I've never known you to go back on something you have set your mind on not doing."

Anna's mind went back to the night under the bridge, looking at the muddy water of the Mississippi River splashing in the rain and a man about to be loaded down with cement blocks so that he could be dropped in the river, never to be found.

"Daddy, never is forever—and as we both know, some of the twists and turns of this life make saying never one great big lie."

"Here is the money I have been saving—no sense in refusing it because I'm not going to let you," he said, handing her an envelope. He then reached into his pocket and offered her a stick of gum. She accepted it and watched him stick a piece into his own mouth.

After all of the unhappiness she had gone through, driving off Anna looked at her father and saw how good and healthy he looked. His chewing gum meant he was struggling to give up the Lucky Strikes that had been an unbreakable habit for most of his life. Whatever her regrets were, she never regretted having the Old Head give him the Healing Tree's strength that had for so long protected her life.

"A parent's love is sometimes difficult for it endures much," he said when they drove up to his restaurant. Her father hugged her to him. Whispering; "I love my little Baby Girl," After kissing her dimpled cheek he got out of the car.

I am free at last, Anna thought, watching her father drive away from his restaurant. She then drove off as her mind wandered back to when summer was over and the kids had returned to school. She had decided to go sit on the only beach she knew down by Carlyle where she had taken them to learn skiing. The blue and white Buick had sat hidden behind another car near her house. It must have followed her for a long time before she realized it, because she had almost reached the beach when she noticed it. Her heart pounding, she had turned into the nearest gas station. As soon as she had parked and started to get out of the car, Jay Man was there at her car door.

"Jake said to wait for him here. He is on his way." In his eyes, Anna saw hate. It must be horrible having no one to love you, thoughts as to what might have caused that hate flashed through her mind, she had wanted to get out and run but she knew the gun he carried was meant to kill. By the time Jake had arrived, she had become a wreck; fear had mounted so heavily in her heart.

"Who were you going to see, little wife of mine?"

"Jake, I was driving down here to the beach to sit alone."

"Why don't you have the kids with you, bitch?" When she didn't answer, he grabbed a handful of her hair, pulling her out of the car.

"They are in school, remember?" His sudden slap had stunned her.

"I don't think you were going to sit by the lake alone. I think you were on your way to see that black-ass nigger of yours. The motherfucker needs to see your ass again for a little loving. Isn't that right?"

"No Jake, it is not right." Sobbing, she fell to her knees. "Why don't you just kill me now and get it over with?"

"Not until I get my hands on your black-ass nigger, bitch. You seem to think that motherfucker is so fearsome, calling for him when you're in bed with me."

"That's you saying I call for him. I don't remember calling anyone." She remembered the ensuing fight after their return home and her escape into her daughter's room locking the door.

Anna's mind returned to the present with her thinking even the past three days in jail had not been as horrible as the prison she had lived in as Jake's wife this last year. All of the beatings and humiliations she had endured were enough for her to swear off men forever. It was Ray that Jake wanted. He had become obsessed with getting his hands on her former lover and killing him. Nothing she had said had convinced him that he did not want that meeting to take place. Ray would have gladly come, but Jake would have regretted it far more than he realized. She knew that for a fact. If it was crazy he was looking for, he would find it quick and in a hurry looking for Ray. He had no idea of the horror of what would be waiting for him—not in this world. No, this was best. He was out of her life forever. She was on her way to Louisiana and her daughter she had left screaming for her too long ago.

Epilogue

The old widow sat on the edge of her front window it's orange back pulsating wildly. Looking into her rearview mirror, Anna felt her heart jump into her throat as she drove through downtown Session. The blue and white Buick that had followed her everywhere for the last six months suddenly came up behind her. Even when she had been with her children, the blue and white Buick had trailed behind her everywhere she went—standing outside any store while she shopped—even outside the beauty salon where she had her hair done. There he was, his smashed-in face with those thick wet lips, staring her down.

Now, here he was again. Her heart pounded as she realized Jake would never give up. Wasn't their son shooting him enough? What was she going to do? She would kill herself before going back to him. "Old Head, I will never allow my life to be controlled by that man again!" Suddenly, she felt the power of the blue light circling inside her car.

"Remember the leaf you consumed from the Healing Tree, Daughter. Its power to endure has helped you get to this point. No man can imprison you when freedom stands before you. Look, Daughter, and see it!"

Anna looked ahead, trying to see what the Old Head meant as she drove trying to escape her stalker. There, walking out of the bank was her father. She almost hit him she drove up so fast beside his car. Jumping out, she rushed up to him.

"Daddy, Daddy, please, don't let him get me!" Grabbing her up into his arms, he looked around to see Jay Man jump back into his car and speed off. Anna was trembling so much that her father had to push her into his car and lock the door.

"Who was that man? Why are you terrified, Baby Girl? Tell me what is going on here."

"Daddy he's the man Jake hired to follow me everywhere I go. He is outside the house after Jake goes to work. No matter where I go, he is there—and a few minutes later, here comes Jake. It has been horrible living like that.

"Baby Girl, I don't understand any of this."

"Daddy, I tried to be a good wife for Jake, but it just did not work out that way. Every turn I took led me further and further into the abyss. Once he and Fred dragged Dee and me out to that racetrack it was all over between us."

"What do you mean?"

"It was out there I discovered he was having an affair with a white woman who works for Raymond's brother out at the racetrack.

"And he . . . found out about the white man you have been with?"

"Daddy, I am still alive. No, when he met Ray, he never picked up on our relationship. He just thought he was a white man looking at a black woman he wished he could have. His wealth, of course, pushed the thought of his being seriously interested in me far from Jake's mind. Jake thinks there is some wealthy black man he needs to kill so that his pride can be restored. But Ray's wife did pick up on it." A look of shame covered Anna's face. "We had an ugly confrontation out there. I have not felt good about it since, even though Jake was so busy with Angela that he never discovered the connection between Ray and me. Ray and his wife divorced soon after."

"Anna . . ."

"I know, Daddy. I went to where we once lived to let him know about Raspy hoping that he would go get her before Jake found out about her. I didn't care what Jake did to me, but I couldn't let him find my baby and hurt her. I knew once Ray got her, there would be nothing Jake could do to harm her."

"Yes, the baby . . . Anna, why didn't you tell him about the child? You know if Jake finds out about her . . . not to mention your mother . . ."

"Daddy, Jake saw her."

"What?"

"Remember when he told Momma about me wet nursing a baby down South? My baby was screaming for me to take her, and I had to turn my back and act like she wasn't mine, I have never been so ashamed in my life," Anna cried, shaking her head as she confessed to her father how she had denied her daughter as she relived the scene. Seeing the shocked look on her father's face she added, "I know, Daddy. I am little more than a disgrace as a mother, but I couldn't allow him to know she was mine. His name is on her birth records. She would be doomed once he got his hands on her. As for telling Raymond about her, I just couldn't after he discovered how his wife had deceived him. He might have rejected her and not believed she was his. She's mine, and I alone am responsible for her, Daddy. That is how it has to be."

"My God Baby Girl, you are living in two worlds. How can that be?"

"Daddy those two worlds can not come together without death resulting."

"Why didn't you tell me all this was going on?"

"Daddy, you already spent a year in prison because of me. I couldn't allow you to spend one more day there because of how Jake has treated me. I had to learn how to endure this hell until I could get away. I tried to leave many times before, but this man you saw jump back into his car is always trailing me. Even the kids tried to help me, but he always caught me. He's Jake's henchman. I don't think that even now Jake plans for me to leave him."

"I must tell you, Baby Girl, you will never go back to that fool. I plan to go see Jake. If he so much as suggests he plans to force you to come back to him, I will kill his ass up in that hospital."

Anna sat stunned. She had not heard her father curse since her mother had beaten her when she was fourteen years old. Having to confess her awful life to him was worst than standing before her grandmother six months pregnant with the baby's father no where in sight.

"I will drive you down to Louisiana, Baby Girl. Neither Jake nor this fool he has following you will think of hurting you with me in the car. I know that."

"No, Daddy. I've had a change of plans," I need you to take me to the airport. I think it is best that I fly out of this country before getting my baby. I don't want Jake to get his hands on her. If he finds me down in Louisiana, chances are he will find her and discover she is my daughter. It would be deadly, and even you couldn't stop the damage he'd do to her. I will call and let you know what country I am in and when I will return."

Ms Anna The Promise Keeper Trouble is coming in the third and final book of the Ms. Anna trilogy. Meow rides the helm as Collier sends two worlds colliding!

CPSIA information can be obtained at www.ICGtesting.com
Printed in the USA
LVOW04s0751020915

452275LV00019B/123/P